Sinners at the Altar

A Sinners Encores Anthology

OLIVIA CUNNING

VULPINE
PRESS

For more information on the author and her works, please visit www.oliviacunning.com.

Copyright 2014 Olivia Cunning

Published by Vulpine Press
Cover Design by Olivia Cunning
Cover Photo by Inara Prusakova at depositphotos.com
Edited by E.L. Hill at www.anoveledit.com

ISBN-10: 1-939276-13-6
ISBN-13: 978-1-939276-13-1

For Sinners fans everywhere,
who wanted more of these naughty rock stars
as much as I did.

Books by Olivia Cunning

SINNERS ON TOUR SERIES:
Backstage Pass
Rock Hard
Hot Ticket
Wicked Beat
Double Time
Sinners at the Altar
COMING SOON:
Sinners in Paradise

ONE NIGHT WITH SOLE REGRET SERIES:
Try Me #1
Tempt Me #2
Take Me #3
Share Me: A Prequel #0.5
Touch Me #4
Tie Me #5
Tell Me #6
COMING SOON:
Tease Me #7
Treat Me #8

LOVERS' LEAP SERIES:
Loving on Borrowed Time
Twice Upon a Time

Writing as OLIVIA DOWNING
Defying Destiny

TABLE OF CONTENTS

SINNERS ON TOUR ENCORE

Appetite
for Seduction

Epilogue to Backstage Pass

OLIVIA
CUNNING

Chapter 1

A LINE OF SUNLIGHT FILTERED through the window blinds and angled across Brian's eyelids. Wincing against the red glare, he turned his face into his pillow. Something felt *wrong* this morning. He recognized the bed as the one at the back of Sinners' tour bus, so it wasn't because he was waking up in an unfamiliar hotel room. He was accustomed to life on the road and opening his eyes to a new city almost every morning, so why did he feel like something was different from his norm?

It was too quiet. The motion of the tour bus and the din of its engine were missing. It was such a familiar lullaby that his mornings felt off if he didn't wake to the sound.

With a sleepy smile, he rubbed his face against his pillow, still trying to grasp full consciousness, and cringed as pain shot across the bridge of his nose. *Fuck*, his face hurt. And not because he'd slept on it again. He felt as if someone had pounded him between the eyes with a hard fist.

Probably because someone had.

All at once his mind grasped *why* the bus was stationary this morning and the reason his nose felt like it had been moshing with a wall in his sleep. They were in Las Vegas. *Vegas*. Myrna had agreed to marry him in Vegas. His botched bachelor party the night before had resulted in his worse-for-wear face, which meant...

Today was his wedding day.

Holy shit!

Instantly awake, Brian shot his hand out into the space beside him to find nothing but an expanse of empty mattress. Had it been a dream? The woman had been throwing off his proposals for weeks, so maybe he had imagined her telling him she loved him. Dreamed that she'd agreed to marry him. Brian's heart panged unpleasantly.

He reached farther, needing the tangible evidence of her skin beneath his touch. More cool and empty sheet met his seeking fingertips. Had Myrna changed her mind and left him? She had been pissed when he'd shown up with two black eyes the night before. He couldn't blame her for having second thoughts after he'd gotten into a fight at a strip club. A strip club he hadn't even wanted to go to, but still…

He stretched his arm as far as it would go, and his fingers found warm, soft skin. He breathed a sigh of relief and spooned against Myrna's back, inhaling her delicate scent. Not a dream. Not his imagination. Sweet reality.

Myrna murmured his name in her sleep. The corners of Brian's mouth turned up, and his heart warmed. He snuggled closer to her back, placing a tender kiss behind her ear.

"I love you," he whispered. It felt so good to say it openly without worrying about her getting upset. The only thing better than verbally expressing his love was hearing her say it in return. He should probably let her sleep—their make-up sex had kept them awake well into the night—but he needed to see the love shining in her hazel eyes and hear her put the sentiment to words. In a few hours, she'd be his wife—Mrs. Myrna Sinclair. As far as he was concerned, the honeymoon started now.

Brian flicked Myrna's earlobe with his tongue and sucked it into his mouth. The breathy sigh she emitted grabbed him by the balls. It was always like this with her; she ignited an insatiable sexual hunger within him. And so many things about her contributed to it. Her openness to any sexual experience blew his mind and challenged him to invent new experiences to share with her. Her scent, her taste, the sexy little sounds she made while their bodies were joined, the texture of her skin, the way the light danced in her auburn hair, the gleam of naughtiness in her hazel eyes, how her pouty lips always begged for his kisses... The entirety of her physical being burned his body with awareness. The music he composed while making love to her inspired his soul. Her hard-won trust set his heart ablaze. He loved everything about her, even her stubbornness. She wasn't an easy woman, but she was the only woman for him. He'd known it the first time they'd made love. And now she knew it too. At least she said she did. He decided she needed a few reminders so she wouldn't forget.

Sucking and nibbling on her ear, he moved his hand to cover her breast. She arched into his palm, her hardened nipple pressing into his flesh.

"Brian!" she gasped.

It would be the one and only name she'd call out in ecstasy for the rest of their lives. He couldn't ever imagine growing tired of hearing her say it.

He slid his hand lower, over her ribs, her belly, seeking the center of her pleasure at the juncture of her thighs. His fingers brushed the crisp curls between her legs, and she shuddered. He already knew what he wanted to do to her. He'd stroke her clit until she came and then press her down on her belly, suspend himself over her back and fuck her slow from behind. Grind his hips each time he buried his cock deep inside. Tease her clit with his balls until she begged him to make her come.

Myrna caught his hand before he could find his target.

"No," she said firmly.

"*No?*" How could she say no? She never told him no. *Never.*

"Not until the honeymoon."

He grinned. "Which I've already decided starts now."

She rolled over to face him and winced. "Oh, baby, your *face!* And I thought you looked bad last night."

"Thanks."

Bar fights never ended well, even when you won. It hadn't necessarily been the brightest idea to get in a brawl at his bachelor party, but the instigator of the fight—one Eric Sticks—wasn't known for coming up with bright ideas. Impulsive ideas? Yeah. Troublemaking ideas? Definitely. But not bright ones. And the cause of the fight—one Jessica Chase. Well, he didn't want his morning ruined by thoughts of that gold digger.

For a few tense moments the night before, Brian had thought Myrna would call off their wedding. Thought his world would end. But after telling him off, she'd listened. She allowed him to explain. And while she hadn't condoned his idiocy—or Eric's—she'd forgiven him. He'd made sure to thank her body profusely for her forgiveness well into the night.

Myrna kissed the bridge of his nose, and his flesh throbbed in protest. Wincing, he drew a pained breath through his teeth.

"Does it hurt?" she asked, rubbing her thumb along his cheekbone.

"Doesn't feel good. Are both eyes black now?"

"Yep. You're the sexiest raccoon rock-god on the planet."

He grinned. "Well, as long as you think I'm sexy."

"Always." She kissed him and pulled away to stare into his eyes.

He stared back, his heart thudding with a mixture of love and lust and unadulterated joy. He couldn't believe Myrna was openly his. That she wanted to marry him. Today.

Holy shit!

"I love you," she said. She burrowed her fingers into his hair. "I love you," she said more firmly. "Do you believe me?"

Almost—it was still very new coming from her lips—but he said, "Yes."

"I think I fell in love with you when I saw you standing in the terminal in Portland waiting for me. Do you remember that?"

"Yeah, but you didn't love me then. I asked you if you were opening up possibilities between us and you said only sexual ones. And then you gave me your panties to make sure I understood exactly what you meant." He still had those panties somewhere.

"Well, I was an idiot. And I did love you, Brian, I just didn't want to admit it. I was scared."

"And you're not scared anymore?"

She shook her head.

"And you promise not to break my heart?" he asked.

"I promise."

"And you'll love me forever?"

"Forever."

"And we can start the honeymoon right now?"

She laughed. "Nope. I'm going to make you wait."

"It's the two black eyes, isn't it?"

He blinked at her, knowing he looked like shit. He felt like shit. He wasn't sure why he'd let his band mates talk him into going to a strip club for his bachelor party. They hadn't believed him when he'd told them he'd rather spend his last night of *freedom* with Myrna. He'd had enough of bachelorhood; it was only more of the same. The love he shared with Myrna was new and exciting. Exactly what he wanted. Needed. His smart and sexy *Myrna*. His heart.

"Nope, it's not the black eyes. It's knowing how hard you're going to fuck me after I tease you all day."

She offered him a devilish grin, and his cock pulsed with excitement.

"Are you sure you're not punishing me for getting into a fight last night?"

"Well, maybe a little." She kissed him again. "But I love you regardless." She stared at him with such intensity he had to look away.

"I *love* you," she said with conviction, and he met her eyes again. "*I* love you. I love *you*. Which way do you like me to say it?"

"Any way is fine with me as long as it's frequent and you mean it."

She continued to stare into his eyes. "I do. *I* do. I *do*. How should I say that?"

He grinned. "You just have to say that once."

She smiled and there was no mistaking that her level of happiness matched his.

"We have a busy day ahead of us," she said. "Rings. Dress. Makeover. Wedding. Sinners concert. Honeymoon. We'd better get out of bed."

"Or we can stay in bed, forget the dress, and get married right here while participating in the honeymoon. I'm a firm believer in multitasking." He grinned hopefully and nodded, encouraging her to mimic his motion and agree with his perfect plan.

The eyebrow she raised at him told him that wasn't happening. *Damn.*

He released a defeated sigh and pulled out of her arms. "Let's go pick out that ring. It'll be huge and expensive—no protests out of you."

· She opened her mouth, and he covered it with one hand.

"No protests."

The corners of her mouth turned up against his palm. He knew damned well he'd get her whatever ring she wanted.

"We're in agreement?"

She nodded, and he moved his hand so he could kiss her lips. "Are you ready to go pick it out?"

He so wanted to put that physical token of his affection on her left ring finger. The slender digit looked hopelessly bare at the moment. He drew her hand to his lips to kiss spot that would soon be obscured by his eternal rock.

She tossed the covers aside. "I need a shower first."

"I'll join you."

She appraised him for a moment, her gaze skimming over his naked flesh from head to toe. Her concentration focused mostly in the middle. When his cock hardened beneath her appreciative attention, her tongue darted out to wet her lips.

"Yeah, you will," she said.

Chapter 2

MYRNA SLIPPED INTO A THICK, red bathrobe and opened the door that lead to the main corridor of the tour bus. Naked, gorgeous, and *hard*, Brian followed her.

The bathroom was to her left. When she tried to slide the door open, she found it locked.

"Occupado," Eric Sticks called from within.

"Hurry up. We have to get ready for the wedding," Brian yelled, and pounded on the door with the heel of his hand.

"Almost finished," Eric called back.

"He's probably jerking it in there," Brian said.

Myrna turned and wrapped her arms around her soon-to-be husband. She'd promised herself she'd never get married again. Not after her first marriage had ended so horribly. But now that her defenses had crumbled, she couldn't wait to start her life with this wonderful man. After putting him off for so long and fighting his affections with an uncompromising—and in hindsight *ridiculous*—stubbornness, she felt she had a lot to make up to him. She wanted Brian to be happy. She wanted him to feel loved. Cherished. She'd never felt that way about her first husband. She had never wanted to put Jeremy's happiness before her own. What she had with Brian was special. Perfect. Forever. She wished she had recognized it sooner.

Sliding her hands up the smooth skin of Brian's back, she pressed a trail of kisses along his collarbone. "How many hours before I get to be Mrs. Sinclair?"

"We have to get a marriage license; that will probably take twenty minutes or so." He burrowed his hands into her hair and tilted her head back to sample her lips with tender, sucking kisses. "After that? As soon as you're ready."

"I'd say immediately, but I want to look pretty for you."

"You look damn fine in this robe, Professor."

"And you look damn fine in nothing, Master Sinclair."

The feel of his warm skin and firm muscles beneath her eager hands had her reconsidering her earlier decision to make him wait until that night. The Beast didn't want to wait either; Brian's cock rose hard and thick against her belly. She grabbed her fiancé's ass with both hands to pull him closer. He produced a sound, half groan/half growl, that made her pussy throb with need.

"I'm going to wear a skirt and spend the entire day without any panties on," she whispered in his ear.

"You can't expect me to control myself knowing that."

Her hand slid down the ridge of his hipbone. His thigh. Up the inside of his leg. She brushed the side of her hand over his balls, and he tensed.

"If you don't stop that, I'm going to fuck you right here," he said.

She repeated the motion. "Oh yeah?"

He pressed her up against the flimsy wall next to the bathroom door. His cock rubbed against the inside of her thigh, and she shuddered. *Yes, Brian, take me right here.*

"You have got to be fucking kidding me," Sed grumbled from his bunk just past the bathroom door.

"Sorry, did we wake you?" Myrna murmured.

Brian nuzzled her neck and ground his cock against her mound.

"Who can sleep with all the lovey, lovey, kissy, screw-me talk three feet from your head?" The usual smoothness of the singer's baritone was uncommonly raspy this morning and his demeanor even grumpier than usual.

"Jace for one," Brian said.

Myrna chuckled. Sinners' young bassist did like his sleep.

Myrna peeked over Brian's shoulder and found Jace unconscious in the top bunk. His cute stubble-adorned face was squashed against the mattress. His bleached hair lay limp instead of poking out in its usual spikes. *Endearing* was the word Myrna would use to describe Jace Seymour. And kinky. Or so she gathered based on tidbits she'd heard from groupies and what she'd seen in his suitcase of carnal delights.

"I think he had a rough night," Sed grumbled and cleared his throat with a wince. "He got in late and passed out in his bunk without even taking off his boots."

Or removing his leather jacket, Myrna noted with a grin.

She snuggled closer to Brian with her chin resting on his shoulder as they waited for the bathroom. Around here, someone always seemed to be waiting for the bathroom.

"You guys should consider staying in a hotel when the bus is parked," she said. "Aren't there around a million hotel rooms in this city?"

She'd grown accustomed to the close quarters of the bus while touring with the band for her research project, but after sharing a bathroom with five guys, she deserved a trophy or a medal or something.

A pair of grass-green eyes peered at her from the bottom bunk across the way. She was glad to see Trey awake. She'd been worried about him. Some overzealous bouncer had cracked him in the back of the head with a ball bat the night before, but he looked better than Brian did this morning, so he must be all right. She smiled at him, but he didn't return the smile. His gaze wasn't focused on her. It was zeroed in on Brian's bare ass. Trey's tongue rubbed against his upper lip, and Myrna could only imagine where his thoughts had drifted. A seed of jealousy sprouted in her chest, and she ran her hands over Brian's smooth ass cheeks. She grinned triumphantly when Brian's ever-attentive cock jerked against her belly.

Brian was hers—every inch of him—and Trey damned well better not forget it.

Trey closed his eyes and rolled onto his opposite side, presenting his back to her.

The bathroom door slid open, and Eric emerged. "All finished!" he announced, as if he expected a smiley face sticker for his accomplishment.

Brian turned his head toward the bathroom and took a hesitant sniff. Apparently finding the place nontoxic, he tugged Myrna into the small room. The bathroom door slid shut, and Myrna's robe landed on the floor an instant later.

"Alone at last." Brian filled both hands with her breasts, massaging gently. His dark eyes were glassy with lust as he watched his thumbs brush against her stiff nipples. "You know the idea of making love to my *wife* is enough to push me beyond control. You don't have to tease me all day to make me crazy."

She grinned at him and hopped up onto the vanity. "Good, because I don't want to wait all day. I want your wickedly fast fingers against me—*inside* me—right now." She leaned back against the cold vanity mirror, bent her knees, and rested her feet on the countertop, opening herself wide to her lover. Her fiancée. Her soon-to-be husband. "Make me come, baby. Make my pussy beg you to fill it."

"Can I taste you first?"

She didn't respond, just grabbed two fistfuls of his shoulder-length black hair and tugged his head between her legs.

He inhaled deeply. "Oh fuck, baby. You smell like sex."

His tongue slid inside her, and she watched him trace her opening. Around, around, around, until she had to close her eyes from overstimulation. He pressed two fingers inside her, and she strained against them, craving his big, thick cock already. His fingers pulled free to spread her juices over her throbbing clit.

"Oh!" she gasped.

He sucked her clit into his mouth and then rammed two fingers into her greedy body, thrusting them harder and harder as he suckled her clit with agonizing gentleness. She called out her pleasure, the sounds of her wet pussy and cries of excitement echoing off the walls of the tiny bathroom.

Brian pulled away and shifted his fingers to her clit, stroking her fast and hard.

"Watch yourself, baby. Watch."

She forced her gaze down between her legs where Brian was working her trigger. He knew exactly how to make her explode. Watching his fingers move against her and thinking about the way those fingers looked when he played one of his guitar solos sent her over the edge. Her ass lifted off the vanity, and he moved his hand away so she could see her pussy pulse with release. Brian rubbed the head of his cock against her opening as her spasms of pleasure tried to grip him. Tug him in.

He slipped inside her easily, and she stared at the spot where their bodies were joined. The way his cock filled her made her breath catch. Her flesh ebbed and stretched with his deep, steady strokes. Brian gyrated his hips as they watched her folds strain to accommodate his girth.

Slowly, her pleasure built again. Oh, but he filled her so perfectly, rubbed her just right.

"Brian." She needed the feel of his name on her lips almost as much as she needed the feel of his hard cock within her.

He lifted his head, and she met his gaze. They stared into each other's eyes as their bodies moved together over and over again. Emotions flooded her being, stealing her breath, making her eyes ache as tenderness overflowed.

"Brian?"

The physical connection, they'd always had that. But opening her heart to him made sex so much more than simple pleasure.

"Yes, baby?"

"I love you," she said.

He cupped her face between his palms and kissed her softly. "I love you." Buried balls deep, he stared into her eyes. "Are you really mine?" he whispered.

"Yes."

"About time you admitted it, Professor." He grinned and pulled out. She gasped in protest, but was too late to pull him back to her.

"Let's finish this in the shower," he said. "I'm determined to marry you today one way or another, and we need to work on some multitasking or we'll waste the entire day fucking in the tour bus bathroom."

"I wouldn't say we were *wasting* the day," she said.

"I will marry you today, Myrna Evans. Got it?"

"Got it," she said, smiling her brightest.

While he adjusted the temperature of the water, she hopped off the counter and moved up behind him to kiss his back with an open mouth and tongue and teeth. She rubbed her hands over his firm belly, his pecs, his strong shoulders. He stepped into the shower and she followed, consumed by her insatiable hunger for this man. Finally admitting that she loved him hadn't lessened her lust for him. If anything, it made it even more pronounced. How lucky was she to be in love and in lust with the same man?

He turned to face her, and her gaze lowered to his thick cock standing at proud attention between them. She wanted his cum in her mouth. Wanted it to pulse into the back of her throat. Wanted to swallow him whole.

She lowered herself to her knees, running her hands up his thighs. The warm water of the shower coursed between her splayed fingers and flowed down her arms. Brian tilted his head back into the flowing water the same instant she sucked his cock into her mouth.

"Ah," he gasped.

She held the base of his shaft with one hand as she bobbed her head fast, sucked him hard, and cradled his heavy balls in her palm. She wanted to reward him for being so good to her. For loving her. She knew what he liked. She moved her free hand between her legs and slid her fingers into her silky depths, seeking slick juices to ease her penetration of her lover. When she'd collected enough of her own fluids on her fingertips, she lifted her hand between his legs.

Her slippery fingers pressed against the opening to his ass, and he grunted before widening his legs. She slid two fingers inside him, gently thrusting in and out until he began to whimper. He knew what was coming. Knew how good she could make him feel. Trusted her with his body. It rocked her world that he let her do this for him.

She released his shaft to free her other hand and shifted it to his balls, drawing them forward and gently massaging them against the base of his cock in slow gentle circles. Inside his ass, the fingers of her other hand curled forward, and she rubbed against his gland. He wasn't the only one who knew how to work a trigger. Brian started spurting immediately. His entire body shuddered as he cried out in bliss. His fluids pulsing into the back of her throat, Brian grabbed her head to slow its relentless bobbing as she sucked him off, but she refused to lay off until he'd spent every last drop. He sagged against the shower wall, gulping for air and shaking with aftershocks of pleasure. Releasing his cock with a loud sucking pop, Myrna teased the opening at its tip with her tongue, still rubbing him inside to prolong his bliss.

Myrna loved how massaging his prostate made him shudder and quake. Loved how he allowed her to do any kinky thing she wanted to do to him. Loved how he made her feel sexy and appreciated. She couldn't wait to spend the rest of their lives figuring out what other things they had in common, because it was blatantly obvious that they had the sex part figured out.

"God, baby," he groaned. "I don't know what I did to deserve that, but let me know what it was so I can do it repeatedly."

"Did you like that? My fingers inside you?"

"You know I like it."

"One of these days I'm going to strap on a dildo and fuck you in the ass."

She pulled her fingers free of his body and climbed to her feet. She wasn't sure why, but the thought of dominating him—of fucking him—really turned her on. Maybe it was because Brian had never allowed Trey to take him.

She sighed. She wasn't sure why she was so flipping jealous of the guy today. Maybe because Trey had loved Brian unconditionally for ages and she was just beginning to offer him the same devotion. Well, whatever the reason for that unwarranted emotion making a reappearance this morning, she needed to get over it. She knew Brian didn't have romantic feelings for Trey, no matter how much

Trey wanted him to. If Brian hadn't started loving the guy by now, he wasn't about to do so anytime soon—or ever, if she had a say in the matter.

His cock twitched at whatever wild thoughts were circulating through that gloriously deviant mind of his.

"Sounds interesting. How about we try it tonight?"

She had expected him to protest her demand a little, but was delighted that he'd agreed. The man was so sexually experimental; so open to anything. It was one of the things she loved most about him and a quality she hadn't realized was lacking in her past romantic interests until she'd found her sexual match in Brian. At first their sexual compatibility had been enough to keep her with him, but somewhere along the way she'd realized that while his body was an amazing gift, it was the man's open and loving heart that was the real prize. And unlike her, Trey had probably realized that before Brian had branded him with lust.

Damn it. Why couldn't she stop thinking about Trey this morning? Had she again dreamed about the way he'd looked when he'd stolen a kiss from Brian? She couldn't deny Trey's love-drenched look of longing still haunted her thoughts and dreams. Her lover had seemed completely unaffected by the kiss she'd witnessed Trey take from him. So if it hadn't meant anything to Brian, why did it bother her so fucking much?

"We'll take a detour to a sex shop after we pick out our rings," she said, forcing thoughts of Trey from her mind. Her misguided jealousy was her issue, not Brian's, and she wouldn't let niggling insecurities about a long-ago tryst between a pair of drunken, testosterone-fueled teenagers to darken her wedding day.

Completely oblivious to her internal struggles, Brian wrapped her in a tight embrace. "God, I love you, woman," he said. "My turn to make you come."

"Yeah, it is."

His ingenious fingers moved between her legs to stroke her clit, his touch sending thoughts of Trey's infatuation scattering and her knees buckling.

Chapter 3

MYRNA HID HER HAND BEHIND her back as Brian came after it with a monster of a diamond engagement ring. The platinum setting had channel set princess diamonds surrounding a round central stone large enough to kill a charging elephant.

"It's too big," Myrna protested. She'd been in love with the stunning designer ring until she'd glimpsed the price tag and had gone light-headed. The thing was worth more than her beloved Thunderbird.

"Try it on before you decide," Brian suggested.

Resolved to tell him she didn't like the way it looked on her finger, she held out her left hand and forced herself not to dissolve into a puddle of mush at the delighted smile on Brian's handsome face. She was going to have to give the guy his way more often; he practically radiated happiness at his small victory.

He sank to one knee at her feet, and her heart dropped.

"Brian, what are you doing?" she whispered, glancing nervously at the store clerk, who grinned broadly, and then looked back down at the man at her feet.

"Asking you properly," Brian said, gazing up at her with love shining in his eyes.

She scarcely noticed the bruised rings around those eyes, they were so filled with hope and happiness.

"Myrna Evans, I love you with all I am, have been, or will ever be. Will you marry me?"

"I already said I would," she said around the lump in her throat.

"You should answer me properly," he said. "In front of this witness who is about to make a huge commission."

Myrna laughed because she was so damned happy. Her only other option was crying. And for the same reason.

"Yes, Brian Sinclair, I will marry you," she said.

The clerk clapped her hands excitedly as Brian slipped the ring on Myrna's left ring finger.

"Now you have to accept it," he said with a crooked grin, "no matter how expensive it is."

"You jerk," Myrna said. She smiled down at her hand and her heart skipped a beat. Her vision blurred as her eyes filled with tears at seeing his ring on her finger for the first time. "You generous, wonderful, sweet *jerk*!"

She practically tackled him to the ground when she dropped into his arms and kissed him desperately. He chuckled against her lips, his arms tightening around her to draw her closer. After a moment, he turned his face toward the jewelry counter, and Myrna moved her kisses to his jaw and neck.

"We'll also take a couple of wedding bands to go," Brian said to the clerk. "As you can see, we're a bit anxious to get to the honeymoon."

After purchasing her ridunckulous engagement ring and their matching wedding bands, they headed to a nearby bridal shop on foot.

Brian jerked Myrna's arm and she gasped in pain. She drew to a sudden halt and turned to him to ask him what the fuck he thought he was doing when she discovered she'd almost walked into the doorframe of the bridal shop. She'd been so busy staring at her engagement ring, transfixed by its sparkle that she'd probably have earned a set of shiners to match his if he hadn't yanked her out of harm's way. The ring might be extravagant for her taste, but it was also stunning and, more importantly, it symbolized how much she meant to Brian.

She gaped at the huge rock at the realization. Holy fuck, he must love her a lot.

Inside the shop, Myrna explained her dire situation, and a bridal consultant shoved ten different dresses into her arms before showing her to a dressing room. She had to find something that fit right off the rack because there was no time for alterations.

After almost an hour of trying on dresses, the growing pile of discarded gowns was starting to depress her. The first didn't fit. The next made her look flat-chested. Another two were downright ugly; were all those bows on her ass really necessary? One not even close to her style never made it off the hanger.

On Myrna's seventh attempt, she was starting to think she should just get married in her business attire. Brian liked when she wore suits. She was sure he wouldn't mind her wearing one at the ceremony. Her bridal assistant, Carla—*we'll find you something perfect, honey, I've never failed yet*—finished zipping the latest dress and stood back to study Myrna. Her breath caught, and she covered her wide mouth with trembling fingers. Myrna lifted her eyes to the three reflections of herself in the mirror, expecting yet another disappointment. She never expected to burst into tears.

"That's the one," Carla said, pulling Myrna, now sobbing uncontrollably, into her arms to rub her back until she got a handle on her emotions.

"I'm sorry. I can't believe I'm crying." Myrna drew away and dabbed at her eyes, feeling like a complete ass for getting so emotional over a stupid dress.

"Happens all the time," Carla assured her. She smiled broadly. "Are you wearing it out, then?"

"I don't want him to see me in it yet."

Brian was sitting just outside the dressing room waiting for her.

"Do you have someone to help you with the zipper?"

She supposed she could ask one of the guys to help her on the bus. "I'll figure something out."

She turned back to the mirror and ran her hands down the rumpled satin bodice.

The white dress was form fitting from breast to hip; the skirt was loose and long and gathered on one side by a decorative design embroidered in silver thread. The hem just brushed the floor. She turned to examine the back, which had a simple train that extended a few feet behind her. The row of pearl buttons that hid the back zipper was a lovely bonus that ended in another design embroidered in silver that bunched the train just below her rump. She'd wanted to look beautiful for Brian when he took her as his wife and, in this dress, she felt beautiful. She held her arms out and shook her hips side to side, watching the skirt sway enticingly. Perfect. The dress was perfect.

"Did you find anything yet?" Brian called from outside the dressing room door. "It's getting late, sweetheart. Just pick something."

"Just pick something," Carla said and rolled her eyes. "Men just don't get it."

But Myrna knew when he saw her in this dress, he'd get it. Because the sap was far more sentimental than she was.

"I think I found something suitable," Myrna called to her eager fiancé. "I'll be out as soon as I take it off."

"I want to see it." The door handle rattled, but it was locked.

"You'll have to wait," Myrna said. "I want it to be a surprise.

Chapter 4

BRIAN PACED UP AND DOWN the aisle of Sinners' tour bus. His four band mates watched him as if they were spectators at Wimbledon. He paused before the closed door at the end of the corridor and listened for sounds of Myrna moving inside the bedroom. Silence assaulted his ears. She *had* to be in there. There was no escaping the bedroom. The window was too small, and he'd have noticed if she'd tried to sneak past him.

Brian couldn't wait to see her in her dress. Couldn't wait to see *her*, dress or no dress. But even though he willed it, the doorknob didn't turn. The door didn't open. His woman didn't appear, leap into his arms, and kiss him senseless. Not yet. What was taking her so long?

Trey had helped her zip herself into the garment ages ago. Well, maybe it had only been twenty minutes ago, but it *felt* like ages, especially since Trey had made a big show about how gorgeous she looked as he'd left her alone in the bedroom to fix her hair or whatever was taking her an eternity.

Brian wrapped the rope of chain that hung from his belt loop around one finger and jangled it repeatedly. His pre-concert jitters had nothing on these pre-wedding jitters. The soles of his feet were cold, as if ice water filled his boots. At least pacing kept his mind off the turbulence in his stomach. Sort of. He turned and headed back up the aisle toward the front of the bus, moving past the bathroom, the bunks stacked on each side of the corridor, and the dining table.

Like a parking garage gate, an arm dropped in front of him. Brian drew to a halt and lifted a questioning brow at his best friend. His best man. His musical soul mate—rhythm guitarist Trey Mills.

"Will you sit down?" Trey said. "You're driving me insane."

"Can't help it. I'm freaking out," Brian said.

Eric stopped tapping his drumsticks on the tabletop and glanced up at him. "Why? You're not having second thoughts, are you? Because if you are, Myrna's gonna need a lot of consoling for her broken heart." Eric grinned, looking entirely too pleased with the idea. "I think I'll go check on her."

When he started to climb out of the booth, Brian sat beside him and shoved him up against the wall to prevent him from trying to console Myrna, who needed no consoling. If anyone needed consoling, it would be him. And Eric would not be the one he turned to.

"I'm not having second thoughts," Brian said. "I think maybe she is."

"She's not." Sed's deep voice sounded just behind Brian's left shoulder. "She's happy. *With* you. I'm not sure why, exactly, when she could have had me..."

Brian snapped his head up to glare at Sed, and Sed chuckled.

"Easy, Sinclair." Sed shoved his shoulder. "Your prize is safe. I'm just fucking with you."

Brian wasn't so sure. Sed had a way with women. Brian's women. And Sed had been moping all day about his ex-fiancée. The one who had left and ripped his heart out. The one he'd seen the night before for the first time in two years. The one who caused grown men to fight burly bouncers for reasons still not entirely clear. Sed might be trying to play it cool, but Brian knew better. Jessica had wrecked the man and until Sed let her go for good, he wasn't ever going to get out of his romantic slump. Or stop imposing that romantic slump on those around him.

"So what are you going to say to her?" Jace asked.

Brian glanced across the table at their bass player. Jace had been on edge all day. The youngest member of the band checked the time again, before briefly meeting Brian's eyes. Something was going on with Jace, not that he'd ever share what it was. But he was acting weird even for Jace.

Perplexed, Brian said, "Say to her?" He had absolutely nothing nice to say to Jessica Chase.

"Your vows," Jace clarified. "They're kind of important."

Oh. He'd meant *that* her. The important one.

"I don't know," Brian said. "I figured it would be best to wing it. So it's more sincere."

"Wrong," Trey said. "As nervous as you are now, how do you think you're going to feel during the actual ceremony?"

The only thing Brian was nervous about was that the wedding might not take place. What was taking her so long to get ready?

"Do you still have the rings?" he asked Trey.

"Yes. I promise I didn't hock them for beer money."

"Let me see."

Trey sighed and lifted his butt out of the bench seat so he could slide his hand into the front pocket of his jeans. He slid his hand deeper, a confused look on his face. "I'm sure they're in here somewhere."

Brian's heart stuttered in his chest.

Trey checked his other pocket. "This is not good," he said. "Maybe you need to check for me." He held his pocket open in invitation.

"Stop fucking around, Trey." Brian reached across the table and grabbed Trey around the neck.

Trey's pained outrush of breath gave Brian pause. He'd forgotten about Trey's head injury. They'd all gotten into that little fight at the strip club the night before and were suffering various afflictions. Perhaps Brian had gotten off easy with his two black eyes. At least he didn't have a huge knot on the back of his head.

"Are you okay?" he asked.

Trey closed his eyes and lifted a finger at Brian. After a moment, he opened his eyes. "Yeah. It comes and goes."

"I still think we need to take him to a hospital," Sed said.

"Brian's getting married today," Trey said.

"So?"

"I'm the best man."

"We'll go after the wedding, then."

"We have a concert."

"And?" Sed's look of warning would have sent most men running, but Trey just shook his head in annoyance.

"Dare will rip off my junk and feed it to jackals if we miss this performance," Trey said.

Sinners just so happened to be opening for Dare's band, Exodus End, at Las Vegas's Mandalay Bay in about four hours.

Eric burst out laughing. "Where's he going to find a jackal?"

"The zoo. How the hell should I know? He's Dare. He has connections."

If Trey needed a doctor, Brian didn't want him to put off getting treatment for any reason. Not even the much anticipated wedding that he and Myrna had been planning for two entire days. "Myrna and I could postpone—"

"I'm not going to the hospital."

"You will if we make you," Sed said.

"I'm fine. Fuck. Get off my back."

"I think you should go," Brian said. "If you're fine, they'll just look you over and send you on your way."

"After I sit in the ER waiting room for five hours." Trey unwrapped a cherry sucker and stuck it into his mouth. "Not going."

Brian heard the bedroom door open. His heart leapt to his throat. He was on his feet even before his bride appeared in the doorway.

The fitted bodice of her gorgeous white dress pressed her breasts up and together in a most beguiling manner while its gathered skirt made her waist look impossibly tiny and her hips look extra curvy. Myrna covered the center of her chest with one dainty hand. Light caught the diamond engagement ring on her finger. The ring Brian had put there a couple of hours ago. The ring that proved she'd agreed to be his. The ring that he'd convinced her to accept even though she'd protested its expense. He was proud of his small victory. The diamond was ginormous. No guy would ever consider hitting on her with *that* rock on her finger.

Myrna's auburn hair was pulled back in an elegant twist with loose tendrils framing her beautiful face. She'd applied her make-up to make the green in her hazel eyes pop, and the coral color that had been applied to her soft, pouty lips made them look even more kissable than usual.

Stunning. His woman was stunning. And his.

Even though Myrna's physical beauty stole Brian's breath, there was something that rocked his world even more than her face and her body. It was the blended look of love, anticipation, and *trust* in her wide eyes as she stared at him from the end of the corridor that had him completely out of his head.

"I think I'm ready," she said, her voice trembling with emotion.

Brian couldn't keep his hands off her for another moment. He dashed down the hallway and swept her into his arms, drawing the full length of her body against him.

"You shouldn't kiss me yet," she said breathlessly.

"Why?"

"I just put on lipstick."

"Then you're going to have to put it on again."

She smiled and wrapped her arms around his neck. "I can live with that."

He lowered his head, pausing with his lips a hair's breadth from hers. His heart thrummed with anticipation, and his cock stirred to attention against his upper thigh. After a moment, her eyes flipped open. He watched her pupils constrict as she focused on his eyes.

"You're right," he whispered. "I shouldn't kiss you."

"Why not?"

"I want to marry you first."

"Then let's get going, because I really need to be kissed. Among other things." Her hands slid over the white dress shirt she'd talked him into wearing. "You look so handsome in this shirt. I want to bite off your buttons."

At her words, he no longer felt like a douche for wearing it for her.

Brian took her hand and walked backward down the bus aisle toward the exit, tugging her with him. He couldn't take his eyes off her even to watch where he was going. "Trey, I hope you found those rings," he said as he passed the dining table.

"I've got them. Where are we going?"

"The first drive-thru wedding chapel we encounter."

"We can't all fit in the Thunderbird," Eric said.

"We'll just shove you and Jace in the trunk," Trey said.

"We'll follow on my motorcycle," Jace said.

"Where's your sense of adventure?" Trey asked, wrapping an arm around Jace's shoulders.

"I don't call a trip in the trunk of a car with Eric an adventure. More of a nightmare."

"Hey," Eric said, "I took a shower this morning." He sniffed his armpit. "*And* remembered deodorant, you lucky motherfucker."

Trey laughed.

Brian hoped the ceremony didn't take too long. He had a powerful need to strip that dress off Myrna's gorgeous body and get her worked up enough to bite off his buttons.

Chapter 5

MYRNA SERIOUSLY NEEDED TO GET a bigger car. Her pink '57 Thunderbird convertible coupe did not seat four comfortably. Hell, it didn't seat three comfortably. Brian, Trey, and Sed sat hip to hip across the white leather bench seat, leaving Myrna to sit on their combined laps and smoother them all with the huge skirt of her gown. Layers of satin did not mix well with the brutal Vegas heat. Still she had no doubt that she hadn't chosen this dress—it had chosen her—so she'd had no choice but to claim it as her wedding gown. To hell with comfort and practicality. She was getting married to fucking Brian "Master" Sinclair—in her opinion the greatest guitarist who ever lived. She was determined to look beautiful for him even if she died of heatstroke.

The car pulled into a drive-thru wedding chapel, the rumble of Jace's Harley following behind them. As they sat in line waiting their turn, Myrna fidgeted with her engagement ring. She'd vowed never to get married again. How had she fallen into this trap? Oh God, what was she thinking? This would never work. Brian was a rock star; she was a college professor. Their worlds were on opposite ends of the spectrum. How would they ever manage to stay together when they'd be forced to spend so much time apart?

Brian's hand covered hers and squeezed. She looked into his eyes, and her concerns instantly evaporated. *This* was how she'd fallen. Exactly this. He was wonderful, and she was incredibly lucky he hadn't given up on her. And they *would* make it work. They would. She wouldn't give up on him, on *them*, ever.

"What are you thinking?" he asked.

"I've fallen."

"And I can't get up!" Eric said from the back of Jace's motorcycle, which sat idling next to the car's passenger side.

"Eric, we're going to have to gag you, aren't we?" Sed said and reached out of the car to make a grab for him. Eric jerked back just in time.

"I have a gag," Jace said. "But it's back on the bus."

If Myrna didn't love these guys as her surrogate family, she would have clobbered them all. "Guys, today is all about me," she said, "so shut the hell up."

Brian chuckled and lifted her hand to his lips. He kissed her knuckles. "That's one reason I knew I had to marry you."

"Because I'm bitchy?"

"Because you don't treat my band mates like rock stars."

"She does bitch at us," Trey said.

"Constantly," Sed added.

"And I, for one, like it very much," Eric said.

The car in front of them pulled away, and Brian eased up to the window. Jace moved the motorcycle next to the car and shut off the rumbling engine. They were greeted by Elvis Presley. Well, a pretty good imitation of him. Elvis slid his large, white-framed sunglasses down his nose and offered a wide smile.

"I say-uh, welcome to the Chapel of Rock, baby."

"Fitting," Trey said.

"Do you got the paperwork, baby? We need a license to make it legit."

Brian handed Elvis the marriage license they'd picked up at the bureau that morning. "Best sixty bucks I ever spent," Brian said.

While Elvis did whatever it was he needed to do with the marriage license, Brian slid up to sit on the trunk of the convertible with his feet resting on the front seat. He drew Myrna up to sit across his lap, wrapping one strong arm around her back. He took her hand in his free hand, holding it gently. She stared into his eyes, and his encouraging smile made the entire world melt away. This was really happening. She was marrying Brian Sinclair. Becoming his wife. Forever. Her smile widened until her cheeks hurt.

"Is this man your hunka hunka burning love?" Elvis asked.

Myrna laughed. "I'll say."

"Does this woman have you all shook up?" Elvis asked.

Brian grinned. "Yeah, she does."

Elvis broke into a decent rendition of "Love Me Tender." Sed joined him in the second chorus. By the time Elvis finished, the entire band was accompanying him at the top of their lungs, even Brian. Myrna couldn't stop laughing. How many women could claim that Elvis and Sinners serenaded her on her wedding day? Only her. And as obnoxious as it was, their willingness to make fools of themselves on her behalf meant the world to her. At the end of the song, Myrna hugged Brian and whispered into his ear, "God, I love you... and your stupid band too."

He chuckled. "That's good, because you're stuck with us for life."

And where that idea had once terrified her, a lifetime suddenly didn't seem long enough.

She looked up into Brian's intense brown eyes, her throat tight with emotion, her eyes prickling with tears.

"Do you have vows you want to recite to your baby?" Elvis asked.

Words tumbled from Myrna's lips like toppling dominos. All the things she'd been afraid to voice, to *feel*, since she'd first met Brian, poured out in one rush of emotion.

"I don't know how you knew what I needed more than I did. Or why you refused to give up on me. I'm just so very glad you didn't. You loved me when I didn't want to be loved. Lifted me when I didn't realize I was down. Gave me so much I was too stupid to take, too afraid that I'd come to need you and lose myself. I thought that by loving you, I'd become weak. I know now that loving you doesn't make me weak, Brian, it makes me stronger." She tugged his hand against her chest over her pounding heart. "I know I've hurt you more than once, and I don't know how to make that up to you other than trust you with my heart and love you the way you deserve to be loved. That's what I vow. I vow to love you and tell you often. I vow to stay beside you no matter what the future brings. Have faith in you. In us. I also vow to be true to you—heart, mind, body, and soul—and *never* cheat on you with Sed."

Brian laughed and touched her cheek. "Never?"

"Never. I want only you. Need only you. Always."

She turned to look at Trey, who looked more than a little nauseated. She wasn't sure if the nausea was due to his head trauma or the fact that she was so openly committing to Brian.

"Ring?" She extended her hand in Trey's direction. He dropped Brian's thick platinum band in her hand. Myrna took Brian's left hand and slid the ring onto his ring finger. "With this ring, you're stuck with me, because I refuse to ever let you go."

He grinned, his eyes turning skyward with a look of elation. How could any woman resist a man who was so overjoyed by her expressions of love? Brian should have been married years ago. She silently sent a word of thanks to Sed for being such a jackass and destroying Brian's previous relationships. In a strange way, she owed Sed one. Or twenty. Hopefully, one day she'd be able to return the favor and help him find a woman who truly made him happy—as happy as she was with Brian. Boy, would that be a tall order to fill.

Waiting for the words he would say to her, Myrna suppressed the urge to hug Brian. She didn't want to distract him. She needed to hear what was in his heart.

Brian cleared his throat and stared at Myrna's chin. "Trey was right: I should have written this down."

"You wish you would have listened to me now, don't you?" Trey said.

"Just tell me how you feel, baby," Myrna encouraged, stroking Brian's hair behind one ear until he looked up at her again.

"I think I'm better at showing."

She lowered her eyes to hide her disappointment. It probably didn't help that his four band mates were witness to the verbalization of his feelings. She knew he loved her; that was good enough for her. He could tell her when they were alone.

Brian tucked a finger under her chin, and she lifted her gaze to meet his.

"I thought I knew what love was, that I understood its depth, its importance, its beauty and the happiness and the heartache it brings." He huffed—a small sound of amusement. "I wasn't even close. When I look at you, I see radiance. I know pure happiness. Everything else pales in comparison. The thought of living a single moment without you tears me apart inside. Just when I think I love you as much as possible, you open your heart to me a little more, and my love expands—grows—wanting to fill every emptiness inside you."

"You have," she whispered. And that was just it—the reason she could love him forever. This moment wasn't the ultimate expression of their love; it was just the beginning. As long as they continued to nurture what existed between them, their affections would burn brighter, lift them higher, bring them closer. Grow.

"I love you, Myrna."

He snatched her ring from Trey's palm. She slipped her hours-old engagement ring off so he could slide her wedding ring onto her finger.

"With this ring, I claim you as mine and give my heart to you. Forever."

He lifted her hand to his lips and kissed the ring he'd just slid in place. She didn't need the material possession. Didn't need the piece of paper that legally bound them. Didn't even need the ceremony before witnesses. The only thing she needed—to know this union was sacred and forever—was the look of love on Brian's handsome face. She carefully slipped her engagement ring back on her finger—keeping her wedding ring nearer her heart—so she didn't drop the expensive thing with her trembling hands.

"I now pronounce you husband and uh-wife," the Elvis justice of the peace said. "I say-uh you may kiss your beautiful bride."

Myrna wrapped both arms around Brian's neck and met his lips with tenderness that quickly burgeoned into insatiable need. There was more to this kiss than a mutual sharing of pleasure. It was a physical expression of their love. She let the emotions take her, holding nothing back, knowing this man was incapable of intentionally destroying her. He *could* destroy her, but he wouldn't. She trusted him completely. As her last defenses crumbled, she wondered why she felt victorious instead of defeated. She'd lost. She'd given in to him, yet she'd won so much for herself in return.

Oh God, she loved him so much, she could just go on kissing him forever.

The guys offered their congratulations. Sed pounded Brian on the back. Eric cheered. Myrna continued to kiss her husband until everyone but Brian was complaining. Even the Elvis impersonator was trying to hurry them along. The kiss consumed her, not with lust, though that physical spark between her and Brian was still strong and true, but with love. *This* was what she'd been fighting? What she'd been afraid of? What a fool she'd been. She pulled Brian closer, wishing that she could dissolve into his body and truly become one with him.

When they drew apart at last, she stared into her husband's eyes and knew he was counting on her to be his rock. His life on the road was not an easy one. That stability he craved in his life? She could be that for him. She could. And he could be everything she'd been denying herself for far too long.

Chapter 6

BRIAN GAZED DOWN AT HIS WIFE—his *wife*—spread across the bed in the tour bus's bedroom. The wide skirt of her white gown concealed all but the three-inch heels on her feet and one trim ankle. She had the tip of her index finger trapped between her teeth and a seductive smile on her lips that said, *I'm all yours.* Damn, she was the most beautiful thing he'd ever seen. She deserved better than a wedding night on a tour bus.

"We could go to a hotel right now," he said. "A penthouse suite."

"You have a concert in three hours."

"So?"

She chuckled in a way that made his balls tighten with need. "Once I get started with you, husband of mine, I'm not going to stop. Which is bound to start a fifteen-thousand-fan riot on the streets of Las Vegas when you miss your gig."

"What if I'm ready to start with you now, wife? Fuck the consequences."

"Come lie beside me," she said and patted the mattress next to her curvy hip.

Damn, that dress was as sexy as it was beautiful. It was as if it had been made specifically for her.

He kicked off his shoes and crawled up onto the bed beside her. She deftly flipped him onto his back and pressed her luscious breasts against his chest as she kissed him.

She drew away and stared down into his eyes. He lifted a hand to trace the contour of her cheek with his thumb. She smiled and then cuddled up against his side, her head resting on his shoulder, her hand splayed over his belly.

"Where are we going to live?" she asked.

The idea that they would be separated for even an hour made his chest ache. "You're finishing out the summer on tour with us, aren't you?"

"Yeah, but that's only six more weeks. How long will you be on tour after that?"

"Until almost Thanksgiving."

Her hand curled into the fabric of his crisp dress shirt. "I don't want to live a day without you, but I'm not ready to give up my career either."

"I wouldn't ask you to. I know you love your work."

"Some of it," she said, her voice wavering with uncertainty. "I'm not sure if my unconventional ways of thinking will ever be embraced by my peers."

"I've always wondered why you specialized in human sexuality."

She laughed. "Seriously?"

"Just curious." He knew she didn't like to talk about herself. She was very guarded about certain aspects of her life. Especially her past.

"Because I love sex. The way it feels. How much it influences people. Its wondrous variety. I'm sure you already know that."

Oh yeah, he definitely knew she loved sex and all its variations. He'd never met a woman who appreciated sex more than Myrna Evans. Erm, Myrna Sinclair. *Sinclair!* His hand moved to the back of her head to press her closer to his chest. He could scarcely believe she was his wife now. *His.*

"But there's more to the subject than just hands-on experimentation. I like to study how it affects people—physically, emotionally, spiritually. It's biology. Psychology. Sociology. I never told you this, but I use guitar riffs in one of my classes and have my students discuss the sexual nature of rock music."

"Really?"

"Yeah, and do you know whose riffs evoke the strongest sensual response?"

He lifted his head to look at her.

"Yours. The way you play is like sex on strings."

He chuckled. "Especially since you came into my life."

"You'll have to play for my class sometime."

"Sure. I'd love to see where you work."

"I'm probably being selfish, but do you think it's possible for you to live with me in Kansas City when you're not on tour?"

"I have this album to—"

She lifted a finger to hush him. "And then I'll consider quitting my full-time job to start a family. I really want to keep working one more year. I'm excited about the groupie project I've been working on this summer, but it's time for a change. As soon as I finish this project, I want to do some other things." She snuggled closer to his chest. "Mostly I want to have a baby with you."

Stunned speechless, Brian's vision blurred. Had he heard her correctly? She wanted to start a family?

"Unless you don't want children," she said, obviously mistaking his dumbstruck silence for hesitation toward the idea. "I know you'll make a great father, Brian. Even though it'll be tough to raise a family when you're on the road so much, you'll be there as often as possible. I realize I'll have to do a lot by myself while you're gone, but the thought of making a baby with you and carrying him or her inside me just makes me happy." She covered her lower belly with both hands and tilted her head to look at him. "Brian?"

Make a baby with Myrna? Yes, please. He was ready to start immediately. In one swift motion, he rolled her beneath him, covering her body with his and cupping her lovely face between his hands.

"You make me so happy, Myrna. I can't wait to start a family with you. Can we start right away?"

A brilliant smile lit her features, but she didn't immediately start flushing her birth control pills down the toilet. "We should wait a few months to get pregnant. It would be best if I deliver the baby at the end of next May, when the school year is over. That would make the most sense."

He chuckled. "My logical little sex professor." He kissed her. Honestly, he was surprised she'd made this decision so easily. It was as if her admission of love changed her entire outlook. He was glad he'd been patient with her and hadn't pushed her too fast or too hard and driven her away. It was nice to get something right and be rewarded for it. "That makes perfect sense, baby. I think it's a good idea. I also think I need to practice baby-making right now. I love you so much my dick is hard."

She laughed. "Sweetheart, you don't need any more practice. You're already at the top of your game."

"Then it's time for the next inning."

There was no way he was letting her put him off until after Sinners' concert. He needed to deepen the connection between them. To lose himself in her. To lessen the ache in his groin. The woman was trying to kill him.

"Hey, Myrna," Eric called from just outside the door. "We got it—come see."

She smiled at Brian. "I'm hungry," she said. "How about you?"

"I hope you mean you're hungry for sex."

"I'm always hungry for sex. Who do you think you married today?"

He grinned. "You. I married you."

When his hands began to wander over the smooth skin of her bare shoulders, she twisted from beneath him and climbed from the bed, tugging on the skirt trapped beneath his body.

"Come on," she said. "The guys have a surprise for you."

"Is that why you're still in your dress? You've been waiting for the guys to do something stupid." He forced himself from the bed, his hard-on-from-hell uncomfortable in his pants.

"They went to a lot of trouble to get this surprise for you. They want to celebrate with us."

"I'm going to fucking kill them all. I don't want to celebrate with them; I want to celebrate with you."

"Well, I'm going to celebrate with them. You can stay in here by yourself if you want."

Damn woman, knowing how to get him to do exactly what she wanted him to do. She opened the door, and Brian caught sight of Eric in the corridor, holding a decorated white cake.

"What do you think?" Eric asked Myrna.

Brian joined her in the doorway. The square cake had a pink '57 Ford Thunderbird printed in the icing. On the trunk of the car was a little sign made out of frosting: *Just Married to the Band.*

"Uh, no," Brian said. "She's just married to *me*."

"When you marry a band member, you always marry into the band," Sed said, his deep voice a bit gruff.

"I love it, guys! It's perfect," Myrna said. "Let's all have some."

Eric, preening like a peacock, placed the cake in the center of the dining table. "I told you she'd love it," he told Jace, who was sitting in the booth looking like he was going to hop out of his skin at any minute. Dude needed to get laid in a bad way.

"Where's Trey?" Myrna asked.

"Sleeping."

"Sleeping?" Myrna drew back the curtain of his bunk. Trey was curled into fetal position around his pillow. Myrna leaned down to brush his bangs out of his face. He didn't stir. "I'm worried about him. How long was he unconscious last night?"

"A few minutes, maybe." Attempting to get a better look at Trey, Sed leaned closer to Myrna.

Brian tensed. He doubted that he'd ever get over his aversion to having Sed near his woman. He trusted Myrna, but women had a way of losing their panties if Sed so much as glanced at them. And Brian knew for a fact that, currently, Myrna wasn't wearing panties. One less line of defense against Sed the Fuckinator.

"Should we just take him to the hospital?" Sed said, flexing his huge biceps.

Brian was satisfied when Myrna didn't swoon at the sight of his impressive guns.

"I think I can hold him down until we get there."

Trey's eyes drifted open, and he pinned Sed with a look of disgust. "I heard that. I already told you I'm not going to any hospital. I'm just a little tired. What's the big deal?" He sat up in his bunk and went white as a sheet.

"Trey..." Brian said.

"Don't you start on me too."

When Trey stood, he swayed slightly. Brian wrapped an arm around him and ran his free hand over the back of Trey's head where that overzealous asshole bouncer had cracked him in the skull with a bat the night before.

"The swelling's gone down since last night," Brian said. "But you still have a lump."

"See, I'm fine."

"Trey, I think you should get this checked out." Brian stared into his best friend's eyes, willing him to agree.

Trey lowered his gaze after a long moment. "I'm fine." He leaned around Brian, instantly alert when he spotted what Eric had set on the table. "Is that cake?"

"With strawberry filling," Eric said. "They didn't have cherry."

Trey beamed. "You asked for cherry? For me?"

"Myrna told me to," Eric said.

Trey tugged Myrna into his arms. "Hey, baby, where have you been all my life?"

When he tipped her backwards and then upright again, she laughed.

"Let's see," she said. "BFE, Missouri."

"Wish I knew where that was." Trey squeezed her against him, rocking back and forth.

"Between a soybean field and a farrowing house."

"What the fuck's a farrowing house?"

"Where piglets are born."

Trey made his impish face. The one that got him anything he

wanted. "Sounds cute."

"Smells bad." Myrna snuggled closer to Trey. "But you smell good. New aftershave?"

"Some fan sent it to me. If you like it, I'll give it to Brian."

Watching Trey and Myrna touch and tease each other didn't make Brian jealous in the least. Truth be told, it turned him on more than a little. He wondered if Myrna had any interest in another threesome. He knew Trey would be game.

"Are we going to cut this cake?" Eric asked.

"It's tradition for the bride and groom to cut the first piece and feed it to each other," Jace said.

Myrna released Trey and turned to grin at Brian. "Yeah, that's what they do with it. *Feed* each other." She laughed wickedly.

Brian lifted an eyebrow at her. Did she intend to shove it up his nose? "Don't even think about it, Myrna."

"Think about what?"

"Dipping your nipples in that frosting. I won't be able to keep my tongue off them."

Her mouth dropped open.

No doubt imagining what she'd look like with her breasts covered in frosting, Eric did an about-face and repeatedly banged his head against the thin wall behind the booth.

Sed pulled open a drawer and handed Myrna a knife. She took Brian's hand in hers and tugged him toward the cake. Hands combined, they drew the knife down into the cake and cut a slice to share. Brian lifted the piece with his fingers and fed Myrna a bite. She then did the same for him. As much as he liked to play around with her, he was glad she allowed him this moment of tender romance. He was kind of a sucker for it. He swallowed the bite of cake and kissed her, the sweet taste of her lips fueling his desire again. After he'd removed all traces of frosting from her delectable lips, he pulled away.

"I love you," she said before flashing her most devilish grin. "But save some of that tongue action for my nipples." She swatted his ass playfully before she took up the knife again and waved it around at the guys. "Who's next?"

"What do you mean?" Eric asked.

"Well, I'm marrying into this *band*. Doesn't that mean I should share cake with all of you?"

Brian grinned, glad his wife got along so well with his band mates. Many a band had fallen to ruin because a significant other didn't understand the dynamics between band members. Myrna got it. And the guys adored her. He couldn't ask for a better situation. Well, maybe if Myrna agreed to go on tour with them indefinitely. But he wouldn't ask that of her just yet. Her job was important to her and therefore important to him as well. But if she came up with the idea to quit her job immediately, he wouldn't object. They had the next six weeks together at least. He planned to spend every moment of them in her arms. The rest of the world would just have to get along without him.

"My turn!" Eric wrapped his long fingers around Myrna's hand and helped her cut a slice of cake.

She lifted the piece and touched it to Eric's nose, leaving a spot of white and pink frosting on the tip. When she fed a bite to him, Brian could practically see Eric melting.

"Do I get a kiss too?" Eric asked. He leaned toward Myrna with his lips puckered, and Brian shoved a hand in his face.

"Those lips are mine, Sticks," Brian said.

"Damn it!" Eric said, but he was grinning.

"Do you want to participate, Jace?" Myrna asked.

"I don't—"

She grabbed Jace's arm and yanked him out of the booth. Blushing ferociously, Jace helped Myrna draw the knife down through the cake. When he took the bite into his mouth, she smiled. His gaze turned to the floor.

"That wasn't so bad, was it?" Myrna asked. "If you don't stop looking so cute, I'm going to make you dance with me too."

His gaze lifted to hers, and he didn't look away. The fact that Myrna flushed in response wasn't lost on Brian. Jace so rarely stared a person in the eyes that when he did, it was disconcerting.

"I don't think that's a good idea," he said. "I'm a little... wound up today."

Eric whacked him on the back. "He means he's horny."

"It's a bit more complicated than that," Jace said.

"I'll dance with you, Myrna," Eric said. He made his way toward the sound system in the living area.

Jace offered Myrna an apologetic smile and disappeared into the bathroom.

Myrna waved a beckoning hand at Sed. "Come on, Sed. Your turn."

Sed eyed Brian. "If I touch you, Brian will have my nut sac made into a coin purse."

Trey burst out laughing. "But who in their right mind would carry it?"

"I'm pretty sure Jessica Chase would," Eric called from the living area. "She's used to carrying his balls around in her purse."

"Fuck you, Sticks," Sed grumbled.

Brian stopped him from smacking Eric in the head by shoving a hand against Sed's chest. "Go ahead and share a piece of cake," Brian said. "I trust her."

The tension went out of Sed's body as he turned to look at Myrna.

Despite his words, Brian still stiffened when Sed moved to stand next to her. His wife looked so small beside Sed's impressive height and broad shoulders. Sed's muscles bulged inside his tight black T-shirt as he wrapped his hand around hers. Brian's heart thudded faster and faster as the pair cut a slice of cake and Myrna lifted it to Sed's lips. She smiled up at him with affection, and Brian's skin crawled the entire length of his spine. He really needed to get over the jealousy he felt every time Myrna was anywhere near Sed. She wasn't like his past girlfriends. She wasn't going to cheat on him with Sed. Mentally, Brian knew that, but instinctively, he didn't want her within ten miles of the man. When Sed stepped away, Brian released a breath he didn't realize he'd been holding.

"Trey?" Myrna said.

Trey moved to stand behind her and wrapped both arms around her body before taking her hand in both of his. "I want lots of frosting," he said, directing the knife toward a corner piece. "And some filling. And more frosting." He scraped extra frosting onto his chosen portion of cake.

Myrna laughed. "You know what they say about guys with a sweet tooth?"

"What?" Trey asked.

"That they're sweet."

"That's not very original," Trey said. "I've heard they have special skills with their pierced tongues." He stuck his tongue out at her and winked.

Myrna chuckled. "I think they just say that about *you*, Trey Mills."

Eric finally found the song he was looking for, which was good because Brian was damned tired of watching his band mates touch his woman. She was laughing at Trey's attempts to lick all the frosting off her fingers when Brian took her hand and tugged her against him. There wasn't much room in the bus corridor for dancing, but that suited his purposes fine. It meant he had to hold her close and just sway to the music, her body plastered against his.

"I love this song," she murmured and snuggled closer.

Her warm breath tickled his neck. His hand slid up her back to her bare shoulder.

"I love *you*," he said.

"I'm happy. Deliriously happy." She leaned away from him and stared into his eyes, the huge smile on her face echoing her declaration. "We're going to make this work."

He had no doubts.

"I hate to cut in, but"—Eric somehow got his lean body wedged between Brian and Myrna—"dancing was *my* idea."

"God, when can we get the hell out of here and be alone?" Brian grumbled.

Myrna chuckled. "Go figure out which hotel you want to stay in tonight. I'll call and make reservations. Eric is feeling left out."

"No, Eric wants to cop a feel," Trey said.

"It's good luck to dance with the bride," Eric said, displaying surprising skill as he led Myrna down the corridor and away from Brian. "And I need all the luck I can get."

"I get to dance with her next," Sed said.

"Absolutely not," Brian said.

"And then me," Trey added. He was making a spectacular mess of the wedding cake by removing icing with his fingers and sucking it off them.

"Okay, party's over," Brian said.

Emerging from the bathroom behind Brian, Jace pressed his hands against Brian's shoulders and leaned close to his back to say, "Don't forget to take off her garter. It's tradition."

Since when was Jace an expert at wedding traditions? But he was right. That was a tradition Brian didn't want to miss out on.

Myrna gasped when he pulled her from Eric's embrace and lifted her to sit on the kitchen counter. "Did you remember to wear a garter?" he asked.

She grinned devilishly. "I'm not telling. You'll have to find out for yourself."

He took her right ankle in one hand and slid the hem of her dress up one inch at a time. The guys hooted and hollered their appreciation. Brian kissed the depression under her kneecap and continued to lift her dress.

"Not too high, Brian," she said to him, her hands pressing her skirt against her lap. "Don't forget I'm not wearing panties."

At this declaration, his band mates sounded like a bunch of Neanderthals at a strip club. Myrna just giggled at them. Brian found the lacy white and blue garter at the top of her thigh-high stocking. He slid his fingers beneath it, tracing the bare skin above her stocking until she emitted that sexy little gasp he adored so much. He slowly drew the garter down her leg to her ankle. Her high-heeled shoe tumbled off as he freed the scrap of material from her body. He kissed the instep of her foot and raised the garter over his head in victory. The guys cheered until they realized one of them would have to catch it. Brian slipped his finger into the garter and stretched it, hurling it toward four very uninterested bachelors. It hit the ceiling, bounced off Sed's head, and landed on Eric's shoulder. The other three men scrambled away from Eric as if he'd contracted an incurable, highly contagious disease.

"Looks like Eric's the next to get married," Jace said quietly.

"Who would marry him?" Trey teased.

"Someone who likes a sucker with a lot of money," Sed said.

"I'm glad Eric caught it," Myrna said. She slipped off the counter and retrieved the garter from Eric's palm. She slipped it over his hand and arm, drawing it upward until it circled his biceps. "It looks sexy on you," she told him.

And judging by the smug look on his face, he believed her. What a dipshit!

"You're going to make some girl very happy one day," she said.

Eric smiled broadly, looking as excited as a man granted his three wishes by a genie.

"But *you'll* be fucking miserable, Eric," Trey said.

Myrna gave Eric's cheek a reassuring pat. "Don't listen to them."

Eric fingered the garter on his arm, lost in thought.

"It's getting pretty late," Myrna said. "You guys should start getting ready for your show."

"Yeah, you all head to the venue and leave us alone," Brian said. He had a powerful need to spend more quality time under her skirt.

"I need to get changed into my suit," she said. "I can get some data on Exodus End's groupies tonight." Myrna's eyes flashed with excitement. "There's no way I'm passing up that opportunity."

Brian caught her as she started to move past him. "You're going to work tonight?"

"Just while you're working."

This was not going as he'd envisioned at all. He figured they could make love all evening, he'd take an hour "break" to do his concert while she spent an hour in bed recovering, and then they'd make love all night. He'd heard that the heat between a couple usually diminished after marriage, but he'd never expected it to happen so quickly.

"Brian, you're pouting," Myrna said.

"I don't pout."

"Yeah, you do," Trey said. "I'm going to take a little nap. Someone wake me in an hour." He climbed into his bunk and pulled the curtain closed.

Myrna tapped Brian's cheek, and he turned his head. "Help me take off my dress?"

Now she was talking.

Chapter 7

BRIAN TRAILED AFTER HIS WIFE, blood surging into his eager cock. He'd known she'd eventually cave to his unquenchable desire for her. He was just glad it had happened sooner rather than later.

Once they were alone in the bedroom together, Myrna folded herself into his arms. "We need to finish that dance."

He rested his cheek against her hair and drew her closer, swaying gently to the music that always accompanied her proximity. When his hands moved to the closure at her back, she didn't protest. He slowly tugged the zipper down until the only thing holding up her dress was the press of their bodies. He caressed her back with slow, firm strokes until she was so relaxed, he thought she might melt into a puddle at his feet. Preferring her excited and responsive, he slid his hands over the sweet swell of her ass. That did the trick. She rubbed her face against his neck and sucked his flesh with soft kisses. Her hands wandered over his back and then she lowered her head to take his top button between her teeth. She tugged. It stayed firmly adhered to his shirt. She gnawed. It didn't budge. She chomped and pulled her head to the side, and it finally came free. She blew the button out of her mouth, and it pinged against his chest.

"I think I chipped a tooth," she said, running her tongue over the ridge of her teeth.

"Let me check."

He kissed her deeply, exploring her mouth with his tongue. She groaned and clung to his shirt with both hands. His buttons might thwart her attempts to *bite* them off, but they were no match for her deft fingers. She attacked the fastenings eagerly, and his shirt was on the floor in seconds. Her dress followed.

She pressed the warm, soft globes of her breasts against his bare chest and tore her mouth from his.

"Damn it, I knew I shouldn't let myself be alone with you," she said.

He drew his eyebrows together. "Why?"

"Because I start lusting all over you like a bitch in heat." She unfastened his belt, released the buttons of his fly, and plunged both hands into his boxers.

"And that's a problem?"

Her stroking the length of his cock with both hands didn't feel like a problem to him.

"Yes. I don't want you to think I only want you for your body. I need you to know that I love you for more than your skills in the sack."

"I do know that, Myrna."

"You do?"

"Yeah."

"Good, because I can't wait another minute."

He grunted in surprise when she grabbed him by one arm and flung him across the bed. She jerked his pants down to his knees, flipped him onto his back, and straddled him. She looked so fucking hot in nothing but her thigh-high stockings. The fuck-me gleam in her eyes sent control beyond reach. He grabbed her by the ass, and she directed his throbbing dick into the center of heaven. She sank down as he thrust up. They collided in bliss.

"Oh," she gasped, following him down as he lowered his hips to the bed.

Head tilted back, eyes closed, Myrna sat impaled by him and rotated her hips to force her body to take him deeper. She whimpered, her fingertips curling into his abdomen. Being buried within her silky heat made him ache. He rocked his hips slightly to urge her to rise and fall over him.

"Do you still hear music when we make love?" she asked.

"Usually."

"How do I make it happen?"

"I'm not sure, but you should probably move a little."

She rose maybe an inch and lowered herself again. Lord, but she was tight around his cockhead when he was buried balls deep. He released a tortured gasp when she repeated the same slight motion again and again.

There was a sharp knock at the door.

"Brian," Sed called through the door. "We need you in the stadium. Now."

"What?" he grumbled. "I'm busy!" he yelled. "Get lost!"

"I'm really sorry, dude, but Dave said he needs you onstage now. Something about the configuration of something or other and a lot of impressive electronics-sounding words I didn't understand

and the threat of your guitar getting fried and electrocuting you."

"Tell him to figure it out on his own!"

"Do I have to come in there and get you?" Sed yelled. "I've always wanted a second look at Myrna naked."

Brian bellowed with rage. "I swear, I'm quitting this fucking band!"

"He'll be there in a minute, Sed," Myrna called.

She lifted her hips, and Brian fell free of her body.

"Uh," he gasped. "No. They can get along without me."

"Sweetheart," she said, "it's okay. You need to get ready for the concert. We'll pick up with this later. Your music is important. I understand. Really."

"It's not okay. Being with you is more important right now."

"It makes me happy to hear you say that." She lowered her eyes and smiled sweetly.

Brian almost choked on his tongue. Myrna Evans, erm, *Sinclair*, was openly admitting that his sentimental drivel made her happy? Oh God, there was no way he could concentrate on anything but making love to her now.

He reached for her, but she climbed from the bed. "I'll catch up with you backstage," she said and went to the closet and tugged out one of her skirt suits.

She chose the trim navy blue one and a silky pink top to wear underneath. Brian groaned. The woman knew what seeing her in conservative attire did to him and how much he liked knowing what she was wearing underneath. Tonight it was nothing but thigh-high stockings. Mercy. She pulled the silky top over her head and the fabric clung to the erect buds of her bare nipples. Oh God, she wasn't wearing a bra tonight either? Fuck him. Fuck him all to hell. He'd never make it through a concert with that knowledge rattling around in his brain.

Myrna's skirt quickly hid her sexy ass from view, and then she shrugged into her suit jacket.

"Get dressed, baby," she said gently. "I'll catch up with you *backstage*."

"Yeah, I heard you the first time." He climbed from the bed and pulled up his pants.

"But I don't think you understood that it meant I'd be fucking you senseless when I caught up with you."

She dropped the bombshell without fuss, as if she were telling him they were having eggplant for dinner.

She slipped into a pair of three-inch heels, exited the room without a backwards glance, and left Brian staring at the door with his mouth agape and his dick hard and his thoughts swirling with images of being fucked senseless.

When he finally remembered that he was supposed to be dealing with band bullshit, he pulled on the tight black T-shirt he planned to wear onstage that night. He had a more difficult time buttoning his jeans over his stiff cock. His difficulty wasn't due to his cock being damp with Myrna's juices. Well, that wasn't exactly true. The reason it was so painfully hard was because it *was* still damp with Myrna's juices, which served as a delicious reminder of the feel of her tight pussy gripping him. So it actually *was* her fault that his dick's perpetual rigidity was putting a horrible strain on the buttons of his fly. This called for a cold lap-bath in the nearest sink. Poor mistreated dick. She'd better make this up to him and soon.

Ten minutes later, Brian found Sinners' front-of-house soundboard operator, Dave, cussing up a storm backstage inside the arena. When Dave noticed Brian, he looked like he'd just witnessed an angel descend from the heavens. A guitar was shoved into Brian's hands, and he spent almost an hour working with Dave to fix some feedback problem Brian swore was imaginary. He didn't hear it at all. Even if it did exist, Brian wasn't sure why one of the roadies wasn't a suitable replacement for strumming and adjusting and strumming some more.

"No one sounds like you," Dave explained, when Brian started to get antsy and tried pawning off strum-duty on their mohawk-sporting roadie, Jake.

When Dave was finally satisfied the nonexistent feedback had been squelched, he let Brian go and started having a coronary over one of Eric's off-sounding bass drums. Dave wasn't typically this high-strung, so his agitation must have had something to do with being in the company of Exodus End's legendary soundboard operator, Mad Dog McFarley. The dude looked like a startled bulldog, but he was second to none in mixing a live show. Dave kept wandering over to Mad Dog's soundboard and peeking over his shoulder, as if trying to photograph top-secret documents with an implanted eye-cam.

Brian shook his head, trusting that the guy would keep his shit together for the show.

He headed toward the dressing room, hoping that Myrna would "catch up" with him soon. He couldn't think of anything but getting lost in her for twenty or thirty hours. As he passed a door, a graceful hand reached out and grabbed him by the T-shirt, tugging him into the dark confines of a closet. She found his mouth in the darkness, pressing her naked body against his. Brian grabbed her bare ass before it dawned on him that several things weren't right. More specifically, that her ass was in the wrong place; it was several inches too low. And she didn't taste like Myrna. Didn't smell like Myrna. *Wasn't* Myrna. He shoved the unfamiliar woman away and reached for the doorknob to escape.

The woman was surprisingly strong as she wrapped both arms around his waist and pulled him away from the door.

"Don't deny me this, Master Sinclair. I want you so bad."

"Let go," he demanded, trying to pry her iron grip from his waist.

"Just let me suck your cock. Please."

Her needy voice made his skin crawl. "I said let go. I don't want to have to get rough with you."

She'd somehow managed to get his belt buckle unfastened. He covered his crotch with one hand and tried to fend her off with the other.

The woman emitted a throaty chuckle. "I want you to get rough with me. Leave marks on my skin. Nail me hard as *fuck* so that my pussy remembers you in the morning."

She grabbed his ass, and his balls tried to climb up into his belly. There wasn't anything about this attempted seduction that turned him on in the slightest. Brian managed to get a hand on the doorknob again and opened the door. His gaze was lowered toward the floor, but the space at his feet wasn't empty. He'd recognize those high heels and shapely calves anywhere.

"Myrna," he gasped, a lump of cold lead settling in his stomach. His head jerked up automatically. "This isn't what it looks like."

"So there isn't a naked woman plastered to your back with her hand on your crotch? You aren't coming out of a dark closet with your belt unbuckled?"

"No," he denied.

"I'm not blind, Brian."

"I mean yes, but—"

"Nor am I stupid," she added.

He forced his gaze to hold hers, but she looked away and glared at the woman accosting him.

"Get your fucking hands off my husband," she said.

Her uncompromising tone made the hairs on the back of Brian's neck stand on end.

"Your *husband*?" the woman gasped.

"Yes, my husband. Mine. Get the fuck away from him."

"I didn't know—When did he—Well, how was I suppo—Just let me get my clothes."

The woman moved away from Brian's back, and he stepped outside the small, dark room. She closed the door quietly.

"Honestly, Myrna, I was trying to get away from her. There's no way I would have done anything with her. She just grabbed me when I walked past the door."

"I trust you."

"I would never destroy what we have over something so stupid."

"Brian, I trust you. Chill."

Myrna slid into his arms.

"You do?" His body melted against hers with relief.

"Of course. Do I have a reason not to?"

"No. All I want is you." They'd just danced to a song with those exact words as the title. Surely she knew he meant what he said.

She lifted a hand to cup his cheek. "I feel exactly the same way."

He kissed her, his soul buoyant with joy.

The door behind him opened again and naked-chick, now mostly clothed, brushed past them as she fled. Still kissing him, Myrna walked Brian backwards into the empty closet and shut the door.

"I'll have to thank your groupie for pointing out this place," she said. "I wondered how I was going to get you alone backstage. I had settled on a bathroom stall, but the last time we tried that, it didn't end well."

Brian laughed. "It ended well for me." He laughed again and squeezed her in a tight embrace. "But not so well for my lucky hat."

"Or Eric."

"Every time he wears that hat, I think I'm going to bust a gut trying not to laugh."

"Less talking. More satisfying kisses."

She clung to his shoulders. In the darkness, her kiss landed on his chin. She nibbled her way to his lips and caressed them with deep sucking kisses. As she warmed, her scent—a sweet combination of coconut, sex, and Myrna—intensified, blotting the scent of antiseptic cleanser coming from somewhere in the closet.

She nipped Brian's lower lip. Lust slammed into his gut, hot and heavy. He moved his hands to her ass—which was in exactly the right location, thank you very much—and ground her pelvis against his rapidly engorging cock. He'd just got the damned thing under control, and hoped to God she wasn't going to leave him unsatisfied again. He wasn't sure he'd survive.

"How long before you have to be onstage?" she asked breathlessly.

She tugged impatiently at his hair—her signal that she needed to be penetrated quickly. It was one of his favorite signals. Second only to the gaspy moan she made in the back of her throat when she was close to orgasm.

"I'm not sure. Twenty minutes or so."

"Are you hot for me?"

"Yeah, of course. I'm always hot for you." He wished he could see her. Read her expression. The closet was completely devoid of light; he could scarcely make out the hairline crack under the door.

"Tell me what you want to do to me," she whispered and caught his bottom lip between her teeth again, this time tugging until it slipped free. She was feeling frisky, was she?

"I want to let your hair down," he said, sliding both hands up her back to press her more firmly against his chest. Something about getting it on with her while she was dressed in a conservative skirt suit always did it for him. Maybe because she was the only woman he'd ever known to wear suits.

"That's it?" she whispered.

"I want to let your hair down, so I can wrap it around my fist while I fuck you from behind."

Her breath caught.

"Are you wet?"

"Getting that way."

He found the clip at the back of her head and released her hair. It dropped around her shoulders, covering his free hand in a curtain of silk. He carefully gathered it in one hand and wrapped it around his fist to tug it evenly, so it wouldn't hurt. Much. He yanked, and Myrna gasped.

"Did I hurt you?" he asked, heart thudding. That wasn't his intention. Rough didn't have to hurt.

"N-no. Fuck me, Brian."

"Pull your skirt up around your waist."

She moved away slightly. He heard the rustle of her clothes. He gave her hair another tug and then lowered his hand to make sure she'd obeyed him. His hand found the smooth skin of her bare ass.

"Touch your cunt."

"You touch it," she said.

He tugged her hair more aggressively. "Don't disobey me. I'm in control here. Slide your fingers inside that pussy and tell me how wet you are."

The back of her hand brushed his fly as she moved to obey him. He gritted his teeth so he didn't reveal how turned on he was. She needed to think he was in control here. Good thing it was dark so she couldn't see his expression; he knew it revealed his deep longing. When the sound of her wet flesh accepting her fingers reached his ears, his belly tightened with need.

"Are you wet?" he asked gruffly.

"Y-yes."

"Are your juices dripping down the insides of your thighs?"

"Almost."

"Rub yourself until they do. I want that cunt hot and wet before I fuck it."

"Brian?" she pleaded.

He tightened his hand in her hair. "Do it."

The sounds of her fingers rapidly stroking her flesh had his balls aching in seconds.

"That's it, baby. Get ready for me."

He released her hair so he could move behind her. He unfastened his pants and jerked them down to his knees. His cock pulsed with excitement the instant he freed it.

Myrna crooned with impending release.

"Are you wet now?"

"Yes… Oh God, yes. I'm going to—"

He slapped her ass with a resounding smack.

"Did I say you could make yourself come? No coming unless I'm inside you. Understand?"

"Y-yes," she gasped.

Fumbling in the dark, he gathered her hair in his fist again. With his other hand he sought her hand, which was still working between her legs. He captured her wrist and shifted her fingers from her pussy to her clit.

"Rub that greedy clit while I fuck you. Don't stop rubbing until I come. I don't care how many times you get off between now and then. Keep rubbing it."

"I don't know what's gotten into you, Brian," she said in a low voice.

He hesitated. Maybe he was being too bossy. He loosened his hold on her hair.

"I don't know what's gotten into you," she repeated, "but I like it."

He yanked her hair. "Do you want to be fucked?"

"Yes. I want you to fuck me."

"Then you better rub your clit like I told you."

"And if I don't?"

He slid a hand over her ass and slapped it again. Her entire body tensed and she shuddered.

"I'll paddle your ass raw."

"Oh God," she said breathlessly. "If we had more time, I'd resist more," she whispered. "Next time."

And there would be plenty of next times. A lifetime's worth.

She groaned as she began to work her clit. "I'll do whatever you say, *Master* Sinclair."

"Good," he murmured to her. "Rub it fast and hard—don't tease it. Get yourself off."

He used his hand to guide his cock into her hot, slick opening. He thrust into her with gentle, shallow strokes to wet himself with her juices. Intense pleasure coursed the entire length of his cock as he plunged deep with one driving thrust. Myrna cried out, her pussy gripping him in hard spasms as she came.

"Don't stop rubbing yourself just because you came," he said.

Her vocalizations grew so loud, he wouldn't have been surprised if someone opened the closet door to investigate. He didn't want her to quiet down though. He wanted her to scream his name.

Brian possessed her with a relentless hard and fast rhythm, one hand tugging at her hair, the other gripping her hip to pull her against him with each thrust. He never imagined the first time he made love to his wife that he'd be fucking her hard and dirty in a supply closet backstage. He'd imagined rose petals floating in a warm bath. Gentle touches. Tender kisses that lasted for hours. But fucking her this way would bring him release quickly, and he needed that tonight. Needed to get his overwhelming desire for her out of his system before he went onstage. He'd treasure her, as she deserved, later that night. For now, he embraced the building urgency in his groin and relished the pleasure rippling through his body. He shouted in triumph as he found release. Bliss flooded every inch of him as his seed pulsed into her body.

He wrapped both arms around her and pulled her upright to hug her back against his chest. His lips brushed her silky hair. "You're beautiful."

She chuckled. "It's too dark in here for you to know that."

"I know it."

"Do you think you can make it through your concert now?"

"Not really. No."

He held her against him, thumbs stroking her bare nipples against the inside of her silk top, until his breath stilled. When he thought he might be able to live without being buried inside her, he slipped free of her body with a regretful wince.

She turned in his arms and drew him close—pressing her soft breasts into his chest.

"I'm going to go clean up." She kissed his jaw. "And make a hotel reservation." Kissed his chin. "Pack a suitcase, but no clothes." Kissed his lips. "I don't want to see you until after the show," she said. "And then I want to see nothing *but* you for the next two days."

She left him in the dark closet. He was too breathless to follow.

When Brian finally managed to find his way out of the supply closet and to the backstage area, someone thrust a guitar in his hands. He lifted its strap over his head and settled his guitar into place. The crowd was already roaring with excitement. His band looked a bit worse for wear after the events of last night, but they were ready to hit the stage. And he was too consumed by thoughts of his bride to suffer from his normal preconcert nerves. He just wanted to get on the stage, rock the roof off the arena, and return to his wife.

"Finally done boning Myrna?" Trey asked.

Brian grinned. "Not by a long shot. The real honeymoon starts in forty-six minutes."

Trey stumbled over the bottom step as he headed onstage. Brian wished he would just go to the fucking hospital and get it over with, but he knew why Trey hated hospitals—he'd spent too many hours in them when his father had been a resident. But that didn't excuse him from seeking medical attention when he needed it.

Brian took him by one arm to help him climb the stairs. "You sure you're okay, buddy?"

"Like you care." Trey wrenched his arm out of Brian's grasp and trotted over to his spot stage right.

Brian shook his head. "Serve him right if it turned out to be something serious," he grumbled to himself.

Chapter 8

THE OPULENT LOBBY OF THE VENETIAN couldn't compete for Myrna's attention; her husband had it all. He had a smudge of eyeliner under his left eye, which was still horribly bruised. His black T-shirt was damp with sweat. Clumps of hair clung to his neck and face. Yeah... hot. Even though he'd assured her that his concert that night had been the worst Sinners had ever performed, she wished she'd seen him onstage. Nothing turned her on more than watching this man delight fifteen thousand fans with his talented fingers. Except when those talented fingers were delighting her alone.

"Your Prima Suite is on the thirty-fifth floor," the clerk said and slid a set of keycards across the counter.

"I want to make sure we understand each other," Brian said to him. "Do not disturb us under any circumstances. I don't care if the hotel is on fire. I don't care if the fuckin' President of the United States needs to speak to me. Do. Not. Disturb. Got it?"

Eyes wide, the attractive olive-skinned man swallowed hard and nodded. "I understand, Mr. Sinclair."

"Has our room service order been sent up to our room already?" Myrna asked. "I placed it when I made the reservation."

"I'll check to make sure." The clerk reached for the phone.

Brian didn't wait for confirmation. He grabbed the keycards off the counter and took Myrna's hand to lead her to the elevator. "I don't need room service," he said. "I need my wife." He lifted her hand and kissed her knuckles. "Uninterrupted for hours."

"We have all night," she said. "And all day tomorrow."

"I hope you aren't planning on sleeping."

She grinned and shook her head.

Because the hotel was so massive, it took them a while to find the right elevator. Myrna could tell Brian was frustrated with the delay. "Sweetheart, relax."

"This isn't exactly how I pictured my wedding day to go. I wanted it to be special for you, and it's just been one interruption after another."

"It has been special for me."

She smiled at him, but he didn't look convinced. When the elevator slid open, she was very happy to find it empty. Brian ushered her inside and set their suitcase down before tapping the button to their floor.

He needed to loosen up and quit stressing over stuff he had no control over. And luckily for him, she knew exactly how to get his mind off his worries.

She grabbed two fistfuls of his hair and kissed him. Hard. "You make me so fucking hot, Master Sinclair," she said, staring up into his intense brown eyes. She knew he didn't like her to call him by his stage name, but she absolutely wanted to live the fantasy with her rock star husband before she lived another fantasy with the amazing man beneath the stage persona. "Can I do something for you, my personal sex god? Anything. I'm your number one fan."

Brian chuckled and wrapped both arms around her. "Don't call me Master Sinclair, that's what you can do for me."

He hadn't seemed to mind the title when he'd been pounding her hard and pulling her hair in a dark closet backstage.

"Is that *all* I can do for you?" Myrna circled his body to stand behind him. Sliding her hands over his lower belly, her pinkies dipped into the waistband of the jeans riding low on his narrow hips. "Because I really want to please you, *Master* Sinclair."

She forced one hand deeper into his pants and carefully arranged his cock so it was pointing up toward his belly. The head of his half-hard dick peeked out just above the waistband of his low-slung jeans. As she stroked it with her thumb, it rose to attention, revealing itself an inch at a time as it grew harder and harder. His head dropped back to rest against hers.

"I want to suck your balls while you jack off," she whispered into his ear. "I brought your butt plug and a cock ring in the suitcase."

"A vibrating one?"

"Yeah. I want to ride you hard. Come over and over again until my juices drip down your sac."

"Oh God, Myrna. I love it when you talk dirty to me in elevators. Or anywhere else."

"Someone might come in and see me playing with The Beast. Does that excite you?"

"Yeah, I hope someone sees how fucking hard you make me."

"We can ride up and down until someone comes in the elevator," she said, still rubbing her thumb over his most sensitive flesh.

"Can I be the one who comes in the elevator?"

She laughed and pressed her hand against the hard ridge in his pants, holding his shaft against his lower belly. "If I can ride up and down." When he began to seep pre-cum, she spread it over his exposed cockhead in gentle circles.

"The way today is going, I'd probably get arrested for public indecency and spend my honeymoon in jail as Big Bart's bitch."

"I wouldn't let that happen. I'm the only one who's gonna fuck you up the ass tonight, Master Sinclair."

His cock twitched in her hand. Did that idea excite him?

Interesting.

"Has anyone ever done you that way before?" she asked.

"N-no," he said breathlessly.

"Not even Trey?" She really needed confirmation on that.

He shook his head. "He was the bottom. Have you ever? Fucked a guy?"

"No," she said, "but I've always wanted to."

"You know I'll try anything twice. With you? Three times."

And that was one of the many reasons she loved this man. Most guys talked the talk, but if you got too kinky with them, they backed down. Brian never baulked at a sexual experience and never made her feel like a whore for pushing the limits.

When the elevator door opened on their floor, they stared into the corridor, anticipating someone entering the car to watch how naughty they were being. They waited. Brian hit the button to hold the door. No one appeared. Myrna sighed. They exchanged looks of disappointment.

"Do you want to go down and try again?" she asked.

"I want to go down all right, but we won't need the elevator."

"I'm going to shave my pussy tonight so you can suck, lick, and eat every inch of it, inside and out. Would you like that?" She certainly would.

He made a sound of torture and pressed her hand over his partially exposed cock to conceal it before dashing off the elevator.

"Suitcase!" she protested. She had a full arsenal of kinky fun packed in that thing.

Brian backtracked for the suitcase. He looked at the keycard in his hand, then at the suitcase on the floor, and then at the hand he had pressed over hers. "I don't have enough hands," he complained.

Myrna carefully tucked his cock into his pants and stepped away. "Now you do."

"That was my favorite occupied hand though." He picked up the suitcase.

She laughed and tugged him down the corridor toward their room.

When he tried the key, the light on the lock flashed red. He checked the room number. "It's the right room."

The rattle of a cart echoed down the corridor. Myrna smiled at the young man who was pushing it in their direction. Their room service had arrived just in time; she couldn't let her husband go hungry. He needed his stamina.

Brian's second attempt to open the door worked. "Hallelujah," he said. "I was thinking we'd just have to go at it in the hall."

The suitcase slid across the floor of the marble entry, and Myrna found herself jerked into the room by one arm.

"Wait, our room ser—"

"No more waiting," he said and drew her against his body.

He removed the clip from her sloppily styled hair and tossed it aside. Her hair tumbled down around her shoulders, and he buried both hands in it before lowering his head to kiss her. The door hit the room service cart with a loud bang.

"Um... room service," the server said in a loud whisper.

"*Argh*. Get out of here," Brian said as he tried to close the door with one hand. The large cart got in the way.

"Sweetheart, just let him leave the cart inside the door. It will only take a second."

Brian dropped his hand from the door and squeezed her ass. She inched him away from the door so the server could push the cart inside the entryway—a lovely entryway, she noted. Myrna assumed the rest of the suite was spectacular, but she doubted she'd get a chance to see it before Brian lost complete control. Performing live always got him worked up. As did being felt up in elevators.

He shoved her against the wall, capturing her hands on either side of her head. Staring at her as if he wanted to telegraph his desire directly to her thoughts, he rubbed the hard ridge of his cock against her mound until she began to gyrate with him.

He released one of her wrists and grabbed her hair. "Let me out of my pants," he growled into her ear. "I'm going to fuck you right here against the wall."

Her pussy pulsated with the first tease of orgasm. If he kept talking to her like that, he wouldn't have to fuck her to make her come.

Her hands moved to his fly, fumbling with the buttons to unleash his huge cock. Oh God, she wanted it. She held it in both hands, and he thrust into her loose grip repeatedly. His broken gasps made her whimper with need.

Someone cleared his throat. Incredulous, Myrna peeked around Brian's shoulder to find their server standing there with a hand out.

"He needs a tip," Myrna said as Brian tugged her tight skirt up her thighs.

"I'll give him a tip. Get the fuck out of here and close the goddamned door. There's his fucking tip."

"Just add a twenty percent gratuity to the bill," Myrna said.

The cart rattled again as the server pushed it out of his way. The door closed. Alone at last.

Brian rubbed the head of his cock against Myrna's hot, needy opening. Her entire core pulsed and ached, begging to be filled. She buried her face in his neck and inhaled his intoxicating scent. She loved the way he smelled after a concert. The blend of excitement and the exertion of performing live added some pheromone to his sweat that pushed every one of her fuck-me buttons. She sucked the saltiness from his throat, delighting in the rapid surge of blood through the pulse point she palpated with her lips and tongue. She nipped him and rubbed her pussy against the head of his cock, which he still hadn't buried deep inside her the way she wanted.

Fighting her tight skirt, she lifted her leg to rest her thigh against his hip. That was enough to move him, and he surged up into her body, filling her with one deep thrust. She tore her mouth from his throat and released a breathless moan. He clutched her suit jacket as he pounded into her and rubbed his open mouth against her throat and jaw. She loved when they took their time and made love for hours, but there was something unequivocally hot about this man losing all control and fucking her senseless. He sucked a path to her mouth and kissed her deeply. When he tore his mouth from hers, her eyelids fluttered open. Their excited breaths mingled as they stared into each other's eyes. She was so lost in him. So lost. She never wanted to be found again.

"I love you," he whispered. "Myrna."

"Yes, Brian," she said, her breath hitching with emotion. She wasn't an emotional person. She internalized. She knew that. With him? With him, she felt safe. She could show him everything within her heart—good and bad—and know he'd treasure it because he loved her and understood how hard exposing her deepest emotions was for her. Or how hard it *had* been. Opening herself to him was becoming easier by the minute, because he *made* it easy.

"I love you." She grabbed two fistfuls of his hair and yanked to ensure he was paying close attention. "I *love* you."

"Love me a little more gently," he complained.

She released her hold and rubbed his head to undo any damage before wrapping both arms around him. She slid her hands up under the back of his T-shirt, needing the feel of his skin beneath her palms. "I love you," she said into his ear.

He inhaled deeply through his nose, as if trying to internalize her words. Physically draw them inside himself.

"Hearing you say it... I can't even describe how amazing it feels." He nipped her earlobe playfully. "But maybe I can show you."

Brian moved inside her. Slow. Hard. Deep. He was very good at showing his feelings. She became hyperaware of the man against her: the texture of his skin beneath her splayed hands; the warmth of his breath against her shoulder; the tickle of his hair against her nose as her panting stirred the longish strands; his strong fingers massaging her ass as he ground into her, filling her body to its limits with his huge cock. But there was a new awareness within her. A swelling in her chest. A tightening in her throat. A prickle behind her eyes. Was she about to cry? Not in sorrow but in joy? What in the hell had gotten into her?

Brian had. He was in her deep and not just with the rock-hard shaft that was working her toward rapture. His essence, his soul, was now part of her. Essential to her existence.

Brian found a tempo that drove her crazy, that built her pleasure steadily. Taking her higher. Higher.

"I hear you," he whispered. "My muse."

Knowing he was hearing one of his musical compositions while he made love to her caused one of those sentimental tears to leak from her eye. She rubbed her face against his shoulder, hoping he didn't notice that the no-holds-barred sex professor he'd married was actually crying during sex. He'd think she'd been abducted by aliens and replaced with some emotional pod person. She swallowed the lump in her throat and asked, her voice raw, "Do you need something to write on, baby?"

He shook his head and repeatedly murmured a series of notes. "I'll remember it."

"I can't wait to hear you play it."

"I'm sorry. You must hate that this keeps getting in the way of our fun."

She kissed his temple, and her arms tightened around him. "Not at all. It's sexy," she whispered to him. "You composing when we make love is sexy."

He chuckled. "Damned inconvenient if you ask me."

"I didn't." She smiled to herself and did nothing to interrupt or change his thrusting tempo while his murmured stanzas grew longer and more complex. She was glad she had something to distract her—she could get all her overwhelming and tender emotions under control. Sort of.

Myrna's legs began to tremble with exhaustion after several minutes.

"Sweetheart," she whispered, wishing she didn't have to interrupt his musical genius. But she was going to slide to the floor in about three seconds. "Can we move this to the bedroom?"

He continued with the same rhythm and tempo, as if he hadn't heard her.

"Brian?"

No response.

"Brian!"

He started and drew back to look at her. "Sorry, I was lost in you. What did you say?"

"I need to find the nearest bed. My legs are tired." So tired she was shaking.

He pulled out with a whimper, and then his eyes widened suddenly. "I forgot to carry you over the threshold."

She cupped his jaw and kissed him. "I want you to do that when we buy our first house together. Our permanent house. Not a hotel room or a tour bus. Not my condo. Not your apartment. *Our home.* The one we'll choose together and where we'll raise our kids."

His brilliant smile made her heart flutter. "I'm married," he said, as if that realization just struck him.

She chuckled. "It's about time."

He scooped her up into his arms. "Well, wife, if you're not going to let me carry you over the threshold, I'm going to carry you to bed."

She wrapped both arms around his neck and kissed his shoulder. "No objections."

He turned toward the living area of the suite. "This place is like a fucking mansion," he said.

No lie. She'd never seen such a gorgeous hotel room in her life. "Let's dirty it up."

"Do you want to start in the bed?"

She scanned the expansive room, and her eyes settled on the black granite wet bar. "The bar." He took a step in that direction. "Wait! Let me grab the champagne."

He made a quick detour to the cart so she could grab the bottle, and then he hurried to the bar. She yelped when the backs of her thighs touched the cold granite, but forgot her discomfort when he settled between her legs and stared up at her. The light in the foyer gave limited illumination to the room, creating shadows that concealed his expression. His hesitation confused her. Didn't he want her? She shook off her doubts. Of course he wanted her. He always did. How could she think otherwise?

"We need to drink a toast." She shook the champagne vigorously, an ornery grin on her face. Before she could pop the cork, Brian took the bottle from her hands and set it on the bar beside her. The intensity of his gaze caused her heart to leap in anticipation. Amazing things always happened when he looked at her like that. She abandoned her plan to hose him down with champagne and waited for amazing.

His fingers moved to the buttons of her suit jacket. He never took his eyes off her face while he removed her jacket and the shell beneath. She helped him with her skirt, which knocked her shoes to the floor and left her sitting on the cool bar top in nothing but her thigh-high stockings. While he peeled the hosiery from her legs in agonizing slowness, she tugged impatiently at his T-shirt with one hand. He stripped his shirt off, and she wrapped her legs around his ribcage, tugging his body closer.

With a wicked grin on his handsome face, Brian took the bottle from the counter and smashed the neck against the bar. A golden geyser gushed from the bottle. Myrna squealed when the chilled liquid sprayed over her chest and throat before running like a river between her breasts. Brian lowered his head to sample the champagne coursing over her skin.

"To us," he said, collecting the Dom Perignon from her heated flesh.

He shook out the entire contents and dropped the empty bottle on the carpet with a thud. His arms circled Myrna's back to draw her breasts to his mouth.

"That was a three-hundred-dollar bottle of champagne," she told him, her fingers burrowing into his hair.

The flat of his tongue collected the expensive liquid from her nipple. He offered the tender peak a sharp nip before sucking it into his mouth and gently flicking it with his tongue. Myrna gasped, and her body tensed before relaxing in his arms. His mouth moved down the center of her belly, seeking more champagne.

"Worth every penny," he murmured, the deep timbre of his voice sending thrills down her lower back. "Delicious. They could charge a million a bottle if they served it this way."

"I didn't get any." She captured his face between both hands, urged him upward, and kissed him, relishing the taste of their wedding toast on his strong lips.

When he pulled away to stare up into her eyes, he offered her a crooked grin that made her heart race.

"I'll give you some."

He lowered her to her back on the wet bar and then joined her. The smell of alcohol mingled with the musky scent of Brian's body when he settled above her. He bit his lip as he used his hand to guide his cock inside her body. His gaze held hers as he moved his hands to link with hers. He searched her eyes, her face, for a long moment before he drew her arms above her head and began to thrust with agonizing slowness.

A trickle of wasted champagne splashed down on the lower counter of the bar, but Myrna didn't need alcohol to be intoxicated when her sensual husband made love to her. She closed her eyes and gave herself over to sensation. The bliss of his thick cock filling her slowly, receding, filling her again. The hard, wet surface at her back. The strength of his fingers intertwined with hers. The warmth of his breath against her jaw. The crisp texture of the narrow strip of hair that ran down his lower abdomen rubbing against her belly when she arched her back.

And then beyond the physical feelings, but working in tune with them, those overwhelming emotions that left her breathless with wonder made a reappearance.

"Show me," he whispered.

She opened her eyes to find him staring down at her. "Show you what?"

"Your O-face."

She laughed. "I don't have an O-face."

"Yeah, you do. I need to see it." He pushed deep, and she gasped. "I need to see what I do to you."

"It'll make an appearance soon enough. I have complete faith in your abilities."

His persistent rhythm quickly brought her to her peak. When she cried out, he said, "That's it." His breath caught, and he shuddered.

She forced her eyes open so she could watch *his* O-face—mouth open, one eye squeezed shut, the opposite eyebrow arched. He bit his lip, and the skin on his nose crinkled as his entire body went rigid. "Mmm," he gasped.

"All I get is an *mmm*?" She mimicked his sound.

He laughed between gasps. "I'll be more vocal next time."

"Next time?" She squeezed his hands. "Maybe I'm finished for the night."

"Maybe you're going to shave your box like you promised so I can feast on your pussy for an hour or two."

A shudder of delight raced down her spine, making her still-quaking pussy clench with renewed excitement. "Maybe I will."

"And maybe you're going to wear your new jewelry for me while I watch you shave it."

Jewelry? "I'm already wearing my rings."

"Your other new jewelry. That we got at the sex shop."

Her belly quivered. How could she have forgotten? "I guess there is going to be a next time." She lifted her head to kiss him.

"I figured you'd see it my way."

He pulled out and slid from the bar before helping her find her feet and avoid the broken bottle on the floor. He kicked off his boots and removed his pants, which were saturated down the thighs with champagne. Myrna headed for the foyer to find the suitcase she'd packed.

"I'll meet you in the bathroom, if I can find it. This place is huge!" He glanced around the expansive main room and went to check an open doorway. "A home theater? Why did we stay on the bus last night?"

"Not sure," she said. "Maybe you like living the life of a bachelor."

He shook his head.

"Well, there's got to be a bathroom around here somewhere,"

she said. "I specifically requested a jetted tub."

He grinned, and her heart stumbled.

"You know, I love you a little more every minute," he told her.

"Just a little more?" she teased, pinching her thumb and forefinger together.

"Trust me—minute by minute, hour by hour, day by day—all that love accumulates."

He switched on a light and disappeared deeper into the suite. She set the suitcase on the sofa and unzipped it, then riffled through the contents looking for the sack containing their new purchases.

"Found it!" Brian called, his voice echoing.

She found what she'd been looking for as well. "I'll be there in a minute! Go ahead and fill up the tub."

She heard water strike porcelain as she dumped her new rhinestone choker into her hand. She fastened it around her throat and inspected the free ends of two slender chains dangling from the necklace. She'd never worn nipple clamps before. Wasn't exactly sure how to attach them. She licked two fingers and rubbed them over one nipple, teasing it to an erect point before squeezing the open ring shut over the tender tip. An unexpected spasm gripped her lower belly as the weight of the chain tugged at her nipple. Her pussy throbbed.

"Oh," she gasped. "I think I'm going to like this."

She attached the other clamp to her free nipple and inspected her reflection in the mirror behind the bar. Three slender chains draped between the mounds of her breasts. The slender strands swayed against her belly rhythmically and tugged gently on both sensitive tips. She thrust her shoulders back, which lifted her breasts high. Brian was going to love this new piece of jewelry. Perhaps even more than his new ring. Well maybe not that much. But the clamps kept her nipples erect and her pussy tingly—just the way they both liked it.

Myrna slipped on her black patent leather stilettos, picked up her shaving kit, and sashayed her way to the bathroom, feeling as sexy as she knew she looked.

She found Brian lounging in a rapidly filling bathtub of steaming water. His eyes were closed, so she paused in the doorway and cleared her throat.

His eyes blinked open slowly, and then he sat up producing an awkward splash.

"Fuck, you look hot," he said with a groan of approval.

The man had a way with words.

Myrna crossed the room with calculated steps, spread a towel on the ledge at the far end of the tub, and left her shoes on the floor as she climbed up to sit across from him. She lathered her pubic hair with shaving cream and opened her legs wide to give him a good view as she drew the razor over her skin in slow, deliberate strokes. She didn't meet his eyes, pretended he wasn't there. But damned if the excited little gasps he made each time a new strip of bare skin was revealed didn't turn her on.

When the tub was full, he turned off the water. She dipped a hand in the tub and rinsed the traces of shaving cream from her skin. She lathered up again and repeated the process. The repetitive sloshing of water drew Myrna's attention to her enthralled husband. He was stroking the length of his massive cock with both hands. Her thighs contracted involuntarily. She watched him discreetly from beneath the veil of her lashes. Watching him masturbate always turned her on. Her pussy pulsed in time with his strokes, dripping fluids in anticipation. Finished with her task, she rinsed her clean-shaven box with water and moved her fingers to rub against her clit. She tugged on the chains of her nipple clamps with her free hand. Her back arched as she lost herself to pleasure.

"I want to come all over that beautiful pussy," Brian said in a low growl.

The water sloshed as he rose to his knees before her. He stroked his cock faster and faster, until with a startled cry he started coming. Myrna drew her hand away just in time. Cum splattered over her shaved mound and lower belly. "Oh God," he groaned, tugging out one last spurt that landed on her inner thigh.

He collapsed against her, his face resting between her breasts. His fingers found the chains attached to her nipple clamps, and he tugged hard. Pleasurable pain shot from both breasts to Myrna's throbbing clit. Her belly tightened with impending orgasm.

"You're so sexy, baby. So sexy." He kissed a trail down her stomach, his destination obvious. He licked her newly shaved lips, sucked on them, nibbled and kissed them until she was writhing uncontrollably.

When she was certain she would die from lack of fulfillment, he slid two fingers inside her.

"Oh," she gasped, her hands flying to his scalp to press his head and encourage him to take her clit in his mouth.

He inched lower, but merely licked at her inner folds while he slowly drove his fingers in and out of her aching pussy.

"Make me come," she demanded. "Please, Brian, I can't stand it."

He reached up, grabbed both nipple chains in one hand, and tugged sharply. Her pussy tightened around his fingers, but she didn't fly over the edge.

"Brian, Brian," she panted. "Help me."

His tongue flicked her clit, and intense spasms of pleasure gripped her core. "Yes, yes, yes!"

"Say my name," he said brokenly.

"Brian. Brian!"

He yanked her into the tub, water sloshing over the rim and spreading across the floor.

"God, I'm fucking hard as a rock again already," he said in that sexy growl that made her crave another orgasm. "Why do you do this to me?"

"Because I get off on it," she said with a giggle.

His fingers dug into her ass as he shifted her onto his lap, facing him.

"I need to be inside you, sweetheart."

"Yes," she agreed.

"Always inside you," he said against her throat.

"You always are."

With one hand, she helped him find her.

As he penetrated her inch by inch, he groaned. When at last he was buried deep, he said, "This is exactly where I want to be."

Myrna rubbed her mound against him, wondering why she'd waited so long to shave it for him. She had a whole new area of bare skin to enjoy. "You feel amazing," she said.

"Amazing," he agreed breathlessly. "I love you so fucking much."

"I love you too."

He cupped her face in both wet hands and stared deeply into her eyes. "So fucking much?" he prompted.

She laughed. "Yes, I love you so fucking much."

Grinning, Brian fumbled with a control panel on the edge of the tub, and the Jacuzzi jets roared to life.

"Hold on," he said before scooting around the tub to sit cross-legged in front of a jet. "Tell me when you're in a good position."

"Let me turn around," she suggested. She rose until his cock slipped from her body and then turned to face the side of the tub.

She sank onto his cock again, her ass rubbing up against his lower belly. "Is that comfortable for you?"

He leaned back, relaxing into the water. "Feels great," he said brokenly.

She started to ride him, the gushing water pulsing against her clit on each up stroke and each down stroke. Brian's hands trailed over her wet breasts, while his lips brushed over her back.

It was too slippery in the tub to get a good rhythm going on her knees. "Where's Eric when I need him?" she wondered aloud.

"Back on the tour bus where he belongs." Brian grabbed her hips to assist her.

"Thanks," she whispered as their combined movements brought her closer to her peak.

Brian kissed her shoulder and then sank his teeth into her heated flesh. Her back arched beneath his rough attention.

"We could call Trey," he said matter-of-factly. "I'm sure he wouldn't mind making our wedding night rock."

Myrna stiffened and stopped moving. "What's that supposed to mean?" she said, her heart clenching in a bitter mix of anger and hurt and jealousy.

"I don't want Eric to touch you, but if you crave more—"

She didn't let him finish, but instead started to rise from the tub. He caught her around the waist and tugged her back down against him.

"I'm sorry, that didn't come out right," he said. "Our wedding night already rocks. We don't need assistance from Eric or Trey."

You're goddamned right we don't, she thought darkly. And she intended to prove it to him.

It took her a moment to clear her thoughts enough to finish what they started. She was pretty sure that Brian didn't think of Trey in their bed as anything more significant than one of their sex toys, but she just couldn't detach enough to think of Trey that way. And she knew Trey was emotionally invested in the act when Brian was involved. She couldn't fathom how Brian managed to keep his feelings out of the mix. The guy normally tossed his heart around like a hacky sack.

Because her thoughts were racing with the perplexity of her husband's complicated relationship with his best friend, it took Myrna forever to find release. Her clit didn't stand a chance against the Jacuzzi jets no matter how hard she was finding it to concentrate. They reached orgasm together and then relaxed in the water to collect their breaths. Resting with her back against Brian's chest, she traced the tattoos on his forearm with one finger. She wasn't insecure about his feelings for her, but she definitely wanted to keep his attention, no matter what it took.

"Would you be against me getting my clit pierced?" she asked.

Behind her, Brian's body tensed. "What? Where did that come from?"

There was no way she was going to tell him what was going through her head. She wanted his attention drawn away from Trey, not toward him.

She gazed down at her reddened nipples. They were a little raw, but still fully aroused. "I really like my nipple jewelry. I thought it might be sexy to connect it to a piercing in my clit."

"That would be sexy," he said breathlessly. "Are you going to get it done?"

"I haven't decided yet. I just wondered if you'd like it."

"I'd like it." He kissed her shoulder and his arms tightened around her waist from behind. "I like everything about you."

"Are you sure?" God, she sounded needy. She suddenly wanted to punch herself in the teeth.

"I'm sure."

She believed him, but he could probably use another distraction to seal the deal. *She* definitely could. "Are you ready for me to fuck your ass now?" she asked.

His body jerked unexpectedly. "Uh, not yet."

"Did you change your mind?" She turned her head to look up at him. "You don't have to go through with it if you don't want to."

"I want to try it. Later. Right now I just want to hold you. I'm exhausted."

She relaxed against him. She was being silly. He wasn't thinking about Trey. It was their wedding night, and he was thinking about her. She was the one who'd been fixating on the guy all day and it needed to stop. *She* needed to stop.

"This is nice," she said.

"Perfect," he murmured.

Myrna's eyelids grew heavy. The next thing she knew, the water was cold and Brian was snoring softly near her ear. She shifted, and he took a startled breath as he regained consciousness. He rubbed his face with both wet hands. "Shit, did we fall asleep?"

She looked down at her hands with dismay. "I'm all pruney," she said, moving away from him so she could climb out of the tub.

She wrapped a towel around her body and handed one to Brian, who was stumbling around in the tub like a drunk.

"Are you okay?"

He pulled the plug, and the water started to drain. "Cold and stiff."

She smiled. "I'll warm you up and make you extra stiff. It's time for an actual bed to make an appearance on our wedding night."

"Give me a minute alone in here to get ready for you," he said.

She knew what that meant: he was ready to participate in her latest experiment with kink. Ah, the man was made for her.

She nodded and wrapped her arms around him. She kissed him deeply and then pulled away to look in his eyes. "Any time you want me to stop, I will. I know you'd do the same for me."

"I trust you, Professor."

She left him in the bathroom and went to collect everything she'd need to live her dirtiest fantasy with her husband. Well, her dirtiest fantasy to date. She'd think up some new ones soon.

In the bedroom, she tossed back the covers and laid all her tools out in a neat row. She wasn't just going to take Brian—she was going to build his desire until he begged her to possess him.

When he joined her, he eyed her implements curiously. "What are you planning to do to me, woman?"

She drew her hand down the length of the small black dildo strapped over her pubis with a harness. "Fuck you properly."

At her confident words, his cock stirred.

Interesting.

"Lie on your back in the center of the bed," she instructed.

"Wouldn't it be easier—"

"Brian."

He did as she asked. She crawled up between his bent legs and licked his balls until he was rock hard and panting with excitement. Settling a pillow under his butt to angle his hips for easier access, she then reached for the smallest butt plug, the one he was used to and she knew he liked. Still sucking on his sac, she lubricated the plug and touched it to his ass. He gasped. He wasn't usually this tense. She lifted her head and sucked his cock into her throat, inserting the plug in the same instant. He shuddered hard, drawing ragged breaths through his teeth. She massaged the end of the plug, moving it around inside him to open him wider. He relaxed and groaned in pleasure. She popped the plug free and reached for one that was quite a bit larger and longer. She lubed his passage with two fingers and then coated the plug. There was some resistance to this one; his body wasn't used to something so thick. She released his cock from her mouth.

"Relax, baby," she crooned. "Relax."

The instant he relaxed, she shoved. He whimpered.

"Are you okay?" she asked.

When his only response was a series of jerky breaths, she grew concerned. "Brian?"

"God, why does that hurt so good?"

"That's a little thicker than my dildo," she told him. "Do you like it?"

"Y-yes."

"What do you want me to do to you?"

"Suck me."

Not quite the request she was looking for, but she complied. She took his cock in her mouth again, giving extra attention to the rim by bumping her lips over it. His stomach tightened as he neared orgasm. She pulled the thick plug from ass, and he cried out in protest.

"Oh please," he gasped.

"Please what?"

"Please put it back in."

"What do you want me to do to you?"

He lifted his head from the pillow to look at her. His face was flushed, his eyes glassy. "Fuck me, Myrna."

She grabbed the dildo strapped over her mound and moved up his body. She pressed the head of the small phallus against his ass, staring into his eyes as she slowly possessed him. His body broke out into a sweat as she slid deeper.

"Okay?" she asked, brushing a hand over his flushed cheek.

His breath came in hard, harsh gasps. "I can't decide if I like it. Go a little deeper." When she complied, his eyelids fluttered. "Oh, yes, I like it."

She claimed him slowly at first, rocking her hips. His hard cock brushed against her belly; pre-cum dripped from the tip. With one hand clutched in the sheet beneath him, he grabbed his shaft in his other hand and stroked his length in time with her thrusts. He was definitely liking this. Far more than she'd anticipated. Maybe he'd always wanted to be taken this way—long before he'd met her.

"Who are you thinking about?" she asked as she pulled back

and pushed forward again. She filled him completely, grinding her hips until he moaned. "Brian."

"Huh?"

"Who are you thinking about?"

"Don't stop. I'm close."

She could see that. She pulled back and thrust forward, taking him hard and deep and fast.

"Are you thinking about Trey while I fuck your ass?" she asked.

His eyes flipped open, and he pinned her with an incredulous stare. "Why the fuck would I be thinking about Trey?"

She wished she'd swallowed the question instead of throwing it out there between them, especially now, when he was so vulnerable. But since she'd already introduced the subject, it was time to tell him how Trey really felt about him and to find out if deep inside himself, Brian felt any of the same emotions.

"I need to tell you something," she said.

"Tell me what?"

She took a deep breath. "Trey—"

A loud pounding banged at the suite's door. Brian tensed and turned his head, staring with wide eyes. "What the hell was that?"

"Shh, shh. It's nothing. They'll go away."

The knocking intensified. Brian stared anxiously toward the door, as if expecting it to fly off its hinges.

"Brian! Open the door!" Sed called from the other side.

Brian's cock immediately went soft and his body tense.

"Dammit," Myrna cursed.

"Let me up," he said, looking like he was about to throw up.

She pulled out of him.

He stumbled out of bed and grabbed a towel to wrap around his narrow hips. Myrna took a hotel robe from the closet and wrapped it around her body to hide what was going on below her waist. She wondered what Sed would think of her makeshift boner. Not that she would ever tell anyone about her experimentation with Brian. Not even Trey. Especially not Trey. And because her husband liked being taken in the ass, it made the guy even more of a threat. Didn't it? Or maybe it made him less of a threat because Brian had given her what he'd never given to Trey. Hell, she didn't know what to think, so she concentrated on something slightly less exasperating—Sed's interruption.

"The guys are probably just playing a joke on us," she said.

"I'm going to fucking kill them all," Brian said. On his way to the door, Brian bumped into the untouched room service cart and careened into the wall, cursing under his breath and rubbing his knee.

Regaining his footing and his hold on his towel, he yanked the door open. "This better be important."

"Is that Sed?" Myrna asked. She peeked around Brian to find Sed standing at the threshold, his ex-fiancée, Jessica, at his side.

Myrna grinned. Her plan to get them back together was already working.

"You two should get your own room. We're using every inch of ours." Myrna poked the five-inch strap-on against the back of Brian's leg to remind him which inches they'd been using most recently.

Sed didn't smile. If fact, he looked like he was about to burst into tears. Myrna didn't know the man was capable of looking that miserable.

Sed took a deep shuddering breath and blurted, "It's Trey."

Myrna's buoyant heart sank to the pit of her stomach. Brian sagged against her. She hadn't expected Brian to need her to be his rock so soon, but she could be that for him. His rock.

Chapter 9

THE TRIP TO THE HOSPITAL WAS BAD enough for Brian without him having to endure Jessica Chase's presence in their taxi. Not only had the fight that put Trey in the hospital started because of her, the woman turned Sed into a complete asshole. Well, her leaving him had. And Brian was in no mood to be in the same country as her, much less the same vehicle. Perhaps he was focusing on his intense dislike for the woman—more precisely his hatred of the woman's effect on his friend's intellect—more than on Trey's injuries because thinking about losing his best friend made him want to vomit. Or scream. Or cry. Or break something. Sitting calmly in the back seat of a cab wasn't going so well for him.

A cold sweat trickled down the center of his back, and every muscle in his body ached from the tension about to destroy him. If Myrna hadn't been gripping his hand, he very likely would have lost his mind.

When the cab stopped in front of the hospital entrance, Sed and Jessica hopped out immediately, but Myrna refused to budge.

He looked at her in question, needing to hurry.

"He'll be all right," Myrna said calmly, stroking the hair from his face. "I know this is tearing you up inside, but you can't let Trey see you like this. He's going to think the Grim Reaper is standing over his bed. You can fall apart later, I promise. But be strong for him now."

Brian didn't know if he could effectively hide his turmoil, his anguish, his *fucking* helplessness, but Myrna was right. He had to pretend to be confident that Trey was going to pull through unscathed, because the alternative was too horrendous to bear. Even the thought was crippling.

He nodded. "I'll keep it together somehow."

"I'm here. You can lean on me, okay?"

He nodded mutely. He wondered how she knew how much he needed to hear that.

"I love you," she said, not waiting for his answering sentiment before she climbed out of the cab.

He'd really needed to hear that too.

Trey was in high spirits when they finally entered his room ten or twelve centuries later. The time blocks had probably been minutes, but each had felt at least a hundred years long. Brian pretended that Trey's head injury wasn't serious—grand mal seizures weren't all that bad, were they?—and joked around with him only because any other action would have reduced him to a blubbering idiot. Trey hooked two fingers into Brian's front pocket and clung to it the entire visit, so Brian was pretty sure he wasn't the only one faking calm and collectedness. Brian managed to keep up pretenses until the brain surgeon shooed them out of Trey's room and Myrna wrapped her arms around him in the waiting room down the hall.

"Are you okay?" she asked.

"N-no," he said. "I said it would serve him right if it turned out to be something serious, and now…" He swallowed the sob trying to choke him.

"You didn't mean that, sweetheart. You know you didn't."

He hadn't, but that didn't change the fact that he'd *said* it. And it had happened.

It had happened.

Oh God.

Brian crushed Myrna against him and turned to face the wall so no one would see the tears swimming in his eyes. He tried to stop them from falling, but his effort was as effectual as trying to stop the sun from setting. He did manage not to weep, by sucking air through the paralyzing fear squeezing his throat like a vice.

When the rest of Trey's support team entered the waiting room, Brian pushed Myrna away and wiped his damnably leaky eyes on the hem of his T-shirt. Jessica entered with Sed, and Brian clung to the anger he felt toward the woman. Anger would keep the tears at bay. Compared to anguish, anger was an easy emotion for him to deal with.

So as he sat beside Myrna waiting for Trey to come out of surgery, he allowed himself to stew. Whenever he found his mind wandering to Trey and how much he would lose if that man was ripped from his life, Brian glared at Jessica sleeping peacefully against Sed's shoulder and welcomed his aggravation at her reappearance in Sed's life. For hours Brian focused on all the trouble the woman had caused—Sed's grief and sleeplessness and his fucking callous disregard for Brian's emotional entanglements with women. The fight at his bachelor party had started because of her. Everything bad thing that had happened to Brian in the past twenty-four hours—Hell, in the past two *years*—was Jessica's fault. His argument with Myrna last night. Trey's head injury. The black eyes Brian had sported on his fucking wedding day. Sed's damaged throat. All of it—Jessica's fucking fault.

Brian clung to his hatred for the woman like a security blanket. His disgust was the only thing that kept him from curling into fetal position under his uncomfortable chair and sobbing.

He had himself worked up into a fine fury toward the strawberry-blond bombshell by the time the doctor came into the waiting room to announce that Trey had made it through his surgery.

When the doctor said, "Brain injuries are tricky," Brian knew he wasn't going to hold it together much longer. Either he was going to have to hit something or he was going to fall apart in front of his new wife, his band mates, one of his rock heroes—Trey's older brother, Dare—and that fucking pain in the ass, Jessica Chase. He was in no shape to sit waiting for Trey's anesthesia to wear off, and his brilliant wife—bless her—seemed to recognize that.

"Brian and I will come back at eight a.m.," she said, bossing around rock stars as only she could.

Eight? Yes, that should give Brian enough time to get his head together, and maybe Trey would be ready for company by then.

God, please, let him be ready for company by then.

"Then Sed and I will come at noon," Jessica said.

As if Trey would want to see her at all. Brian glared at her. She didn't belong here. He didn't want her here. He knew Trey wouldn't want her around either. But maybe Sed deserved her, because he was hanging on her every word like a lovesick tool.

Myrna had a bit more tact. The traitor actually seemed to *like* Jessica. Brian's need to lash out grew exponentially by the minute. He said his goodbyes quickly, but avoided Sed, lest he punch him in the face. He couldn't very well punch Jessica. He grabbed Myrna by the elbow and hurried to the elevator, hoping to God that they could get the hell out of this oppressive fucking hospital before he was forced to confront Sed face to face. He wasn't sure he could control his rage at this point.

"Why are you so mad?" Myrna asked as he hammered on the down button at the bank of elevators.

"I'm not."

"Bullshit, baby. You're like a ticking time bomb."

He couldn't deny it, so decided to vent. "Why did *she* have to come back now of all times?"

"Who?"

"Jessica."

"Do you have a problem with her?"

"Yes, I have a problem with her. I hate her fucking guts."

"Why?"

"Because," he yelled and commenced to lean solidly on the down button.

Myrna gathered him into her arms, and he stopped harassing the elevator.

"You don't hate her," Myrna said.

"I do."

"No, you hate that she turned one of your best friends into a pussy-whipped douche."

He almost chuckled. It came out more like an exasperated gasp.

Myrna squeezed him, and he relaxed slightly. He knew he'd gotten himself overly aggravated on purpose; it was a whole lot easier to focus on hating Jessica than on loving Trey. Brian would never play the guitar again if they lost that ornery little shit. No one would be able to replace Trey in Brian's life or his career. No one.

"Take a deep breath and let it go," Myrna said. "You're not going to change Sed's mind about her. If they're right for each other, you're going to have get used to her and if they're wrong for each other, they have to figure that out on their own."

"I know," he said. "I just can't deal with it on top of everything else."

"We'll sort it out when Trey's better."

He knew she was right. He needed to focus on the more important tragedy in his life. And when Myrna kissed him, he was sure he could let go of his disapproval of the romantic relationship between a rather large douche and the pussy that whipped him. At least he thought so until Sed stepped up beside him with the woman in question hiding behind his broad back.

"Hey," Sed said.

"Hey," Brian answered, and it would have stopped at that if Sed hadn't been dumb enough to talk about what was bothering Brian.

Brian's heated and *loud* argument with Sed escalated quickly.

The idiot couldn't see what a blight Jessica was on everyone's life, not just his own. When the elevator finally arrived, Myrna shoved him inside with Sed and said, "We'll meet you at the bottom. You two have a little talk. Or slug it out. Whatever."

Oh, they were going to have it out. Minimal talking, maximum slugging.

"How could you take her back?" Brian yelled at Sed. "Do you realize how much shit you put me through while you were trying to get over her?"

"Is it my fault your chicks like to fuck me better than they do you?"

Perhaps he should have been grateful that Sed knew how to push his buttons. He'd needed to explode, and Sed had just pulled his trigger. Brian punched Sed in the jaw, his knuckles protesting the force of the blow. Sed hit the back of the elevator car and then launched himself at Brian just as the elevator doors slid shut. Sed popped him a good one in the mouth, and Brian let loose all the fury that had been building inside him since his honeymoon had been so unceremoniously interrupted by the jackass and his trophy stripper. Brian was completely winded by the time he realized how one-sided the fight had become. Sed was far larger and a much more experienced brawler than he was, so why was he landing two or three punches for every one of Sed's? His anger spent, Brian took a step back and glared up at Sed, breathing hard and clenching his fists.

"Feel better?" Sed asked before he tongued at the blood on his split lip.

"I won't feel better until you dump that fucking bitch."

Sed wiped the sweat from his forehead with the back of his hand. "You're going to live a miserable life then, my friend."

If Sed kept Jessica around, that would make two of them. Or rather as soon as she up and left him again, Sed would back to his miserable ways. She'd dumped him once over money—did he really think the money-grubbing bitch had changed so much in two years? Brian closed his eyes and let out an exasperated huff.

"If you need to punch me some more, you better get on with it," Sed said. "We're almost to the lobby."

Brian laughed and scrub the tension out of his forehead with his palms. "Fuck, Sed. You're an idiot around that woman. Don't you recognize that?"

"Yeah. But does it change how I feel about her?" He shook his head. "Not one bit."

Maybe seeing her in a different light would change his mind. "If it wasn't for her, Trey wouldn't have been injured. He could have died. He could still die."

Sed lowered his gaze and shook his head. "If you're going to blame someone for what happened to Trey, blame me. She didn't ask me to grab her off that stage." He chuckled and rubbed his jaw. "In fact, she was pretty pissed off about it."

"So pissed off she landed on her back with you between her legs?"

Sed scowled. "I know you're upset, but watch your fucking mouth. I won't let you talk about her that way."

The elevator dinged as they reached the ground floor. Brian stumbled as a pair of hands reached into the car, grabbed him by the shirt, and slammed him face down on the hard tile floor.

"Whoa," Sed said. "Easy with the guy's junk. He has a new wife to bone tonight."

Brian doubted he'd be doing very little boning for the rest of the night, but he did appreciate Sed's concern for the well-being of his junk. He wouldn't mind equal concern for his chest and face.

"Hospital security. We saw the pair of you fighting in the elevator," a voice said from somewhere above where Brian lay sprawled with a sharp knee in the center of his back.

"We're friends," Sed assured the guard. Somehow *he'd* avoided getting forced to the ground. Maybe the pair of guards didn't think they could take him on. "Just needed to work out a bit of tension between us. We're good now. Right, Brian?"

"Peachy," Brian said with a grunt of pain.

"Haven't you ever needed to knock some sense into a friend?" Sed asked the guard.

"Not in a hospital elevator," the guard said. But he removed his weight from Brian's back.

"Sorry about that. We could do a repeat in the parking lot if Brian's game," Sed said.

"No thanks," Brian said. "I'm good."

Someone helped Brian to his feet, and Sed wrapped an arm around his shoulders. Brian wasn't sure if the bro-hug was for show—so that the security guards would believe they were friends—or because he needed someone to lean on, but Brian didn't mind. In fact, Sed's arm around him gave him a sense of strength and well-being. Sed had that kind of effect on people. He just had horrible taste in women.

As much as Brian liked hearing the guards reminisce about ass-whuppin's they'd delivered and received at the hands of friends, he was awfully glad to see his beautiful new wife step off the elevator a few minutes later. He didn't even care that Jessica was with her. Soon he and Myrna would be alone together in their hotel room and Brian could pretend he was okay about Trey, without everyone watching.

Chapter 10

BACK IN THE HOTEL ROOM, Myrna circled the suite to turn off all the lights except the lamp next to the bed. Brian sat on the edge of the mattress and fiddled with the alarm clock.

"We have to be up in two hours," he said, his voice hollow with exhaustion. "Sorry our wedding night didn't go so well."

She sat beside him on the bed and took the alarm clock out of his hand to set it on the nightstand.

"Me too," she said. "But we can take an extended honeymoon in a few months. Once the tour is over. And Trey is better."

He lifted his head, allowing her to see his dark eyes strained with fatigue. The bruises around them weren't helping him look any more alert.

"I could try to make love you to you if you want," he said.

"We don't need to have sex again," she said and almost laughed when his shoulders sagged with relief. The poor guy was used to having to satisfy her insatiable sexual appetite for him. "I've had plenty of sex today, but I do need to make love to you."

She scooted off the bed and settled on the floor at his feet. She untied one of his boots and pulled it free, tossing it aside before massaging his instep through his soft, white cotton sock. He murmured a sound of pleasure in the back of his throat. She repeated her attention on his other foot and then urged him to lie back on the bed with his legs dangling over the edge so she could unfasten his jeans. He lifted his hips and she tugged them off. Staring up at her wearily, he held his arms open to her.

"Come here, wife. I need to hold you, remind myself that you're really mine, and think about all that's good in my life when everything else has gone to shit."

She blinked back tears, her heart panging with empathy. She knew he loved Trey—not in the way she'd been fixating on for most of the day, but as a friend, a colleague, and someone he could always depend on.

"I was going to massage your back," she said. "Help you relax."

"I'll feel most relaxed with your head right here."

He patted the center of his chest, and she couldn't deny that she very much wanted to rest her head over his heart. He tugged his shirt off, and she shed most of her clothes. She left her panties in place, hoping to remind her eager pussy that she didn't have to fuck Brian to show him how much she loved him.

They snuggled together beneath the covers, her head on his chest and his heartbeat thudding steadily against her ear.

"I'm sorry I behaved like a regular asshole at the hospital," he said, his voice rumbling through his chest. He covered his eyes with one hand and sighed.

"That was behaving like a *regular* asshole? What are you like when you behave like a *huge* asshole?"

He chuckled halfheartedly. "You don't want to witness that."

She stroked his belly absently, willing her mind to calm down so she could get some sleep.

"What am I going to do if he doesn't recover?" Brian whispered.

"I told you not to let yourself think like that."

"I can't help it."

"He'll be fine. He's Trey-motherfucking-Mills. A little head injury won't keep him down for long."

Brian traced lines over the bare skin of her hip. "Maybe once he's better we can invite him back into our bed. It would be okay when it's not our wedding night, right?"

Myrna bit her lip. As sexually fulfilling as her threesome with Brian and Trey had been, it had been more of a mind-fuck than she'd anticipated. "I don't think that's a good idea," she said after a long moment.

"Why not? I thought you enjoyed it."

"I did," she admitted.

"Well, I enjoyed it. He enjoyed it. What's the problem?"

She was almost afraid to say it. "He loves you."

"I love him too."

The words slashed her heart to ribbons, even though she was almost certain they were talking about different kinds of love. "But are you *in* love with him, Brian?"

"Huh?"

"Nothing," she said, afraid that by discussing it, Brian might realize he *was* in love with Trey. She couldn't lose Brian. Not now. Not when she'd finally given him her heart. It would destroy her.

Brian was quiet for a long moment. "Do you think he's actually in love with me?"

She bit her lip and nodded. "I know he is," she said, mortified when her voice cracked.

Brian's arm tightened around her, but he didn't say anything. She was almost in tears by the time she found the courage to say, "I'm so afraid he'll end up coming between us, and I feel so bad for feeling that way—especially now that he's hurt—but I can't help it. I don't want to lose you, Brian. I *can't* lose you. I just can't."

There. Her greatest fear was now out in the open. A hot tear leaked from the corner of her eye, and she dashed it away angrily.

"You won't lose me, baby, and Trey won't ever come between us. I'm in love with you. I was never in love with him. It was just sex, Myrna. Even when Trey and I fooled around as teens, it was just sex."

For Brian maybe, but she was sure it had meant a lot more than that to Trey. "I know," she said, though her heart was still clouded with doubt. "I just... It makes me jealous to share you with him. Don't you get jealous when he touches me?"

"No, I get a raging hard-on when he touches you."

Yeah, and that wasn't normal.

"But when Sed touches me—"

Brian stiffened. "Did he fucking touch you? I'll break his goddamned fingers."

Myrna slapped his belly. "No, he didn't. Why are you so jealous of Sed, but not Trey? I don't understand."

"Because... Because he's *Trey*."

As if that explained anything. "And?"

"Well... I trust him implicitly with every aspect of my life. Even with you." He tipped his head to kiss the top of hers.

And yet Brian claimed not to be in love with the man.

"But if you're not comfortable allowing him into our bed—"

"I'm not," she said hurriedly.

"That's fine. We'll find something else to give us pleasure."

She snuggled closer to her husband's chest, her heart swelling with affection. She believed what Brian said. He wasn't in love with Trey. She had nothing to fear but her own insecurity.

"All I want is you, Mr. Sinclair."

"You have me, Mrs. Sinclair. Always. If there ever comes a time when I feel Trey might threaten our happiness, I won't hesitate to set him straight."

"Promise?" she said, feeling a bit juvenile for asking, but she needed him to say it.

"I promise. I'm yours, Myrna. Only yours."

She was counting on that. And counting on Brian to never break her heart. She knew if he did, she'd never take a chance on love again.

"And I'm yours, Brian," she whispered. "Always."

SINNERS ON TOUR ENCORE

Sweet
Love of Mine

Epilogue to Wicked Beat

OLIVIA
CUNNING

Chapter 1

SITTING AT A RED LIGHT, Eric banged his head to the music blaring from the speakers and drummed his fingers on the steering wheel of his beloved '67 Corvette. He followed the song's drum progression around the circle with his improvised drumsticks and reached over to the passenger seat to tap his cymbal—Rebekah's pert nose. His *most* beloved giggled, which warmed him far more than the California sunshine streaming in through the car's open convertible top. It also prompted him to use her thigh as his cowbell and her nose as his cymbal again.

"You're in a good mood," she said, smiling crookedly at the dashboard.

Well, what did she expect? He was in love. He paused his *live* in-traffic performance to look at her. Really look at her. His Rebekah. His heart.

She couldn't possibly love him with the same all-encompassing intensity with which he loved her, but he was okay with that. He was used to being unloved. And Rebekah hadn't done anything to make him doubt her feelings. On the contrary, she did things to remind him of her devotion on a regular basis. He just had a hard time wrapping his head around the idea that someone could love him. Correction: that someone *did* love him. Perhaps if he stared at her long enough, his head would catch up with what his heart already knew.

A breeze caught her chin-length blond hair—accented with splotches of purple dye—and blew it against her adorable face. She pushed the silky strands aside impatiently and tucked them behind her small ears. Everything about her was tiny. Except her heart. And her sexual appetite. Two characteristics he happened to hold in high regard. When Rebekah realized he was staring, she turned her head to him and he immediately got lost in her sky-blue eyes.

Eric released a contented sigh, certain that he had a loopy expression on his face, but he didn't care who knew he was one hundred percent invested in this woman. He saw forever in those eyes. He could scarcely believe she was his, really his. He hadn't had to kidnap her or drug her or anything. He lifted a hand to touch her face and make sure he wasn't just imagining her gazing at him with adoration. But that loving look really was directed toward him. He wanted her to look at him just like that forever.

Only forever would do.

When they'd been waiting for her biopsy results at the hospital that morning, he'd thought his world might end then and there. Her oncologist's concern of metastasis had been a false alarm, so Eric had decided he wanted to celebrate her clean bill of health by marrying her. Immediately. *Our forever starts now, baby.* But as they made their way across town toward the courthouse to make it official, he thought perhaps he'd been a bit hasty. He wasn't sure if Rebekah was as keen on the idea as he was. He hadn't consulted her, after all. He had just assumed that she was as ready to be legally wed as he was.

The car behind Eric's honked obnoxiously, reminding him that he was supposed to punch the gas pedal as soon as the light turned green. Normally he'd have sent the impatient jackass a one-fingered salute, but nothing could put a damper on his spirits today. Not when the woman beside him was alive and healthy and *his*.

"I love you," he said before he dropped his hand to the gearshift, slammed it in gear, popped the clutch, and took off with an impressive squeal of tires.

"I love you too!" Rebekah yelled, clinging to the dashboard as the car fishtailed slightly, found its grip, and jetted forward.

Unfortunately, traffic was too thick to have any real fun and Eric had to stop at the next light. And wait. God, he was sick of waiting. While he drummed his overabundance of energy into his steering wheel—*again*—a faded wooden sign hanging over a storefront on the next block caught his attention: *Malachi's Costume Emporium*.

His pulse surged with excitement, and he glanced at Rebekah. Would she go for it? A regular courthouse wedding was a bit too *normal* for the two of them, but perhaps…

"I have an idea," he said.

She stiffened and peeked at him from under her long lashes. She was usually gung-ho for any crazy idea that crossed his mind, so he wondered about her uncharacteristic hesitation.

"What kind of an idea?" she squeaked.

"Maybe we should get married in costumes."

"Costumes?"

"Yeah, costumes!" The idea was really catching on with him. "Wouldn't that be fun?"

"I'm not sure," she said and worried her small hands together.

He lifted an eyebrow at her. She wasn't having second thoughts about marrying him today, was she? Maybe he shouldn't rock her boat too much. He knew her emotions were all over the place after that appointment. But he couldn't help but want to make their wedding as memorable as possible considering their complete lack of planning and provisions.

Not waiting for her to be sure, Eric parallel parked in one of the five unoccupied spaces in front of the costume shop and turned off the engine.

"Come on," he said, taking her hand. "Let's go see how much trouble we can get into."

Still she hesitated.

"Don't you want today to be special?" he asked.

She tore her gaze away from the store window, which had several costumes on display, including some fancy old blue dress that Rebekah had been examining with interest. Her eyes bored into his with all the enthusiasm for life and adventure that he'd come to expect from her.

"It's already special," she said. "Marrying you will undoubtedly be the most memorable five minutes of my life."

"But don't you want it to be an experience unique to us?" He leaned in closer, hoping to sway her with his *obey me, woman* look.

She just laughed at him. "Will it make you happy?"

He beamed a grin at her. "It will."

"Okay," she said. "Then I guess I'll make a fool of myself."

His brief kiss of gratitude soon turned into a hands-pawing, tongue-mingling, cock-raising expression of his undying lust for the woman. His heart raced as he tugged her closer. Kissed her deeper. Loved her a bit more every moment they were together for making him so deliriously happy.

When had he become such a fucking sap?

She tore her mouth from his and sucked in a deep breath. "Easy there, tiger," she said. "You're making my panties all squishy."

"Mmm," he said in appreciation. "Those are my favorite kind of panties."

Maybe they should forgo the selection of costumes and get to the courthouse as soon as possible. He had a sudden urge to start the wedding night festivities sooner rather than later.

A bell over the door jangled as they entered the musty-smelling shop. A wrinkled old man in a white shirt, black suspenders, and red bow tie sat behind a long wooden counter near the door. On second glance, Eric noticed the thin man's eyes were closed. Was he actually asleep sitting up?

"Are you open?" Eric asked loudly.

He didn't stir.

"Are you *alive*?" Eric yelled.

The man started and smiled a greeting when his slightly cloudy eyes squinted at the pair of them.

"Welcome to Malachi's Costume Emporium," he said from his seat in a tall ladder-backed wooden chair next to the wall. "If you need assistance, let me know. Otherwise, enjoy your browsing experience."

He rubbed his beak-like nose with the back of his wrist, leaned against the wall, and closed his eyes once more. Within seconds his breathing had become deep and even. He was undoubtedly asleep again.

Eric glanced at Rebekah to share a moment of mutual surprise at the proprietor's trusting disposition—he supposed costume-shop business would be especially light in December, but still...

Rebekah wasn't paying attention. Some costume had already caught her eye. She released Eric's hand and immediately gravitated toward the ugliest wedding dress Eric had ever seen. The yellowed and limp lace collar looked like an enormous bib that covered both shoulders and half of the front. The skirt was layered with wide ruffles and some net-like fabric that looked as if had been caught in a paper shredder. Rebekah touched the ugly thing as though it were made of solid gold.

His heart panged as he realized what was bothering her. She didn't want to get married in a courthouse. She wanted a real wedding. One with flowers and bridesmaids and a church and an extravagant white dress.

"You look around," he said. "I need to call Jace and let him know we'll be at the courthouse a little later than anticipated."

His best man and witness wouldn't appreciate spending his entire day waiting at the courthouse while he and Rebekah goofed off in Malachi's Costume Emporium.

"I should call my mom and let her know too," she said, turning the dress to stare at the equally ugly reverse side. Five bows exploded from the rump in shameless celebration of the dress's gaudiness.

"I'll call her," Eric said.

Rebekah tore her gaze from her strange obsession and blinked at him with her mouth hanging open. "*You're* volunteering to call *my* mother." She pointed at him and then at her chest.

He'd had a moment of bonding with Rebekah's mother at the hospital that morning, and he wanted to use it to his advantage before he screwed something up and she went back to hating him again. He figured he had a couple days in Mrs. Blake's good favor. Tops.

"Yeah, I'll call her. No problem."

Rebekah shrugged and went back to worshiping the ugly wedding gown.

Eric bit his lip as he watched her, wondering how to make her happy. He had a pathological need to bring her as much joy as she brought him. He figured it was time to call in a few favors. He stepped outside to make several calls because he didn't want Rebekah to overhear his sudden change of plans. He hoped his friends would be willing to drop everything for him today and wondered how long he'd be able to stall his bride at the costume shop while they made his plan happen. His stomach was doing all sorts of acrobatics as he dialed his soon-to-be in-laws' house and waited for someone to answer. He prayed his hesitant bride liked his impromptu surprise. He'd be crushed if he couldn't make her burst with joy by the end of the day.

Chapter 2

REBEKAH BLAKE—SOON TO BE REBEKAH STICKS—peeked over the rack of costumes she was contemplating and gazed at her very tall, very handsome, very tattooed, very *fidgety* fiancé. She was supposed to be deciding what to wear to their spur-of-the-moment courthouse wedding, but she couldn't stop looking at the man. Couldn't stop thinking about how sweet he was. How gorgeous. How generous. How wonderful. How thoughtful and understanding. How absolutely perfect.

Just how did she get to be so lucky? And why was she so fucking nervous? Her belly wouldn't stop writhing no matter how much she told herself that this was what she wanted. And it was. Her heart and her mind were ecstatic about marrying Eric. It was only her stomach that seemed against the idea.

Having just rejoined her after making some twenty-minute-long phone call outside the store, Eric pulled a costume from the rack and held it up to his neck, glancing down at the green tights, brown tunic, and felt hat dangling limply from the hanger.

"Ah, perfect," he said. "I'll rob from the rich and give to the poor."

"You are not wearing that to our wedding," Rebekah said with a shake of her head.

"Green looks great on me," he said, glancing up at her and sporting a dreamy grin the instant his blue eyes touched on hers. "And Robin Hood is the type of hero who makes the ladies swoon."

Eric was the type of hero who made Rebekah swoon.

"But you're too tall for tights," she said.

"Too skinny, you mean?"

"No, you're not skinny, you're too *tall*. You'll end up with your crotch at your knees."

"I think you have me mistaken for Tripod."

Rebekah laughed. Eric's best friend, Jace, apparently had some monster cock, the sheer size of which scared the eggs out of chickens. Or maybe it scared them out of the ovaries of all species.

"What did you pick out?" Eric asked, lifting his cleft chin and then cocking his head in interest.

"Cleopatra?" It was far more a question than an assertion. If they were going to dress up for their courthouse wedding, she figured they should play at being one of the great couples in history. Robin Hood and Maid Marion would have worked, but Cleopatra and Mark Antony had been naughtier. Much more comparable to herself and her rock star lover. Well, except for the double-suicide thing. That was a no-go for her. She loved life too much to give it up willingly.

"So I get to choose between tights and a skirt?" he said, eyeing the pair of costumes Rebekah had taken off the rack and turning his nose up at the Marc Antony toga she'd selected. "Maybe we should go for Romeo and Juliet. But wait—doesn't Romeo wear tights too?" He shook his head and paused, tapping his chin. "How about Bonnie and Clyde? I could dress like Clyde without looking like a tool. Gangsta!" He rattled an imaginary Tommy gun, making all the appropriate sounds. *Loud* sounds.

The shop's proprietor remained undisturbed in his chair behind the counter.

Cleopatra and Mark Antony. Romeo and Juliet. Bonnie and Clyde. Those couples had died horribly for each other.

Rebekah's scrunched her eyebrows together. "Ever notice how the most memorable couples all died way before their time?"

"I guess suicide is more romantic than paying the mortgage and folding laundry."

She chuckled. "Depends on who you ask. I'd much rather fold your laundry for the next seventy years than prove I love you by falling into an early grave."

"Ah, baby," he said with a crooked grin, "where's your sense of suicide pacts?"

Rebekah lifted the Cleopatra costume and gave it a shake for emphasis. "As much as I love you, I won't be kissing a spitting cobra to prove it. So don't go shoving any swords through your chest on my behalf."

"I have a snake you can kiss," Eric said and slid his hand down over his crotch. "It's not poisonous, but if you kiss it just right, it does spit."

She snorted and shook her head before shoving the Mark Antony toga against his chest. "Go try this on," she said.

"Also, I believe Cleo kissed an asp, not a cobra," he said.

"I'm not kissing your asp *or* charming your snake before the wedding."

"But after…" He lifted his brows and wiggled them at her.

She grinned. "Count on it."

Eric glanced over at the proprietor sitting behind the front counter. The elderly man—who was apparently mostly deaf, even though his ears were uncommonly large—was still sound asleep with head resting against the wall. Eric grinned and sidled over to the front door, locking it with a barely audible click. Old Malachi emitted a soft snore, but didn't open his eyes.

"What are you doing?" Rebekah whispered loudly.

"Ensuring us a little privacy."

"For what?"

Glassy-eyed and grinning, Eric led her to the enlarged wheelchair-accessible dressing room near the back of the store. He already looked like his cobra was ready to spit on her. The man's sexual appetite knew no end. Not that Rebekah had any complaints. Hers happened to match his. At least it had since she'd met Eric Sticks, Mr. Libido himself.

When they were inside the large stall, he locked the door and immediately stripped her T-shirt off over her head.

"Don't they have cameras in these things?" she asked, covering her bra with crossed arms.

Eric glanced around the stall and located a suspicious-looking black lens. He tossed her T-shirt over it and after checking carefully for additional points of observation, said, "Feel better?"

"What if Malachi wakes up?"

"I don't think a nuclear explosion would rouse the man from his afternoon nap."

She shrugged and stripped off her jeans and flip-flops. She slipped into the skirt and top of the costume and studied herself in the mirror while Eric tried to figure out how to fasten a leather sword belt over his toga.

Rebekah tugged at the hem of her short white skirt as she examined the outfit.

The bodice and skirt were trimmed in gold and faux jewels. It was cute and a little reveling—several inches of her belly showed— but it wasn't exactly what she'd envisioned wearing when she said *I do.* Of course she'd never imagined she'd be marrying someone like Eric, so quirky and fun and enthusiastic and spontaneous. Someone who completed her and made her feel alive and radiant with joy. She figured she'd settle for someone a bit more even-kilter. In other words, boring. Thank God she'd come to her senses.

"I'm not sure this is proper wedding attire," she said.

"You look sexy, baby," a deep voice whispered in her ear. She shivered at the sound, her body recognizing the tone as some surrender-to-his-passion cue.

A pair of strong, masculine hands slid around her bare midriff and splayed over her belly, which began to quiver in anticipation. The man's hands always enflamed her into a raging inferno of lust.

She watched Eric touch her and smiled at the pair they made in the mirror, him all tall and dark and rugged and her all short and light and... she hated to admit it... *adorable*. Ugh! She couldn't help but quirk a brow at the sight of Eric's long bare legs peeking from beneath his own skirt. Well, technically his toga.

"I remember reading somewhere that Cleopatra sailed down the Nile topless." Eric's breath teased her ear, lifting gooseflesh along her spine. "Don't you think you should stay in character?"

"I think you're making that up," she said.

"I'm not. Some famous historian discovered Ms. Patra had a bit of exhibitionist in her. They've recently started calling her the Lady Godiva of the Nile."

"Oh really? What was this famous historian's name?"

He shook his head. "I'm sure you've never heard of him."

"I'm sure you're right, because he doesn't exist."

Eric unfastened the gold clasp between her breasts and slipped the small top from her shoulders. The garment dropped to the floor. Eric traced the cup of her bra with one finger.

"Well, this will never do. I know Cleo never wore a bra," he said.

She lifted an eyebrow and met his gaze in the mirror. "Are you going to try to convince me that she was the first feminist?"

"No, nothing like that," he said, grinning as he watched his finger glide over the soft swell of her breast in her reflection. "Bras hadn't been invented yet."

Rebekah snorted with laughter.

Eric fumbled at her back, and the hook of her bra popped loose. The white lace landed at her feet on the strangely patterned red and green plush carpet. The décor of the costume shop probably hadn't been upgraded in at least thirty years, but the ambiance of the place didn't matter. Rebekah was having fun.

She always had fun when she was with Eric.

His hands slid up her ribs to cup her breasts and pinch her nipples. Her body jerked as her pussy throbbed with appreciation of his attention.

She also always had sex when she was with Eric.

Eric rubbed both her nipples with his thumbs until the pink tips grew hard and achy beneath his persistent touch. Rebekah sighed and lifted her arms over her head to bury her fingers in his thick black hair. It felt like warm silk against her fingertips. Some people thought his unusual haircut was weird, but she found it delightful. If she felt like stroking soft short hair or burying her fingers in medium-length hair or wrapping long strands around her hand *or* playing with stiff spikes, she could. All on the same head. Fingers delighting in the medium-length strands at his nape, she urged Eric's head down so he'd use that delicious mouth of his on her flesh. Eager to please, Eric trailed kisses along her shoulder as she watched him in the mirror.

"Mark Antony's sole purpose in life was to stroke his queen's nipples so they looked pert and inviting to all who faced her," Eric continued with his fabricated history lesson.

"Is that so?" she asked skeptically.

"Why do you think she was able to bend so many all-powerful kings to her will?"

"Maybe because she was intelligent and cunning?"

"Nah," Eric said, rolling her tender nipples between his thumbs and forefingers. "She had a fantastic rack."

He tugged hard at the taut buds until they slipped free of his fingers. Spikes of pleasure spiraled through Rebekah's flesh. She moaned and squirmed against him.

"You might not have the right hair color to be an authentic Cleopatra, but you definitely have the perfect tits to bring kings to their knees."

Rebekah chuckled at his compliment. "So what did Mark Antony do when his constant nipple stimulation made his queen's pussy all hot and achy? Surely she found it to be incredibly distracting. It must be difficult ruling an empire when all you can think about it being filled with your lover's hard, thick cock."

Her lover's hard, thick cock jumped against her lower back at her declaration, and he bent his knees to poke her in the ass with it.

"That's where wearing a man-dress came in handy," Eric said.

She giggled. "You mean a toga?"

"Yeah, that's what I said: man-dress." He nibbled at her ear.

"Take your panties off, my queen, and I'll fill that hot, achy pussy right up for you."

She flushed at his suggestiveness. If she took her panties off, things were going to get out of hand in a hurry. "Don't we have to be at the courthouse soon?" she asked.

"We have at least an hour to waste."

"And you're sure the owner of this shop isn't watching us on the security camera right now?"

"I doubt he knows where the security camera is. Besides, we covered the lens, remember? And I locked the front door, so we have the entire place to ourselves."

"I should have known you were up to something naughty when you did that."

"I'm always up and always naughty."

She glanced up at the pink T-shirt covering the camera lens in the corner of the dressing room and then reached under her skirt to slide her panties down. She kicked them off and squirmed when cool air bathed the hot and achy flesh between her thighs. Truthfully, she had no problem when things got out of hand in a hurry as long as the hands were Eric's very capable ones.

When Eric slid his palms down from her breasts, she caught them and returned them to her chest.

"Now, Mark Antony," she said, "you wouldn't shirk on your sole purpose in life, would you? Keep those fingers where they belong."

He plucked at her nipples, watching her in the mirror. "Maybe Mark Antony had two sole purposes. One pleasing nipples and another pleasing pussies."

"I hope you mean *pussy*. I only have one." And he would not be pleasing any but hers for the rest of their lives.

"And if I remember correctly it's the best one," he said. "But maybe you ought to show me so I can determine if it's worth devoting my life entire to."

"Not your life," she said with a grin. "Just your cock."

"And my lips and tongue and fingers too, I suppose."

"And your eyes."

Her man was very visual. Recently he'd become more hands-on, much to her delight, but he still liked to look and she still liked to show. Rebekah propped her foot on the wall next to the mirror and lifted her skirt so her naughty fiancé could see in the mirror's reflection all that was usually hidden between her legs. She spread her lips with two fingers and used the one in between to massage her throbbing clit.

"What do you think? Is this worth your eternal devotion?"

"I don't just love you for your fantastic pussy," he said. "You know that, right?"

"I know."

She slid her finger down her seam and dipped it into her slippery hole.

Eric groaned and rubbed his arousal against her ass. "But I do have a certain unmistakable attraction to it. Come for me, Rebekah," he whispered.

"*Here?*"

"Please. I want to watch."

"We're going to get caught," she whispered.

Even though Malachi seemed hard of hearing and was obviously a deep sleeper, Rebekah tended to get a bit vocal when she was being more daring than usual. And masturbating in a dressing room so her man could watch her get off was fairly daring. Even for her.

"Don't worry," he said. "The entry door is locked. No one is here but us."

"I still don't know how you talked me into coming here," she said.

"I talked you into coming? *Here?*" He grinned. "You never disappoint me, baby."

She smacked his thigh. "If we spend our wedding night in jail, it will be all your fault."

He chuckled. "You could always say no."

"To you?" She grinned at him in the mirror. "You know you have me wrapped around your little finger, don't you?"

He curled his lip at her. "I'd rather have you wrapped around something else."

She laughed. "You have me wrapped around that too."

With her free hand, she reached behind her, flipped up the hem of his toga, and freed his cock from his boxer briefs. She grabbed his shaft in a firm grip.

"On your knees, my handsome general. I don't just want to come *for* you. I want to come *on* you."

She'd have left him standing if he weren't so damned tall, but he had more than an extra foot on her own five feet three inches, and she didn't want his cock poking her in the back or even her ass.

She wanted it between her legs. Right where it belonged.

She released his hard, veined shaft so he could sink to the floor behind her. She squatted over him and leaned her back against his chest. "Don't let me fall," she said.

He held her thighs and used his chest as leverage as she suspended her crotch over his cock. She positioned him so the shaft was nestled in her seam and his enlarged head pressed against her clit. His dick looked even more erotic nestled there than she had imagined it would. She massaged her clit with her fingers while at the same time teasing his cock's sensitive head. In the mirror, Eric's gaze was riveted to what she was doing between her legs, but she was watching his lean face. She loved that heavy-lidded enraptured look he got when he was turned on. And if his expression was any indication, he liked the way his cock looked buried in her folds as much as she did.

As her excitement built, she couldn't stop her hips from rocking into her hand. The slight motion of her pussy rubbing his length was apparently driving Eric insane because he began to rock with her, sliding his length against her, his cockhead bumping against her fingertips with every forward motion. She flattened her palm against the underside of his cock and pressed it up against her sensitive clit, rocking harder to use his rim to get off. The tip of his cock appeared each time she rocked back and disappeared from view when she shifted forward.

"Oh," she gasped. "That feels good." Much better than her fingers had felt. The thick ridge of his shaft rubbing her from front to back made her crave deep penetration.

"Can't take it," Eric said, sucking air into his lungs. "Need. Inside."

He moved her forward, and she lost her balance. She caught herself with her hands against the mirror and drew an excited breath through her teeth as Eric reached between them and slipped just inside her. He inched forward on his knees to find a better position and surged upward, burying himself deep. When she glanced down, she could see everything in the mirror. His thick, glistening shaft disappeared into her swollen pussy as he thrust into her, and then it reappeared as he withdrew. Watching him take her was almost as hot as hearing it, but not nearly as fantastic as feeling both her body stretch to accommodate him and the maddening friction that rubbed her just right deep inside.

"Can you see?" she asked, unable to take her eyes off the

joining of their bodies. Off the way her pussy swallowed his rigid length. Off his flesh glistening with her fluids as he claimed her over and over again. She could also see her name inked on his lower belly, and seeing her brand on his skin made watching him fuck her even hotter.

Eric shifted his head slightly to the side, and his hot breath bathed the back of her shoulder as it came out in an excited gasp.

"I can now," he said. "Fuck, baby. There is nothing more beautiful in this world than your pussy stuffed with my cock."

Apparently being able to watch himself move inside her inspired all sorts of pleasing motions in his slim hips. Her body adjusted to him, her lips and folds stretching as he filled her and churned, pulled back and filled her again at a different angle. Her legs began to tremble from holding a crouched position for so long, but damn, it turned her on to watch him work her pussy into a frenzy. Her excitement built. And built. Higher. Higher.

"Oh God, Eric," she groaned, rocking to meet his thrusts now. Wanting to come. "Oh please. Fuck me harder."

His motions became more vigorous, making her tits bounce with each penetrating thrust.

"Beautiful," he whispered. "You're so fucking beautiful."

She didn't realize she was mewling with pleasure until Eric whispered, "Need a little help?"

She nodded, and he released her thigh to stroke her clit. She cried out at once, unable to hold in the sound, and came so hard, her fluids gushed down his cock and trickled onto his balls. Her pussy clenched rhythmically around him, driving him, coaxing him, sending him over the edge to join her in bliss.

Eric grunted. His cock twitched as he buried himself deep and let go. She saw his shaft jerk in the mirror and felt it move inside her.

Oh God.

Legs trembling, she forced herself to kneel. Eric slipped out of her—a pity—but she couldn't hold that crouched pose for another second.

"Love you," he murmured against the nape of her neck, remembering Mark Antony's sole purpose in life and moving his hands to hold her breasts and stroke her sensitized nipples.

"Love you too."

"You shouldn't lie to me on our wedding day," he said, nibbling her ear and making the back of her neck tingle.

"I didn't lie to you," she said, scowling. "I *do* love you!"

"Not that. You said you weren't going to charm my snake until after the wedding. And, baby, my snake was fully charmed."

She chuckled. "I'm *so* sorry," she said, her voice full of as much sincerity as she could muster. "I promise I'll never lie to you again."

"Apology accepted." He winked at her and gave her a squeeze. "Will you lie to me about kissing my asp too? Please."

"You don't expect me to go back on another promise, do you?" she teased. "I want you to be able to trust my word."

"I do trust your word. You said there'd be snake charming and asp kissing after the wedding, and I know you'll keep that promise."

"The sooner we get married, the sooner I can keep my word."

"Let's go! Is this what you want to wear to our wedding?" he asked, slipping a hand up her thigh and into the skirt that was mostly around her waist. "It's really sexy. Especially now that I've seen your O-face while you were wearing it."

"Eric!"

"You have to wear the top too, though, because I don't want anyone to see this fantastic rack but me. Kings be damned."

She considered the costume in the mirror and decided she didn't like it much after all.

"Now that I've been fucked by Mark Antony, I think I need something a little different to get married in. Something a little less revealing, perhaps."

He chuckled and kissed the back of her shoulder. "Any ideas?"

"I'm not sure. Let's go browse some more."

"King Arthur and Guinevere? I can slide Excalibur into your stone. Pull it out. Slide it back in again. Repeat and repeat until the magic happens."

Rebekah stifled a giggle. "I'm not familiar with my stone, King Arthur. Where's that exactly?"

"I think it's between your boobs." He cupped them in both hands and pressed them together.

"Damn," she said. "I was hoping my stone was a bit lower."

She winked at him in the mirror and climbed to her feet, tugging out of his grip as she rose.

Rebekah found a packet of tissues and wet wipes in her purse—a necessity when dating Eric Sticks—and used them to clean herself up before they redressed and went back to the racks of costumes as if they hadn't just been fucking in the dressing room.

Not that anyone but the two of them would have noticed.

Malachi was still fast asleep.

Rebekah looked at Bride of Frankenstein costumes and one of an astronaut. She considered a Southern belle gown that would have made Scarlett O'Hara green with envy, but for some reason she kept returning to the white dress she'd first spotted. It was probably meant for the ghost of a heartbroken specter, but technically it was a wedding dress. Rebekah lifted it from the rack and held it against her body.

"Did you find something?" Eric asked, thumbing through a rack of mobster attire.

"Bride costume," Rebekah said, showing him the mass of lace and frills she couldn't help but gravitate toward again and again.

"I guess that's fitting," he said. "But not terribly creative."

She hung the dress back on the rack and tried to find something more creative. If he thought she was going to get married in one of her usual, naughty costumes with her tits and ass more bare than covered, he had another think coming. Her mother would be at the ceremony as Rebekah's witness. And for once Rebekah didn't want to stir things up with the woman.

Rebekah slid hangers down the rack one at a time as she looked at flapper dresses and regency gowns, ballerina tutus and army fatigues. She started when a large hand splayed over her lower back. The tattoo she'd recently had inked there was still a bit sensitive to the touch. Eric thrust the frilly white wedding dress into her arms.

"I think you should wear this."

"But it's not terribly creative," she reminded him.

"I don't mind. As long as you promise to wear it to bed tonight," he said. "The thought of you in a wedding gown has me in a state that would make those Robin Hood or Romeo tights several inches too short, if you catch my drift."

She laughed and gave him a hearty squeeze. The man was gifted at making her feel good about herself, and he could get his dick hard more times in a day than three average men combined.

"Then maybe you should wear the wedding dress to hide your perpetual hard-on," she said, "and I should be the one to wear the tights because I'm super short."

His eyebrows drew together. "Would it turn you on if I said yes to the dress?"

"Uh, no. Not at all."

"Then forget it."

She laughed at the thought of him dressed in a wedding gown. If she lied and told him that cross-dressers made her horny, she had no doubt that her eager groom would say his eternal vows to her in a frilly white wedding gown. She wouldn't do that to him though. Even if it would be hilarious.

"So I'll wear the bridal gown and you wear this," she said, hurrying to a nearby rack and jerking out a tuxedo—007 version, very smooth and cool—that looked like it might fit him.

"Honey, do you want to wait? Maybe you'd like to get married in a cathedral with the dress and the twelve bridesmaids and the cake and the—"

She kissed him to shut him up. She knew he wanted to give her the world, and he had. He *was* her world, so as long as he stayed by her side, she had everything she could possibly want.

"I don't want the bridesmaids or the cake or the cathedral," she said. "I do want the vows and the kiss and even though I didn't expect to, I apparently want the stupid dress."

"Personally, I'm most looking forward to the kiss," he said. "I think I need to practice it a couple dozen times to gauge the appropriate amount of tongue to give you. What do you say?"

She swatted his shoulder. "No more kissing until you say *I do,* or we're going to end up screwing in the dressing room again and miss our own wedding."

"Fine," he said with a resigned sigh. "I'll just fantasize about kissing you while you go try on that dress. And then we'll head to the courthouse."

She held the gown up and examined it closely. It was horribly outdated, the enormous lace collar was yellowed from age and stained with what appeared to be fake blood—probably from some bride of Dracula from a past Halloween.

"It's not a very pretty gown," she said.

"If you want, we could go to a real wedding shop and buy you a better dress," Eric said.

"Off the rack? That's kind of tacky."

"There isn't anything tacky about your rack, babe." He caught a finger in the top of her T-shirt and tugged down to give himself a nice view of her cleavage.

She slapped a hand over her chest. "I don't think we have time to go shopping somewhere else anyway," she said.

"We have some time," he said. "I do want you to be legally mine as soon as possible, but your happiness is my number one priority. At the moment, your cleavage is a close second."

He made a grab for her boob, and she smacked his wrist.

"I'd be happy marrying you dressed just like this," she said, sweeping a hand down the front of her pink T-shirt and faded jeans. She even wiggled her toes, clearly visible in her cheap flip-flops. "Coming here to pick out costumes was *your* idea, remember?"

"Are you sure?" he said. "That doesn't sound like some lame idea *I'd* come up with."

She said nothing, just lifted her eyebrows at him in challenge.

"We could get married naked," he said. "There's an option."

Grinning, she shook her head at him in disgrace. "Now *that's* really a lame idea. My mother was just starting to like you. I don't think she wants to get to know your balls on a more personal level."

Eric's face paled visibly. "You're right. I don't want to say my vows while sporting wood in front of your mother."

Rebekah giggled. "And why would you be sporting wood?"

"I always sport wood when you're naked."

She slipped her hand into his and pressed her head against his arm, loving him a little more with each passing vulgar declaration.

"And half the time when you're fully clothed," he added. "And if you're wearing one of your sexy costumes"—he made a cat sound in the back of his throat—"I'm completely gone. But you already know that."

She did know that and used the knowledge to her advantage. Initially she'd been stunned that he'd wanted to dress up for their wedding. It was definitely something they liked to do in the bedroom, but weddings weren't supposed to be about sex. Wedding nights, on the other hand, were meant for a whole different expression of love. Was it time for their wedding night yet? She glanced at a wall clock and noted that they'd been in the costume shop for well over an hour.

How had they wasted so much time already? At that rate, they'd never get out of the place and would miss their opportunity to get married today. She was starting to think he was trying to stall her. Maybe he secretly wanted the courthouse to be closed by the time they got there. If he had cold feet and honestly wanted to delay the wedding, she just wished he'd tell her instead of goofing off all afternoon in this dusty old store.

The loud rumble of an engine outside caused Eric to glance out the window, his shoulders high with eagerness. When it continued past the shop, his shoulders dropped again.

He was up to something, she just knew it.

"Are you going to try it on?" he asked when he caught her trying to read his mind.

She probably shouldn't. Wearing an ugly costume wedding dress kind of defeated the entire purpose of their exercise in spontaneity. "Maybe I should go for something else. That Victorian gown is really pretty," she said, gazing across the store at the beautiful blue gown on a mannequin in the window, "but is definitely not my size. I hate being short."

"You look beautiful just the way you are."

She highly doubted that. It had been an exhausting morning at the oncologist. She was mentally drained and was sure it showed outwardly. Thinking that her uterine cancer might have metastasized when they'd found a suspicious spot in her MRI had shoved her head first under the oppressive boulder that dwelled at rock bottom. She'd been there before, knew that place all too well. Cancer had already fucked her out of her chance to have babies; she couldn't believe it would be so cruel as to fuck her out of her chance at happiness as Eric's wife. Even when she'd been near death on chemotherapy a couple of years ago, she had never felt as utterly defeated as she had that morning.

Then hours later, she'd been handed a clean bill of health and her mood had elevated her back to the land of the living—she'd let herself hope for a future again. A future for herself. A future with Eric. Eric's insistence that they get married immediately had sent her soaring with happiness. Yet the up, down, down, so far down, up, up, way up of her emotional roller coaster had taken its toll. Her bottom lip trembled as she thought about how much she stood to lose if she got sick again. Even though Eric had assured her that he would stand by her if her cancer returned, she wanted their times together to be filled with joy and love, not sorrow and pain.

"What's the matter?" Eric asked.

She forced her emotions back inside, struggling to keep them out of her expression. He didn't need to know how upset she still was. She was supposed to be letting that fear go—not allow it to continue to churn inside her—but that was more easily imagined than accomplished.

She rubbed her face with one hand. "I'm just a little tired; it's already been a long day. And I could stand a little rest. When are we supposed to be at the courthouse?"

"I was told we should get there no later than five."

According to the wall clock, it was already almost four.

"Then we'd better make a decision on these costumes and fast. We're almost out of time."

"I'm sure they'll wait for us if we're a bit late."

Rebekah chuckled. "A government office? I highly doubt that."

He glanced at the time again. "No rush," he said.

"There's something you're not telling me," she said. "You're stalling for time, aren't you?"

"What? No, of course not." He shoved the wedding gown in her arms and turned her toward a dressing room.

He'd never lied to her about anything important before. She hoped he wasn't starting now.

She glanced over her shoulder and caught him sneaking a peek at his cellphone.

She bit her lip, more than a little annoyed that he was focused on something besides her on their wedding day.

He glanced up, slid his phone back in his pocket, and pushed her in the back again. "Go try it on. Then we'll decide."

"Only if you try on the James Bond getup."

He grabbed the spy wear off the rack. "Will do."

She sighed, not satisfied with the dress in the least, and went to the dressing room at the back of the shop with Eric on her heels. She closed the door in his face when he tried to follow her inside. She wasn't going to fall for that again. They'd definitely be late if he joined her in the dressing room a second time.

Rebekah shimmied out of her jeans and shirt before she slipped the dress on over her head. She almost cried when she saw her reflection and not the good kind of emotional oh-my-God-this-dress-was-meant-just-for-me cry. She was not marrying the love of her life in this travesty of a garment.

"I hate it," she called.

When he didn't answer, she cocked her head toward the door, listening intently. Eric was whispering loudly to someone, apparently on his cellphone.

"What is taking you so long? I can't stall her much longer," Eric said in a poor attempt at a whisper.

Ah, so she'd been right. He was trying to keep her here as long as possible. But why? She hoped it wasn't because he'd changed his mind. She opened the door, and his eyes widened as she caught him on his phone.

"Who are you talking to?" she asked.

"That dress is hideous on you, babe."

He wasn't lying, but her emotional rollercoaster had taken one dip too many, and the tears started falling before she could stop them.

"Oh God," he said. "Don't cry, don't cry. It's just Jace." He thrust his phone in her direction. "Here, you talk to him."

"I don't want to talk to him. I'm not crying because you're talking to Jace! You said I look hideous."

His face fell. "No, I didn't. I said that *dress* is hideous."

"Same difference." She rushed into the dressing room, slammed the door and locked it.

"Reb," Eric said, knocking on the door. "Let me in. You don't look hideous at all." Not to her—to Jace presumably—he growled, "Just hurry the fuck up, will you?"

She yanked the dress off over her head and threw it over the top of the dressing room door, satisfied by the sounds of Eric trying to disentangle himself from the yards of taffeta and lace and satin and ugly.

"I promise everything will be fine as soon as Jace gets here," Eric said.

That was a weird thing to promise. Rebekah wiped the stupid tears from her face with the back of her hand. She couldn't believe he'd asked Jace to come there in the first place. What? Did she need two guys to tell her she looked hideous in that fucking dress?

"Rebekah? Are you okay?"

"Give me a minute," she said breathlessly, still trying to get a handle on her emotions. What she wouldn't give for a hot bath and a soft bed and a hard body to cuddle against.

"I love you," he said at the door crack.

Well, that little sentiment didn't help her get her emotions under control in the least. She stared at the ceiling, blinking her eyes, willing them to stop leaking like a pair of broken faucets.

"Rebekah?"

"I love y-you too," she said, cringing when her voice cracked.

"Are you crying in there?"

She sniffed loudly. "N-no."

"Baby, I didn't mean to hurt your feelings. Let me in."

"That's not why I'm crying," she said.

"Then why? Let me fix it."

She laughed half-heartedly. "I don't know why. I'm just... I'm a complete mess all of a sudden." She ground the heels of her hands into her eyes and took several deep breaths. "It has nothing to do with you." And yet it had everything to do with him. She feared she'd loved him too fast, too hard, and now she feared burning out, running out of time, of *life*, too soon—like those tragic couples they'd spoken of earlier. But he wasn't at fault for those fears. He was just the reason she cared so much that she lived. Really *lived*. Beside him.

"Let me in," he said calmly.

She wiped at the residual tears, took a deep steadying breath, and unlocked the door. He entered the dressing room, closing the door behind him, and looked her over from bottom to top. She stood in the bright room in her bra and panties, but didn't feel self-conscious about it. He'd seen her in much less twenty minutes before.

"I have just the thing for those tears," he said.

With Eric, there was no telling what he thought would cure tears. She looked up at him skeptically.

He patted his chest. "You. Right here. Right now."

She collided with his chest, and he wrapped her in a tight embrace. She clung to him, her arms stealing around his waist to draw him closer. In his arms she felt safe and loved. Complete. None of those things made her feel like crying. They made her feel like smiling. If she spent a month, a year, a decade, or a century in his arms, she'd cherish every moment. No one knew how much time they had to live. She had to let the fear go and make the most of the time she did have, no matter how long that happened to be. Rebekah relaxed against him, the corners of her mouth already drawing upward. He kissed the top of her head.

"Better?" he asked after a moment.

She nodded. "Today is supposed to be the happiest day of my life."

"It isn't?"

She grinned and tilted her head back to stare up into his pretty blue eyes. "Not yet, but it's getting better." She reached up and captured the long purple lock of his hair and gave it a tug. "Thank you for knowing that I needed you to hold me."

"You did?" he said, blinking at her. "I just wanted to see you in your underwear again."

"Then we're both happy." She patted his butt, knowing his greatest defense mechanism was inappropriate humor. He used it unabashedly when he was feeling his most vulnerable. She supposed they were both on the emotionally raw side today.

She got lost in his gaze until he lowered his head to kiss her, and her eyelids fluttered shut. His affectionate embrace turned a bit more passionate as his hands slid down her back and over her bottom. She melted into him, wanting his bare skin against hers, wanting him buried deep inside her, wanting to be one with him. It didn't matter that she'd just had all those things half an hour ago. She wanted them again already.

"Do you know what I think?" he whispered against her lips.

"That you should press me up against that wall and fuck my brains out?"

"Uh, no, that wasn't what I was thinking. For once."

"Were you thinking I should drop down to my knees, yank your pants down, and suck you off while you watch in the mirror?"

He groaned. "Lord, woman, you do know how my mind works, don't you? But no, that's not what I was thinking either."

"Then what?" she asked, sliding her hand down his belly to cup the growing bulge between his legs. She gave his always attentive cock an appreciative squeeze.

"I think Jace got lost."

She gasped in exasperation. "Why are you so fixated on Jace?"

An unmistakable low rumble grew louder as Jace's Harley came up the street and drew to a halt in front of the store.

"There he is. Finally." Eric pecked her on the lips and drew out of her arms. "You stay here," he instructed. "I'll be right back."

"Eric, what's going on?"

He grinned, boyish charm seeping from every pore. "It's a surprise."

She crossed her arms over her chest. "I don't like surprises."

"Liar." He let himself out of the dressing room, and she peeked out around the door to watch him stride toward the entrance. He had to unlock the front door to let Jace in. The bell over the door jangled.

"Welcome to Malachi's Costume Empori…" The gravelly voice that came from behind the counter ended in a pronounced snore.

Rebekah giggled. She was surprised the old man hadn't been robbed blind by now.

Dressed in leather and denim, Jace entered the store carrying an enormous white box and looking more out of sorts than usual.

"You owe me one," he said to Eric in greeting.

"I owe you ten. Whatever." He pounded Jace enthusiastically on the back, sending him careening into a rack of adorable fruit and vegetable costumes for babies and toddlers.

Eric snatched the box out of Jace's arms and headed in Rebekah's direction. Her eyes widened, and she slipped back into the dressing room, pretending she hadn't been eavesdropping.

"Do you know how hard it is to hold a giant box while on a motorcycle?" Jace complained. "The wind kept catching it, and I almost wiped out three times."

"Not my fault you're an idiot. You should have borrowed Aggie's car." Eric spoke just outside the dressing room door.

"You didn't tell me the thing was so fucking huge."

"I didn't know."

A sudden knock on the door made Rebekah jump.

"Yes?" Rebekah said, trying to sound nonchalant even though her heart was hammering out a rapid staccato.

"I have something for you to try on."

"What is it?"

"A dress."

"Where did you get it?" she asked.

"Open the door."

"I'm in my underwear. Remember?"

"Turn around, dude," Eric said to Jace. "He's not looking, Reb. Open the door."

She eased the door open. Eric beamed a smile at her, shoved the giant box into her arms, and then closed the door behind her. She set the box on the floor and stared down at it. The oversized box was shockingly familiar.

"Eric?" she said, covering her lips with a trembling hand.

"Does it make you happy?"

"Eric? How did you get this?" She didn't have to open it to know what was inside.

"I asked your mom if she had something you could wear and sent Jace to your parents' house to get it."

She gnawed on her lips, knowing those tears she'd just gotten under control were going to start falling again the second she glimpsed her mother's wedding gown, which was undoubtedly nestled inside. She'd seen it a hundred times as a girl and had dreamed of getting married in a fairy-tale church wedding to a handsome prince in that beautiful sentimental dress. Well, the church would be a courthouse and her prince was a tattooed metal drummer with a crazy hairstyle and no manners, but this day was definitely her dream come true.

"Thank you," she whispered.

"Hurry, baby," he said. "We're going to be late. Jace is being a slowpoke today."

"It's a miracle I didn't crash," Jace said.

She heard several thuds as a punching match ensued between the two friends.

Rebekah lifted the lid from the box and pulled the dress out, shaking it and smoothing the wrinkles with her hands. Seeing it didn't trigger the tears she'd expected; instead, her emotions took a completely unexpected trajectory. Rebekah beamed at the dress, her heart fluttering with joy, and hugged the garment to her chest. She put it on over her head and stared at herself in the mirror. She looked like a bride. Eric's bride. She couldn't help but smile even more broadly.

"Perfect, perfect, perfect," she said, hugging the loose bodice to her chest and doing a happy dance. She opened the dressing room door and crushed Jace in a huge and hasty hug for risking his life to bring the gown to her before grabbing Eric by the arm and tugging him into the dressing room. He stared at her with his mouth agape.

"Oh my God, baby. You look amazing."

She touched her fingertips to her lips and nodded, too choked up to speak.

"Did I do good?" he asked.

She nodded again and tried to swallow her happiness. It settled somewhere over her heart and swelled in her breast.

Her words came out all breathless as she forced them through the knot in her throat. "You did wonderful, Eric. I'm overjoyed that you did this, that you *thought* of this and made it happen. It never occurred to me to wear my mother's dress today." She touched his jaw. "This means so much to me. *You* mean so much to me."

He smiled, his eyes uncommonly shiny with moisture. "I'm glad," he said, a breathless hitch in his own voice. "On both counts."

She pecked him on the lips and then turned her back to him. "Button me?"

His fingers trembled against her skin as he fastened the long row of pearl buttons up the center of her back.

"You two better hurry—Brian says they're ready," Jace called through the dressing room door.

"Dude," Eric yelled at Jace. "Shut up!"

"Ready for what?" Rebekah asked, peering over her shoulder. "What are you up to, Eric Sticks?"

"Nothing," he said, working his way up the row of buttons more quickly.

"Eric..."

He huffed out a breath. "You made my birthday special for me, so I'm trying to make your wedding day special for you. Stop asking questions and deal with it."

She chuckled. "Consider it dealt with."

She stopped pestering him about his surprise, though her mind was racing with possibilities, and she held still so he could finish buttoning her gown. She watched him in the mirror, too enamored with the look of concentration on his face, and the devilish tongue pressed against his upper lip, to take note of her transformation into a bride. This was a far different scene from what they'd shared in this dressing room mirror the first time, but she felt even closer to him this time. Not sexually closer, but him helping her dress was infinitely intimate.

"This thing is going to be hell to get off of you tonight, isn't it?" he said as he finished up with the last few buttons.

"I'm sure we'll figure out a work-around."

"Done!" he said and tagged her bare shoulder before lifting both hands in a sign of victory.

"A new record," she said as she gathered the wide embroidered skirt in both hands to turn toward the door. The dress style was fairly simple. Her shoulders were bare except for the slender straps just thick enough to cover her bra straps. A band of satin several inches wide completely circled the dress at the level of her collar bones, continuing around her upper arms and back. The rest of the bodice was fitted to the waist, and the A-line skirt continued to the floor and trailed into a long train behind her. The only embellishments to the humble style were the pearl buttons at her back, the beautiful floral embroidery work that decorated the matte satin, and a delicate trim along the hem of the skirt and train. No lace. No bows. No ruffles. Just elegance

Before she could turn the knob to exit the dressing room, Eric covered her hand with his.

"Okay, time to get you back out of that dress."

"*What?* What's wrong with it?" She smoothed her hand over the fabric looking for the tragic flaw she'd apparently missed. If he said it looked hideous, she'd likely pull a Cleopatra or a Juliet and end it all right then.

"There is no way I'll be able to concentrate on anything but my dick with you looking that beautiful."

She breathed a sigh of relief and slapped at him. "Stop goofing around, Eric Sticks."

"She thinks I'm joking," he said to his reflection.

She laughed and opened the dressing room door.

Jace glanced up from his cellphone, and his jaw dropped.

"Wow," he said. "You look amazing."

Which earned him another unwanted hug from Rebekah and a thunk in the forehead from Eric.

Eric glanced at the clock and went pale. "When did it get so late?"

"When you were seeing the bride in her dress before the ceremony," Jace said. "That's bad luck, you know."

"I'm currently the luckiest motherfucker on the planet. I'm not worried about some lame superstition."

Jace blinked at him and shook his head. "Okay, that's a first. First you deviate from your 'dye your weird hair a different ugly color every forty-nine days' routine, and now this?"

"I always wondered why you dye it every forty-nine days," Rebekah said. "Sixty-nine seems a more likely number for Eric Half-Porn-Star/Half-Rock-Star Sticks to base a superstition around."

Eric grinned, probably thinking of sixty-nines past.

"While sixty-nine might result in two people getting lucky, seven has always been my lucky number."

Rebekah's brow furrowed. "There's no seven in forty-nine," she said.

"There are *seven* sevens in forty-nine. Which makes it the luckiest number in existence."

"That's exactly why I'm so surprised you've stopped caring about your luck," Jace said.

"I used my lifetime supply to win the girl," Eric said. "Now that I have everything I want, I don't need luck anymore."

Rebekah melted at his declaration. Jace gagged and pantomimed shoving his finger down his throat. Eric checked out the clock and grabbed Rebekah's hand.

"Is everyone there already?" Eric asked Jace as they raced

toward the exit. "Thanks for letting us use your store!" he called to the proprietor on his way out the door. "We'll come back again soon."

"Welcome to Malachi's Cos..." the man murmured in his sleep.

"You might want to empty out the trash in the dressing room," Eric added. "Just saying."

Rebekah felt her face go warm as she thought about all those used tissues and wet wipes they'd placed in the trash.

"They're still waiting on Trey," Jace said when they stepped outside. "But I think he's on his way."

"Just how many people did you invite to our small private ceremony?" Rebekah asked. Not that she minded. She was just surprised. When had Eric even had time to invite them? Had that been why he'd slipped outside and spent twenty minutes on the phone? And kept annoying her by checking the damned device instead of giving her his undivided attention?

"I invited only family," he said.

And since he had no real family to speak of, that meant his band. When she was on the road running Sinners' soundboard, they were like her surrogate family too. She was glad Eric had invited them. The dress meant a lot to her, but it would mean even more if those she cared about got to see her wear it when she pledged to love Eric for the rest of her life. She hoped that would be a very long time.

Chapter 3

ERIC OPENED THE PASSENGER DOOR of his recently awesomified vintage Corvette and helped his beautiful bride get her dress into the car without catching it in the door. When he leaned over the open convertible top and kissed her forehead, she smiled up at him, her blue eyes twinkling with happiness.

That look right there—he wanted to be the cause of that look on her face for the rest of his life. His heart swelled so big that he found it difficult to draw air. This woman meant everything to him and for those few horrible minutes while they'd been waiting for her biopsy result that morning, he'd thought he might have to figure out how to live without her. He wasn't sure he'd have been able to do it. He was determined to fill every moment they spent together with joy and love because even if she lived to be a hundred and twenty, there still wouldn't be enough time to show her how much she meant to him.

"You're looking particularly sappy at the moment," Rebekah said. She reached up to tap his nose with her index finger.

"Do you prefer my horny look? I'm sure I can find it if I stare at your cleavage for a couple of seconds."

She did look spectacular in her wedding dress. Her *mother's* wedding dress, some cock-blocking synapse in his brain reminded him.

She laughed. "Get in the car. I need to marry you now."

"Well, that's not going to get rid of my sappy look. If anything, it'll intensify it."

She took his hand and kissed his knuckles before pressing them against her cheek. "I'll figure out a way to put up with it somehow," she whispered.

She released his hand, and he stole a quick kiss before climbing behind the wheel and starting the car. It roared to life with none of the knocking, glugging, or grinding it used to produce. Produce, that is, when he was actually able to get it started. "You're a genius mechanic, baby," he said, flashing a grin at his bride-to-be.

"Are we going to work on my Camaro tonight?"

Eric laughed. "Not unless we're using the back seat for consummation purposes."

He pulled into traffic and drove to the courthouse, wondering if Rebekah would be okay with all the quick plans he'd made to make their day a bit more special. He knew women liked to plan these things, and he'd never heard of a groom making all the arrangements, but they weren't a typical couple. Nope. He was sure they were much happier.

Jace waited outside next to his motorcycle while Eric helped Rebekah out of the car and into the courthouse.

"Isn't he your witness?" Rebekah asked. "I should call my mom to let her know we've made it."

Her mom had miraculously agreed to be Rebekah's witness, but she wouldn't be meeting them here. They had somewhere else to go after they picked up their license, but he wasn't going to tell Rebekah where. He wanted to surprise her. Even more so now that he'd seen how she'd reacted to her wedding gown surprise.

"We have to get the license first," he said. One of many things he'd learned when he'd called the courthouse late that morning. He'd also asked who could perform the ceremony. Which had started his mind churning on another way to make Rebekah's wedding day more meaningful.

People were grinning at Rebekah as she passed them in her wedding dress. They were probably wondering why she was with the tall goofy guy in jeans and a T-shirt. He hoped Trey was able to find the tuxedo in Eric's closet. He'd worn it to the Grammy's a couple of years ago and was pretty sure he still had it stuffed it in a box somewhere. Eric also hoped that the guy didn't get distracted by something far more interesting than wedding attire on the way to his house.

While he and Rebekah were waiting in line to get their license, Eric discreetly checked his text messages. He was glad he'd been able to keep Rebekah distracted with trying on costumes while others put together his preparations for him. It hadn't been easy orchestrating things right under her nose.

One text from Brian: *Still waiting on Trey. Everyone else is here and ready to roll.*

One from his soon-to-be mother-in-law, Mrs. B: *Thanks for making today special for her. I'm sorry for the way I've been treating you.*

One from Sed: *Don't you think I have better things to do on my day off than attend your wedding?*

Eric knew he was just messing with him, so didn't take offense.

One from his soon-to-be brother-in-law, Dave: *If you ever break her heart, I'll run over your balls with my wheelchair.*

Eric winced and shifted uncomfortably at the very idea.

One from Rebekah's ex-fiancé, Isaac: *You didn't have to invite me, but thanks. I'm glad she's happy.*

And one from Jon: *Sorry, can't make it. But kiss her once for me.*

"You're certainly popular today," Rebekah said, craning her neck, trying to see who he was texting.

He tucked his phone into his pocket. "Me?" He placed a hand on the small of her back and urged her closer, even though it buried his legs in her cumbersome skirt and made him feel off balance. "Everyone is looking at you today."

"I feel kind of dumb wearing this huge, fancy dress in the courthouse," she said. The train was draped over one arm. She lifted the skirt in front and gave it a shake.

"You shouldn't feel dumb, you should feel beautiful," he said. "Because you are."

When they reached the front of the line, they showed the clerk their IDs to have their marriage license prepared.

"How do you want the names to read?"

Eric froze. They hadn't exactly discussed that. His birth name was Anderson, but his legal name was Sticks. Would she even want his name? He wouldn't blame her if she didn't. He knew it was chosen-by-an-eighteen-year-old lame.

"Rebekah Esther Sticks," Rebekah said without hesitation.

"Are you sure?" he asked.

"Of course. Unless you think I should lose my horrible middle name while I have the chance?"

"I was referring to the last name."

"I definitely want that one," she said, beaming up at him.

He didn't understand why her taking his chosen last name filled him with pride. "You're the boss, Mrs. Sticks."

"Where do we go next? Is a judge performing our ceremony?" Rebekah asked.

"Nope, not a judge," he said.

"A magistrate?"

"Nope."

"Justice of the peace?"

"Nope."

Rebekah's brow crinkled. "Then who?"

"You'll see."

"You are certainly being mysterious today," she said.

"I'm always mysterious."

She laughed. "You're never mysterious. Your openness is one of the things I love most about you." She slid a hand up his neck, and there was no way he could resist that open invitation to indulge in a lengthy kiss.

When he drew away, he cupped her cheek. "Sometimes surprises can be good things."

"I can't wait to see what you have in store for me," she said. "I'm sure it will be *memorable*."

She said memorable as if he'd hired a circus clown to spell out their vows in balloon letters and marry them on a trampoline. He grinned. She really was going to be surprised when she saw what a hopelessly traditional sap she'd agreed to marry.

Marriage license in hand, he escorted her out of the courthouse and back to the car.

"Um, where are we going?" she asked.

He grinned at her, working hard at maintaining the mystery when all he wanted to do was tell her every little detail of his plan.

"You'll see," he said.

While they'd been inside, Jace had done his part and tied a collection of empty cans to the bumper of their car. He'd also attached a sign to the trunk that read, *Almost Married*.

Rebekah giggled when she saw it and gave Jace another hug. This time he actually hugged her back.

"I know today is all about making the bride happy," Jace said quietly, "but take good care of that crazy man of yours. He's sort of important to me."

Eric rolled his eyes and slapped Jace in the back of the head, as if hearing Jace spout sentimental drivel didn't make him one happy bastard.

"Did you bring a blindfold like I asked?" Eric asked.

Jace pulled one out of his back pocket. "I always carry a spare."

Eric chuckled and took the black leather from Jace's hand. "Of course you do."

"Why do you need a blindfold?" Rebekah asked.

"I don't," he said, and slipped it over her head. "You do."

"Eric?"

He covered her anxious eyes with the blindfold and was

shocked by the surge of lust that flooded his groin at seeing her blindfolded in leather while wearing her very proper wedding gown.

"Damn, baby. We're going to have to use that thing again later tonight."

"Just don't get your love goo all over it," Jace said. "It's one of my favorites."

"No promises," Eric said as he took Rebekah's hand to lead her to the car. "Goo sometimes winds up in the most unusual places."

"Such as lucky hats?" Jace chuckled.

"Exactly."

Rebekah's fingers trembled against his palm, but she put her trust in him and allowed him to direct her into the passenger seat. He wasn't used to people depending on him or trusting him explicitly. It was a huge responsibility that he was ready to take on.

When his woman was safely tucked inside the Corvette once more, Eric got in, started the car, and headed in the direction of his surprise venue. The aluminum cans clanked against the pavement behind them and several nearby drivers honked their horns in congratulations. All of which made him very happy. On this particularly loud and obnoxious drive, he didn't have the urge to flip off *any* of the honkers.

As he drove around several blocks looking for the place they would say *I do*, Eric hoped that Rebekah wouldn't be mad that he hadn't consulted her on the location he'd chosen. What if she hated this idea? What if it made her change her mind about loving him? Or worse, made her realize she'd never loved him, not even for a second?

He glanced at her sitting so trustingly beside him and decided her coming to her senses would be the worst thing that had ever happened to him. And Eric had lived through some pretty fucked up shit in his youth.

Chapter 4

REBEKAH HAD NO IDEA where Eric was taking her, but she'd learned in the months that they'd been together that he was far more thoughtful than he looked and far more romantic than he acted. When he surprised a girl, it was a very good thing. She stroked the warm metal of her engagement ring, remembering the last time he'd surprised her. There was no way he could top that. Or could he?

"Are you going to give me a hint about where we're going?" she asked, shifting her blindfold to a more comfortable position, but not removing it. She was determined to be a good sport about his plans, even if they did turn into a fiasco. So far he was doing well, but she never knew what to expect out of Eric. Usually that was a good thing. But sometimes…

"Nope. No hints."

She could hear the smile in his tone even over the road noise and the clunking of the cans trailing the car.

"Can I try to guess?" she asked.

"You can try, but I'm not going to tell you if you guess correctly."

The car bumped over a curve, jostling Rebekah into clinging to the dashboard. She had a hard time with Eric's driving when she could see where they were going; it was a true test of her trust to ride in his passenger seat wearing a blindfold.

"Are we going to the tattoo parlor?" she asked. They did plan to have their vows permanently etched on their skin. They'd discussed it several times. She'd already written her vows and had them memorized. She wasn't sure if Eric had given his much thought yet.

He chuckled. "You're way off, sweetheart."

"But you said you wanted to have your vows tattooed into your sleeve, and I definitely want mine made into a beautiful work of art. Did you change your mind?" She stroked her bare upper arm, imagining a colorful and intricate design with flowers and butterflies and musical notes and words that expressed her love for Eric.

"No, I still want to do that with you—for sure, can't wait—but we can have the work done when we have more time. A big piece like that will take hours, and everyone is waiting for us now."

"Where?" she asked.

"At your—" He broke off with a laugh. "You almost got me to say it."

"At my…" she said, pondering places that belonged to her and coming up lacking. "At my… At my *what*?"

Not her parents' house surely.

He didn't answer and met the rest of her questions and guesses with silence. Eventually the car pulled to a stop and she could hear voices speaking in a crowd, but they were too far away to make out any threads of conversation or identify who the voices belonged to. The blindfold suddenly dropped from her eyes to cover her nose as Eric tugged it down. She blinked in the glaringly bright light of the early evening sun and willed her eyes to adjust. Was that a circus tent? she thought as her aching eyes glimpsed something huge and white with two vertical stripes in some bright color. She squeezed her eyes shut again.

"Are we getting married on a trapeze?" she asked.

Eric laughed. "No, are you blind? We're at your father's church."

Her jaw dropped. She lifted a trembling hand to her lips, her eyes swimming with tears. She opened her properly adjusted eyes and there it was—just like Eric had said. Rebekah had so many happy memories of the little chapel with its tall stained-glass windows and white façade. Even though she'd been on the road and unable to attend church for months, she still recalled the worn but gleaming pews. The tall pulpit. The joyous choir. And her warm and welcoming father spreading the word of love to any who would listen. She didn't have to go inside to feel her connection to this place. It was ingrained deep in her heart.

"I probably should have asked, but I thought you might like your father to marry us. Since he's in the business."

"Did my mother put you up to this?" she asked, knowing the woman could be a bit overbearing and that Eric was not a religious person. She couldn't imagine him wanting to get married in a church, and she loved him enough to be okay with that. God would understand. He knew love, and he would never stand in its way. He didn't care about gender or race or age or anything but the spread of his love. Rebekah had always believed that. Her father had been preaching it her entire life.

"*Okay*," Eric said with a heavy sigh, "this was obviously a poor decision on my part. I'll just turn this car around and make a speedy getaway."

She covered his hand with hers before he could put the gears in reverse. "I would *love* my father to marry us in the church he adores, but I don't want you to feel forced into doing something you aren't comfortable with just because my mother happens to think she's queen of the fucking universe." She rolled her eyes and shook her head. The woman had always been a bit too righteous. Even for a minister's wife.

Eric grinned. "She never suggested it. Like the dress, it was my idea. I called your parents' house and when your father answered, I asked him if he'd be willing to marry us instead of giving you away. I think he was crying by the time I hung up, so if I feel any pressure at all, it's because I don't have it in me to break that man's heart. But if you don't want to get married here, I'll drive away now and let *you* tell your daddy later."

She grabbed both of Eric's hands and clutched them to her chest over her pounding heart. "But I *do* want to get married here. I do. I do."

"Hey, save all that *I do* stuff for the ceremony," he teased.

She flung herself into his arms and kissed him, the gearshift digging into her thigh—not that she cared just then.

After a moment, she pulled away and examined his face. God, she loved him. How did he know what things were important to her? She'd never told him how much her daddy's church meant to her. When they were off tour, she attended service on Sundays when she could, but Eric had never wanted to accompany her. He said church made him feel uncomfortable. So she'd gone by herself.

Eric caught a stray tear from her cheek with the pad of his thumb. "These better be happy tears, damn it," he said.

"The happiest," she assured him.

Eric captured her face between his hands and pressed his forehead to hers. "So you said I do and we kissed and everything, so does that mean we're married and can start our wedding night? Because I really want to do things to you right now. Things I shouldn't be thinking about in a church parking lot."

Before she could answer, there was a loud thud on the hood of the car. Eric jumped up and shot out of his seat to lean over the windshield and grab someone by the shirt.

"You deliver a guy's lucky tuxedo…" Trey said, both hands raised in surrender.

"Don't hit my car," Eric said through gritted teeth. He shoved Trey in the chest as he released him.

"I've been standing here trying to get your attention for several minutes," Trey said. "But I see why you were distracted. Hellooooo, Rebekah Blake."

"Sticks," Eric corrected.

"Not yet," Trey said with a wink directed at Rebekah. "She's still on the market as far as I'm concerned."

Rebekah's face flushed with heat. She wasn't sure what it was about Trey Mills that made him such a walking aphrodisiac. She wouldn't trade her Eric for a hundred Treys, but she wasn't dead. The man was sexy in a flustering sort of way. She'd always thought so. Maybe it was strange that she could still find him attractive after knowing that he'd stolen her ex-fiancé Isaac's heart and his cherry, but damn if she could hold that against the guy.

"You already missed your chance at a threesome with Trey," Eric whispered in her ear. "You better get over him fast."

She slapped him in the shoulder. "If I'd really wanted to have a threesome with Trey, I would have," she said, just as her mother arrived at her side of the car. Thankfully her mom hadn't heard what she'd said. Her mother freaked out over sections of Rebekah's hair being colored blue or purple—as it currently was. Rebekah couldn't imagine how many 360s the woman's head would do if she'd known some of the things Rebekah had done on the Sinners' tour bus outside the sanctity of marriage. Or even outside the propriety of a legitimate relationship.

"So glad it fits you, baby girl," her mom said, smiling brightly at her wedding dress. "See, I wasn't always so big boned."

"You still look fantastic, Mom."

"I would totally do you, Mrs. B," Trey said with an ornery grin.

Rebekah was pretty sure that if any other man had said that to her mother—perhaps even her own husband—he would end up with a few less teeth, but Trey slipped a red sucker into his sensual mouth, clicking his tongue jewelry against it, and to Rebekah's utter astonishment, her mother blushed and flicked her gaze to the ground.

"Ah, well. Maybe twenty years ago," she said, obviously flustered.

"I like mature women," he said. "And younger women. And

women my own age."

"You like any woman with a pulse," Eric said.

Rebekah was glad Trey didn't mention that he liked men of all ages as well. She wasn't sure how her mother would handle knowing about Trey's lack of preference or that Isaac—the man her mother had been convinced was perfect for Rebekah—had been just as charmed by Trey Mills as every woman in the immediate vicinity.

"Will you stop fawning over Trey?" Eric complained.

"I'm not fawning over Trey," Rebekah said. "I'm too in love with you to even notice him."

"So you say."

"Trey never would have asked my mother to borrow her wedding dress."

"I'm a lot of things," Trey said, "but a cross-dresser isn't one of them."

Rebekah would flip him off for that later.

"He never would have thought to ask my daddy to perform the wedding ceremony."

"Yeah, because I'm never getting married."

"Trey, I'm trying to have a private conversation with my perfect groom. Please see your way out of it."

"Rebekah Esther Blake, that was very rude," her mother said.

Rebekah sighed. "Maybe we should just go back to the courthouse and avoid our respective families."

"It's closed by now," Eric said.

"Then let's get hitched so we can hurry home to celebrate in private."

"I would very much like to celebrate your privates." Eric sprang out of the car without opening the door and reached inside to scoop Rebekah into his arms. She laughed as he struggled to lift her out of the car through the open convertible top.

"This seemed like a good idea," he said, groaning in protest as he hefted her up and against his chest. "I think I broke my back."

"Then let me walk," she insisted.

"I don't want you to get away," he said and squeezed her against his chest.

"I'm not going anywhere without you at my side."

"Promise?"

"Pinkie swear." She extended her little finger, and he set her on her feet so he could save his back and loop her little finger with his to give it a congenial shake.

Their fingers were broken apart as Rebekah was instantly surrounded by chattering women. Her mother was determined to remove thirty years' worth of wrinkles from her borrowed wedding gown by tugging and smoothing the skirt with her palms. Everyone else had just discovered the bride had arrived and required a piece of her attention.

Sed's gorgeous fiancée looped an arm through Rebekah's and started towing her toward the church.

"We did the best we could with the decorations previous brides left behind," Jessica said. "It's a bit of a hodgepodge of styles, but it doesn't look bad considering Eric demanded we fix it up less than two hours ago. Come see if there's anything you want changed."

Rebekah glanced helplessly over her shoulder at Eric. She just pinkie swore that she'd never leave his side and there were already several feet and a couple of extraneous bodies between them. He grinned at her over the crowd and waved her toward the church as the members of his band descended upon him with a bevy of fist bumps, bro hugs, and huge smiles.

"I'll meet you at the altar," he yelled.

"I'll be there," she hollered back.

Chapter 5

ERIC WATCHED Myrna, Jessica, and Mrs. B usher Rebekah toward the church entrance until they were out of sight. Everyone around him was talking at once, and he was too distracted to make sense of any of it.

A crumpled mass of black fabric was shoved into his arms. "You better wear this damned thing," Trey said. "Besides a lucky tuxedo, you have some really weird shit in your closet, dude. I believe I'm scarred for life."

Eric snorted. "Yeah, right. I don't even want to know what's in your closet."

Eric and Rebekah did have a lot of kinky implements in their stash of carnal delights, but there was no way their sexy costumes and sex toys rivaled Trey Mills's stockpile of apparatuses. Now, if Trey had been going through Jace's closet, Eric might have understood the affront to Trey's feigned propriety.

"I guess I'm supposed to act like a girl today," Aggie said, staring after where the rest of the women had vanished, anything but longing in her blue-eyed gaze. "You know I'd rather stay out here with you guys, right?"

"Is that because women are less likely to be intimidated by you?" Eric asked. He'd never known a woman to wear black leather pants and an off-the shoulder red sweater to a wedding. Until now.

"Aggie has a couple of female slaves," Jace said, slipping an arm around Aggie's waist and kissing her. "I guarantee they are plenty intimidated."

Eric's brows rose in interest. "I didn't know you swung that way, Mistress V."

Aggie grinned deviously. "There's a lot you don't know about the way I swing, Sticks. There's my overhand swing," she said, demonstrating. "My underhand swing, and my all-time favorite, the backhand swing."

Jace chuckled. "She doesn't do anything but spank them. And I'd much rather watch her spank a submissive woman than whip a man."

"Aggie lets you watch?" Eric said, his jaw attempting to get acquainted with the ground. "Seriously? Damn... How do I get in on that?"

"It's more like *make* him watch. For disobeying," Aggie said.

She whispered something in Jace's ear that made him blush to the dark roots of his bleached-blond spikes. That thick, brown beard stubble of his didn't hide his embarrassment one bit. Aggie gave Jace's ass one hard smack and a punishing squeeze before turning away and striding off after the rest of the women.

"Okay, what did she say to you to make you blush like that?" Eric asked.

"If I tell you, she'll punish me," Jace said with a grin.

"And that would be a negative for you why?" Trey said around the sucker in his mouth. "We know you get off on that shit. And if she punishes you by making you watch her spank chicks, sign me up for some of that." His words were further garbled by the barbell in his tongue.

Eric wondered what he'd interrupted when he'd called Trey earlier. Eric knew the guy only wore the barbell for special occasions. And Eric was pretty sure that weddings didn't count as special occasions to Trey.

Jace stared at his boots as he said, "Mistress V has a group of six coeds coming over tonight. They think they want to try out some BDSM after their book club read some kinky novel."

"Ooo," Trey said. "Maybe I should lend you a hand. Six women at once. Not sure if even Sed's gone to *that* extreme."

"Maybe a few times," Sed said with a deep laugh.

"So what did you do to deserve this hellish punishment, Tripod?" Eric asked with a snort.

"Not a thing. She needs my assistance is all. Aggie thinks she can turn at least half of them into dommes when they use me as their plaything for the night. And watching a bunch of young women spank each other after I've been worked over for a couple of hours is bound to make my alone time with Aggie extra hot."

"I totally understand the appeal of hitting you, Tripod. I just don't get why Aggie lets other people abuse her sub."

"I'm not her sub, Eric," Jace said, pinning him with an annoyed stare. "I just get off on the pain."

Eric lifted both hands in surrender. "My mistake." He knew how hard Jace could hit when he was ticked off. And the only stars Eric wanted to see for the rest of the day were the ones in

Rebekah's eyes when she looked at him.

"Okay, Eric," Sed said, scratching his neck and finding the cloudless sky a bit too interesting. "Shouldn't you be getting ready or something? I thought you were getting married today."

He was. Every other concern fled his mind in an instant. He shook out his tuxedo to find Trey had brought the pants and jacket, but no shirt or vest or tie or shoes.

"Trey?" Eric questioned. "Where's the rest of it?"

"The rest of it?"

"The shirt and shoes and stuff."

"You said to bring your lucky tuxedo. You didn't say anything about a shirt or shoes."

"You don't expect me to wear this with a T-shirt and my Cons, do you?"

After a moment of reflection, all four members of his band nodded in unison.

"Yep," said Brian. "I'd totally expect that."

"Reb won't mind. She gets you," Jace said. "Like the way Aggie gets me."

"And Myrna gets me," Brian added.

"And Jess gets me," Sed said.

"Psh, no one gets you," Eric said. "Jess just puts up with you."

That earned him a teeth-jarring smack in the back of the head, which he probably deserved.

Eric slipped the tuxedo jacket on over his white T-shirt. He stared down at his belly, but couldn't really tell how ridiculous the well-cut jacket looked without a proper shirt and tie.

"She won't care," Jace assured him and patted him on the back.

"I'm sure her mother will."

"And that bothers you why?" Trey asked.

Eric shrugged. Maybe because his only memory of his real mother was her saying goodbye when she'd left him with child protective services. To tell the truth, he didn't really remember *her* at all. Not what she looked like. Not the sound of her voice. He didn't remember any of it. He just remembered what it felt like to wait for her. And wait. And wait. Only to finally realize that she wasn't coming back because he wasn't worth her time. The stupid bitch wasn't worth his time either.

Eric and Mrs. B hadn't started off on the best of terms, but he legitimately hoped that one day she'd let him call her Mom. Not that he would say any of that to the guys. Well, maybe Jace. Jace could understand where he was coming from, but the other guys wouldn't really get it. Trey's mother was eccentric but unabashedly loving, Sed had the poster mom for woman of the year, and Brian's mother was a hottie who could not be ignored. Claire Sinclair wasn't very affectionate, Eric supposed, but what the woman lacked in nurturing, she more than made up for with a fine body and supermodel face. Brian obviously wouldn't care that his mom looked hot in a bikini, but all of their mothers were better than Eric's. Even Jace's mother wasn't all bad. At least she'd taught him to play the piano before she'd died. It was something. Eric had nothing to cling to. Not even memories or photographs.

Eric wasn't sure why he was even thinking about his junkie whore of a mother today. He'd abandoned her memory the way she'd abandoned him long ago and was better for it. He hadn't really thought about her for over a decade. Not since he'd changed his last name from Anderson to Sticks. The name he would give his new wife. The one he'd chosen for himself. Now that he was no longer an eighteen-year-old punk with a chip on his shoulder, he realized Sticks was a pretty silly name for a drummer. Regardless, he was proud that Rebekah had chosen Sticks to be her name as well.

"Are you still with us, Sticks?" Brian asked.

"Yeah," he said, surprised by how raw his voice sounded around the tightness in his throat.

It rattled him that even after all this time his mother could still get to him. She'd probably died long ago, and he was sure the world was a better place without her. He refused to give her another thought today. At least he'd *try* not to think of her. Or wonder if she'd be happy for him.

"Let's get you married off then," Brian said. He placed a hand between Eric's shoulder blades and gave him a shove toward the church. It was the only prodding Eric needed. "You *were* slated to get married next."

"I *was*? Since when?" Eric said.

"You caught Myrna's garter, remember?"

Eric chuckled. He'd completely forgotten about that. "I still have it," he said. "I saved it for luck. It's in the glovebox of the Corvette. I was going to hang it from the rearview mirror when I got it fixed, but I forgot."

"Maybe Rebekah should wear it today," Brian suggested. "It could become a Sinners tradition."

"One lucky garter coming up," Jace said and trotted back toward Eric's car.

Inside the church, Eric was shown to a small room behind the altar so he could change from his jeans into his tuxedo pants. He kind of liked that he was stuck wearing his Converse. He still wasn't sure about wearing Hanes under Armani, but he had little choice. Unless he went bare-chested under his tux. He scratched that idea as soon as it occurred to him.

He hadn't seen any sign of Rebekah as he'd walked through the welcoming church, but he had noticed that the bouquets of artificial flowers on the ends of the pews were bright pink and didn't match the golden yellow roses on the big candelabras near the altar. Considering that the lady Sinners had had less than two hours to pull it together, they'd done an amazing job of giving Rebekah a real wedding. He figured Jess owed him one after he'd gone to jail for her proposal to Sed, but he'd have to think of something nice to repay Myrna and Aggie for helping out.

The door opened, and Rebekah's father poked his head into the room. He was dressed in full ceremonial garb, which made Eric even more nervous, but the pudgy balding man smiled a welcome and walked in, closing the door behind him. He sat beside Eric on the bench and clasped his hands between his knees.

"I figured I'd have more time to prepare my talk," Father Blake said.

Eric glanced at him, his stomach churning with nerves. He wanted this man's respect, but wasn't sure how to earn it.

"You don't have to say anything," Eric said.

"But I do. That's my little girl you're marrying."

Eric steeled himself for the barrage of criticism that was sure to follow.

"For most fathers, letting go of a daughter so she can offer her love to a man is probably one of the hardest things he'll ever do, but after watching my little girl get so sick and lose all her hair and almost die, *this* is easy."

"If she gets sick again, I'll be there for her," Eric promised.

Father Blake smiled warmly. "I know that, son."

Son… All the air evacuated the little overwarm room.

Father Blake patted Eric's back and gave his shoulder a squeeze. "A lot of people will be there for her if she gets sick again. What I ask of you is that you're there for her when the sink gets clogged or she burns the eggs or her car won't start."

Eric chuckled. "She'd be better at getting the car started than I would, but I've got the eggs covered."

"That's not what I mean. You don't need to be there to fix everything for her. Just be there for her. And love her. Even when she doesn't seem to need a reminder of how you feel, she does. Don't forget to tell her. Show her. Not only when her world comes crashing down, but when it really matters most. Every day."

"That will be absolutely no problem at all," Eric said without pausing between words.

"Good. If you forget, I'll be sure to remind you none too gently."

"I won't forget. Your daughter—*Rebekah*—she's my everything. My *everything*."

Smiling, Father Blake searched Eric's eyes and then after a long moment, he cleared his throat. "Uh, we don't need to have a sex talk, do we?"

Eric's face went numb as the blood drained from his head. "Uh, no, sir." He shook his head emphatically.

"Good. Because that would be awkward." Father Blake laughed.

Awkward? Uh, yeah. Just a little.

"I also wanted to ask if you were overly attached to the wedding bands you bought for the ceremony."

"Wedding bands?" Eric shot to his feet. "Crap! We forgot to get wedding bands."

"Good." Father Blake said. He fumbled in a pocket in his robe.

"Good?" Would they have to call off the wedding? Was that what Rebekah's father thought was good about forgetting something so important? Had he changed his mind? Did he not really want to marry them? Rebekah would be crushed. So crushed she'd probably call the whole thing off.

"Sit down, Eric."

Eric sat. Partially because his knees were weak, partially because he was slightly terrified to do anything that would make this man dislike him. Father Blake pulled his hand out of his pocket and opened it to show Eric two silver rings resting on his palm.

"These have been in my family for five generations. It would mean a lot to me if you would use them for the ceremony today."

Eric was so stunned—so *touched*—that he couldn't find any words. His family didn't have heirlooms. Hell, he didn't have a family, so the idea that Rebekah's father would offer something so precious to him completely threw Eric for a loop.

"I…" He couldn't talk through the sudden tightness in his chest.

"If you don't want them, I understand. They are a bit tarnished, even though I tried to clean them up this afternoon. A rich guy like you would probably rather have platinum."

Father Blake pressed his lips together and closed his hand, moving to return the rings to his pocket.

"Don't," Eric whispered. Having something so meaningful snatched away before he could even adjust to the idea was like a knife to his heart. "I want…"

Father Blake didn't say a word. He simply took Eric by the wrist, dropped the two silver bands into his palm, and folded his hand closed over the two bits of aged metal. They sat side by side for a long moment. Eric wanted to thank him for entrusting him with the rings and more importantly, with his beloved daughter, but his emotions were high and he didn't want to embarrass himself in front of his soon-to-be father-in-law by sobbing like a little girl.

"I still say you're too tall for her," Father Blake said, "but I know you have a good heart and that's what really counts, isn't it? The love between you."

Eric gave a curt nod. "I'll treasure these," he said opening his hand to stare at the bands nestled there. The smaller of the two rings had settled inside the larger, partially filling the gaping space in its center. "And I'll treasure her."

"You know they say women tend to marry men who are a lot like their fathers," Father Blake said.

Eric blinked at him in surprise. A Baptist minister and a degenerate rock drummer couldn't possibly have anything in common. But the man's eyes were a bit misty, and Eric recognized that same sentimental quality in himself. At least when it came to Rebekah. So at minimum they shared some syrupy feelings about one tiny yet strong purple-haired woman.

Father Blake laughed. "I just don't see it."

"Well, we both love her. That's enough to have in common, isn't it?"

The older man nodded and patted Eric on the thigh. "Are you ready to get married?"

Eric smiled, his stomach suddenly a jumble of nerves and excitement. He closed his hand over the rings and squeezed. "I am now. Thanks for saving my ass, Father Blake."

"Watch your language in the house of the Lord, son," he said, rising to his feet.

"Sorry," Eric said at once.

"And for the love of God, stop calling me Father Blake. I'm not a priest."

Eric's heart sank. Great. He'd insulted the man. Was it possible for him to get absolutely everything wrong with Rebekah's parents? Because he was doing a spectacular job at fucking things up. He opened his mouth to apologize again, but Whatever-honorific-the-man-preferred Blake continued.

"Members of my congregation call me Brother Bill," he said and blessed Eric with a warm and welcoming smile. "But you; you should call me Dad."

Again Eric couldn't find the ability to speak, so he just smiled and nodded. Father Bla— Brother Bil— *Dad* left the room and closed the door gently behind him, leaving Eric alone to collect himself. He prayed he wasn't one of those douchebags who fainted at his own wedding. He was feeling a tad light-headed and incredibly overwhelmed. He opened his hand and stared down at the two silver bands, tracing them with one finger. He knew these rings would mean as much to Rebekah as they meant to him. He only wished he could give her half as much as she was giving him by offering the one gift he'd never dreamed of having—a real family. What did he have to offer her in return? Just one banged-up heart and any material possession her heart desired. He hoped they would be enough.

There was a knock at the door, and it opened before he could answer it. Sed popped his head around the gleaming mahogany structure.

"Are you decent?" Sed asked.

Eric grinned, suddenly feeling calmer for no reason other than Sed always had a strange settling effect on him. "I'm never decent. You know that. Is it time?"

"Not quite. Jessica decided Rebekah needed a veil and took off in my car to find one."

"She'd better hurry. I'm not sure my nerves can take much more of a wait."

Sed closed the door and took a seat on the bench beside Eric. "You're not thinking about backing out, are you?"

"Not at all. I just want to get this over with and get on with our lives."

Sed chuckled. "I can relate to that. Jessica's mother is driving me insane with reception preparations. Seems your mother-in-law is a ballbuster too. We can commiserate for all eternity."

Eric laughed. "I think Mrs. B has settled down a bit now that she's figured out Rebekah isn't going to marry Isaac, no matter how much she wanted her to."

Sed squeezed his eyes shut and shook his head. "The woman seems pretty taken with Trey, considering he's the one who ruined Isaac for all women."

"She's recovering nicely since her mental breakdown at her daughter's fake engagement party."

Sed nodded empathetically. "I don't envy you, but I still say my future mother-in-law is ten times worse."

"What about Jace's? Have you met Aggie's mom?"

"Can't say that I have."

"Be sure to invite her to your wedding. She's a party waiting to happen."

Sed chuckled. "I just might. Jessica's mom is so worried that some low-class loser will show up at the reception, she's rewritten the guest list three times."

Eric lifted a brow at him. "Has she seen your friends? We're *all* low-class losers."

"Who happen to have a lot of money, so that's okay by her. She keeps adding A-list actors I've never met and taking Sinners' road crew off the guest list. Without our road crew, we're nothing. Those guys work their asses off for us. What's weird is that Jess's mom is not a part of high society. She just wants to be. Her ridiculous posturing drives Jessica crazy. Every time Jess talks with her mother, she gets pissed."

Eric grinned at him, knowing how much Jessica's temper pushed all of Sed's buttons—good buttons, bad buttons, and everything in between. It especially wreaked havoc on his lust button. "Which I'm sure makes her completely irresistible to you."

Sed laughed. "I'm just glad her anger isn't directed toward me for a change."

"Do you want a little advice?"

"From you?" Sed laughed, and then his face hardened. "Yeah, I guess I do."

"Put your foot down with Jessica's mother. It's your wedding and your reception; you should celebrate it with the people important to you."

"I just want Jessica to be happy," Sed said. "I don't even need a wedding. It's all for her."

"Is she happy with her mother running the show?"

Sed made a sound almost like a growl. "Not at all."

"So let her mom pick out the table decorations and the champagne, but make it clear that the guest list is yours. Don't compromise. Put her in her fucking place." It occurred to Eric how odd it was that he was offering Sed advice. Sed had never needed nor wanted his advice in the past. This wedding shit must really be eating the guy up if he was listening to anything Eric had to say.

"I still think you and Brian have the right idea," Sed said. "Quick and painless."

"Not quick enough. You realize I'd probably be married by now if your woman hadn't decided Rebekah needed a veil."

Sed pounded him on the back enthusiastically. "A thirty-minute wait isn't so bad. Try putting up with this bullshit for eight months."

"No thank you."

"So what was her dad doing in here? Threatening your life? At least I have only one insane in-law to deal with."

Eric shook his head, and his hand tightened over the rings still clutched in his fist. "He was welcoming me to his family. He's a great man."

"Well, Dave has informed everyone that he will be attempting to put you out of your misery on a regular basis, so be prepared."

Eric chuckled. "He's all talk. If his little sister is happy, he's mush, and I guarantee his little sister will be happy. I'll make sure of it."

Another knock sounded on the door. "Yeah!" Sed called.

The door opened, and Trey peeked through the opening. "Did you finish having the sex talk with him yet?"

"Yep," Sed said and climbed to his feet. "He now knows which hole to stick it in."

"All of them?" Trey said.

"Yep, but we went over the proper sequence," Sed said, giving Eric a hand up and another encouraging pound on the shoulder.

"Take the ass first, right?" Eric said, glad they were joking around. It helped with his gargantuan case of unexpected nerves. "And then it goes right in the mouth."

"Repeat after me," Trey said. "M-P-A. Mouth. Pussy. Ass."

"P-A-M?" Eric asked.

"Not unless she likes the taste," Trey said.

"M-P-A," Eric said, pointing to imaginary body parts in the air. "Mouth. Pussy. Ass. Got it."

"I prefer M-V-P," Sed said. "I'm not much for A."

"What's M-V-P?" Trey asked.

"Mouth Vagina Pussy."

"Aren't V and P the same thing?" Eric said, scratching his head as if confused.

"Yeah, but I always take two goes at it," Sed boasted. "First I make sweet love to the vagina. And then I fuck that pussy raw."

Someone cleared his throat in the doorway.

"Hey, Mr. Blake," Trey said, as if they'd been discussing the World Series MVP and not the one Sed frequented. "Is it time to start the ceremony?"

Eric could count on one hand the number of times he'd seen Sedric Lionheart blush. It seemed he would finally get to use the fingers of both hands to record the activation of Sed's blush-o-meter. He was so red Eric could have toasted a grilled cheese on the man's face.

"Yes, it's time to start," Father Bl—*Dad* said before he shut the door again.

"Really smooth, Sed," Eric said.

"Do you think he heard me?" Sed whispered.

"The entire church heard you," Trey said.

"Oh God. I'm going to Hell for sure now."

"Was there any doubt before?" Trey asked.

Sed chuckled. "Well, at least I'll be in good company." He wrapped an arm around Eric's shoulders and escorted him out the door.

Eric scanned the pews.

Myrna, Aggie, and Jessica were seated in the front pew on his side. On Rebekah's side sat Isaac, who stole a glance at Trey, stiffened as if someone had slapped him in the face, and then diverted his gaze to the front of the church where Mr. and Mrs. B were already standing at the altar. Jace was also up front waiting for Eric. He gave Eric an encouraging wink as Sed and Trey abandoned him to sit in the front pew with the women. Brian was nowhere to be seen. And neither was Dave, which Eric thought odd. His perplexity vanished—as did the rest of the world—when the massive double doors at the back of the church opened and a wheelchair whirred into the aisle. The first note of the wedding march wailed from an electric guitar that could only be under the skilled fingers of Master Sinclair. But even the sounds faded under the thudding pulse in Eric's ears as he glimpsed his bride standing beside her brother's wheelchair. Her lovely face was obscured by a gauzy white veil, but he could feel her gaze on his and he couldn't look away or do anything as ordinary as breathe.

Don't faint, he thought as she took a step in his direction. Do not faint.

Chapter 6

REBEKAH'S HEART FLUTTERED in her chest like the wings of a butterfly as she stared down the aisle at Eric. She grinned when she noticed he was wearing his Converse and a T-shirt under an expensive tuxedo. Perfect attire for him. Perfect man for her.

Dave's wheelchair sputtered and zoomed, sputtered and zoomed as he tried to keep pace with Brian Sinclair's electrifying rendition of the wedding march. Rebekah tore her gaze from her waiting groom to look down at her brother.

"Having problems?" she whispered.

"I hate this thing," he grumbled before hooking an arm around her waist and tumbling her onto his lap. She patted the wide skirt of her dress down, laughing as Dave zoomed up the aisle at a more constant speed. They must have made quite a sight because every person in the room was laughing by the time they arrived at the front of the church with her train dragging the floor beside his chair. They waited for Brian to finish his Wedding March guitar solo and then her dad said, "Who gives this woman to this man?"

"That would be me," Dave said.

Dave tipped her off of his lap, and she swept her dress out of the way of his chair. He surprised her by clutching her forearm and hauling himself to his feet. He took her hand, placed it on his arm, and labored forward three steps. He handed her off to Eric. "Take her, she's a pain in the butt, and all yours," he said before lifting her veil. "I love you, baby sis," he said.

"I love you too."

He kissed her cheek and forced his uncooperative legs to take several more steps before collapsing in the pew next to Isaac, leaving his wheelchair abandoned in the aisle.

Rebekah smiled when Isaac's eyes met hers. She was so glad he was there. They were no longer lovers, but he was still her dearest friend. She hoped one day he and Eric could get along. They were a lot more alike than they were different. Neither of them seemed to recognize that, but she did.

She lifted her head, and her breath caught. The smile on Eric's face could have cleared the cloudiest of days. It made her glow beneath its radiance.

She stared into his loving blue eyes as her father outlined the expectations of marriage and as they repeated their standard vows. She was scarcely aware of what she was saying, but she felt every word deep in her heart.

"Do you have the rings?" her father said.

Rebekah's heart skipped a beat. They'd forgotten to get rings!

Eric turned to Jace, who handed him two slightly tarnished silver bands. Her lip quivered when she recognized them, and she tore her gaze from Eric's palm to her father's misty-eyed stare.

"Daddy?" she whispered.

He smiled and nodded reassuringly.

She couldn't believe he was letting them wear the rings that had been passed down his side of the family for five generations. She knew how much those rings meant to him. He wouldn't have given them to Eric unless he truly accepted him as part of the family. *Oh, thank you, Daddy. Thank you.*

"Wear them well," her father said, and then he blessed the rings and their wearers with words she'd heard dozens of times. Yet this time the lifelong blessing, the forever blessing, was for her and Eric. Before she could get too choked up, her dad said, "Do you have anything you'd like to say to Eric as you take him as your husband?"

Rebekah nodded, her vision blurry through the tears in her eyes. She took the larger of the two rings from her father's palm and slipped the ring onto Eric's left ring finger. Her heart gave a little skip of joy to find it fit his long, slender finger perfectly, as if he were destined to be a part of the family. She stared up into Eric's eyes as she said the words she'd prepared. The ones she would later have tattooed on her skin.

"Eric, I promise to live beside you like there is no tomorrow, love you like you're the only perfect man on Earth, and laugh with you like no one is watching. You bring so much joy into my life, give so much love, awaken my passion, stir my soul, rock my body."

She heard her mother click her tongue with disapproval, but she didn't care. These were her words to Eric, and they had nothing to do with her mother or anyone else.

"You're my heart and soul, Eric. I can only hope that I will make you half as happy as you make me. I want to spend my whole life trying. I pledge my heart, my soul, my life to you, my love. My husband."

Eric gnawed on his lower lip, looking at her like he'd just won the lottery.

"Do you have anything you'd like to say to Rebekah as you take her as your wife?" her father asked.

Eric jumped, as if he hadn't realized they weren't alone. Rebekah completely understood that feeling.

He swallowed hard, took the ring from her father's hand and with trembling fingers, slid it on her left ring finger. He blew out his cheeks, squeezed his eyelids together, and then opened his eyes to gaze into hers. His trembling lessened as he stood there for a long moment just searching her gaze and then he spoke.

"Forever was just a word until I met you. Now it's a promise. A dream. My cherished reality. I love you forever, Rebekah. My love. My wife." He lifted her hands to his lips and kissed her wedding band, staring deep into her eyes. "Forever."

"Forever," she repeated, unable to take her eyes off his.

Her mother sniffed loudly behind her. There were several other sniffles from the front pew.

"Do you all have allergies or what?" Eric asked. His voice sounded extra loud in the quiet church.

Rebekah's laugh was accompanied by several others.

Eric glanced at her dad. "Well?" he said, eyes wide with expectation.

"By the power vested in me, I now pronounce you husband and wife. You may kiss your bride."

"Fucking finally," Eric said and drew Rebekah against his body.

To a background of laughter, catcalls, her mother's open weeping, and one incredibly sensual guitar solo, Rebekah Sticks kissed her husband for the first time. The press of Eric's lips against hers was even more tender, emotional, and passionate than she'd anticipated. Her throat and eyes ached with unshed tears. Happy tears. The happiest.

Eric's strong arms tightened around her, drawing her closer, enveloping her in love and tenderness and heat. She couldn't ignore the heat between them.

"Get a room!" Trey yelled.

She felt Eric smile against her lips, and he drew back to gaze down into her eyes.

"Best advice I've gotten all day," he said.

She had to agree.

Her dad cleared his throat and spoke in a loud, clear voice. "This day Rebekah and Eric entered as two and now leave as one soul united," he said. "May I present Mr. and Mrs. Eric Sticks. May their love shine more brightly with each passing moment."

She beamed at her daddy, who was blinking far more than necessary. Her mother squeezed her arm, and Rebekah turned to find her smiling through her tears. Eric shook her dad's hand and then helped her down from the single step at the front of the church so they could exit.

They didn't get far.

Chapter 7

ERIC JERKED UNEXPECTEDLY as he was hugged vigorously from behind. He turned his head to find Jace—all denim and leather and tough guy and maybe a few tears—with his face buried in Eric's back. Eric grinned and patted the pair of hands clasped tightly together at his waist.

"Now, Tripod," Eric said, "you had your chance with me and settled for Aggie."

He caught the stunned look on Rebekah's face and offered her a wink. The tension immediately drained from her body and she smiled, cocking her head to peek at the man behind him.

"Fuck you," Jace said, his words muffled by Eric's back. He attempted some strange variation of the Heimlich maneuver. "Just… Fuck you."

After a moment, Jace took a deep breath, drew away, and settled for pounding on Eric's back with enough force to fracture bones.

"Yes, you like me," Eric said, chuckling. "I get it. Stop trying to break me. Aggie, control your sub."

"You're such an ass," Jace said.

Well, what did Jace expect? If he didn't turn Jace's uncharacteristic emotional display into a joke, he'd have to put on an uncharacteristic emotional display of his own.

Jace circled Eric's neck with both hands and pretended to choke him. Not one to be left out of a gag, Eric let his head loll loosely and stuck his tongue out as if he were in true distress.

Rebekah's mother tried to step in—presumably to save his life—but Rebekah caught her arm and shook her head. That slight motion made Eric love her all the more. The woman understood him in a way that completely baffled him. He figured most women would be pissed to have her first moment as a newlywed standing beside her husband interrupted by a bunch of immature male-bonding bullshit, but not his Rebekah.

Since it didn't seem like they would ever make it back down the aisle, the spectators rose from the pews to offer their hugs and congratulations.

Eric kept one eye on his bride, who kissed his hand and then released it so she could hug her family—now his family too, he thought with a smile. Aggie stepped up to help Jace get his out-of-control emotions back under his command. She pinched his ass, and he immediately dropped his hands from Eric's throat. Eric grinned to himself. Nope, he obviously wasn't her sub at all.

Sed took the opening to give Eric a customary slap on the back of the head before capturing his arms in a full-nelson so Trey could bless Eric's nose with his sticky cherry sucker.

"Hold still," Trey said, tracking Eric's jerky head motions with his lollipop.

Brian emerged from the choir loft, where he'd been playing his guitar, and wrapped a protective arm around his pregnant wife's shoulders before approaching Eric.

"Words of wisdom from one married man to another," Brian said, turning his head side to side as he tried to track Eric's gaze. After an exasperating moment, he released his wife and hugged Trey from behind, pinning his arms and his sucker to his sides. Trey immediately went still.

"Guys, really?" Brian said. "The man just got married. Show him some respect."

"Yeah," Eric said. "What he said."

Sed released Eric's aching arms.

"You can harass him after I'm through with him," Brian added.

"And I thought you were on my side."

"I am. I'm going to help you out here. So listen carefully."

Eric nodded, having rarely dealt with any of his band members speaking to him with such earnestness.

"You only need to remember three words to keep your wife happy," Brian said, releasing Trey so he could draw Myrna against his side.

"I love you?" Eric said.

"No. Any idiot can try that route. The three words are: she's *always* right. If you remember that, your life will run smoothly."

"But what if she's wrong?"

Brian stuck a finger in Eric's face. "No, dude. Listen to me and remember. She's *always* right."

"She's always right," Eric repeated obediently.

Myrna laughed. "But if you need to spice things up a little, falsely accuse her of being wrong."

Brian patted Eric's chest with the flat of his hand. "Just make sure you admit she's always right after the hot, angry make-up sex."

"Got it," Eric said.

"Brian?" Jessica said, laying a hand on Brian's arm.

Brian turned his head to look at her. "Yeah?"

"Will you please have this little talk with Sed?" she asked.

"Sure. When's your wedding again?"

"Don't wait until we're married. He needs to learn this now!"

Everyone laughed, even the Blakes, who were huddled in a perma-hug around Dave and his wheelchair. Eric noticed the only one still sitting in the pews was Rebekah's friend Isaac. It was probably hard for him to see Rebekah marry someone besides himself and even harder to be completely ignored by Trey, who he was obviously still mooning over. Poor guy. Eric separated from his group of admirers and joined Isaac on the gleaming wood bench. Isaac glanced up, his hazel eyes wide with surprise.

"Why are you sitting over here by yourself?" Eric asked.

"I just wanted to be here for Rebekah. I don't want to intrude on her happiness."

"She'd probably like that though," Eric said. "Personally, I don't know why she likes you so much. You're sort of a douche."

Isaac blinked at him in shock.

Eric grinned. "I'm joking," he said. "I do that sometimes." And sometimes he hid behind jokes so he could speak his mind freely, but Isaac didn't need to know that.

"Oh."

"But even though you're a douche and really hurt her feelings, she's forgiven you. I don't get it. I'd have cut you from my life and buried you in the backyard."

He did sort of get it, actually. He had a friend who had hurt him repeatedly and still he couldn't remove that man from his life. But unlike Isaac, Jon hadn't had the decency to show up for the wedding. At least Isaac cared enough about Rebekah to show the fuck up. Jon didn't even have that going for him.

"Her forgiveness is far better than I deserve," Isaac said.

"So don't you think you should go tell her that you're happy for her, even if it's a lie? I know she'd like to hear that from you."

Eric glanced over at Rebekah and caught her watching them. He smiled at her and her answering smile was a bit hesitant. She probably thought he was being mean to Isaac. And yep, that had been his first instinct. The man had ripped Rebekah's heart out, and Eric didn't take kindly to anyone who hurt her. He also didn't appreciate Isaac's attempts to drive him and Rebekah apart. But in the end, Eric had won the girl and Isaac had lost her. Eric figured that was punishment enough for the pretty guy. He did seem to have a good heart under all his confusion.

"I don't know what to say to her," Isaac said. "This past week has been hell for me."

"You can start by not focusing on yourself," Eric said and rose to his feet. "Maybe ask her how her cancer screening went this morning."

"That was today?" All the blood drained out of Isaac's face. "Is she okay?"

"Does she look okay?" Eric asked.

They both stared at the woman in question, who was showing off her enormous, expensive engagement ring and her cheap, meaningful wedding ring to the ladies surrounding her.

"She looks radiant," Isaac said. "She never looked like that when she was with me."

As if she could feel Eric's gaze on her, Rebekah lifted her head and met his eyes over the small crowd of admirers. She smiled brightly, and Eric's chest swelled with a strong sense of pride. No one made her as happy as he did. Not even Dr. Perfect. Now that was something to crow about. Before he could swoop down on her and carry her out of the church to celebrate, Isaac strode purposefully to her side, took her hand, and pulled her behind the pulpit for a more private word. Eric hardly struggled with his spike of jealousy at all. He trusted Rebekah. It was the impossibly-good-looking physician that he didn't quite trust.

Chapter 8

REBEKAH STARED AT THE MAN who'd been her best friend since childhood and decided she didn't really know him anymore. Or maybe she'd never known him. She'd always thought of him as perfect in every way. Everyone around him had placed him on a pedestal and held him there his entire gifted life. Now that he'd taken a few hits to his ego like everyone else in the world, she decided that she didn't think less of him. No, now that she could see him as imperfect, she liked him even more.

Isaac took both of her hands in his and gazed deeply into her eyes. "Your husband said I shouldn't talk about myself today. He said I should focus on you. So here goes." He took a deep breath. "I'm happy for you, Rebekah. I think you've found your match."

"I don't mind if you talk about yourself. I know you're having a rough time. Have you talked to your father since the party?"

He shook his head.

"He'll come around," she said. "I'm sure you're not the first gay man in history to come out to his father and hundreds of onlookers at his surprise fake engagement bash."

Isaac chuckled, the sound warm and full of heart. "I'd like to meet others who've lived through this. Maybe they could tell me what to do with the rest of my life. My plans to take over his practice when he retires have completely fallen through."

"Well, I can tell you exactly what you should do. Stop feeling sorry for yourself and find a *new* dream," she said. "Do you know how many times my own plans have fallen through? How many times I've had to admit defeat? How many times I had to reinvent myself?"

Ever a man of logic, Isaac shifted his gaze to her forehead as he did his mental calculations.

"Uh, six?"

She chuckled. "Something like that. I've lost track."

"How do you do it, Rebekah? I know there had to be times when you just wanted to give up and go into hiding."

She lifted her eyebrows at him. "Do you really think so?"

He gnawed on his perfect lower lip with his perfect white teeth. "I should have known you've never felt that way."

"I feel that way all the time. I really felt that way this morning," she said.

"At your screening?"

She nodded, and her eyes filled with tears as a sudden rush of emotion caught her by surprise.

His face went slack. "They found something, didn't they?" He grabbed her by both shoulders and gave her a shake. "That's why you got married so quickly. Why you invited me. How bad is it?"

"First, I didn't invite you, Eric did." She peeked over Isaac's shoulder and found Eric smiling and laughing with his friends while he kept half his attention trained on her. "This morning they thought they'd found a spot of cancer growing in my pelvis."

"Oh God, Reb, why didn't you call me?"

"Because it was a false alarm. Do you see what you're doing here?"

He shook his head.

"You're really good at scraping other people up off the floor when they're down. But when it's you who's taken a hit, you can't find your bootstraps to pull yourself up. Why is that?"

He shook his head slightly, sending his soft brown curls dancing about his head.

"I don't know. Maybe because it's easier to analyze a situation when you're on the outside looking in."

"So remove yourself from your situation. Stand outside yourself and look in. What do you want?"

"Trey," he said without hesitation.

"And if I told you that he'll never love you?"

Isaac lowered his eyes. "I already know that."

"So what else do you want?"

"I thought I wanted what my father has: a successful practice, load of cash, a big house with lots of colleagues who pretend they're my friends. A wife and kids. A killer golf swing. But…"

She squeezed his hands encouragingly, because she already knew Isaac wasn't much like his father. Never had been, never would be. And he'd never find happiness as long as he chased his father's dream. He glanced up and met her eyes.

"But?" she prompted.

"When I was in Africa, I felt I was really making a difference. I woke up every morning with purpose and connection. I don't know.

It just felt… right. Like it was what I was supposed to do. My calling. Does that make sense?"

She nodded eagerly. "I feel that way when I mix Sinners' music. I've never felt that way before about anything. That's why I kept failing at everything I tried before. I hadn't found my *thing*. You need to find your thing, Isaac. If it's in Africa treating patients who can't afford to pay you in anything but gratitude, then go back. There's nothing holding you here."

He glanced at Trey, who was laughing at Jace as he tried to remove the sucker adhered to his jacket between his shoulder blades. Playing his part, Jace spun in one direction and then the other, slapping his back and shoulders as the stick remained just out of reach. But Isaac wasn't even looking at Jace. He had eyes only for Trey. Trey didn't seem to know Isaac existed.

Isaac sighed and lowered his gaze to the carpet. "I wish you were wrong about that," he said, "but you're not. Trey doesn't have to get over me. He was never into me at all. He just wanted sex and I gave it to him all too willingly."

"I know what that's like," Rebekah said with a laugh.

Isaac's head jerked up. "You had sex with him too?"

"Eh, almost," Rebekah said. "So what are you going to do, Isaac? Do you need a kick in the ass?" She kicked up the hem of her wedding dress. "I'll do it!"

Isaac stared into nothingness for a moment and then smiled slightly. Nodded slightly. Shook his head. Blew out a breath.

"Isaac!" Rebekah shouted and gave him a shake.

"What?"

His eyes met hers, and she could still see the uncertainty there.

"Fine," he said. "I'll *think* about going back to my patients. They do need me far more than anyone here does."

She wrapped him in her arms and gave him a friendly squeeze. "Don't think, Isaac. Do."

"But maybe my father—"

"Stop worrying about what your father thinks of you," she said. "God knows my mother hates everything about my life, but I have to live the life that makes me happy, not one that satisfies her. You…" She patted his chest. "…need to live the life that makes *you* happy. Fuck him, Isaac. *Fuck* him."

Isaac chuckled, his cheeks slightly flushed. "You're right. Fuck him. *Fuck you, Dad. If you don't love me for who I am, then I don't need your approval.*"

"That's right. Feel better?"

He smiled his perfect smile and ran a perfectly manicured hand through a perfectly tamed set of light brown curls. "Yeah, actually. I do."

"Good, because I really need to be with my husband right now. I hope you understand."

"I've taken too much of your time already."

"You're still my bestie, Isaac. Nothing will change that. If you need to talk or need a hug or want to go shopping, I'm here. Just not on my wedding night, okay?"

He laughed. "I'll miss you," he said, giving her a hug that forced all the air from her lungs. "While I'm doing my *thing* in Africa."

Rebekah hugged him back, hoping Isaac would end up as happy as she was. Yet she kind of doubted it was possible. Her level of happiness was almost criminal.

Chapter 9

ERIC SMILED DOWN at his wife when she slid her hand into his and leaned against his upper arm. She gazed up at him with beguiling blue eyes, and he was glad they'd decided to put off the customary reception for a couple of weeks. How did new husbands make it through an entire evening without making love to their women? Maybe that's where the booze came in.

"Did you have a nice talk with Isaac?" he asked.

"Yep," she said. "Can we leave now, before someone else decides to interrupt?"

"Oh good, you're still here," a familiar voice called from the church entrance. "I thought I'd missed it."

"You did miss it, Jon," Sed called. "They're ready to leave."

Jon rushed down the aisle. He looked surprisingly good as he took Eric's hand and eagerly pumped it up and down.

"I thought you weren't coming," Eric said.

"Wouldn't miss it," he said.

"Jon," Sed said, shaking his head. "You *did* miss it."

"I did? Right. Hope it was special. Anyway, I think I found us a drummer."

The entire band swiveled their heads in Eric's direction, various levels of shock registering on their faces.

"You aren't going to leave the band, are you?" Jace said, grabbing Eric's sleeve.

Sed tilted his head back and shook it at the ceiling. "Happens all the time. Guy gets married. Wife takes over his life. Guy leaves band. Band is screwed."

"I'm not leaving Sinners," Eric said. "I just… want to start a second band. A band with fewer fan expectations so I can try some experimental things. And sing. And play guitar." Which would step on every band member's fucking toes.

Rebekah squeezed his hand in encouragement. He hadn't wanted the guys to find out like this. He'd wanted to have some songs for them to listen to so they could see how different the two bands would be and why he didn't expect Sinners to share his new vision.

Nice, Jon. Thanks for that.

"So do you need a bassist?" Jace asked.

Eric couldn't even bring himself to look at Jace when he said, "Jon's playing bass."

"Oh," Jace said flatly.

Shit. The last thing he wanted to do was hurt Jace. Eric wished that Jon knew how to keep his big mouth shut. That way Eric could have broken the idea to the guys himself and ensured that they realized he wasn't going anywhere. The side project would always take a back seat to Sinners.

"This thing is in its infancy," Eric said, hoping to lessen the impact of his news. "I'm not even sure if it will get off the ground."

"It will definitely get off the ground," Jon said excitedly. "I was talking to Caiden James when you sent me the wedding invite this afternoon. It took some encouragement and quite a bit of alcohol, but he's agreed to join us. Well, he will if you ask him. I don't think he really believed me. But he was stoked by the thought of working with you, Sticks."

"He'll get in touch with you in a couple of days," Rebekah said to Jon, taking Eric firmly by the elbow. "And you can hash out all the details about your band then."

Jon's smile faded, and he scowled slightly as he looked down at Rebekah.

"My *husband*," she continued, "is mine for the next seventy-two hours or so. After that, I *might* give him a few minutes to himself, but don't count on it. The man promised me a lifelong honeymoon, and I plan to hold him to his word."

Eric grinned and drew her against his side to give her a hearty squeeze. "That's right, I did. We'd better get started on that. Later, dudes."

He scooped Rebekah off her feet and into his arms, and carried her toward the church exit. There was only so much waiting a guy could be expected to tolerate.

Chapter 10

REBEKAH HUGGED ERIC'S NECK and giggled against his shoulder. Thank God he'd decided to make an escape. There was only so much waiting a girl could be expected to tolerate.

They'd almost made it to the door when rapid footfalls approached from behind.

"Wait!" Jessica called. "Don't forget to throw your bouquet. And we have rice. For luck!"

"And the garter," Myrna added.

Eric blew out his cheeks and set Rebekah on her feet. "Almost made it," he said.

Rebekah tossed her bouquet over her shoulder without looking.

There was a loud thud, and Rebekah turned to find Jessica on the floor, her body obscured by a pew, her feet sticking out into the aisle. "Warn a bride-to-be!" Jessica complained from between the pews. She lifted a hand into the air, clutching the bouquet in victory.

Sed chuckled and shook his head as he helped her to her feet. "Did you hit your head? Why did you dive for it like that?"

"Because no other woman in this room is getting married before me!" Jessica said, brushing off the skirt of her dress.

"Aggie might," Jace said quietly. "If we find the right time and place."

Jessica huffed out a breath. "Well… too bad. I caught the bouquet at risk of grievous injury, so we're next." She looked up at Sed. "And you'd better catch the garter or you're sleeping on the couch tonight."

Rebekah squeaked in surprise as the skirt of her dress was suddenly pushed up. Eric's long warm hands grasped her bare thigh and then shifted to the other to slide the garter down her leg. He was surprisingly matter-of-fact about it. He tugged it over her foot and tossed it directly to Sed, who caught it against his waist with one hand.

"Are you happy?" Eric said to Jessica.

She flushed. "Yes," she said quietly.

"Good. Now go cook your man some rice; we don't need it."

Rebekah snorted at Jessica's wide eyes and even wider mouth. Jessica hadn't managed to deliver a comeback before Eric tossed Rebekah over his shoulder, gathered her cumbersome train in his other hand, and practically sprinted the last few feet to the door. Giggling, Rebekah waved goodbye to all the smiling people in the church. Even Jon was grinning like a fool as he patted Jace on the back.

At the top of the church steps outside, Eric yelled, "My wife!" before jostling her uncomfortably as he bounded down the stairs with her still over his shoulder.

"My husband!" she yelled back.

He swatted her on the butt, which she barely felt through the layers of fabric. And then at last he set her on her feet next to the passenger side of the Corvette. Her heart threatened to beat itself right out of her chest as she gazed up into his smiling face. He leaned down to kiss her. Before his lips brushed hers, he was interrupted by a loud, "Wait! You're not married yet."

Her dad came rushing toward them waving a piece of paper. "You haven't signed the license."

"So much for a speedy getaway," Eric said, "but I guess signing the license is pretty important."

They signed their names, using the hood of the car as their writing surface. Jace and her mom signed as their witnesses, her dad signed as the officiating clergy, and it was finally official. They were married.

"Can we go now?" Eric asked. "I never realized that marrying her would keep me out of her arms for so long."

"You can go," Dad said. "Congratulations."

The rest of the party had made their way to the car by this time. So everyone required another hug, another handshake, another kiss on the cheek, another pat on the back. Eric opened the passenger door and slowly herded Rebekah away from well-wishers and into the car.

He closed the door resolutely, took a deep breath, and circled the car to get into the driver's seat. Jessica took out her camera phone and made them smile so she could snap a few photos. She'd taken some of the ceremony too. And Myrna had gotten a video on her phone. Rebekah spent the next several minutes thanking them profusely. She leaned out of the car to give Myrna a hug. And removed her veil to return it to Jessica, thanking her again for letting her borrow it. She turned toward Eric to find him with his jaw set, rolling his eyes at the steering wheel. He started the car, apparently ready to run over anyone still in their path.

From behind the car, Aggie said, "I think you need to change your sign. It says *almost* married."

Eric slapped his forehead. "You people are driving me nuts! I don't need all this ceremony. I just need her. *Comprende?*"

He shifted the car into first and revved the engine in warning.

"We'll celebrate at the reception!" Rebekah called to the apprehensive friends and family backing away from the car. "It'll be fun. We'll even get a cake and dance and everything."

Eric eased forward, waiting somewhat patiently for Dave to maneuver his wheelchair out of the car's path. When they were finally clear to leave, Eric drove off, honking his horn all the way out of the parking lot.

Rebekah turned in her seat so she could wave at everyone over the open back of the car. When they were all out of sight, she turned around and sighed happily. She didn't mind a bit of ceremony, but she'd much rather spend her evening with Eric than with well-wishers.

"Do you want to stay at a hotel tonight?" Eric asked, his eyes on the road.

"No, I want to stay at your house."

"Our house," he said.

"*Our* house," she repeated with a tender smile.

Maybe the reason the ceremony was necessary was so a person felt married. She didn't really feel as if anything had changed between them. Was she supposed to feel different? She'd given him her heart well before she'd said *I do.*

Rebekah looked down at her hand and then rubbed the wedding band on her finger. It was a well-worn ring, comfortable as an old pair of sneakers. She almost felt as if she'd always worn it.

"I'm glad Daddy let us use these rings." She glanced at Eric, her eyes a bit on the watery side.

"I figured you'd feel that way."

He reached over and cupped the back of her head, his own eyes shinier than usual.

"Did he tell you the story behind them?"

He shook his head.

"His great-great-grandparents immigrated to the United States from England during the mid-eighteen hundreds. The husband,

Walter, was a skilled cabinet maker, but they struggled at first because any profit they made had to go back into the business. Apparently they had to sell their wedding bands to buy shoes for their children so the kids could go to school. After many years, the cabinet-making business began to make a profit. Walter and his wife were able to buy a house and shoes for their kids. Figuring the man they'd sold their rings to had melted them down for the silver long before, they even bought new wedding rings. One day old Walt was designing new cabinets for a used-jewelry dealer and what did he see in the display case?"

"The rings."

Rebekah reached over to squeeze his knee. "Right. The rings. So it became a tradition that newly married couples in the family would start their marriage wearing these very same rings until they could make their fortune and afford new ones. Then they'd replace them and save the silver rings to pass on to their children. By the time of my dad's generation, things weren't so tight financially, so he and Mom did use the rings in the ceremony, but they traded them for new rings right after."

Eric lifted his hand over the steering wheel to look at the ring on his finger. "So we aren't supposed to wear them forever?"

"We can wear them as long as we want," she said. It wasn't as if they'd be able to have children to pass them on to. Well, at least not blood-related children. She wondered if her ancestors would be okay with an adopted child wearing the rings.

"What if Dave wants them when he gets married?"

Rebekah smiled, hoping someday soon her brother would find someone he wanted to spend the rest of his life with. "Then I say we let him have them. They've been blessed with many generations of love, including ours. We can't really expect him to give that up."

Eric smiled sadly. "I wish I had a cool story to tell you about my ancestors, but I know nothing about them. I probably come from a long line of derelicts and criminals."

"I doubt that," she said. "You have too good a heart, Eric. I have to think at least some of that is genetic."

He concentrated extra hard on the road. They were still miles from home.

He was silent for a long while, and she didn't press him further. She didn't want him to be sad today. She almost wished she hadn't told him the story about the rings, how they connected generation after generation of her family. It had to make him feel completely disconnected from his own family.

They turned onto the gravel road that led to Eric's sunny yellow Victorian-style house in the country. He stopped in the driveway and shut off the engine, but didn't make a move to get out of the car.

He took a deep breath and turned toward her. "I never really thought much about my family—what I was missing by not having one—until I found you."

Her heart panged. "Baby, if you want to try to figure out where you come from, we can go look through records and stuff, figure out who your relatives are. I'm sure there are plenty of interesting stories in your ancestors' pasts."

"I wouldn't know where to start."

"With your birth certificate. Also, as a former ward of the state, you have a file somewhere."

He laughed. "Oh, I have a file all right."

"If you don't want to know, that's fine," she said. "I don't mind being your entire family."

"You and my band. It's enough," he said. He took her hand in his and kissed her knuckle just below her wedding ring. "But I'll think about it. Maybe knowing the truth about who I am and where I came from will be a bit less terrifying with you beside me. You make me feel I can overcome any obstacle."

Her shoulders drooped, and she relaxed into her seat with a dreamy grin. "You'd better stop making me swoon," she said. "I'm liable to melt right into this seat."

He grinned. "I like to make you swoony. Never had a woman get swoony over me before."

"Then you must have not shown a single woman who you really are."

"You don't think this sentimental sap is really me, do you? I just act this way to get in your pants."

Blue eyes twinkling with mischief, he winked at her.

She laughed. "It is effective in that regard," she admitted. "But I'm not wearing pants. And I'm not sure your swooniness is enough to get you under my skirt."

"When we get in the house, you won't be wearing your skirt either."

She opened her mouth to tease him further, and he added, "Or your panties."

She laughed. He knew her well; she had been going to tease

him about the extra swoon requirement for getting in her panties.

His teasing smile faded and he simply stared at her for a long moment. His eyes searched her face as if he was trying to decide if she really could handle being there for him for things other than great laughs and hot sex. Her heart rate accelerated when his eyes finally settled on hers and she steeled herself to support whatever he'd decided. She wouldn't force him one way or the other. She might push a bit, because she believed knowing what he came from would give him some closure, but she wouldn't force him to face it if he didn't want to.

"I've spent the last twenty-five years trying to forget I ever had a family," he said. "I've lived my entire life focusing on the present. For the first time, I'm ready to concentrate on my future and building it with you. And I don't think I want my past to intrude on that."

Planning their future was more important, but for her, the future was far more terrifying than the past. They'd already survived their pasts. The same could not be said for their futures.

"That's fine, baby." She touched the cleft in his chin with one fingertip and then cupped his face between her palms. "I'll always support you. Always."

His eyes flicked up to stare at her forehead, and he flashed a perfect set of white teeth at her when he grinned crookedly. "You realize I'm going to have to test that promise, don't you? Make sure you mean it by being obnoxious and picking fights."

"Well then, I'll start looking forward to a lot of make-up sex." She pulled his face to hers so she could kiss him.

She drew away when his fingers began to work the buttons at her back. "Not here," she said, reaching for his door handle to exit the car.

"Yes," he said firmly. "Right here."

"But the neighbors will see us."

He glanced over his shoulder at the nearest house, nearly a mile away and set back away from the gravel road by a driveway almost as long as theirs. The roofline was barely visible. He turned his gaze to her again.

"I highly doubt that," he said. "Do you remember the very first thing that we bonded over?"

She thought back to their earliest meetings. "This car," she said.

He nodded. "That's when I fell in love with you, you know.

The minute you started talking about head gaskets and carburetor intakes, I was a goner."

"You're being swoony again," she accused.

He unzipped his pants and directed her hand into his fly, filling her palm with hard, hot cock. A spasm clenched deep in her pussy, and she gasped with the intensity of her sudden lust.

"Still think I'm swoony?"

"Yep," she said, and tugged his cock free of his pants. "Have I ever sucked you off in this car?"

"Not yet."

She wiggled her eyebrows at him. "Well, that's about to be remedied."

He pulled a lever and pushed the seat back as far as it would go. Knowing how much he liked to watch, Rebekah bent over his lap and tilted her head. She slowly drew her tongue along the underside of his cockhead, blowing breaths over the wetness she left behind. Eric stroked her hair tenderly as she delivered hesitant licks to his flesh.

"Am I doing it right?" she whispered hesitantly.

"You know you are," he said.

"I wasn't sure, what with me being a virginal bride and all," she said, wickedly grinning up at him and winking.

He winked back, his silent affirmation that he realized she wanted to play.

"It feels good when you suck it," he said.

"Like this?"

She covered her teeth with her lips and clamped her mouth over his shaft from beneath.

"Usually you go at it from the tip and suck it down your throat," he instructed helpfully.

Still latched on to the underside of his cock, she rubbed her tongue against the thick ridge in her mouth and then slowly turned her head side to side to work his flesh from base toward the crown and back.

"Fuck." He sucked the word deep into his chest. "That's another option."

She forced herself not to laugh and continued working her mouth up and down the underside of his cock. With each repetitive motion, she moved a fraction of an inch upward. The corners of her mouth were becoming tender, so it was a bit of a relief when she reached his tip and tilted her head a bit so that the head of his cock popped into her mouth. She continued her up and down motion, still sucking hard on the underside. She could feel his cockhead push her cheek out with each downward slide and knew he'd be able to see that he was in her mouth as well as feel it.

Eric's belly began to quiver beneath her hand. His breaths came out in overexcited gasps.

"You are so fucking sexy," he growled, rocking his hips to push harder against the inside of her cheek. "Ride me, Reb. I want to come inside you our first time together as husband and wife."

She lifted her head, his cock popping free of her mouth, and looked up at him with wide eyes. "Ride you?" she whispered, as if aghast.

"We'll play later," he promised, grabbing her by the arms and pulling her into the narrow space between his body and the steering wheel. "I don't have the patience at the moment."

"Even if you don't want to pretend I'm an untried virgin, I just don't think sex is doable in this huge dress in this little car, baby."

The man was determined to prove her wrong. Within a minute he had the white train of the dress flipped over the dash and windshield, trailing across the forest-green hood of the Corvette. The front of the voluminous skirt was bunched up between them, separating their bodies far too much for her liking. She managed to get her legs beneath her and her knees in his seat so she could straddle his hips.

His fingers slipped beneath the leg of her panties and found her as hot and eager as he was.

She fleetingly thought that her mother would kill her for getting her wedding gown dirty, but Eric slipped inside her and then nothing mattered but him. He pulled her onto him and buried his face in her throat. His hot breath warmed her chest. His hard cock filled her just right. She rocked her hips, encouraging deeper penetration. Eric's arms wrapped around her back and held her close. He didn't seem interested in fucking, just being inside her. Or maybe he was finding maneuverability in the tiny car as impossible as she was.

"I love you so much," he murmured against her skin, his voice raw with emotion. "So much."

"Shh. I know." She hugged his head against her and kissed his hair. Her body was filled with him, but her heart was overflowing.

"So much, Rebekah. So much."

"I love you too, Eric."

"I want to give you everything, baby. Anything in the world. In the universe. What do you want? Name it and it's yours."

She placed a finger under his chin and lifted his head to stare into his tormented blue eyes. She stroked his brow to lessen the crease there and then cupped his face between her hands. "I already have everything I want right here."

"But if you could have anything? What would it be?"

Apparently he didn't believe she was being sincere. "What if I asked you the same? What do you want—besides me—at this very moment?"

"Nothing. Just your happiness."

"Then you have everything you want too."

He bit the corner of his lower lip and stared at her forehead. "I'm sorry," he said. "I just... I feel like I should buy you things. To prove how much I love you."

"Do you think I should buy you a bunch of things to prove how much I love you?"

His brow furrowed, and he shook his head.

"Then why do you think I would require it? Do I come across as materialistic or something?"

"No," he said hastily. "Of course not."

"You're enough, Eric. Okay?"

She could see the battle raging inside him, but wasn't sure what was causing it.

"Why don't you think you're enough—*more* than enough—for me?"

"I don't know," he said, avoiding her eyes. "I just... I want to believe it. I know you mean it. I just wonder if one day you'll realize I'm *not* enough, I was never enough, and you'll... leave."

"I won't leave," she said. She grabbed him by the chin and forced him to meet her eyes. "Look at me, damn it." His blue eyes lifted to hers. "I won't leave you. I won't. I'm not your fucking mother."

He grinned at her. "Thank God for that. My cock is still inside you."

She slapped his shoulder angrily, and he flinched. "Don't make this into a fucking joke, Eric. I know it hurts you."

"You do hit hard for a girl," he teased.

She growled in frustration. She understood that he used humor as a defense mechanism, but God, she could strangle him when he used it to shut her out. She opened the car door and struggled to get off his lap. He clutched both hands in the fabric of her cumbersome gown and kept her from rising.

"You liar, you're going to leave me already!" he said, his voice uncharacteristically hard.

"I'm not *leaving* you," she said. "I'm going into the house. Let go of my dress."

"And if I refuse?"

"You get to tell my mother how it got ripped."

She wrenched her body away from his, and the seams strained to stay together. He let go at once, and she staggered out of the car. Lips pursed, she gathered her skirts in her arms and dashed for the house.

How could she possibly prove she was strong enough to support him if she ran away at his first sign of adversity? Fuck, she had to pull it together. He'd never get over his insecurity about deserving love if she let his defense mechanisms hurt her. But she couldn't help it. Deep down she knew his inability to accept that she loved him was his issue, not hers, but damn, it hurt to think that she wasn't meeting his needs. If she were, he'd have an easy time accepting her assurances. How did she show him what was in her heart? How did she get him to understand that she wasn't just saying she loved him and going through the motions? She loved him unconditionally—how could she not? But how did she prove it to him? And why should she have to?

She dashed tears away as she climbed the steps. Her heels echoed on the wide sunny porch as she hurried to the door. She grabbed the handle and found it locked. She growled in frustration and rattled it, as if that would have any affect. A hand covered hers on the doorknob. Eric moved up solidly against her back, effectively preventing her escape. She went still, the flesh between her shoulders tingling.

Even in her frustration and pain, her skin craved his touch.

"You are not allowed to be mad at me today," he said in her ear and handed her the house keys.

"I can be mad if I want to be mad!" She shoved the key into the lock and struggled to turn it. Why were her goddamned hands shaking so badly?

"Why are you mad?"

"I'm not!" She wasn't lying. She wasn't mad. She was hurt and she was scared. Scared that she'd never be enough to make up for all the neglected years of his youth.

"We promised never to do this, remember?" he said. "We said we'd always communicate with each other, even when it's hard. So tell me what's bothering you so we can make it right."

She took a deep breath and tilted her head to look up into the spired roof on the interior of the porch. She'd never noticed the interesting architecture of the white beams up there before. She wondered what other details she'd failed to notice about Eric's showcase Victorian. She was wondering this now because communication *was* hard.

"Rebekah," he whispered, his lips brushing the hair above her ear. "Talk to me."

She bit her lip and looked down at his hand covering hers on the doorknob.

"Sometimes," she said. "Sometimes you make me feel like I don't love you enough. Or maybe it's you don't *believe* I love you. Not really."

"I do struggle with that," he said quietly.

"Why? H-how do I prove it to you, Eric? How do I make you believe it?"

"For starters, you could kiss that spitting cobra that likes you so much," he said in a teasing tone. His free hand slid over her shoulder and plucked at the buttons at the back of her gown. "Cobras prefer their women naked."

Would she ever get him to be serious for more than five seconds at a time?

She huffed out a breath, trying to remind herself why he acted the way he did. Tried to remember how much she enjoyed his infallible sense of humor.

"That would only prove I lust after you. I know you believe that. I can't keep my hands off you."

"Are you sure? You left me in the car with my hard dick hanging out of my pants. I thought wedding-night sex was a guaranteed thing."

She chuckled slightly, unable to help herself. It wasn't like her to be too serious either, but figuring out *why* he struggled was important to her. She needed to know what she was doing wrong so she could help him believe that her love was as true and unending as his own. That she had enough love to give him. Enough to fill his life with it.

"Sex *is* guaranteed, Mr. Sticks. *After* you answer my question."

He sighed and leaned heavily against her back. Her bodice

loosened, and she realized he hadn't just been playing with her buttons—he'd been unfastening them.

"Why did I pick *now* to remind you that we promised to communicate? I want to get laid." He turned the doorknob and pushed the door open. "Will you let me carry you across the threshold now, wife?"

"After you answer my question."

"What was your question again?"

"Why don't you believe I love you?"

"I do," he said.

"Do you think I love you as much as you love me?"

"That's a loaded question I refuse to answer."

"Why is it loaded?"

"Because if I say I love *you* more, then it becomes a competition, and if I say you love *me* more, then you get your feelings hurt, and if I say we love *equally*, you'll want evidence of something that can never be proven, something you can feel, but can't touch. Can't see. You can't hear it or smell it. How do you know it's real if you can't experience it with anything but your heart?"

"You don't think love is real?"

"I trust that it's real. I believe that it's real. I know what I feel for you inside my heart, my *soul*, is real. But when I *think* and try to *know*, that's when I start to wonder and doubt and… remember."

She was pretty sure his sudden bout of remembering was really eating at him.

"You can tell what you remember," she said. "You never talk about your past."

"I don't want or need to talk about my past. It's over. I can't change one second about it. Can't we just be happy with what we have now? Does it really matter that I have a hard time believing you love me because no one has ever *wanted* to love me before? I mean, shit, Reb, you can't possibly *want* to love me. I'm a fucking train wreck. I keep waiting for you to say, *I'm over it. Thank God I finally came to my senses. I must have been drugged or something. Who would ever* want *to love that weirdo?*"

Her heart twisted until she thought her chest might implode.

"*Eric*, I want to love you," she said. "I do. I'm glad I love you. Can I help how I feel? No. I think I pretty much have to love you at this point—you are beyond wonderful to me, but I also want to love you. You deserve so much love in your life. I willingly give you all I have. I promise you that."

But would it ever be enough? The thing that could fill his life with more love, all the love he could possibly ever need—*a child of his own*—she could never give him. So he needed a whole lot of loving to compensate. She just hoped she had enough.

"If I promise to believe you love me, can I carry you over the threshold, strip that dress off you, and fuck you like there's no tomorrow?"

She sighed, knowing this would go nowhere as long as his thoughts were consumed with lust.

"I'm not sure what you're waiting for," she said with a smile, resolved to tackle the issue when he was ready. At the moment he was only ready for one thing, and she knew she could meet that need for sure. "Are you going to make me wait for it, husband? My pussy is dripping for you, you know."

"*Woman*," he growled, "why do you torment me?"

"Because I love you," she said.

She squeaked in surprise when he scooped her into his arms and carried her over the threshold.

"Welcome home, Mrs. Sticks," he said.

"Welcome home, Mr. Sticks," she returned.

"Now for that bed." He only managed a few steps before getting caught in her train and stumbling into the wall behind the open front door. "I'm sorry, but this dress has to go. Who invented these things? Fathers who wanted their daughters to remain virgins on their wedding night?"

Laughing, Rebekah clung to his neck. "Take my virginity now, husband," she said. "Please!"

"I was going to carry you to bed before fucking you like there's no tomorrow," he said.

"If there was really no tomorrow, would you bother taking me to bed, or would you fuck me right here on the foyer floor with my skirt over my head?"

He paused for a second, glancing out of the corner of his eye as he contemplated her logic. "Good point."

Eric set her on her feet and the door slammed closed. Startled, she turned around, and it took her a long moment to register what she was actually seeing.

"Eric!" she squeaked. "Where are your pants?"

He grinned down at his stiff cock, standing proud just beneath the hem of his white T-shirt. "I left them in the car. Didn't think I'd need them."

She snorted with laughter, wondering if any of their neighbors had driven by and witnessed bare-assed Eric in his tuxedo jacket and Converse tennis shoes standing on the front porch.

She crooked a beckoning finger at him, her cheeks aching from smiling so broadly. "Come here, you."

"Am I in trouble?"

He took a hesitant step forward, and she clutched his shirtfront in one hand before dragging him to the floor on top of her.

"You're in huge trouble," she said, tumbling him onto his back. "I'm sure the cops are on their way at this very moment to arrest you for indecent exposure."

His eyes widened. "Quick! Hide the evidence."

She grinned wickedly. "My pleasure."

She straddled his hips and carefully arranged her skirts around them. "They'll never find it now," she said. "No one would ever think to look under there."

His mouth dropped open as she rubbed her ass against his hard length. She wasn't sure what had him so excited. Actually, Eric was always excited. She'd have been surprised if he weren't.

"I think they might check under your skirt," he said breathlessly. "Can't you think of a better place to slip it into? Someplace warm and soft and slick."

If her panties hadn't been in the way, she'd have already slipped it into someplace warm and soft and slick.

One of his hands yanked her loosened bodice down so he could palm her breasts. His other hand was lost somewhere beneath the billowy cloud of her skirt.

"You'll have to give me a hint," she said. "Where do you want it?"

Beneath her skirt, his hands stroked her skin, slowly making its way toward the moist heat between her thighs. His fingers slipped beneath the elastic at the crotch of her panties. Her eyelids fluttered as he stroked her inner folds and teased her opening.

"This feels about right," he whispered.

"It feels right to me." She lifted her hips so he could guide himself into her.

She sank down on him with a sigh of pleasure. The panties cutting into her tender flesh delivered an unexpected thrill as she began to rise and fall over him. She took her time, rotating her hips to work him deep inside her body, staring into his eyes to work him deep inside her heart.

She didn't fuck him like there was no tomorrow. She made love to him like there were infinite tomorrows that still wouldn't be enough.

Chapter 11

ERIC WATCHED REBEKAH through half-closed eyes because the feel of her above him, around him, made it difficult to hold his eyelids open at all. The floor at his back was hard, cool, and unyielding, but the woman above was all softness, warmth, and comfort—his personal bliss. The fading sunlight glowed orange through the windows on either side of the entry door and bathed his wife in the surreal golden aura of the divine, of someone gifted to him directly from the heavens. An angel. His angel.

And he was certain the pussy squeezing and tugging him toward oblivion was lined with warm, molten gold. Eric had had his share of Certified Grade A Pussy in his life, but Rebekah's out-fucked them all. Which made it all but impossible to hold his desire in check.

He closed his eyes a moment and allowed himself to concentrate on nothing but the hot, slick flesh surrounding him. Tugging. Rubbing. Encompassing. His belly clenched and his balls tightened. He gasped as a hard spasm at the base of his cock made it jerk inside her.

"*Rebekah?*" he called breathlessly.

"Not yet, baby. Almost."

He dug his fingertips into the hardwood beneath him and forced his orgasm back—knowing exploding inside her would feel fan-fucking-tastic now but would be even better if he could delay his gratification longer.

He pried his eyes open, needing to focus on something other than the feel of her rising and falling over his over sensitized length.

She was still aglow with the light of the sunset. Her chin-length blond and purple hair swayed each time her hips lowered. His gaze traveled down the delicate curve of her jaw, slender neck, prominent collarbones, and the gentle swells of her breasts above the cups of her lacy bra.

If only he'd thought to unhook it when he'd been pressed against her back earlier. He knew he couldn't reach the hooks without shifting positions. As if reading his mind, Rebekah reached behind her back and released the clasp. When he glanced up, she smiled at him. Apparently his fixated gaze had made him easy to read. She slipped the straps down her arms and tossed the bra aside. His gaze wandered downward and he was blessed with the sight of her perky tits bouncing enticingly above the loosened bodice of her billowing white dress. He lifted a hand to cup one breast, stroking the rosy nipple at the center. She moaned, churning her hips to work her clit against him. She was close, he realized. He considered fumbling around beneath her dress until he found her center—he knew he could send her flying with a few strokes of her clit—but damned if she didn't look hot with her tongue pressed against her upper lip and her eyes squeezed shut as she sought her release.

He plucked her nipple, and her back arched.

"Yes," she groaned.

She rose and fell over him faster now. Harder. Pausing every few down strokes to rub herself against him, seeking fulfillment. Her moans became cries of ecstasy.

"Almost," she said in a breathless gasp. "Eric. Eric!"

This still wasn't easy for him—timing their orgasms so they could come together—but she was well worth the effort to try. He could hold back just long enough for her to come. He hoped. He fought the urge to help her along and clenched his eyes closed, concentrating on the feel of her around him, waiting, waiting for the feel of her pussy's involuntary clenching as her body tumbled into the abyss. He was concentrating so hard on not coming that his orgasm took him by surprise.

"Oh shit! Rebekah," he groaned. His hips lifted off the floor as hard pulses of pleasure gripped the base of his cock.

Rebekah cried out as her pussy squeezed him rhythmically, tugging hard at his jerking cock, intensifying his pleasure, drawing it out, making his entire body quake with unparalleled bliss.

She shuddered for several intense moments and then collapsed on top of him, still shaking with aftershocks of ecstasy. He wanted to wrap her in his arms and press her closer to his chest, but he couldn't move his arms.

"I love you," she whispered. "My sex-god husband."

He grinned crookedly at her praise. "I owe that all to you."

She giggled, her pussy tightening around his softening cock with the shake of her body. "I knew you had it in you. We just had to bring it out."

"You bring it out tirelessly several times a day."

"It's a tough job…" She snorted and lifted her body from his to sit astride his hips. "Well, we're married. It's been consummated in the foyer. Now what? Watch TV?"

He lifted an eyebrow at her. "Are you serious?"

She shrugged, but couldn't hide the devious gleam in her pretty blue eyes. "Isn't that what typical married couples do?"

"I refuse to be typical. And I'll tell you what we're going to do." He was starting to feel the uncomfortableness of the hard floor. "You are going to take off that dress, and then we are going to bless every room in this house with an orgasm."

Rebekah's eyes widened. "There are six bedrooms."

"And a kitchen. Dining room. Parlor. Living room. Conservatory. Four bathrooms."

"Even *you* can't come that many times in one night."

"Mrs. Sticks, I didn't say I was going to have an orgasm in every room, but one of us will."

She leaned over to kiss him and then propped herself up with her hands on either side of his head to gaze into his eyes. "I think I'm going to like this game."

He grinned. "Yes. Game. We're currently tied one orgasm to one. He with the highest score by the end of the night gets breakfast in bed in the morning."

"*He* with the highest score?" Rebekah shook her head slowly, sending soft blond locks caressing her flushed cheeks. "I think you mean *she* with the highest score. I'm planning to win this competition."

Eric grinned. He actually *planned* to make her win, but he wasn't going to tell her that. "The game starts as soon as you're naked."

"You're going to have to help me with that. I can't reach the buttons."

"I think I can manage," he teased and winced as he struggled into a sitting position. His body protested the ache in his lower back. "I need to add a rule to this game," he said.

"You can't change the rules after it's begun."

"You aren't naked yet, so it hasn't begun."

"Fine," she said. "What's the new rule?"

"No more fucking on the floor. At least not tonight."

"But I can kneel on the floor, right?"

His cock twitched with interest as he pictured her kneeling at his feet while he drove his cock down her throat. "Only if you put a pillow beneath your knees."

"Deal," she said. "Now get this goddamned dress off me. I want to play."

He wrapped his arms around her and unfastened the rest of the buttons at her back by feel. His lips moved across the warm skin of her throat and collarbones as the tiny pearls came free from their satin loops one pop at a time.

When he freed the last of the buttons, he splayed his hands over her smooth bare back and drew her naked breasts against his T-shirt. She pushed his tuxedo jacket from his shoulders and tugged at his T-shirt impatiently. Within moments they were naked and kissing, touching and groaning, but still in the foyer.

"Where next?" she asked eagerly, her eyes alight with adventure and longing and love.

Was it even possible to love someone as much as he loved her? Fuck, she was perfect.

He helped her to her feet before climbing to his own. He switched on the lights, took her hand, and led her into the chef's kitchen. The large but country-cozy room glowed invitingly under the soft lighting.

"Welcome to our kitchen," he said. "This is where I eat."

"Don't you eat in the dining room?" she asked.

"Formally. I'll show you how I eat formally next." He wiggled his eyebrows at her and she giggled. "But this is where I eat most of the time, because it's quicker and more convenient. Are you hungry?"

"I'm always hungry for you, baby."

"But are you hungry for food? We haven't eaten all day."

She scrunched up her forehead and covered her belly with both hands. "Now that you mention it… I guess I was so full of wedded bliss that I didn't notice."

Eric opened the refrigerator and hunted for something edible. There were still leftovers from his birthday feast. He went straight for the mostly demolished cake. "How does cake sound?"

"I thought maybe you'd prefer pie," she said from behind him.

He turned and almost dropped the cake. She was sitting on the counter with her feet planted on the granite surface and her legs wide open. She rubbed at her clit with two fingers. "You want some? It's not an ordinary pie. The more you eat it, the creamier it gets."

He loved how his sweetheart of a wife could get raunchy

without any provocation or warning. It was one of the things he liked best about her.

"That is one delicious-looking pie," he said, his mouth watering with anticipation and his cock stirring with interest. He managed to regain his composure enough to carry the cake across the space between them and set it safely on the counter beside her.

"Isn't that counter cold?" he asked, moving to stand between her legs.

"I'm so hot for you, I hardly noticed."

His chest swelled with what had to pride and he kissed her deeply, nudging her hand from her self-inflicted pleasure so he could claim the victory of making her come. He slipped two fingers inside her and massaged her clit with his thumb. She groaned into his mouth. Unable to resist the allure of watching his fingers claim her, he tugged his mouth away and stared down to where they were buried in her silky heat. He worked them in and out, churning them in wide arcs to watch her flushed and swollen flesh accept his invasion.

Rebekah's hands moved to rest on his shoulders, and she pressed down almost imperceptibly, but he knew what she wanted. She wanted him to eat. And he was suddenly starving. He kissed his way down her chest, pausing at her breasts to kiss and suck and nibble her pebbled nipples. Her fingers dug into his scalp, and she rocked against his hand, murmuring soft moans of encouragement as he rammed his fingers deeper, stretched her wider, and tapped her clit with his thumb to remind her where his lips would soon be. He moved lower, sucking feather-light kisses down her trembling belly. He nibbled her clean-shaven mons, delivering sharp nips that made her beg for what she actually wanted.

"Oh please, Eric. Please," she whispered.

He grinned. He would win this round for sure. When his tongue slid into her seam and brushed against her clit, her body jerked. He flicked her clit rapidly with the tip of his tongue, gave it a hard suck, then rubbed it with the flat of his circling tongue.

Her pussy was soaked—from their combined cum from earlier and her freely flowing juices. The excess lubrication made it easy for him to slip his little finger into her ass.

"Oh God, Eric!" she said. "You are the best multifunction vibrator ever made."

He chuckled and used her compliment as inspiration, pressing his lips against her clit and blowing steady vibrations through her flesh. She cried out as she shattered with orgasm. He finger-fucked her while her body, consumed in the throes of passion, strained and jerked violently.

When she settled a bit, she pulled him up against her so she could wrap her arms and legs around him and rest her head against his shoulder. Her heart thudded hard and fast against his chest, and her breath warmed the skin over his collarbone in shaky bursts. His right hand was still buried between her thighs, but he wrapped his left arm around her back to hold her close.

"I win," she said with a breathless chuckle. "Current score: two big Os for Rebekah, Eric one."

"I can still catch up," he said.

"If I let you," she said in a teasing tone.

"That sounds like a challenge. I can still go back to my old ways, you know." He'd always been able to come frequently. It was the duration of the buildup that he used to struggle with.

"After all my hard work to get you past that?" She leaned back to look at him, and her smirk belayed her willingness to *work* with him again if necessary.

His smartass remark was interrupted by her belly grumbling with hunger. He jerked back to give her tummy an appraising look and pulled his hand free from the snug passages between her thighs.

"The pie was divine," Eric said. "But how about some cake and maybe some leftover lasagna? Even though I just sampled pie, I'm still hungry and *you* haven't eaten anything."

"Maybe I'll have a large, hard sausage for dessert. I'll eat it formally in the dining room."

He grinned. She was ready for their third match already? There would be no complaints out of him.

She kissed him briefly and then hopped off the counter. "I'll be right back," she said and sauntered off to the half bath in the hall. He wanted a piece of that hot ass next, he decided, so he could stare at the name tattooed across her lower back. *His* name.

When she disappeared from sight, he washed his hands in the sink and humming under his breath, popped the leftover lasagna in the microwave. Myrna had made it for his birthday celebration a few days before. The smell of tomatoes, Italian herbs, cheese, and sausage began to fill the room as the food warmed. A pair of soft lips kissed the middle of his back, and Rebekah's small hands circled his waist. His cock had started to soften again but rose with distracting rapidity as she stroked his length gently between her palms.

"Damn, woman, can't a man eat before you demand additional satisfaction?"

"You just had pie," she reminded him. "I'm the one who hasn't eaten yet."

He groaned as her thumbs massaged his cockhead gently. Neither one of them was going to get any sustenance if she kept that up.

"We already christened this room," he reminded her. "Save it for the dining room."

"I figured if I make you come here, the dining room will be my victory as well."

"You're willing to resort to cheating?" He chuckled and opened the cabinet next to the microwave to pull out a pair of plates, loving the fact that he needed two. "I never realized how competitive you are."

"I love to win," she said, her hand moving between his legs to cup his heavy balls. "Especially when the prize is you."

"The prize is breakfast in bed, remember?" He set the plates on the counter and closed his eyes, pretending nonchalance as his flesh pulsated with pleasure beneath her gentle touch.

"You're the real prize," she whispered and kissed trails of tingly delight down his spine. "I'm so glad I won you."

"You didn't have to work very hard," he admitted with a laugh. "You had no competition."

The microwaved beeped, and Eric retrieved the container, somehow managing not to drop it as Rebekah trailed after him, her hand now lingering at the base of his cock.

"I'd fight for you," she said. "You know that, right?"

He shrugged. "Doesn't matter to me. You're mine and I'm yours and that's the way it's going to be forever. No take-it-backsies."

"No take-it-backsies," she agreed.

He scooped steaming lasagna onto two plates, having to pause several times as her hand did marvelous things to his attentive cock.

"If you keep that up, I'm going to have to paddle your ass," he said finally.

"If I keep what up?"

"Playing with my dick while I'm trying to get dinner ready."

Her palm skimmed his length, and he shuddered.

"Then I guess you're going to have to paddle my ass."

She squeaked in surprise when he turned abruptly and lifted her off the floor by her upper arms.

"Eric!"

He hauled her into the dining room, turned her to face the long white-washed table, and pressed between her shoulders to urge her to bend forward. She complied without hesitation. He drew back his hand to swat her ass and stopped short when confronted by her panties.

"Why did you put your panties back on?" he asked.

"I'm a bit… wet," she said breathlessly. "I didn't want to make a mess on the chairs."

"I don't give a fuck about that," he said. "Take them off."

She glanced over her shoulder at him, apparently taken aback by the uncharacteristic harshness in his tone. He didn't falter. And he *was* going to paddle her ass while he fucked her. He wouldn't spank her particularly hard, but he would make sure she felt it.

"Off!" he said when she did nothing but blink at him over her shoulder.

Leaning over the table, she slowly lowered her panties, exposing her perfect rump to his appreciative stare. She got them as far as her knees before his need for her became too much. He swatted her ass with his palm. She gasped in surprise. He massaged the soft globe of flesh and then spanked her again. Her pale skin reddened beneath his hand.

Perhaps he was being too rough with her tender backside.

She widened her stance slightly, her legs held together by the panties at her knees, and flattened her chest and belly to the table, inviting more. He swatted her untouched cheek, and she jerked before moaning brokenly.

"Do you like your punishment, naughty wife?"

"Oh yes," she whispered.

He used his free hand to direct his cock into her hot pussy. He slid deep without resistance.

"Oh God," she said, her voice muffled by the table. "Fuck me hard."

He was glad they were of the same mind. And he planned to claim his orgasm in the dining room. Even up the score a bit. He thrust into her hard and fast, slapping her ass every few dozen strokes to prevent her from coming. At least he'd anticipated that the stinging pain would hold her orgasm at bay. Instead it sent her flying. Her screams of release dragged him along for the ride. He pulled out at the last moment to watch himself come over her lower back in several vigorous spurts. He massaged his cum into his tattooed name and then rubbed her bright red ass with both palms.

"You liked that?" he asked, a bit surprised that she'd responded so enthusiastically to rough handling.

"Mmm hmm," she purred. "I like everything you do to me. I do believe the score is now three to one in my favor."

"I just came all over your back, Rebekah Sticks," he reminded her. "The score is two to two."

"I believe I came first. So the point goes to me."

"Maybe you were faking it."

"You know I never fake it."

"Not even to win?"

She rose from the table and turned to look up at him with her pair of baby blues. He melted on the spot.

She shook her head slowly. "I never fake it. I came first."

"Fine, we'll call it a tie."

"Sore loser," she accused with a grin. "Fine. A tie. That makes it three to two. I'm still winning."

She kicked off her panties and practically skipped back into the kitchen to claim her plate of now cool lasagna.

She settled for sitting on a dishtowel while they ate at the dining room table. Naked. He hoped they'd take all of their meals naked. She was so beautiful sitting across from him—completely comfortable in her own skin—that he scarcely tasted the delicious lasagna he shoveled into his mouth.

"So I think Isaac is going to go back to Africa for a while," she said, poking at a bit of sausage with her fork.

He didn't like that she looked so depressed about the notion of Isaac leaving the continent. Eric was fucking stoked about the news himself.

"I'm sure he'll be happier there," she said.

"You're going to miss him, aren't you?" Eric asked, trying to ignore the stabs of jealousy spiking up his throat.

She nodded. "He just got back. We haven't even had time to go shopping together."

"*Shopping?*"

She grinned. "I should have realized he was gay a long time ago. The man loves to shop. We used to have so much fun together. Well, except when we tried to have sex. That never did feel quite right with him."

"Your vagina was trying to wait for me," Eric claimed. "It knew he wasn't the right dick for you."

She laughed. "Smart vagina. I should have listened to it. It knows a thing or two about dicks."

"I'm insanely jealous of that guy. Do you realize that?"

"Why?" she asked. "He's just a friend."

"A friend who fucked you before I did. A friend you loved before you loved me."

Her eyebrows crinkled together as she stared at her plate and took several small bites.

"I'll always love him, Eric."

His heart wrenched in two.

"But it's nothing like the love I feel for you," she continued. "He's just a friend." She shrugged. "Apparently he was always just a friend and I wanted it to be more, not because I felt more for him, but because..." She tapped her fork against her plate, still not looking at him. "Because it made *sense*. It was a logical relationship, not a passionate one. I never felt as if my world would end if Isaac was no longer in my life. I never got giddy with happiness just looking at him. I never thought I'd die if he didn't fuck me immediately. I never felt as if he completed me. Complemented me, yes, but he never *completed* me. Never made me feel whole, as if everything that was missing in my life was wrapped up in a perfect package and delivered directly to my heart."

She finally met Eric's eyes.

"Isaac never made me feel for even an instant the way you make me feel every moment since I met you, Eric. He's not your competition, he's lost somewhere in your shadow. So don't be jealous. There is nothing for you to be jealous of. The love I feel for Isaac is friendship, that's all it ever was. I just never realized what it was until I had real love. With you."

"I'll never be jealous of that douchebag again," Eric said, too overwhelmed with emotion to say anything more meaningful.

Rebekah laughed. "Good."

"But I am glad he's leaving the continent." Maybe a lion would eat him.

Rebekah rolled her eyes and shook her head. "He's not a threat to you, Eric."

"I know. I just like him better not being a threat halfway around the world."

"You'd like him once you got to know him," Rebekah said.

Eric doubted that, but he let it drop. He didn't want to talk about Isaac. Now that his belly was full, he was ready to do a bit more celebrating with his bride. "Are you ready for dessert?"

"I'd love some cake," she said.

"You're having big hard sausage for dessert. Remember?"

"If I promise to be very good—having learned my lesson after your *brutal* spanking." She smirked at him. "Can I have two desserts tonight?"

"Of course." He slipped from his chair and leaned over to kiss her before taking their plates to the kitchen and cutting two mostly intact pieces of birthday cake.

When he returned to her, she was staring down at her wedding ring, twisting it around her finger. She had *that* expression on her face. The one of sad longing she wore when she thought about not being able to have a baby.

"What's wrong?" he asked, slipping into the seat beside her this time.

She shook her head slightly. "Everything is perfect," she said and smiled up at him.

"We'll adopt a baby," he said. "We can head to an agency right now if you want."

She huffed on a half laugh. "How did you know I was thinking about babies?"

"You have a thinking-about-babies expression," he said. "I've seen it frequently enough that I recognize it."

"I was just thinking I'll never be able to pass this ring down to my children," she said.

"Why not?"

"Well, because even if we adopt a dozen of them—"

"A *dozen* of them?"

She patted his hand. "They won't be blood."

He lifted an eyebrow at her. "What's more important? Blood or love?"

When she paused in reflection, he took her hand and squeezed it. "Love is more important," he said. "Love. I have no blood ties, but I have you. It's far more important."

She nodded. "You're right. I'm being foolish. I just... Sometimes I..."

He stroked the silky hair at the back of her head. "I know. You never have to say it. I know you feel you've lost something irreplaceable, but there are kids out there who've lost something irreplaceable too. They've lost the love of their mothers. You can give them that. It will mean everything to them. Trust me on that."

She gave him a rather watery smile and wrapped her arms around him. "I love you," she whispered.

"Eat your cake," he said after a long moment.

"And then sausage," she said with a giggle.

"You didn't think I'd forget that, did you?"

He won a point in the living room, when Rebekah sucked her dessert into submission on the sofa. Rebekah's point on the stairs came easily—literally—and they agreed to call their tryst against the tile wall in the master bathroom shower a tie. They hadn't even started on the first of their six bedrooms when Rebekah called a timeout.

"Can we finish tomorrow?" she asked, leaning against the inside of the bathroom door, a fluffy white towel wrapped around her exhausted body.

"Are you giving up?" he asked.

"If I give up, do you win?" she asked wearily.

He rubbed the water from his sopping hair with a towel as he watched her. "Yep."

"Well, that ain't happening. To bed with you, husband," she said.

She crawled up onto the bed, flopped onto her back, and held her arms out to the ceiling. "Take me. I'm yours," she said.

He was going to have to pull out some marital aids, he decided, and headed toward the closet. He knew he'd be unable to get hard again for at least an hour and surely Rebekah would need more stimulation than usual to come after that gusher she'd just had in the shower.

By the time he made it to bed with a six-pack of vibrators pressed against his bare belly, Rebekah had fallen asleep. He grinned and whispered, "I win," but he knew damned well he'd have no problem reinstating their competition in the morning. They couldn't leave this game between them unfinished.

He set the vibrators within reach on the nightstand, planning to give her one hell of a morning wakeup call, and lit a candle. He switched off the overhead light and climbed into bed with his wife. She sighed contentedly when he drew her into his arms and flipped the comforter over their entwined bodies.

His body was tired, but his mind was so full, he doubted he'd ever sleep. So he held her and instead of shutting the world away, he let his thoughts wander. Unfortunately they wandered in ways he didn't necessarily like.

Near sunrise, Eric rested on one elbow so he could stare down into the sweet face of his wife while she slept. The candle on the bedside table flickered wildly as it burned up the last of its fuel. Eric's mind was still too full to sleep. His heart too full to move from her side. He traced one of her eyebrows with a fingertip, overwhelmed by the tenderness she stirred within him. At times he wanted to cradle her against him gently, afraid she'd break. At other times he longed to squeeze her tightly, to make sure she could feel the strength of his love. God knew he'd never be able to express it with the depth he felt it. She filled so much within him he'd never realized was hollow. But there were still a few places she couldn't touch. Couldn't fill. He wondered if he could love Rebekah better if he were whole.

If he tried to fill those spots of emptiness that had been left behind early in his childhood, maybe he could be a man worthy of her attention.

Maybe it was time.

Time to seek out his mother. Time to know the truth about why the heartless bitch had abandoned him. He didn't even know if the woman was alive. Wasn't sure if he *cared* if she was alive. But if she was... If she was, he wanted to know. Needed to face her. He'd thought that by burying her abandonment beneath years and years of disregard, she would cease to haunt him, but he'd been pretending. With Rebekah by his side, for the first time in his life Eric had the courage to find answers to questions that had eaten at him for years. With Rebekah by his side, he could face anything.

He was no longer alone.

Eric tugged Rebekah's small body solidly against his chest, his heart thudding painfully beneath her temple. She stirred, her arm moving to circle his waist.

"Eric?" she murmured.

He remembered a time when she'd woken from sleep and, unfamiliar with having strange men in her bed, she'd called him Isaac. Now the only name she whispered when pulled from her dreams was Eric's. He fucking loved that.

"Is it morning?" she murmured, her voice slurred with sleep.

"Not yet."

"Are you horny again already?" And instead of grumbling about his ceaseless libido interfering with her sleep, she turned her head to kiss his chest.

"Getting that way," he said with a grin.

Her hand reached up and sought his face, rubbing at the beard stubble she found beneath her fingertips. "Did you sleep well?"

Her breath warmed the skin of his chest and the achingly full heart within.

"I haven't slept at all," he said. "I've been watching you sleep."

"Why didn't you tell me you were the creepy stalker type?" she asked.

"You're on to me," he said with a grin. "Can't seem to help my limitless infatuation for you, Mrs. Sticks."

"Completely understandable. I'm pretty awesome, you know." She rasped her fingernails gently over his beard stubble.

"I know." He pressed a kiss to her hair and forced himself to be serious, even though every instinct preferred to continue their light-hearted banter. "Do you really think we can find out about my mother?" he forced out.

Rebekah stiffened slightly and then tugged away from his chest so she could look at him in the low flicker of the candlelight. "I'm sure we can. Do you want to try?"

He worried his lower lip for a moment because he had promised not to lie to Rebekah and once he voiced this desire, there'd be no returning to his path of indifference. "I think so. The entire process will probably turn me into an emotional wreck or an insufferable asshole. You sure you can handle that?"

She nodded. "Yes, I know I can. With you beside me, I can handle anything."

He smiled. "Yeah, I feel that way too. It's the only reason I think I'm ready to face her."

"Then we'll find her and no matter what happens, I'll still love you." She gripped his chin in her hand and stared intently into his eyes. "You believe me, right?"

He gazed at her for a long moment, absorbing her affection, her love. He would probably never feel worthy of her, but he did believe her. She loved him. He could feel it in her touch, see it in her eyes, hear it in her voice when she spoke his name. Taste it in her kiss. It was real. She loved him. He believed. He'd never doubt it again.

"I do," he whispered and kissed her just as the candle flickered out and they were bathed in darkness. "I do believe, sweet love of mine."

Patience

Epilogue to Rock Hard

OLIVIA CUNNING

Chapter 1

GROGGY FROM SLEEP, SED ROLLED OVER in bed and reached for Jessica. When he found nothing but empty pillow, he felt a moment of panic. He lifted his head to see if the bathroom light was on and then checked the clock. Even though it was past eight, the room was more dimly lit than was typical for a southern Californian morning. It probably had something to do with the storm clouds he could see outside the French doors to the balcony. And the absence of his heart and soul probably had something to do with it being his wedding day.

And hers.

Jessica had wanted to stay in a hotel room the night before so they wouldn't see each other before the wedding, but three orgasms had exhausted her enough to keep her in his bed. At least for the night. She must have risen early and vacated the place. He could almost picture her with her hand over her eyes as she scooted out of the bed to avoid glimpsing him even in sleep. He made a mental note to tease her about it later. He'd only agreed to a traditional wedding because his family were expecting it and Jessica said she wanted one. He didn't care how the deed was done as long as he could make that woman his in the eyes of God, his friends and family, and the fine state of California. That way she would never leave him again.

Sed rolled out of bed and stood naked before the French doors, scowling at the angry clouds overhead. Jessica would be heartbroken if it rained today. He wanted her to be happy every day, but especially today. He wondered if the band's manager could do something about the weather. Jerry was a miracle worker when it came to keeping the band from falling apart, even though they'd gone through plenty of tragic events in the past couple of years. Surely the guy could stop a few rainclouds from dampening his day.

Sed's cellphone rang and he recognized the guitar-solo ringtone of his best man, Brian Sinclair.

"Are you up?" Brian asked in greeting.

Sed glanced down at his morning wood, which would have been stone hard if Jessica was in his morning routine, but it was already subsiding in her absence. "Not quite," he said.

"Jessica and Myrna just left with an entire van full of giggling women. We need to go round up the guys and pick up our tuxedos."

And how Jessica had ever talked him into wearing one of those, Sed would never know. At least she hadn't insisted he wear one of those ridiculous bow ties. That was not happening.

"I'll be over as soon as I get out of the shower."

"You nervous?" Brian asked.

"No," he said, but as soon as the words were out of his mouth, his stomach lurched in protest. "Not much," he amended.

"Jessica is a wreck this morning. Not that I blame her. Look who she's marrying."

One corner of Sed's mouth lifted in amusement. "Great, Brian. That's just what I need to hear this morning."

"Just remember I'm the nice one. Wait until Eric gets going."

"I'm looking forward to it," Sed said with a laugh. Nothing anyone said or did would keep him from marrying Jessica today. Not even Eric Sticks.

He found it hilarious that Jessica had set out proper socks and underwear for him in the bathroom. He'd gotten her really worked up the night before when he'd told her he was wearing white tube socks with his black tux and dress shoes. He did enjoy riling her. But he'd behave himself today. She was already under enough stress. Tonight, on the other hand, her temper was bound to get poked. And that wouldn't be the only thing he poked.

Like a good husband-to-be, he wore those dumbass, thin black dress socks with his basketball shorts, T-shirt, and cross-trainers. He just hoped no paparazzi were waiting at the gate of his condominium complex this morning. He felt as lame in the dress socks as he looked.

When he arrived at Brian's house, a party of cars was already parked in the long driveway. He recognized Aggie's black Mustang, his sister's Toyota, Eric's Corvette, and the big van that Rebekah drove to haul her brother Dave and his wheelchair around. Jessica's car was there as well. He really wished he'd gotten to see her that morning. His day never started right when he had to start it without her.

Sed rang the doorbell and was ushered into the house by Brian. He was surprised the man wasn't holding his son. The kid was always attached to Brian's arm except when he was on stage playing his guitar. He occasionally let Sed hold him. And nothing filled Sed with wonder more than snuggling his friend's baby against chest except the knowledge that in seven months he'd be cuddling one of his own.

"Where's Malcolm?" Sed asked.

"With his mother," Brian said. "Come in. Did you have breakfast? Myrna said to make sure you ate something. She doesn't want you fainting at the altar."

Sed laughed. "Why the fuck would I faint?"

"It happens more than you think. Remember when Trey fainted at Malcolm's birth?"

"Shut up, assmunch," Trey said as he entered the room on cue.

"I missed that, unfortunately," Sed said.

"Invite him to Jessica's delivery," Brian said, "and behold the hilarity for yourself."

"I don't think Jessica will want an audience of Trey."

"I don't know," Trey said. "It's not like I've never witnessed the two of you fucking in the bed right beside me."

"We thought you were asleep," Sed said.

"Dude," Eric said, loping into the foyer to join the festivities, "where the fuck did you get those socks?"

"Jessica said I have to wear them with my tux." Sed looked down at his socks and scowled.

"You could have brought them and changed into them later instead of wearing them now," Eric said.

He punched Eric in the shoulder. "But I want to make sure they're nice and smelly before the ceremony."

The mechanical whir of Dave's wheelchair announced his arrival into the increasingly crowded foyer.

"Why are we all congregating out here?" Dave said. "The strippers are getting lonely."

"Strippers?" Sed's band and crew had thrown him a wild and rather incriminating bachelor party a few nights before. He didn't need any repeats this morning.

Brian chuckled and shook his head. "Myrna's having some work done in the dining room. They're stripping wallpaper off the walls this morning."

"Good one, Dave!" Eric said with a hearty laugh.

"I think I've been hanging around with you too much," Dave said. "Your lame sense of humor is wearing off on me."

"Five minutes is too much when it comes to Eric," Sed teased.

"That's what she said," Dave added with a laugh.

Eric had no qualms against smacking his brother-in-law in the forehead.

"Where's Jace?" Sed asked, noting the absence of the final member of his band.

"Asleep on Brian's couch," Trey said. "You know he doesn't function before noon."

"I think Aggie got a little vicious with him last night in the dungeon," Eric said. "It's got to be rough for them on the road without their St. Andrew's cross."

"I heard that," Jace called from the living room off to the right of the foyer.

"What are you going to do about it, Tripod?" Eric asked.

"Gift you an hour-long session from Aggie when she's on her period."

"Eww, why when she's on her period?" Eric asked, his long nose crinkled in disgust.

"Because she's twice as vicious when she's in a really bad mood."

Sed still hadn't taken Jessica for a training session with Aggie. He wasn't afraid or anything. But now that Jess was pregnant, he couldn't imagine that her using a cane on him to work through her frustrations would be good for the baby. Yeah, good excuse. It was bad for the baby.

Brian presented Sed with a piece of paper. "Jessica said you are to follow this schedule and not deviate from it at all."

Sed scanned the contents, scowling at things like *trim nails* and *brush teeth*. What? Was he five? He glanced at his fingernails and decided they could use a trim, but still... He could plan things on his own. In fact, he'd planned their entire wedding dinner on his own. When he'd realized that a morning wedding and an afternoon reception meant they'd have the evening free, he'd taken it upon himself to arrange something special so he could celebrate his new wife in style. Having sex in another unusual location had only been part of his motivation for devising his plan. He'd rock her world tonight, he had no doubt. But he knew how important it was for her day to go without a hitch, so he'd follow her stupid list without argument.

Eric handed him a pink box that looked like something a three-year-old would store her beloved plastic princess tiara in.

"What's this?" Sed asked.

"This is where you'll keep your balls once you're married," Eric said. "Jess probably doesn't want to continue keeping them for you."

Eric ducked in time to avoid Sed's retaliating slap.

"It only hurts for a minute," Brian said, "and then you'll wonder why you ever insisted on holding on to them in the first place."

This bit of teasing was nothing compared to the massive ball and chain they'd manacled to his leg during his bachelor party. They hadn't removed it until late the next day. Luckily, Jess thought it was hilarious when he came to bed that night and had to sleep in his jeans with his leg dangling outside the covers. It had been Jace who'd finally come to his rescue. Probably because the manacle had originated in Aggie's dungeon.

"I need mine for baby making," Sed said and handed the box back to Eric. "And keeping my woman in line."

Even the strippers in the dining room laughed at that claim.

Chapter 2

JESSICA LOOKED SKYWARD and frowned at the heavy black clouds rolling in. Not a good omen, she decided. Especially since her wedding was scheduled to start in two hours and was supposed to take place on the beach.

"It can't rain," she said to Myrna, who was driving her from her nail appointment to her hair appointment. "It just can't."

Myrna scrunched her neck so she could see the sky better out the windshield of her minivan, a vehicle Jessica couldn't believe the woman owned, much less drove. But the soft coo from the back seat—where four-month-old Malcolm was secured in his car seat—was the only excuse Myrna needed. Jessica supposed any mother would give up driving her '57 Thunderbird convertible to keep her baby safe. And the van came in handy for lugging Jessica's bridesmaids from one appointment to the next. It even had room for the only male tagging along for the day.

"Can't is a strong word," Myrna said.

"We've been planning this for months."

"And what was the backup plan for rain?" Aggie asked from the seat directly behind Jessica.

"There is no backup plan for rain."

"It won't rain," Reagan called from the very back seat of the van, where she was sitting with Eric's wife, Rebekah, and Sed's youngest sister, Elise. "I won't let it."

Jessica hoped Reagan's confidence had the desired effect. She wanted this wedding to be over with. The planning of it had been driving her nuts. She needed everything to be perfect and everyone to have a memorable and enjoyable time, but mostly she just wanted to be Sed's wife. God, she couldn't wait to see him in his tux. He'd worn one to the Grammy's during the two years they'd been separated and when she'd seen him in it on television, she'd nearly swallowed her tongue. Not that she'd ever admit to watching the awards in hopes of catching a glimpse of him, because at that time she'd hated his fucking guts. At least that was what she'd been trying to convince herself. Good thing she'd finally figured out that beneath the arrogance and domineering behavior beat the heart of a good man. A man she loved more than anything. A man who made her toes curl and her heart thud.

Maybe *he* could stop the rain.

"I can call the crew and ask them to set up a beer tent," Rebekah offered.

Uh, no. Jessica refused to get married in a beer tent. She'd rather be drowned by rain.

"Thanks for the offer, sweetie," she called, "but it can't rain. It just can't."

"You should have eloped," Sed's sister, Kylie, said from her seat between Aggie and Malcolm's car seat.

"I tried to tell Sed that," Elise said. "But would he listen? Of course not. This is bullheaded Sed we're talking about here. He doesn't listen to anything anyone tells him."

Sed would have eloped if Jessica had wanted to, but silly her, she'd thought having a big wedding with seven bridesmaids, seven groomsmen, and who even knew how many ushers would be fun. So far, not so fun. And if it rained on their big day... Jessica wasn't going to let herself think about that.

Feeling as if she were forgetting some important detail, she ran a mental checklist and toyed with the engagement ring on her finger, rubbing the band into her flesh. The inexpensive piece of jewelry meant the world to her; it was by far her most cherished possession. And not because it meant she belonged to Sed, but because he'd carried it around with him for two years while they'd been separated. He might have behaved like a horny imbecile for the entirety of their time apart, but he'd never stopped thinking about her, just as she'd never stopped thinking of him.

"Don't forget to put that on a different finger for the ceremony," Myrna said as they sat waiting for a red light to change to green.

She glanced up. "What?"

"You're getting a new ring today," she said. "You're supposed to wear the wedding band close to your heart."

"This is the one that's closest to my heart," she said, but she slipped the ring off and put it on her right hand. It felt weird there, but she didn't want to mess up at the ceremony. Everything needed to be perfect because as wonderful as it was to be engaged to Sed, being his wife would bring her even more joy.

"I feel like I've forgotten something," Jessica said, going through her mental checklist one more time.

"You haven't forgotten anything," Myrna assured her and

smiled into her rearview mirror as she checked on her son who was giggling at Kylie's game of peek-a-boo.

"Beth!" Jessica shouted as her subconscious churned out the missing piece of her morning. Her best friend was a rather important part of the ceremony.

"Did I forget to tell you she called?" Myrna asked sheepishly.

Jessica's breath caught. "Is she okay? She's coming, isn't she?"

"Everything is fine. She overslept and is running late. She's going to meet us at the salon after she picks up the dresses."

Even though the bridal shop was on the opposite side of town near Beth's apartment, Jessica probably should have picked up the dresses herself. If Beth didn't show with them in time, they might as well call off the whole wedding.

"Breathe, Jess," Myrna said and reached over to pat her shoulder.

Jessica sucked a breath into her lungs and attempted to put her head between her knees but was halted by the seatbelt cutting into her shoulder.

"Ow." She laughed at her own stupidity and rubbed at her sore collarbone.

Everything will be fine, she told herself, but herself wasn't buying it.

At the beauty salon, Jessica's hair was yanked, teased, curled, braided, coiled, pinned, and tucked until her wedding veil and long strawberry-blond hair were an entwined work of art.

"Wow, Jess," Myrna said, her own hair in the small and mighty fist of the son she had resting against one shoulder. "You look stunning."

She smiled. "So do you," she said just as Malcolm grasped the pearl adorning one of the bobby pins in his mother's auburn hair and tugged it free. This sent half of Myrna's carefully styled up-do cascading down one shoulder.

"Mal," Myrna said with exasperation, "those aren't to play with."

The adorable, black-haired baby, who looked so much like his gorgeous guitarist father his mother didn't stand a chance, laughed with an orneriness rivaling Trey's. The tyke was immediately forgiven.

"Will someone hold him while I get the damage repaired?" Myrna asked, holding Malcolm around the middle and out of reach of another pearl he was staring at intently.

Rebekah claimed the honor. She touched Malcolm's tiny fingers and traced the lines of his face. She was obviously completely enamored. And who could blame her? Jessica would have loved to have held Malcolm, but if Myrna's tiny pin pearls weren't safe from his grasp, Jessica's veil would never survive the interaction.

As soon as the make-up artist was finished with Aggie, she went to work on Jessica's face. Though the woman had been unable to talk Aggie out of wearing her typical red lipstick, she'd toned down her usual heavy eyeliner for a more understated look. Jessica wouldn't have minded Aggie showing up looking the way she always did, though she was glad she wasn't planning on wearing her corset and thigh-high boots. Jessica's grandparents would likely have keeled over on the spot if she had.

The salon door flew open and Beth dashed into the waiting area, her blue eyes wild and her tangle of brown hair even wilder. "I'm here," she announced.

Jessica's shoulders sagged with relief. "Took you long enough."

Beth spotted her and rushed to her side. "Oh God, I'm so sorry, Jess. I was up late studying and fell asleep on the sofa and didn't hear the alarm go off and then I couldn't find my keys and finally found them in yesterday's jeans, but then I was halfway to the salon and remembered I needed clean underwear and had to go back to the house to get them out of the drier and—" She finally sucked in a deep breath. "Can you ever forgive me?"

"Did you remember to pick up the dresses?" Jessica asked.

"Of course. They're locked in the car."

"Then you are forgiven. But you owe me ice cream for making me worry." Jessica winked at her.

Beth hugged her. In her haste, she knocked aside the eye shadow brush the make-up artist was using on one of Jessica's lids. The woman scowled and reached for a cloth to undo the damage.

"You're the best," Beth said loudly in Jess's ear.

"You're the best," Jessica returned. "Thank you for picking up the dresses."

"No problem."

Beth was hurriedly directed to a chair so her bed hair could be tamed into something more appropriate for the occasion and Jessica relaxed. A little.

When all seven ladies were properly beautified, they returned to the van. Beth climbed into her dated sedan to follow them to the venue with her cargo of dress. Jessica would have ridden with her to keep her company, but every inch of Beth's trunk was stuffed with books so the backseat was full of bridesmaids' dresses while Jess's wedding dress rode shotgun. Jessica hoped she'd have time to catch up with Beth later. She didn't get to see nearly enough of her friend since their lives had taken different paths.

Jessica scowled up at the clouds as soon as she was belted into Myrna's van. The sky was even darker than when they'd entered the salon, but the rain was still holding off. Thank God.

Jessica continued to stare at the sky all the way to the beach location where the ceremony was to be performed. Perhaps it was just gloomy and the clouds would clear up before she walked down the aisle at eleven. Maybe she should have scheduled an afternoon wedding instead of a morning ceremony. She bit her lip. Maybe it was too late to change any plans so she should stop worrying so much. She was supposed to be enjoying her time today.

She fought the urge to call Sed to ask him to commiserate. He'd understand why she was so worried about this; he'd been dealing with her insanity over the wedding for months. Sometimes she was astonished that he still wanted to marry her.

Myrna parked the van near the small building where they were to change into their dresses. Closer to the shore, the small white tent where she'd wait to make her entrance had already been erected and the rows of white wooden folding chairs set up. Several people were decorating the aisles with red roses and sprigs of baby's breath, trailing lace, and satin ribbons in red and white. The decorating was going rather smoothly, considering how breezy it was.

Maybe she was worried about nothing. The women chatted among themselves as they entered the little beach house. Jessica paused at the dining room table to admire the bouquets set in a neat row. All eight of the smaller bouquets matched hers. The only difference was that the bridal bouquet was larger and had white lilies worked into the red roses. She bent to draw the sweet lily scent into her nose and sneezed unexpectedly.

She drew away and sneezed again. And again.

"Are you allergic to your flowers?" Beth asked.

Jessica's eyes and nose began to itch and ache. "I must be," she said, her voice nasally from the sudden swelling in her face. She sneezed again and again, backing away from the offending allergens wafting from her bouquet.

"What am I going to do?" she asked. "I can't say my vows if

I'm"—*ah ah ahchoo*—"sneezing the entire time." She sniffed, searching the room for a box of tissues.

"I'm allergic to certain flowers," Myrna said. "You just have to pinch off the anthers. Or is the stamens? Gets rid of the pollen."

"I'll take your word for it," Jessica said, hoping she was right.

Myrna picked up the bouquet and headed into the small kitchen near the back of the cottage. Jessica sneezed again as she passed by, but felt less bothered once the flowers were taken from the room.

"I didn't sneeze when they showed me their samples," Jessica said to Beth, who handed her a tissue. Jessica blew her nose and blinked to prevent her watery eyes from ruining her make-up.

"Because their samples were fake flowers," Beth said. "Remember?"

Beth had gone with Jessica to pick out most of the items for the wedding since Sed had been on the road touring with Sinners almost the entire time she'd been planning the occasion. But she'd sent him pictures of everything and asked his opinion on every detail. He hadn't lost his patience once, even though she must have been driving him bonkers. He probably didn't give a rat's ass if the red ribbons in the flowers were matte or satin, but she had required his opinion on the matter, by God, and he offered one. She'd wanted him to feel he was a part of every decision, every step leading up to this day. She wasn't the only one getting married today.

Jessica chuckled. "You're right. I guess that would explain why I wasn't allergic to them at the florist."

"I hope removing the anthers does the trick," Beth said. "Are you ready to put on your dress?"

Jessica nodded eagerly. It had been a couple of weeks since she'd seen it. They'd done a few last minute alterations so that it would fit perfectly. Which reminded her again that she couldn't wait to see him in his tux. She sighed aloud at the thought of those wide shoulders filling out a perfectly tailored tuxedo jacket. The man cleaned up real nice and looked delicious in and out of his clothes.

In one of the two bedrooms, Beth helped Jessica slip into her gown. At Jessica's back, Beth tugged the zipper, but it wouldn't budge.

"Is it stuck?" Jessica asked, glancing over her shoulder to see what the problem was.

She went light-headed; the problem was that the edges of the zipper were over two inches apart. There was no way they'd ever get it zipped.

"Oh no," Jessica said. "Sed told me I was showing already, but I didn't believe him."

She covered her lower belly with both hands where Sed's baby grew inside her.

"If I'm this fat now, what am I going to be like in seven months?"

"You're not fat," Beth said. "The baby is just big. Like his hunk of a father."

Jessica wasn't sure if she believed that explanation, but it made her feel marginally better. "What are we going to do?" she asked.

"Can you suck it in?" Beth asked, yanking on the open sides of the dress.

Jessica drew her breath upward into her chest, trying to make her stomach as flat as possible. But the problem wasn't her stomach, it was her lower belly. Perhaps she should have chosen a gown that had an empire waist instead of one that was fitted down to mid-hip. She'd thought she'd have plenty of time before her baby bump made any sort of difference in the fit of her clothes.

"I can't," Jessica said as she released her breath with a gasp.

"I will get you into this dress if I have to kick you into it," Beth said.

"I think I have a corset that will fit you," Aggie said.

Jessica hadn't heard her approach. She was standing in the open doorway, appraising her carefully.

"It's white, so it shouldn't show, and it goes down past the crests of the hipbones, so it will cinch you in tight. But it's leather. You don't have anything against leather, do you?"

Could Jessica really wear a white leather corset under her wedding gown? What would Sed think of that? She decided he'd be so turned on that he wouldn't be able to think.

"Do you think it will work?" Jessica said.

Aggie nodded. "For sure. I'll have to go get it though. Do we have time?"

"I can't very well go down the aisle with my dress unzipped," Jessica said. "I'd be grateful if you could get it if you think it's worth a shot. It won't hurt the baby, will it?"

"No, we won't squeeze you breathless. You just need a couple of inches. I'll be back.

Aggie turned on her heel, her long straight black hair spinning out away from her body as she moved.

"Thanks, Aggie!" Jessica called after her.

"Not a problem," Aggie called back.

Beth lifted her eyebrows. "A white leather corset? The things my cousin comes up with."

"She's been selling her handmade corsets from a little merch wagon that's pulled behind Sinners' tour bus. Her wares are so popular, she has to turn customers away. Have you seen them?"

"No. I didn't know she was running a business now. I thought she was still stripping in Vegas," Beth said.

Jessica laughed. "You two don't talk much, do you?"

"Her mom and my mom don't really get along," Beth whispered. "Aunt Tabitha's the black sheep of the family. And then Aggie... Well, she's just kind of different. Intimidating?" Beth's dark brows scrunched together. "Or maybe the word is scary. Yeah, Aggie is scary."

Jessica grinned and shook her head. Aggie just pretended to be scary, but underneath the leather and cold stares, she was a pussy cat. "Aggie's fabulous. You really should get to know her better, Beth. Don't let the whips and leather scare you away."

Beth laughed. "Do you even hear what you're saying?"

"You're the one who sent me to Vegas to be taken under her wing, remember?"

"Yeah, well..." Beth shrugged. "Maybe I was living vicariously. All I do is study, study, study. At least you get to have a life. I don't think I'm ever going to pass the bar."

"You'll pass," Jess said, patting her on the back.

"Easy for you to say, brainiac who passed on her first try."

"Jessica?" The unmistakable high-pitched voice of her mother carried through the entire cottage. "Jessica?"

"Oh shit," Jessica said. "She's here? I thought she'd be kept occupied at the reception hall until the ceremony."

"Jessica, where are you?" her mother called.

"I don't want her to know my dress doesn't fit," Jessica whispered to Beth. "You know what she's like. She'll never let me live it down."

Wide-eyed, Beth glanced around the room and then pulled the quilt from the bed. She tossed it over Jessica's back, who crinkled her brow at her in confusion.

"Pretend you're cold," she said just as Jessica's mother entered the room.

Jessica pulled the quilt more securely around her shoulders, huddling into it as if she was in the Northwest Territories in January instead of Southern California in June.

"There you are," her mom said, breezing into the room. "Why didn't you answer when I called?"

"You called?" Jessica played dumb. "I didn't hear you."

"The reception hall is all ready to go. I told you that you could count on me to make your day perfect."

Jessica's day had been far from perfect thus far, but she smiled at her mother.

"Thank you for working so hard on the reception arrangements."

The woman had tried to take over the entire wedding. And then Sed's mom had gotten in on the planning, and the preparations had turned into a constant argument. Sed's mom thought they should get married in a church. Jessica's mom thought they should fly everyone to Paris and get married there. Jessica had cherished memories of her and Sed atop the Eiffel Tower replica in Vegas, but Paris? She wasn't sure where that idea had come from. She'd certainly never mentioned wanting to visit Paris, much less wanting to get married there. She assumed her mother had always wanted to get married abroad and was attempting to live vicariously through her only daughter. The entire time they were planning the wedding, Jessica had felt pulled in a thousand directions. She'd tried to find a compromise, but sometimes there just wasn't one to be had. Luckily, Sed gave her the support necessary to tell both mothers where *she* wanted to get married. On the beach.

Sed's mother had taken the news without batting an eyelash and had immediately starting collecting information on possible locations. Her mother, on the other hand, said a beach wedding wasn't grand enough for her daughter. Jessica wasn't sure when her mother started thinking she had much value. Probably the minute she'd become engaged to a rich rock star.

"Why are you wrapped up in a blanket?" Mom asked, eyeing her speculatively.

"Just a little cold," Jessica said, tugging the blanket closer and pretending to shiver.

"Are you sick?"

"No," Jessica said, shaking her head. "I think it's nerves."

"Well, don't get cold feet now. The deposits are nonrefundable."

"My feet are perfectly warm," Jessica assured her.

"I know you'll be disappointed, but Ed isn't coming," Mom said. "He had something important to attend to."

A date with his favorite sports channel, Jessica presumed. She nodded, not really caring that her stepfather wouldn't be there. They weren't exactly close. She'd only invited him because it was expected of her. Ed was pretty much a creeper and had been since her mother married him just after Jessica had turned seventeen.

"That's all right, Mom. I know how hard he works." To help you live above your means, Jessica added silently.

"Where's Monica?"

Jessica shrugged. Unlike her mother, who needed constant recognition for the smallest of tasks, Sed's mother got things done and required no supervision.

Sed's youngest sister, Elise, spoke up. "Mom's out with the florist helping with the arbor over the altar. They're trying to figure out how to keep the flowers in place with all the wind."

"She probably needs my help," Jessica's mom said and she turned to go.

Jessica felt a touch sorry for Monica, but at least her mother would be out of her hair for a while.

"I wonder if Sed is here yet," Jessica said. She hadn't spoken to him all day. She missed him. Usually when he wasn't on tour, they were inseparable. And when he was on tour without her, she was miserable. It had only been twelve hours since she'd seen him last, yet it felt like ages. Maybe she should have watched him sleep for a while that morning instead of covering her eyes with her hands when she sneaked out of bed to avoid seeing him before the wedding.

"You should text him," Beth advised. "Make sure he got up."

Sed had still been asleep when she'd left. She trusted that he'd gotten out of bed on time, and if he hadn't, she knew Brian would retrieve him if necessary. Before the bridal party left that morning, Brian had given her his word to keep Sed in line, though the thought of anyone keeping Sed in line was rather ludicrous now that she thought about it. Perhaps she should have enlisted the aid of his mother. But Monica had enough to keep her occupied as she was in charge of overseeing the setup of the beach for the ceremony. Still, Jessica couldn't resist texting Sed. Not to check up on him. Even though today was about celebrating their closeness, she felt very far away from him at the moment.

Happy Wedding Day, she texted. *I can't wait to marry you.*

After she sent the text, she helped Beth zip up the long red bridesmaid gown she'd chosen. All of Jessica's bridesmaids would wear the same color but because each member of her bridal party was unique, she hadn't forced them all to get the same dress. They'd picked gowns they liked, that she hoped they could wear again. She wasn't sure how Sed would feel about the sexy dresses his little sisters had chosen, but she wasn't going to tell them they couldn't wear them. They were grown women, not the girls in pigtails he still thought of them as. Jessica had had enough angst thrown in her direction over the decision when her mother had found out that the bridesmaids weren't going to be dressed as clones. Mom had thrown a huge fit about them looking like a mismatched group of beggars. Jessica had ultimately won that battle, however. And though they were all dressed differently, the deep red color made them look harmonious enough. She liked that they didn't all look exactly the same.

Jessica was pacing by the time Aggie returned over half an hour later with the corset. What if she was too fat to get into the contraption? And why hadn't Sed texted her back? And was her mother still harassing Sed's mom? She hadn't returned yet. And why was Malcolm crying again? She needed the baby to be in a good mood today. Or at the very least, asleep.

"Did you really make this, Aggie?" Beth said in breathless awe as she rubbed her hand over the pale pink orchids embroidered into the leather of the white corset.

"Yeah."

"Where did you learn to sew like this? It's gorgeous."

"Grandma taught me."

Beth chuckled. "Yeah, she tried to teach me too, but I ended up pricking all my fingers and never finished anything. I guess you had a natural talent."

Aggie bit her lip. "No, I just persisted because I wanted an excuse to sit with her. She was always too busy to slow down, except when she was sewing."

"Oh," Beth said and she smiled, no longer looking terrified of her own cousin.

Jessica tried not to gloat. She slipped out of her dress, with Beth holding it up, and then stepped toward Aggie.

"This was supposed to be your wedding gift by the way," Aggie said to Jessica. "I had to dig through hundreds of gifts in the reception hall to find it and then the caterer thought I was trying to steal it."

"Sorry you had to go through so much trouble due to my unquenchable cravings for rocky road ice cream," Jessica said, poking at her belly that was not all baby. Most of it was her.

Aggie wrapped the corset around her.

"I didn't mind," Aggie said, cinching the lacings at Jessica's back. "Too tight?" she asked, concern in her voice.

"No," Jessica said. She felt very tall for some reason. If the corset didn't make her a bit thinner, at the very least it gave her fantastic posture. "You can tighten it more."

"You have me worried about the baby now," Aggie said.

"He's about the size of my thumb at the moment. Doesn't take up much room."

"Can you get enough air, though?"

Jessica nodded. "I'm fine. Really."

"You look sexy as hell in that thing," Beth said. "I almost wish I was a lesbian. Will you embroider one for me, Aggie? Not that I have a man to wear it for, but I can wear it while I study. Maybe it would help me think."

Aggie chuckled. "Of course, hon. And maybe you'll meet someone at the reception. There are at least ten thousand people coming, judging by the size of that reception hall."

"Only five hundred," Jessica said, rolling her eyes. She would never in a million years figure out how her mother had found five hundred people to attend the reception, much less RSVP that they were coming. Jessica didn't know five hundred people. Maybe they were all Sed's acquaintances. She hadn't recognized many of the names on the guest list. At least she and Sed had gotten the final say on the guest list for the wedding, though her mother had kept sneaking people onto that as well.

She slipped her dress back up over her shoulders, closed her eyes and held her breath as Aggie zipped it. The gown zipped with ease. Jessica released a sigh of relief. She turned and hugged Aggie before bursting into tears.

Aggie hugged her tightly and patted her back. "Don't cry, kitten," she said. "You'll ruin your make-up and then we'll have to listen to your mother bitch some more."

Jessica laughed. More of a huff. It turned out that laughing was a chore when one was cinched tight into a corset. Maybe that's why Aggie didn't laugh very often. At least she hadn't been very joyful when she'd been acclimating Jessica to the stripper world in Vegas. Aggie laughed a lot more now that she was with Jace, and she still wore corsets.

Wiping at her tears, Jessica drew away from Aggie and plastered a smile on her face. "I owe you one, Aggie."

"I'll be getting married soon enough," she said. "I'm sure you'll help me out of a disaster or two."

Jessica lit up. This was the first time she'd heard Aggie actually mention her wedding, though she'd been engaged to Jace for almost a year. "Have you picked a date?"

She shook her head, straight black bangs dancing across her forehead. The woman had the most flawless white skin. She must never go out in the sun.

"We're waiting for a location to speak to us. There are things you just know are right, you know?"

Jessica nodded.

"So we'll get married when and where it feels right," Aggie said. "No rush. It's not like we're planning on having kids anytime soon."

"You'll have to change your dungeon into a kid friendly playroom instead of an adults-only one," Jessica teased.

Aggie chuckled, her laugh deep and throaty. "That's the main reason I'm in no hurry. I'm rather fond of that dungeon just the way it is. And Jace likes it even more than I do."

"Are all the corsets you make white?" Beth interrupted. From the expectant expression on her face, she'd been looking for an opening.

"Most are black." Aggie cupped the back of Jessica's head. "Feather looks gorgeous in white though."

Jessica flushed and then burst out laughing. "I'm never going to live that stripper name down, am I?"

"Not with me, kitten." Aggie winked at her and then turned to her cousin. Seeing them side by side, Jessica realized they looked a bit alike. Beth was far more understated than Aggie, so it was easy to overlook her beauty. Beth's hair was brown instead of black and she was tanned from the Southern Californian sun, but the cousins had the same bright blue eyes. Same thick lashes, lush lips, and knockout smile. Yet Aggie was vibrant, and Beth seemed ready to crawl into bed to take a nap. The poor dear needed to study less, Jessica decided. Maybe she could find some spare time to help her out. They'd always studied together when they were roommates.

Plus she hadn't seen near enough of Beth since moving in with Sed.

"Let's measure you for your corset, Beth," Aggie said. "I think you'll look great in black. What kind of design do you want embroidered?"

While Aggie and Beth discussed corsets, Jessica excused herself to go check on the rest of her bridal party. She found Elise and Kylie on the deck at the back of the house, watching the waves. The sky looked blacker than ever, but so far it hadn't started raining. Jessica just wanted it to hold off until she was married to Sed and then it could rain as much as it wanted. Reagan and Rebekah were talking music in the second bedroom—a conversation Jessica couldn't hope to participate in. She found Myrna in the living room with Malcolm in her arms. She was feeding him. Jessica practically melted as she leaned over the back of the sofa to watch him suckle. He had one hand splayed over his mother's breast. His dark brown eyes were fixated on her face as he sucked. Jessica couldn't wait to hold Sed's child to her breast and have him look up at her with his father's eyes. She could already picture it.

"He's so beautiful, Myrna," Jessica said.

"I can't argue," she said with a chuckle and rubbed the baby's cheek with one knuckle. "I happen to agree."

Malcolm paused and smiled up at Jessica around his mother's nipple. Jessica cooed at him, completely in love with the little guy.

"I think he has a crush on you," Myrna said. "He's going to be heartbroken when you marry his rival in an hour."

An hour? Jessica glanced at the clock over the television in the corner. It was a few minutes until ten. She would be married in just over an hour. Feeling suddenly light-headed, she moved around the sofa to flop down on the cushions.

"I should probably go check to make sure everything is ready," she said.

"Trust the people you put in charge," Myrna said. "Everything will go exactly as planned and if it doesn't..." She shrugged. "It doesn't matter as long as you end up married to the man you love, right?"

Jessica wasn't so sure, but she nodded at Myrna's words of wisdom. "Right."

When Malcolm finished feeding, Myrna settled him over her shoulder and patted his back. He let out a mighty belch.

Jessica giggled. "Well, there's something he got from his father."

"No, I do believe he inherited that from me." Myrna laughed as she patted her son's back.

"Can I hold him?" Jessica asked. Nothing would calm her nerves more than cuddling with her favorite future guitarist for a few moments.

Myrna handed Malcolm to her and rose to her feet. "I'm going to go find my shoes," she said, adjusting the bodice of her elegant red gown. "I'll be right back."

"No rush," Jessica assured her.

Malcolm immediately reached for Jessica's veil, but she moved him out of reach just in time, holding him at arms' length.

"Are you being naughty?" she asked in a high-pitched voice and made a face at him.

He giggled and blew a raspberry at her.

"Did you learn something new?" She blew a raspberry back at him.

He blew another raspberry, which was more an exercise in creating as much drool as possible and spraying it in all directions. They continued their giggling raspberry war until Malcolm's brown eyes widened unexpectedly and he spat milk. Jessica hadn't been fast enough, and the warm liquid landed on her dress between her boobs and slid down her front to pool on her lap.

"Shit," she said, leaping to her feet, still holding Malcolm at arm's length as she glanced down at the damage. "A little help here!" she called. "Malcolm just puked all over my dress."

Malcolm's lips twisted together, his little chin quivered, and his eyes filled with tears. His wails of apology tugged hard on Jessica's heartstrings.

"Shh, it's okay," she crooned and bounced him slightly. She couldn't very well cuddle him against her and spread the muck from her dress to his adorable miniature tuxedo.

Her entire bridal party rushed to her aid. Myrna took her son and tried to calm him down. Beth wiped. Elise blotted. Aggie ran to the kitchen to wet a towel.

"At least it's white," Reagan said. "It won't show much."

Could anything else go wrong this morning? Jessica wondered.

The front door opened, and her mother breezed into the little beach house, looking more grave than the Grim Reaper at his own funeral.

"We're going to have to delay the wedding," she said.

Apparently there was plenty more that could go wrong.

Chapter 3

SED WATCHED HIMSELF TRY TO FIX his weird-ass tie in the mirror. It wasn't like a regular tie at all. It was very wide and the fabric thin. It reminded him of an elongated cloth napkin. Morning tuxedo, Jessica had called it. Stupid was more like it. As he attempted to knot the tie for the fourth time, he wondered if Jessica would be incredibly upset if he tossed it in the garbage and claimed to have lost it. Finally giving up when the tie ended up looking like a clown collar, he stepped out of Brian's bedroom to ask for help. Yeah, him. Badass lead singer and rock star asking other dudes how to dress. The things he did to keep the love of his life happy.

"Does anyone know what to do with these stupid fucking ties?" he said.

He noted that all the members of his wedding party were fully dressed—with ties. Apparently he was the only dumbass who couldn't figure out how to tie the fucking thing.

"Over, under, around and through," Eric said, swirling his hands around as if translating Pig Latin into sign language.

"Jace tied ours," Brian said, and Eric scowled at him for not giving him sufficient time to fuck with Sed's head.

"Jace?" Sed asked.

"He's like a wedding expert," Trey said about the man in question, who was blushing furiously and trying to look like a tough guy at the same time. "Weirdest shit I've ever seen."

"My mom used to play piano and organ at weddings," Jace said. "She didn't want to hire a babysitter, so she forced me to go with her and I learned a few tricks over the years." He shrugged as if it were normal for a young male to pick things up about weddings. "What can I say? I was a cute little boy."

"Don't short-change yourself just because you're short," Eric said. "You're still a cute little boy." He pinched Jace's cheek, distorting his face into something comical.

"Fuck you, Sticks," Jace said, slapping at his hand.

"Aww, will you look at that face?" Eric said, stretching Jace's cheek into an even more distorted shape. "He was obviously a fairy wedding princess in a past life and is using this cute little boy claim as a cover."

He released Jace's face to punch him squarely in the shoulder.

Jace ignored the assault, but Sed didn't doubt that Jace would get even with Eric later. When Eric was least expecting it.

"Sit and I'll tie it for you," Jace offered to Sed.

So Sed sat on a spare ottoman and Jace stood behind him, reaching around his neck to tie his tie. Sed was going to have to beat up someone after subjecting himself to this level of feminization and having a man who wasn't his dad tying his tie for him. It couldn't be his dad because Dad had passed away a couple months before. Had he lived, would he have known how to tie the ridiculous accessory? Sed doubted it. His dad had been very blue collar. He'd only owned one tie—a clip-on, at that—and had only worn it on Sundays and to his grave.

Jace slapped Sed's shoulder when he'd finished. "There you go," he said.

"Thanks," Sed said gruffly. He glanced down at the neat knot at his throat and the perfect creases on either side of it. "Wow, Jace really is a fairy wedding princess. What. A. Pussy."

Sed wasn't expecting to be tackled to the floor by Jace. Eric body-slammed Jace into Sed's chest, and soon they were all buried in a dog pile of hard bodies and flailing arms and legs. He wasn't able to deliver a single blow of retaliation. Sed supposed they were all feeling a bit tense and domesticated. So acting like a sextet of immature idiots—even Dave had abandoned his wheelchair to join the wrestling match—did wonders for Sed's level of anxiety. It didn't do much good for the perfectly pressed condition of his tuxedo, but fuck it. If today didn't go as planned for him and Jessica, they'd get past it. The only thing that could possibly ruin his day was if she stood him up at the altar. But she wouldn't do that to him. She couldn't leave him in misery again. She wouldn't.

Would she?

Of course not.

Sed grabbed someone's arm and heard a yelp of pain from Trey. A knee landed uncomfortably close to Sed's crotch, and he stiffened. Okay, destroying his junk would also ruin his day. He had big plans for his fifth appendage that evening.

"Off!" he yelled and then added, "*Umph*," as an elbow connected with his stomach.

It took a while for everyone to feel as if they'd gotten in all the licks they were entitled to, but eventually they collected themselves enough to get into the Blake's wheelchair-accessible van and head for the beach.

Through the windshield, Sed scowled at the dark sky overhead. He glanced at Eric in the driver's seat.

"You don't think it would dare rain on my wedding day, do you?"

"Rain on *The* Sedric Lionheart's wedding day?"

"Yeah."

"Rain on Mr. Lead Singer, Rock God, Control Freak, Boss of the Entire World's wedding day?"

"It wouldn't, would it?" Sed asked, scowling darkly at the rain clouds to put them in their fucking place.

Eric smirked. "Of course not."

"That's what I thought," he said, but he wasn't sure if the clouds had gotten his all-important memo.

Eric parked the van in one of the few disabled parking slots still available. The street in both directions was full of parked cars, as was the very small parking lot.

"Well, Dave," Eric joked, "you're good for more than mixing a live show after all. Premium parking!"

Sed reached over and slapped him for being an ass, but Dave just laughed.

"I'm keeping those plates even after I lose this chair," he vowed.

Which Sed feared would be never. Dave had progressed in his recovery to taking a few steps when necessary, but not much farther. His physical therapy was continually disrupted by their tour schedule and while his sister, Rebekah, helped him strengthen his wasted muscles, she wasn't a professional therapist. Maybe Sed should hire someone to handle that for him on the road. He didn't have any issue with Dave's inability to get around without his wheelchair and they'd had Dave's sound equipment modified for accessibility before they'd gone on tour with Exodus End, but he knew that Dave wanted to progress, and he couldn't do that on the road. This two-week-long break in the tour before they headed to Europe had been necessary to get all their equipment overseas. And for Sed to get married and have a decent honeymoon before getting back to work with a new wife in tow.

While he stood waiting for all the guys to get out of the van, Sed stared at the small beach house where he knew Jessica would be getting ready for the ceremony. A pang of longing set his feet in motion. He wanted to see her so bad, he couldn't wait another moment.

"There you are!" His mother's voice called from the beach. "I thought you were going to be late to your own wedding."

He stopped abruptly. Part of him was glad she'd stopped him before he'd ruined everything by barging into the house and demanding to see his bride before the ceremony. Another part of him cringed at her intrusion.

"Oh my," she said as she hugged him. "You look so handsome."

Sed gave her a vigorous squeeze in return, lifting her onto her tiptoes.

When he released her, she dabbed at her teary eyes with her fingertips.

"I promised myself I wouldn't cry today," she said, "and here you come looking all handsome and grown up in that tuxedo. You've ruined any chance I have at keeping that promise."

"What did you expect, ma? That I'd show up in leather and a T-shirt?"

She laughed and reached up to pat his cheek rather harder than necessary. "Maybe I did," she said. "I wish your father could have been here to see this." Fresh tears swam in her eyes.

Sed grabbed her in another hug so he didn't have to see the sorrow in her tired blue eyes. She'd aged in the two months since his dad's passing. "He's here," he whispered to her. "You know he wouldn't miss it."

She nodded and drew away, dabbing at her tears again.

"I think he's up in those dark rain clouds causing me undue anxiety," Sed admitted.

His mom laughed. "Exactly like something he'd do. He'd be proud of you today. He was always so proud of you."

"Ma, if you make me cry, you'll ruin my mascara." He fluttered his mascara-less eyelashes at her.

She laughed again and looped her arm through his. "Come. I'll show you where you're supposed to stand."

She peered over her shoulder at the tuxedoed rock stars goofing off in the parking lot. Trey was the only one not tussling. He had Ethan, one of the ushers, pressed up against the side of the van expressing his undying lust with deep passionate kisses.

"Guys," his mom said, and they all looked at her for direction.

Even Trey paused in his make-out session to see what was up. "Go into the house. They'll give you instructions there."

Trusting that his friends would do as they were told, Sed followed his mother onto the beach. They'd laid plywood in a strip between the white folding chairs and covered it with red carpeting that matched all the roses decorating every available spot.

"Is it normal to lay plywood?"

Mom shook her head. "We were worried Dave's chair would get stuck in the sand."

He smiled. "You thought of everything, didn't you?"

She released a weary sigh and touched her fingertips to her lower lip. "I hope so. I want today to be perfect for you and Jess. If I hadn't, I would have murdered her mother with a candelabrum and tossed her to the sharks hours ago."

"You have more restraint than I do. And isn't she supposed to be dealing with the reception setup? Why was bugging you?"

"Beats the hell out of me. She's been here driving me nuts for the past two hours. Making changes when I'm not looking. Reserving seats for A-list actors you don't even know. She had your grandmother sitting in the third row; she wouldn't have been able to see a thing back there."

"Memaw?" Sed craned his neck over the crowd and located his grandma's distinctive blue-haired coif in the front row.

"I won that particular battle," his mom said.

"I think I'm going to have to have it out with that woman today. Both Jessica and I have been beyond patient with her, but she's overstepped her bounds one too many times."

"Don't start your marriage in a war, Sed. It will all be over soon, and she'll go back to ignoring your existence."

"We can only hope."

His mother led him around the outer edge of the seated guests and toward the ocean. The waves were really churning and crashing loudly against the beach; apparently there was a heavy storm at sea. A strong frontal boundary held the blackest clouds just offshore— he could actually see the demarcation in the sky. Sed decided his dad wasn't in the clouds, he was in that boundary, holding them back. "Thanks, Dad," he whispered under his breath.

Sed greeted his guests—mostly family, road crew, and musicians who'd toured with him. It was a little off-putting to see rock stars in formal wear—suits and piercings, ties and tattoos. Sed didn't have much time to spend saying hello to Jessica's side of the makeshift chapel, though he greeted a few he knew by name. Her family and friends seemed a bit intimidated by the mix of hoodlums and everyday Joes on his side, though a few of the lawyers in her crowd greeted the less law-abiding musicians with familiarity. He thanked a couple of people that he recognized from television for attending the wedding, but he couldn't put names to any of their faces. He wondered if Jessica knew them. She'd never mentioned knowing any television stars, but it wasn't uncommon in Los Angeles to be friends with famous people.

He took his position next to the chaplain. He shook hands with the bored-looking Jesus look-a-like and then turned to face the tent at the end of the aisle where his bride would soon appear.

A hush fell over the crowd as the quartet of harp, flute, cello, and violin paused and then began to play the song Jessica and he had chosen for the processional. She hadn't taken to his idea of using "Bark at the Moon", but at least she'd asked for his opinion before shooting it down. Sed wiped his hands on his pant legs, wondering why his palms were uncommonly moist. He wasn't the type of guy who got stage fright, but his stomach was suddenly churning.

Sed's heart leapt into his throat as the gauzy white curtains were drawn back. But it wasn't Jess at the front of the procession, it was Jessica's friend Beth and Dave in his wheelchair decorated with flowers and with red and white ribbons trailing behind. Sed smiled when Dave showed off some of his impressive upper body strength by doing a wheelie halfway down the aisle. This made Beth grin and blush. In fact, Dave seemed to be showing off for the cute brunette, which wasn't like Dave. Sed wondered if there was any attraction between them. When they reached him, Beth and Dave separated, with Dave going to the far end on Sed's side and Beth staying next to where Jessica would eventually stand. She smiled at Sed and he realized she'd seen Jess today even if he hadn't. God, he couldn't wait to see his bride. He was about to jump out of his skin with anticipation.

They'd taken a few liberties with the traditional order of the processional to make maneuvering easier for Dave, so next down the aisle was his best man, Brian, and his wife, Myrna. Between them they held a baby carrier decorated with red roses and sprays of little white flowers. Baby's breath, Sed believed it was called. Fitting, since nestled in the carrier with a pillow on his lap—two gold rings tied to it with ribbons—was the cutest ring bearer to ever sleep through his duty. Myrna and Brian started toward Sed, carrying their son between them. He smiled at them both, knowing his dimples were showing, but for once he was glad for the added emphasis of his joy.

The wind whipped Myrna's stunning red gown about her legs as she walked. Sed peeked at the dark sky and prayed for it to hold back the rain until Jessica was his wife. He wanted the moment to be perfect for her, and a downpour was no one's idea of perfection. Unfortunately, the frontal boundary had moved ashore. Shit. If it would just wait another ten minutes, he could say *I do* and it could rain all it wanted. He knew how upset Jessica would be if her dream beach wedding was ruined. She'd worked so hard at planning the occasion and so hard to include him in all the arrangements. He would do anything to make the day what she wanted. But how did one stop the rain?

When Brian and Myrna reached the end of the aisle, they separated. Brian took the carrier with him and set it on the sturdy table to Sed's left so the crowd could see the ring bearer and *ohh* and *ahh* over his adorableness. As usual, Malcolm's coal black hair was standing on end. Sed couldn't stop himself from reaching over and touching the baby's tiny hand. God, he couldn't wait to see his own firstborn in seven months. The baby growing in Jessica's womb already owned him heart and soul. But until he got to hold his own child, he was content fawning over Brian's young son.

Malcolm's hand gripped Sed's finger tightly. His other little fist went directly into his mouth and though still asleep, he sucked it in earnest.

"He inherited the grip from me," Brian whispered, "but that strong suction is all on his mother."

Sed laughed and glanced at Myrna, who was oblivious to her husband's claims.

Movement at the head of the aisle caught his attention and his head snapped up. *Jess?*

No.

Not yet.

Eric and Rebekah were now making their way down the aisle. Where Myrna's gown was long and elegant, Rebekah's was short and sassy—like her. It was the exact same shade of red as Myrna's and also matched the crimson splotches in Rebekah's hair. Eric's trademark lock of colored hair was also dyed red to honor the occasion. The pair of newlyweds had the audacity to share a lingering kiss at the head of the aisle before they separated to opposite sides. Eric shifted to the spot behind Brian and Rebekah took her place behind Myrna.

Aggie and Jace were next down the aisle. Her dress had a plunging neckline, with a short strap between her large breasts to keep them in place and draw appreciative attention to her substantial cleavage. Her long black hair did a better job concealing her porcelain skin than the red silk fabric hugging her curves managed. Aggie's lipstick and red-tipped fingernails matched her dress, stilettos, and bouquet of red roses, as well as the blush currently staining Jace's cheeks. Sed had no idea what the guy was embarrassed about at that particular moment. His woman was something to be proud of. Or maybe he was just hot and bothered by his fiancée. Couldn't blame the guy. Aggie was sex on heels.

When the pair paused before Sed, Aggie pinched Jace's ass and then patted it, her grin a bit devilish. She winked one bright blue eye at Sed before moving to stand behind Rebekah. Walking a bit stiffly, Jace moved to his spot behind Eric. Sed was pretty sure Jace's stance wasn't the only thing stiff about him.

He caught a flash of white out of the corner of his eye and his head swiveled toward the head of the aisle. *Jess?*

No, damn it. Just the breeze blowing the gauzy fabric around the tent at the head of the aisle.

Sed clenched his hands into fists and blew out a steadying breath. This had to be the longest five minutes of his life.

Trey and Reagan walked the aisle next. Jessica's female friends from college immediately started twittering among themselves as Trey charmed them with his on-your-knees smile. Reagan was wearing her trademark combat boots with her formal. She kept nervously sliding her hand over her retro fifties dress and glancing at the front pew, where Ethan, her other boyfriend, sat. Ethan had assured her time and again that he was fine not standing up for Sed since Sed and Ethan hardly knew each other. Trey was the one he and Jessica had asked to be in the wedding party, and Sed had made him pick which of his lovers he wanted on his arm. Trey had seemed to think that ex-cop, bodyguard Ethan wouldn't appreciate having to wear a dress and standing on Jessica's side as a bridesmaid. Though Ethan had readily agreed, Reagan hadn't thought Trey's joke was funny at all. Sed wondered how in the hell they made their relationship work. Awkward situations had to come up on a regular basis.

Ethan blessed Reagan with a wide smile, and she relaxed at Trey's side. Maybe she just thought Ethan would have hurt feelings for being left out. Trey was oblivious to the dynamic. He just accepted the little hiccups as part of the relationship that made him happy. Sed wondered if the man was capable of not going with the flow.

As Trey passed him, Sed twisted to look at the four men standing behind him. He'd never doubted his band of brothers would be here for him. They were always there—come Hell or high water or crazy mother-in-laws. But to see them lined up that way—fidgeting in those stupid ties and fancy tuxes on his behalf—made him smile. There was no one he'd rather have at his back than these guys and no one he'd rather have at his side than his Jess.

Surely it was time for her to take her rightful place.

He sucked in a steadying breath and turned back to the aisle to wait for her approach. The anticipation was killing him. This was far more extreme than waiting in the wings to take the stage.

Elise came down the aisle next, on the arm of their cousin Wayne.

Oh for fuck's sake. How many people were in this wedding party? A thousand?

Elise was smiling so brightly at Sed, she could have lit the heavens. And even though it meant he had to wait a while longer to see the star of his show, he was overwhelmed by the pride he felt at seeing her. He wasn't sure when his baby sister had become a woman, but that red dress was showing entirely too much skin. He would have words with Jessica later about why Elise wasn't wearing the dress he'd liked. The one with the high neckline and matching jacket. Elise winked at him before taking her spot. Sed actually groaned aloud when his other—usually more sensible—sister came into view. Kylie's dress was even less nun-like than Elise's. If any of those guys from Jessica's law practice so much as looked at his sisters, he'd be having lawyer gonads for his wedding feast. The guys in his band knew better than to make a move on his sweet sisters, though he was glad they were all hooked up with women of their own so he could let his guard down a little. But just a little. There were other rock stars in the crowd that could stand a close eye. Especially that Dare Mills character. Sed knew firsthand what Dare's little brother was like and he didn't want his sisters having any part of that.

The first notes of the wedding march sounded, and Sed

straightened, his head whipping around to catch sight of the only person he needed to see today. His heart. His Jessica.

Two ushers swept the gauzy white curtains aside to reveal the bride to the standing crowd.

As he stared, Sed's breath escaped him in a rush.

His heart shattered into a million pieces and all the light went out of his life.

Jessica wasn't there.

Chapter 4

JESSICA YANKED HER BOUQUET out of her mother's hand. "I've had enough," she said. "You have been making me crazy for months. If you want to watch the ceremony, fine, but this is my day, not yours. I don't even want to look at you right now! I don't give a flying fuck that Johnny Depp didn't come, and no, we are not going to wait a few more minutes to see if he arrives late."

In the brief pause of her tirade, Jessica heard the unmistakable sound of the wedding march scrambled by the blowing wind. Eyes popping wide with panic, she gathered her skirt in both hands and dashed into the tent where she was supposed to be standing before the march began. The curtains had already been drawn back, so her entrance had been completely ruined.

None of that mattered when her gaze landed on her groom.

Sed's jaw was set in a harsh line, his stare fixed on the ground before him. She could tell by the look of devastation on his face that he thought she'd stood him up.

No. No, no, no. This was not how this was supposed to go.

The ushers were supposed to sweep the curtains aside and her eyes would meet Sed's from a distance and she'd slowly take her practiced steps in his direction, her gaze never leaving his. The love would flow between them as they anticipated touching, anticipated becoming physically connected, just as they were psychically connected.

But he wasn't even looking at her.

"Sed!" she called.

Jessica was running down the aisle toward him even before he moved. His head popped up and when his gaze landed on her, he staggered against Brian as if his knees had given out. She wanted to apologize for making him worry. She wanted to yell at him for thinking she'd leave him at the altar. But mostly she just wanted to stare at him in adoring awe. He'd never looked more handsome. More loving. More hers.

She stopped dead as she reached the front row of the carefully decorated chairs with their bows all blowing flat and the flowers crumpled, the ribbons flying in every direction in the punishing breeze. But that didn't matter. The only thing that mattered was the man. The man was perfect.

The wedding march faded to silence, allowing her to hear the whispers discussing the scene she'd just made. But these people knew her. They should be used to her causing scenes.

"Who gives this woman to this man in wedlock?" the chaplain said, as if he were going through the motions and not really part of what was going on.

The murmured conversations quieted as everyone stared at the empty spot beside Jessica where her mother was supposed to be standing and giving her away. At least that's how they'd rehearsed.

"I give myself to him," Jessica blurted. "My mother doesn't own me anyway."

Sed chuckled, his dimples flashing in his cheeks. He held out a strong, masculine hand in her direction. Her heart thudded, as it always did when she was near him, and she took his hand, stepping to his side. She didn't know which of them was trembling more, but neither of them was at all steady as they waited for Myrna to arrange Jessica's train as best she could in the wind so they could have their picture-perfect exchange of vows. The backdrop was far from the perfection she'd imagined: the sky was near black with clouds, the ocean churned with angry waves, the wind caught her carefully chosen veil and whipped it about her in chaotic plumes, and her poor bouquet would never look the way it should. But the man....

The man was gorgeous in his tailored black tux with his smile unending and his eyes full of love and a bit of humor.

If he laughed at her for this, she would, she would... laugh right back. Actually, she was moments from breaking into hysterics and she couldn't figure out why. Her perfect day was far from perfect and for some unknowable reason, she didn't care. Not as long as Sed recited his vows and meant them as much as she meant hers.

She could scarcely hear the chaplain over the howling wind, but since she and Sed had written their vows, she didn't need the cues. She knew them by heart.

"You are the reason I breathe," Jessica said, lost in Sed's striking blue gaze until a piece of sand found its way into her eye and she had to rub at it, undoubtedly smudging her make-up into a one-eyed-raccoon look.

"What?" Sed yelled. "I didn't hear you."

"You are the reason I breathe!" she yelled.

"Yeah, I feel the same way!"

Had he forgotten the words? Understandable. He was probably nervous, and it wasn't as if either of them could hear the drone of the chaplain. She blinked the sand out of her eye and then squinted up at him. He had his lips pressed together as if he was barely able to hold it together. She continued. It was important that they recite their vows to each other even if they were the only ones who could hear them.

"I love you more with each passing moment!" she yelled.

"Me too!" he returned.

"I promise to stand beside you always, weather any storm—"

"Any storm?" he yelled.

"Yes, any storm. Even this one."

"I love you!" he yelled. "You matter to me more than anything. I don't want to live a single moment without you in my life."

"I love you too!" Those weren't the words they planned, but considering that she was getting hoarse from yelling, they would have to do.

"Do you want to be my wife?"

"Yes! For always. Do you want to be my husband?"

"Of course I do, or I wouldn't be here."

Sed flung out a hand toward Brian, who started.

"Rings!"

Brian hurriedly unlaced the rings from the pillow on Malcolm's lap and handed them to Sed.

"This ring tells the world you're mine and no one else's," Sed said, then he slipped the ring onto Jessica's finger.

"This ring tells horny bitches that you're off-limits," she countered and slid his ring over the knuckle of his left ring finger.

She couldn't even remember what they'd planned to say. These words were organic. Real. They were both jealous and possessive of each other, so why not just get that all out in the open and into the ceremony?

They both looked at the chaplain, who stared at them as if they were raving lunatics. Jessica was pretty sure they were at that moment.

"Uh, is that it?" the man said.

Jessica and Sed nodded in unison.

"Then I pronounce you husband and wife. Kiss your bride."

Sed drew Jessica against his length and the instant his mouth found hers, the heavens opened and rain began to pour in a torrent. Jessica was vaguely aware of the startled cry of baby Malcolm, the disgruntled shouts of the wedding party, and the scramble for cover by the guests, but all of it faded as Sed continued to kiss her. She dropped her bouquet to the ground so she could cup his cheek. Cool rain slid down his face, over her hand, down her wrist, and dripped from her elbow. The wind finally claimed her veil, ripping it free of pins and combs and hurling it into the air. She didn't care. All she cared about was kissing her husband. This disaster of a day might have taken every perfect moment from her, but it would not take her kiss.

Sed's tongue brushed her upper lip, and she parted her lips, drawing him deeper. If his strong arm hadn't been wrapped around her lower back to press her firmly against his belly, she'd have collapsed at his feet.

He drew away after a long moment and stared down into her eyes, raindrops clinging to his spiky lashes and tracing rapid courses down his strong jaw. The wind had calmed and the rain fell steadily, but it no longer fell in a torrential downpour.

"You're so beautiful," Sed told her, fingers stroking the sopping tangle of her hair. Hair that had been a gorgeous mass of loose curls moments before, but was now wet and limp. She could only assume that her mascara was making her do her best impression of Alice Cooper.

"If you say so." She grinned up at him and touched his face. "Why didn't you tell me how sexy you are in a soaking-wet tuxedo?"

"I didn't want to ruin the surprise."

"So you ordered this rain?" she asked, her eyes flipping skyward.

He leaned close and whispered in her ear, "No, but I think God was afraid if I got too overheated I'd have fucked you right here in front of all our guests."

"I didn't realize a little rain could effectively cool your ardor."

"The effect was short-lived."

"I'm sorry I was late," she said, wrapping her arms around his waist and nuzzling into his wet chest. "My mother wanted us to wait for Johnny Depp."

Sed burst out laughing, the sound rich and deep against her ear as it rumbled through his broad chest. "For a minute, I thought you'd changed your mind. That you finally realized you didn't want to marry me."

She reached up and cupped his face in her hands, staring intently into his eyes. "Never. Who in their right mind would go through all this wedding bullshit if they weren't one hundred percent committed to loving their spouse for the rest of their life?"

"Not me," he admitted with a chuckle. "I'm sorry rain ruined your perfect day."

"You don't know the half of it," she said, "but we're here and we're married. That's all that matters."

"I do love you, Mrs. Lionheart."

He claimed her mouth in another kiss. Her entire body trembled against him. Whether it was from the chill of the rain on her skin or the heat of lust swirling through her blood, she wasn't sure.

Sloshing footsteps approached and the rain suddenly stopped directly overhead, replaced by the sound of drops against nylon. Sed tugged his mouth away and turned his head.

"Are you two going to stand out here in the rain all day?" Eric said, holding an umbrella over their heads.

"Not all day," Sed said. "Just until I've had enough of kissing her."

"So all day then," Eric said with a knowing grin.

Sed chuckled. "Maybe." His blue eyes lifted toward to the black fabric above them. "Bit late for the umbrella."

"Jessica's mother was wailing about ruined dresses, so I had no choice but to save her daughter's poor garment."

"It was mostly ruined by baby puke anyway," Jessica said.

Sed's fingers found the zipper at Jessica's back and eased it down several inches. "She's welcome to the dress. I just want the woman inside it."

"Don't you dare, Sed," Jessica gasped and slapped a hand over the zipper at her back.

"Did she just dare me?" Sed asked Eric.

"I think she did."

"Tell our guests we'll see them at the reception."

"Should I bring her dress to her mother?" Eric asked, winking at Jessica, who couldn't seem to shut her wide-open mouth.

"That won't be necessary," Sed said with a rakish grin that displayed one dimple. "I'll bring it to her myself."

He eased her zipper down another inch, and Jessica backed out of his reach. "Sed!" she said in warning, both hands flying out before her.

He ducked his head slightly and ran his tongue along the ridge of his upper teeth, looking as hungry as any voracious predator. "Maybe you should run," he said in a low growl.

Her breath came out in a startled gasp, and the tips of her breasts tautened. Her hardened nipples had nothing to do with the chill in the air and everything to do with the tone of Sed's voice. Jessica pressed one hand against the bodice of her loosened gown and swept up the train in her other hand. She turned and headed for the waves of the deserted beach. She stumbled as the sand pulled at her kitten heels, so she kicked them off and sprinted as fast as she could move—wanting him to chase her. Wanting him to catch her. But not without some effort.

Cool water washed over her feet as she reached the surf. A hand brushed her arm, and she darted in the opposite direction, laughing breathlessly as she dodged his grip. Water splashed against her ankles and calves as she sprinted down the beach. She could hear his footfalls just behind her. This time when he caught her arm, she turned abruptly and collided with his chest.

His breath escaped in a startled huff. She dropped her train, not caring that the waves and sand were churning it into a puce-tinged mess, and pressed her palms against his chest. The bodice of her dress slipped low, scarcely covering the white leather of her corset. Still breathing hard from exertion, she looked up at him. Tiny stinging raindrops against her eyelids made her blink.

"Why does chasing you make my dick so hard?" he grumbled at her.

"Because it knows when you catch me, it's in for a treat."

She slid her hands down the slick fabric of his red and black brocade vest to find the fly of his trousers. His cock leapt against her palm as she stroked him through his clothes with one hand and fumbled with fastenings with her other.

He claimed her mouth in a deep kiss, hands gripping her bare shoulders. He groaned into her mouth as she freed his massive cock from the confines of his pants. She loved that he'd gone commando beneath his tux. It let her know that he'd planned on fucking her somewhere besides the privacy of their hotel suite in Malibu tonight. Maybe he had ordered that rain after all. It had turned into a blessing in disguise, allowing them precious moments alone together on a deserted, private beach in a storm.

She held his thick length in both hands, gently stroking him as he kissed her. And kissed her. Kissed her as if he planned to never stop.

He tugged his mouth from hers. "Here?" he asked breathlessly. "Are you sure?"

"Are we being watched?" she asked.

He gazed over her shoulder to the near demolished wedding pavilion. "Everyone's gone."

"Then yes, here," she whispered. "Right now."

He touched her face, his eyes searching hers. "Are you really mine now?"

"I've been yours since the day we met," she said. "The only difference is now you have it in writing."

He chuckled. "A little insurance never hurt."

He leaned in to steal a kiss—and her senses. They sank to their knees in unison. He gently eased her onto her back atop the wet sand. An occasional wave teased her toes and pulled at the train of her dress. Sed tugged his mouth free from hers and kissed a gentle trail down her throat and chest. He cupped one breast in his hand and nudged her corset down with his chin so he could suck her sensitive nipple. They were so tender these days because of the pregnancy. Her eyes drifted closed and she gasped, lost in the sensation of his mouth on her. His hand shifted to cradle her lower belly, impeded by the corset cinching her in. Sed was so proud that he'd gotten her pregnant. She could scarcely wait to see him hold their baby—cradling their precious gift in his large, caring hands— for the first time. He would be such a wonderful father. She was honored to have been selected the mother of his children. And to be his wife.

Sed shifted lower and rested his head on her belly. She stroked his hair gently, consumed with tender feelings for the man and the part of him that inseparably linked them—the life growing inside her. When he crawled down her body and shifted his hands beneath her dress, her tenderness was quickly consumed by lust. His hands slid up her thighs and hips, seeking the waistband of her panties. When he found none, his head popped up and their eyes met over the bunched fabric of her gown.

"You're not wearing panties," he told her.

"I'm not?" She grinned at him wickedly. "Hmm. I wonder why I made that decision."

"Because you're the smartest woman I know," he said.

His head disappeared beneath her skirt. She moaned when his mouth found her. He licked and sucked her clit, quickly making her pussy the wettest part of her body, though it was about the only part of her that had escaped the rain and waves.

"Sed!" she cried as her thighs began to quiver and the flesh between them throbbed with impending release. "Don't make me come without you. Not our first time."

She almost regretted her request when he pulled back with a loud sucking pop and slid up her body. When he found her and slid deep inside, claiming her inch by inch with repetitive hard thrusts, he filled more than her body. He filled every part of her.

Sed buried his hands in her wet hair and alternated kissing her passionately and staring into her eyes as he thrust with a slow, deep rhythm that matched the rhythm of the ocean. Her toes curled. Her belly quivered. Her fingers dug into his back so she didn't drift away in the current of her desire. He churned his hips each time their bodies came together, grinding himself against her, making her moan with pleasure as he rubbed his pelvis against her throbbing clit.

Waves were creeping ashore as far as her calves now. An urgency consumed them both, as if they were racing the tide. Sed's strokes hastened—driving his rigid length hard and deep. His fingers—which had been gently tangled in her hair—dug into her scalp, and his tender kisses became hot and desperate.

He tore his mouth from hers, gasping as he fought for control. Watching the twitch of his eye and the set of his jaw as pleasure consumed him sent Jessica flying over the edge. She cried out, her back arching off the beach as her pussy clenched in waves of bliss. Sed gasped brokenly, ramming into her—once, twice—and then he held himself deep inside as his cock jerked with hard spasms of release.

Breathing heavily, he collapsed on top of her, crushing her beneath a mass of firm muscles and heated male flesh. She wrapped her love in a warm and rather sandy embrace, holding him tight as she caught her own breath. But not her wits. Her wits were never within reach when Sed was between her thighs.

"You realize I plan to top this before the night is through," he murmured into her ear.

She rubbed her lips against his jaw, her heart thrumming with anticipation. With expectation. He never let her down.

"I'd like to see you try," she challenged.

Chapter 5

SITTING IN THE BACK OF THE LIMO on the way to the reception, Sed held Jessica's left hand between both of his. He stole glances at her as if he were in elementary school and experiencing his first crush. Her dress was soaking wet and stained with dirt and something green he hoped was just algae. Her make-up was entirely gone, except for the two dark smudges beneath both eyes. Her hair was a limp, tangled mess with a twig of seaweed lost in its strawberry-blond waves. He refused to inform her of the ocean's reminder of what they'd done in its surf.

His woman had never looked more beautiful. Not even the first time he'd seen her and she'd stolen his heart. She'd been riding a Ferris wheel on the boardwalk and he'd stood there at its base like an idiot the entire time, watching her laughing face return with each loop around. She hadn't looked more beautiful when he'd proposed the first time or the second. Nor the first time he'd witnessed her sexy O-face or the hundreds of times he'd seen that blissful expression since then. She hadn't been lovelier when she told him she was pregnant. Not even when he'd stared up the aisle when she'd called his name and he saw her racing toward him in her wedding dress, dazzling in detailed perfection. No, he decided, she was most beautiful at that very moment—sitting beside him quietly, completely bedraggled, and unaware of how giddy it made him that she was his wife.

Of course, giddy wasn't an emotion Sed Lionheart displayed outwardly. That didn't mean he didn't feel it.

Jessica fiddled with her wedding ring, rubbing it into her flesh as she stared at her lap.

"My mother is going to kill me for showing up at the reception looking like this," she whispered.

"I thought you decided you don't care what she thinks."

She pressed the back of her wrist to her mouth and swallowed several times.

"Are you okay?" he asked. The woman had seen her share of morning sickness the first couple months of her pregnancy, but recently it had become a rarity.

"All things considered." She dropped her head back to look up at him. "I don't care what she thinks, but it still hurts my feelings when she yells at me."

"I thought she just made you mad."

"Well, yeah, that's how I always react when I get my feelings hurt." She blinked at him. "All this time with me and you didn't realize that?"

"Uh…" He flicked his gaze to his clasped hands, which were resting on his knees. "Of course I realized that. But sometimes you get mad because you're angry, right?"

"Sometimes," she said. "But not often."

All those times she'd been spitting mad at him was because he'd hurt her feelings? Why hadn't she told him that sooner? And why was he such a bonehead that he hadn't figured it out on his own?

He slid an arm around her lower back and pressed her against his side. "I'm sorry for making you mad all the time."

She released a breathless laugh. "No, you're not. You purposely make me angry so the passion blazes between us. I'm on to you, Lionheart. I know what you're up to."

"Well, I do think you're hot when you're pissed off, but I didn't mean to hurt your feelings."

"I know you don't mean it. Otherwise I would have killed you in your sleep by now."

He laughed. "I'm glad you're more intelligent than violent."

She looked down at her folded hands and then licked her thumb and tried to rub a spot out of her skirt. "I just hope Mom doesn't nag me. I'm happy—the ceremony, the beach, *now*. All the moments I've been alone with you today have felt perfect, even if they weren't what I envisioned. The rest of the day has been one disaster after another. I can't imagine what will be thrown at me next."

"I'll run interference," Sed said. "I honestly don't mind. Your mother can't stand me anyway. I doubt she'll ever forgive me for knocking you up before we were married."

Jessica snorted. "She still doesn't believe that I got pregnant intentionally. Like I'm too stupid to remember to take my birth control pills. Just because that's the reason she had me, doesn't mean I'll make the same mistakes she did."

"If she gets too unbearable, I'll send her packing. Okay?"

Jessica shook her head. "No, I want her there, even though I'm sure she'll be unbearable. She's going to be heartbroken that I didn't wait for her to give me away."

"Unfortunate." Sed smiled. "But not really. It meant a lot to me that you gave yourself to me."

Her jade-green eyes widened, as if she hadn't realized how perfect that little split-second decision had been. Because the woman struggled to let go of even an inch of her independence, he would never forget her giving herself to him so willingly.

"It did?" she asked.

"Yeah, because I know how independent you are. I think by giving yourself to me you've finally realized that resistance is futile. You're mine and mine alone. I'll never let you go."

"As long as I allow it," she challenged.

"And how long will that be?"

She smiled. "Until the day I die."

"Beyond death," he insisted.

"That's still up for negotiation."

"You know you'll never be able to resist me with a halo." He winked at her.

"A halo? Won't that get in the way of your horns?" She extended her index fingers on either side of her head.

"I'll just wear my halo at a cocky angle over one horn. It'll be sexier that way. You won't know what hit you."

She laughed and wrapped both arms around his neck. "I do love you."

"Beyond death?" he asked.

She looked up at her eyebrows as if contemplating what his request entailed. "Yes, beyond death."

He grinned. "I love it when I get my way."

She poked him in the ribs. "I let you get your way," she said.

"And why's that?"

"Because you're even more wonderful when you're happy."

"I am definitely happy."

"And I'm dedicated to keeping you that way."

"I want to do the same for you. So about your mother…"

Jessica released a heavy sigh and rubbed at her forehead with her hand. A hand, he noted, missing the ring that she'd been wearing for months—the one he'd carried in his pocket for two years after she'd flung it at him in anger. Had she finally decided she could be done with the cheap piece of shit once and for all?

"I'll try to get along with her," Jessica said wearily.

"And if you can't?"

"I'll ask her to leave," she said.

"I don't mind stepping in and—"

She covered his lips with a finger and shook her head. "No sense in increasing the tension between the two of you. I can handle it."

He nodded, knowing she liked to handle her problems on her own. He'd just be there to support her if and when she needed him. Sometimes he wished that she'd let him rule her life, fix anything that needed fixing, but then she'd be a lot less interesting and he'd probably have never fallen so hard for her. It was the challenge of Jessica Chase—*Lionheart*—that kept him coming back for more. Their compatibility in the sack didn't hurt either.

"Where's your ring?" he asked, lifting her left hand in his.

"Are you blind? It's right there where you put it."

"Your *other* ring," he clarified.

"Oh." She showed him her right hand. "You're supposed to wear the wedding ring closer to your heart, so I switched it to my other hand for the ceremony and forgot to switch it back."

He took her hand in his and grasped her engagement ring with his fingertips.

"Allow me," he said.

He removed the ring from her right ring finger and slowly slid it onto her left to rest against her wedding band.

She shuddered beside him, and he glanced up to find her smoldering gaze on him.

"Why was that so erotic?" she murmured.

"Slowly sliding things into holes is always erotic," he said with a grin.

"It is when you do it."

The limo pulled to a halt. Sed tugged Jessica into his arms and kissed her deeply, knowing the next few hours would be chaos and they'd have no opportunity to be alone. And when they finally were alone together that evening, he had some romantic dinner plans in store for her and some rather lame words he planned to sing while there. He couldn't wait to see her face when they reached their rendezvous point. He was a bit less sure about the song. It wasn't like anything he'd ever written before. She might hate it.

The door was opened from outside, and Sed reluctantly pulled away from Jess's soft, warm lips. He stared into her eyes and said, "I love you."

"I love you too."

"You can count on me, you know. For anything you need or want. You can always count on me."

She cupped his face between her hands and pecked him on the lips. "I know that. You can count on me as well."

Sed slid from the limo and extended a hand inside to help Jessica out of the car. All their friends and family were standing in a huge crowd outside the reception hall waiting for them. Their cheers of excitement died as soon as Jessica exited the vehicle. Their slack jaws and wide eyes were probably due to Jessica looking like she'd been rolling around on the mud in her wedding dress. And that was pretty close to the truth.

"Oh, sweetheart." Sed's mom separated from the crowd and rushed over to them. "What a terrible time for it to rain."

Jessica offered Sed a naughty smile before turning her attention to her new mother-in-law. "I actually thought it was good timing," she said. "I know I look a mess, but I couldn't be happier."

Mom wrapped both arms around Jessica and squeezed, swaying slightly with girly giddiness. "I'm so glad you're not upset. I was worried that you'd be devastated."

"You can't stop the rain," she said.

But nothing had forced them to make love on the beach in it. Except their insatiable lust for each other.

"It's a good thing you're level-headed," his mom said. "You're going to need a lot of patience to put up with my bullheaded son for the next sixty years."

"Level-headed? Jessica?" Sed sputtered. "I think you have her confused with someone else."

His mom gave him a loving smile over Jessica's shoulder. "Compared to you, doll? Yeah, she's the level-headed one. I can't wait to see how your kids turn out. I predict they'll be a bit challenging to raise."

Sed's stomach did a back flip. He wanted eight of them, but if they were all as stubborn as himself and their mother—*combined*—perhaps he should pare that number down by a few.

His mom tugged away and searched Jessica's face. Scowling, she pulled the strand of seaweed from Jessica's hair. "How did you end up with seaweed in your hair?"

Jessica's eyes widened, and she glared at Sed. He shrugged and shook his head as if he hadn't noticed it.

"That was some wind," Jessica said, her cheeks pink.

The photographer sidled over to join their little group. "Do you still want me to take pictures?" he whispered.

"Of course," Jessica said. "Just pretend I look beautiful."

"You do look beautiful," Sed said gruffly. His chest puffed with pride because she was his.

Without warning, Jessica's mother came at her with a hairbrush. "Dear lord, what a disaster! This will be remembered as the worst celebrity wedding *ever* in the history of Hollywood. Thank God I was only responsible for the reception."

Jessica tried to avoid the hairbrush while Sed worked very hard at holding his tongue.

"*A*, I'm not a celebrity," Jessica said, cringing when the brush landed in her hair and caught on a snag. "*B*, we are not in Hollywood. And *C*, I don't care what you think."

"And *D*," Mom said, "what's important is the kids are happy. Right?" She smiled in her ever friendly way, but Stella just scowled at her.

"Celebrities owe it to the world to have fairy-tale weddings," Stella said. "It gives us regular people something to dream about."

Sed opened his mouth to argue that celebrities didn't owe the world anything—not that he considered himself a huge celebrity in the first place. Celebrities had the right to privacy and bad-hair days and cellulite and stretch marks just like everyone else. But he remembered his promise to Jessica and slammed his mouth closed. His teeth clicked together so hard, his ears rang. It was damn hard to hold his tongue when Jessica's mother was around. Stella was far more outspoken and opinionated than her daughter. And as his opinions always clashed with the woman's, it wasn't as if he enjoyed arguing with her. Or watching Jessica try to hold her own. He had half a mind to shove Jessica back in the limo, steal her away without attending the reception, and deal with his wife's fury later.

While Jessica and her mother argued about Jessica's ruined hair and her ruined dress and her ruined flowers and her ruined wedding, Sed's muscles grew tighter and tighter with tension. If his mother hadn't placed a comforting hand on his elbow, he would have exploded.

"Are you going to say something?" Mom asked quietly.

"Jessica doesn't want me to interfere."

"Do you always let her get her way?"

Sed flushed. "Pretty much."

"You have to pick your battles," Mom said.

"Yeah." At his mother validation of his choice, he felt a bit better about staying out of Stella and Jessica's escalating argument.

"I think this might be the one you should pick." Mom patted his back. "I'll see you inside."

So she wasn't validating his choice after all. He considered clinging to his mother's leg and begging her not to leave him with the mother-in-law that came with his new wife, but he wasn't a three-year-old. He felt almost as helpless as one at the moment. And what must Jessica be feeling having to deal with Stella directly?

"Um, excuse me," Sed said, trying to gain their attention.

"Those stains will never come out of that dress!" her mother was screeching. "Jesus God, do you even remember how long it took you to pick it out, Jessica Chase? You must have tried on a thousand gowns."

"Jessica Lionheart," she corrected. "And it's *my* dress, mother. If I want to tie-dye it and wear it in the Thanksgiving Day parade, that's my prerogative."

"Do you know what your problem is?" Stella said, eyes narrowed dangerously.

"You! You are my problem."

Stella shook her head, sending silky blond locks dancing about her spray-tanned shoulders. "No, your problem is that you think only of yourself, Jessica."

Sed took a step back as Jessica's jaw went hard, and her eyes sparked with anger. She'd leveled him with that look on a few occasions. They never ended well.

"It's my wedding day!" Jessica bellowed. "I'm supposed to think of myself today. My love for Sed and his for me are the only things that are supposed to matter today. You're the one being a selfish shrew." She threw her hands up as a plea to the heavens. Or maybe she was praying for a lightning strike to be sent in her mother's direction.

"Um, sweetheart?" Sed again tried to break into their tirade exchange. He happened to agree with his wife, and not only because he didn't want to face her wrath.

"Me, selfish?" her mother yelled. "Do you know how much time and effort I put into planning this reception?"

Jessica pressed her fingertips to her forehead. "How could I not know that? You've reminded me no less than a million times."

"Our guests are waiting." Sed placed a hand against Jessica's back, hoping to propel her gently in the general direction of the front door. "We're already late. We wouldn't want the lobster bisque your mother selected to get cold."

"I don't even like lobster bisque!" Jessica yelled and stormed up the cement steps to the entry doors of the reception hall.

"She's under a lot of pressure," Sed explained to the startled photographer who had yet to find an opportunity for a candid shot that did not involve flailing hands and angry faces. But at least they were on their way inside. Perhaps Sed could keep Jessica and her mother separated for the rest of the afternoon.

Where was a brick wall when he needed one?

"Speak to her, Sedric," Stella said. "She's being completely unreasonable."

"Look, Stella, I promised Jess I would not interfere unless she asked me to, but I'm not above locking you outside and pretending it was an accident. If you push me, I will push back."

He caught a brief glimpse of her outraged face just before he stalked off. He found Jessica caught in the group embrace of her best friend, Beth, and Sed's two sisters. He breathed a sigh of relief at seeing the wide smile on Jessica's face. The photographer, who had followed him into the building, hurriedly snapped several pictures. He probably wanted something to show for his efforts before chaos reigned over the event once more.

They were supposed to be standing side by side and greeting their assembly line of guests in cool, calm formality. Apparently that plan had also been abandoned. Eric was the first to wrap Sed in an enthusiastic hug. Eric tilted back, lifting Sed's feet off the floor, and shook him for good measure. But Eric didn't keep Sed airborne for long since Sed outweighed the drummer by dozens of pounds.

Eric punched him in the biceps several times. "That was a total Sed move, sending the guests scattering with a rainstorm and getting the goods immediately following the ceremony."

Sed grinned. "Yeah, well... Old habits die hard."

"Did you even say I do?" Trey asked. "I couldn't hear a thing over the wind."

"We said something I-do-like." Sed drew his eyebrows together. "But not what we were supposed to say." They'd chosen their vows carefully. He'd have to say them to her that evening when they were alone together.

"Is she upset?" Brian asked. "She has to be upset. Myrna said their morning was hell."

"She seems fine until her mother starts harping. She just can't handle her today."

Brian glanced behind him and shook his head slightly. The woman in question had just stormed into the building, wielding her hairbrush like a broadsword. "Speaking of her mother…"

"Would you guys do me a huge favor and keep her occupied? If she confronts Jess one more time today, it's not going to end well."

"I'm on it," Trey said.

Sed turned to watch the man in action. Trey walked directly into Stella as if he wasn't watching where he was going. When he hauled her against him to rescue her from falling and said something in her ear, her knees buckled and she swayed against him.

"He's still got it," Brian said with a smirk. "He better hope Reagan doesn't catch him flirting with another woman."

"As if he'd actually do anything with Jessica's mother." Sed shook his head in disgust.

"Are you kidding?" Brian said. "He loves older women. If he wasn't currently in a committed relationship—"

"Two!" Eric threw in.

"Two committed relationships—isn't that an oxymoron?" Brian shook his head. "Anyway, if he wasn't in love, he'd have no problem keeping your mother-in-law entertained for the entire evening."

"I bet she was hot in her day," Eric said. "Not as hot as Brian's mom, of course. I already told Rebekah that Claire Sinclair is my free pass, should the opportunity ever present itself."

Sed laughed at the green tinges that suddenly graced Brian's light skin.

"Ugh, God, stop," Brian said. "If you ever bone my mother, I will cut your dick off and use it to disembowel you."

"Sounds painful," Jace said.

Sed sidled over to his bride, who was laughing at something his grandmother had said. Knowing his memaw, it had probably been something entirely inappropriate.

"Are you ladies up to no good?" Sed asked, slipping an arm around Jessica's waist and holding her securely at his side.

"Memaw said your parents had their reception at a roller rink," Jessica said.

"That's right. It was an eighties thing," he said. "You wouldn't understand."

"Harold and I had our reception at a bowling alley," Memaw said. "Now how did she ever talk you into this big ol' fancy place,

Sedric? It doesn't seem like something you'd pick out for your celebration."

"I picked out something else for our celebration, Memaw, but she doesn't know about it yet, so shhh…" He covered his lips with one finger.

Memaw blushed. "I'll never tell." She pinched Sed's cheek and patted Jessica's before ambling off to find her place card in the dining room.

"What are you talking about?" Jessica asked, appraising him closely with those devastatingly gorgeous jade-green eyes of hers. "You picked out something else? How come this is the first I've heard of it?"

Sed grinned. There was no way he was telling her about their dinner plans in advance. He wanted it to be a surprise.

"Shhh…" He covered his lips with a finger again. "I don't want Jessica to know anything about it." He jerked away with feigned shock. "Oh, hey, Jess. When did you get here?"

"You'd better tell me."

"Nope," he said, brushing his lips against her temple and inhaling her scent. "You smell like the ocean, by the way."

She stiffened slightly.

He whispered into her ear, "It makes me want you."

"We should probably change out of these wet clothes," she said.

She grabbed his crotch and gave it a squeeze. Stunned, he glanced down and was relieved to see her intimate and inappropriate action was hidden behind the skirt of her gown.

"After we dance," he said. And after he worked her body into a frenzy under the dining table.

He took her hand off his thickening cock and smiled like a simpering idiot as every person from the wedding, plus a few hundred additional guests, entered the reception hall and required a personal greeting. When he and Jess were finally able to sit down, the wait staff rushed forward with plates of salad and bowls of soup. Most of their guests had long since finished their soup and salad. The loud din of their chatter filled the cavernous room as they awaited the main course. Sed was starving. He'd refused breakfast despite Brian's harping, and it was already after noon.

The lobster bisque was exceptional. He would have to thank Stella for her excellent taste. He didn't even want to know how much the meal cost him. He and Jess could live off generic mac and cheese for the next few years, no problem.

Jessica leaned close to his ear. "I need to get out of this corset," she said. "There's not enough room for me, the baby, and my lunch in here."

"Why are you wearing a corset anyway? Is that usual?"

"I was too fat to fit in my dress without it," she said, pouting down at her salad.

"You've never been more beautiful." And he wasn't just saying that to make her feel better. "I like a little meat on your bones."

"I think there will be more than a *little* meat on my bones by the time I have this baby," she said.

"More cushion for the pushin'."

She smacked him.

"Sit still and I'll loosen you up a bit," he said.

He leaned behind her and lowered the zipper on her dress. He untied the stays of her corset and worked them loose by a couple of inches.

"Better?" he whispered into her ear.

"Mmm hmm," she murmured. She peeked at him from beneath her eyelashes and slid a hand up his thigh. "Let's let you loose too."

He leaned his belly against the table, hiding his lap in the folds of the tablecloth as her hand found home.

"Baby, as much as I'd love for your hand to be wrapped around my cock at the moment, we're going to have to stand up soon, and I don't want to scandalize my entire family."

Her thumb rubbed the sensitive head of his dick through his pants.

"I'm not planning on making you come," she said. "I just want to make sure you remember you're mine."

"I'll never forget," he vowed.

"Though your cum is a lot more appetizing than this lobster bisque," Jessica said, stirring her soup with her nose crinkled in displeasure.

"Did she just say what I think she said?" Trey asked from behind Jessica's chair. He was filling the empty seat beside Jessica with her giggling mother. Apparently Trey had introduced her to the champagne before the toast. Or perhaps she was just giddy from Trey's attention.

"She said come sit down and have a lot more of this appetizing lobster bisque," Sed told Trey, forcing a smile in Stella's direction.

"Don't mind if I do," Trey said, sitting on Stella's lap and helping himself to her soup.

Stella's raucous laughter caused the entire room to fall silent as everyone turned their heads looking for the source of the obnoxious sound. Trey paused with his spoon to his mouth, his gaze meeting Reagan's across the room. He dropped the spoon in the bowl with a splash that flecked the once spotless white tablecloth.

"Sorry, Stell," he said. "The old ball and chain summons."

He rose from her lap and leaned over Jessica to whisper at Sed. "That's all the neck I'm sticking out for you, dude. You're on your own."

Sed tried making shut-the-hell-up motions with his eyes, but Jessica was too sharp to miss the gist of Trey's words.

"What's he talking about, Sed?" she asked.

"I'll tell you later."

"Are you going to eat that soup?" Trey asked Jess.

She shook her head. He picked up her bowl and carried it with him back to his table. He took a seat next to Reagan, but it was Ethan who looked the most displeased with Trey's farcical seduction of the mother of the bride.

Stella sighed. "He's really good looking."

"Trey?" Jessica lifted an eyebrow at her mother.

"Oh, is that his name?" Stella asked, giggling as she tugged her partially eaten bowl of soup toward her chest. "He was so interested in me that he never said what it was."

She smiled at her soup as she took a bite. At least she was in a good mood now.

A loud clanging drew everyone's attention to their table again. Brian stood from his seat and lifted the glass he'd been striking with his spoon.

"It's tradition for the best man to say a few words about the newlyweds at the wedding reception," he said, smiling warmly at Sed and Jessica. "But I was never the traditional sort." He sat down again.

The entire room burst out laughing.

Myrna shoved him until he stood again. "Well, I guess I have to say something or tonight my wife will have me sleeping in the dining room with the strippers."

Sed laughed, but Jessica twisted her brows together at the inside joke. "I'll explain later," he said under his breath.

"Raise your glasses in a toast to Sed and Jessica," Brian said, "the most sexually explosive couple to ever rock the Vegas strip."

Jessica tossed a roll at Brian. It hit him in the arm and bounced onto the table.

"Here, here," several guests shouted.

Brian tipped his glass toward them. "May your marriage be as long and healthy as Sed's—"

Myrna grabbed her husband's arm and yanked him back into his seat. "What?" Brian said, trying to look innocent. "I was going to say battle cries."

Sed glanced at Jessica to find her laughing. She lifted her glass of non-alcoholic bubbly, and Sed clinked his glass of alcoholic bubbly against it. They linked their arms together and did their best to drain their glasses in the uncomfortable position while a camera flash repeatedly went off near their faces.

The waiters immediately began to serve the main course—steak tartare, seasoned long-grain rice, and steamed asparagus.

"I think it's still mooing," Jessica complained, prodding the piece of meat with her fork. She grabbed a waiter by the sleeve. "Can I get the vegan selection instead?" she asked.

"Sure thing," the man said and hurried off to the side of the room where the meals were being kept warm.

"You don't like the food?" Stella asked. "It cost forty-seven dollars a plate."

Sed cringed, but didn't say anything. He'd just have to sell autographed CDs and calendars of himself naked to avoid bankruptcy. No big deal.

"My stomach can't handle rich food these days," Jessica said, her tone surprisingly steady and not argumentative. "Must be the baby." She covered her belly with one hand, looking slightly nauseated.

Stella nodded in acceptance, and Sed released a sigh of relief that their exchange hadn't escalated into another argument.

Sed loved his steak so much, he ate Jessica's as well. He felt sorry for her as he watched her pick at a plate of steamed vegetables while the flavorful meat practically melted on his tongue. She didn't know what she was missing. As the dinner plates were cleared, Sed rose and took Jessica's hand. She caught her loosened bodice with one hand as the weight of her skirt pulled it down. As discreetly as possible, he zipped the back. It was a struggle, but with a bit of muscle, he brought the pieces of her dress together.

"You got it?" she whispered.

"Yeah."

"I should have had you help me dress."

"That would have been bad luck."

"But less stressful," she said. "I cried so hard when it wouldn't fit. Thankfully, Aggie came to my rescue."

He gave her a gentle hug. Her morning really must have gone horribly if she'd cried *and* allowed someone to rescue her. "I'm sorry I wasn't there to help."

"We figured it out," she said. "Don't feel bad."

"Cake, cake, cake!" Trey began a chant that soon circled the entire room.

Sed took Jessica's cool hand to lead her to the five-tiered wedding cake that had four additional round cakes circling its square base. Nine cakes? Who needed nine cakes? He assumed they'd be eating leftover cake for the next millennium. Either that or they could use it to celebrate their children's birthdays for years.

As they joined hands and sliced through the largest tier, Sed watched Jessica for direction. He didn't particularly want to shove cake in her face, but if she did it to him, he was prepared to retaliate with a vengeance. No one got the better of him. Not even his beloved wife.

She slowly lifted a bite of cake toward his mouth, staring up into his eyes with tenderness and affection. He got lost in that green-eyed gaze, which is probably why he didn't realize she was smearing icing up his chin all the way to his lower lip until it was too late to avoid it.

She grinned crookedly as she placed the bite gently in his mouth. She probably should have let him go first. Determined to retaliate, he grabbed her piece of cake, but before he could lift it, she looped an arm around his neck, rose to her tiptoes, and kissed the icing off his chin and lower lip with enough passion to melt his socks. Catcalls from the guests encouraged her daring, and the photographer caught it all. When Jess drew away at last, he was uncomfortably aroused. Very uncomfortably because his memaw was watching.

"Delicious," Jessica murmured, staring into his eyes. "Can I have some more?"

He lifted the bite of cake to her mouth and fed it to her. She chewed slowly, making his mind race through dozens of naughty things he wanted to do to her sensual mouth. After she swallowed, she released him hastily and backed away. A grin of triumph graced her beautiful face. She even lifted a hand in the air to claim herself the victor of the cake battle. That's when Sed realized he'd been had.

Chapter 6

JESSICA KEPT HER DISTANCE from Sed as he cut a rather large slice of cake, set it calmly on his plate, and returned to the table without her. He wasn't going to retaliate? Was he actually mad? She'd only been teasing. He could shove all nine cakes in her face if it would prevent him from being mad at her. She really counted on him to be calm and levelheaded for her today, which was somewhat hard to admit to herself. How much she counted on him.

Chin up, if not a bit quivery, she collected her own slice of cake and went to join her unreadable husband at the main table. The servers began to cut the cakes into uniform slices and set each slice on the gold-rimmed china dessert plates her mother had chosen.

The rest of the table was empty as she sat beside Sed. He didn't so much as look at her when she sat beside him. Well, fine, if he was going to be a big baby because she'd outsmarted him, then—

She gasped as an entire piece of cake was squashed on her chest. Sed used his plate to spread it over the tops of her breasts and into the cleft between them.

"You may have won the battle, sweetheart," he said. "But I won the war."

Her mouth dropped open as he lowered his head to lick the frosting off her chest, nibbling bits of cake as he very effectively one-upped her. She reached under the table and grabbed his fly, unfastening a button before he caught her hand.

"You do realize where I have to put my cake now, don't you?" she said.

"Can't let me win, can you?"

"Nope."

He chuckled. "I honestly don't mind losing to you, Jessica Chase."

"Lionheart," she corrected.

He grinned up at her, both dimples on full display, and then lowered his lips to sample more frosting from her cleavage. When his tongue slid beneath the leather of her corset—shockingly close to her nipple—waves of pleasure made the tip of her breast tighten. She squirmed in her chair, uncomfortably aroused.

"Are you really going to allow him to do that in public?" Jessica's mom said as she returned to the table with her piece of cake. Monica was right behind her and took her seat on Sed's opposite side.

Jessica wanted him to do even more to her in public, but she forced herself to push him away. "He was cleaning up his cake, Mother. You wouldn't want to let two-dollar-a-slice cake go to waste, would you?" Jessica said tersely.

Jessica stiffened when Sed's hand brushed the bare skin of her inner thigh. How he'd gotten it under her skirt, she didn't know.

"It is delicious," Monica said. She gave her son a disapproving look and his hand disappeared from Jessica's quivering thigh and reappeared above the table.

"What time is it?" he asked. "We have to be out of here by four."

"Four!" Jessica's mom said. "But we have the hall rented until eight."

"And you are more than welcome to stay and party until eight, but Jessica and I have plans for this evening."

"What kind of plans?" Jessica asked.

"Good plans," he assured her with a nod, but he remained tight-lipped about the details.

She leaned close to his ear and, careful not to be overheard, whispered, "Does it involve you filling me with this?"

She grabbed his semi-hard cock through his pants. It jumped against her palm, rapidly engorging with excitement. So he was as hot and bothered as she was. Good to know. Fortunately, her ardor was a bit easier to hide.

"It might," he said.

He took her hand from his lap and lifted it above the table to brush a kiss over her knuckles.

"Patience, love. We have to dance soon," he said.

She supposed she should try to be patient, but it wasn't easy to keep her hands to herself with her virile hunk of a husband within reach.

She ate her cake—which was a far cry more delicious than a plate of steamed vegetables—and allowed her mind to conjure up all sorts of naughty adventures Sed might have planned for their wedding night. She somehow refrained from showing her enthusiasm for the idea and kept both hands above the table.

"Can I have a bite?" Sed asked after a long moment of

watching her eat her cake.

"Didn't get enough off my boobs?" she teased. They were uncomfortably sticky. She was looking forward to getting out of her ocean-stained dress and hopping in the shower. Of course thoughts of showers conjured thoughts of Sed naked in the shower with her. Her hand was trembling as she used the side of her fork to cut a bit of cake from her rapidly dwindling piece.

She offered it to Sed, who leaned forward to take a bite.

"It's okay this way," he said after he swallowed. "But it tastes a lot better when eaten off you."

A sudden loud thud made Jessica jump. The wail of an electric guitar followed an instant later. The band had taken up their instruments, and the entire crowd of wedding guests turned toward the open dance floor beyond the sea of tables; it wasn't every day that Exodus End played at a reception.

"Sed told me that we were to begin exactly at two thirty," the vocalist, Maximilian Richardson, said into his microphone. "Something about wanting to dance with the most beautiful bride ever to be drenched in a downpour."

Sed pushed his chair back and helped Jessica to her feet.

"Congratulations, Sed and Jessica," Max continued. "I'm not sure your song will sound quite right played by a metal band. Dare insisted on changing it up a bit when we rehearsed yesterday."

Dare played a rapid-fire string of notes on his electric guitar that shot sparks of excitement down Jessica's spine. The man had a gift with six strings.

At first, Jessica didn't recognize the song they were playing. Exodus End's cover of Elvis's "Can't Help Falling in Love" took certain liberties with the tempo, and she didn't remember any wailing guitars in the original. And Max's voice, while deep and edgy, didn't quite have the slow sensuality of the King's. Sed stared at her, mouth and eyes wide. She was just as flabbergasted about how to dance to the song as he was. It felt like an opportunity to head bang and mosh to her, so she went with it. Sed caught her against him when she bounced her chest off his. He was laughing so hard, his entire body shook.

"I do love you woman," he said, "but this isn't what I had in mind when I selected this song."

"It sounds awesome!" Jessica said. And she wasn't lying. If anyone could take a sappy love song and turn it into a work of metal perfection, it was Exodus End.

"Stay here," he said.

He released her and stalked across the empty dance floor to the stage. The astonished look on Max's face was priceless as Sed yanked the microphone out of his hand.

The guitar stopped instantly. The drums faded after several more thudding progressions around the toms.

"Max apparently doesn't know how to sing this song properly," Sed said into the microphone.

The band stared after him as he crossed the dance floor toward Jessica. Her heart was thudding like a jackhammer when he wrapped one arm around her waist and tugged her against his body.

"He must not have realized that I picked this song so I could hold my gorgeous wife close, and feel her heart beat against my own." He smiled and she flushed with pleasure.

Staring deep into her eyes, he started the iconic love song, taking no liberties with the tempo or the perfection recorded by Elvis decades past. "Wise men say…"

Lost in his gaze and his serenade, Jessica swayed in time to the music in her heart. She was vaguely aware of a piano starting to play along and a moment later a very subdued drumming filled out the tune, but it was Sed's satin-smooth voice that carried the melody.

By the time he sang, "Take my hand…" she could scarcely see him through the tears in her eyes. She blinked rapidly, sending warm droplets cascading down her cheeks. His hand moved from her waist to the back of her head, and he pressed her face into the hollow of his neck. She tightened her arms around him and pressed a kiss to his throat, immersing herself in his scent, his warmth, and the broad, hard length of his body. She was drowning in the sound of his voice and the emotions it stirred as she clung to him.

The song ended much too soon. Why couldn't he have chosen "In-A-Gadda-Da-Vida" as their song? Not nearly as romantic, but it would have lasted much longer. He extended the microphone from his body until Max came to reclaim it, and then wrapped her in both arms, kissing the top of her head. She lifted her face so she could look at him.

"I really couldn't help falling in love with you," he said.

She nodded, unable to find her voice or strong enough words to describe what she was feeling for him. Love seemed too ordinary a word for the overwhelming rush of emotion swirling in her chest, clogging her throat.

"Can we play our version now?" Max asked through the

microphone. Sed gave him a thumbs-up.

Jessica turned to the stage. Jace climbed out from the piano that had been hidden near the back of the room, and Eric handed a pair of drumsticks back to Exodus End's drummer, Stephen. Knowing that a pair of Sinners had taken over to make her first dance with her husband as romantic as Sed had intended warmed her heart. What a couple of saps.

"How many more traditions do we need to endure before I can get you naked?" Sed whispered.

"Hmm... tossing of the bouquet and garter," she said, speaking loudly since Exodus End had begun to play. The band didn't know the meaning of understated or quiet. "That's about it."

Monica tapped Sed on the shoulder. "May I have this dance?" she asked her son.

"You forgot the mother/son dance." Sed beamed and kissed Jessica before releasing her and tugging his mother into his arms.

"Not sure how to dance to this kind of music," Monica said.

"Just improvise," Sed said, and then he swept her across the dance floor.

Jessica smiled as she watched. She hadn't forgotten. There would be no father/daughter dance for her. She started to leave the floor, not wanting to be completely conspicuous in her lack of a paternal parent. Before she could find a spare seat, she ran headlong into a very tall and lean body. Surprised, she stared up into the smiling face of Eric Sticks.

"Now that Sed is occupied, I'm faced with the opportunity to finally seduce you," Eric said.

She laughed, so grateful that he'd spotted her dilemma that she could have kissed him. In a totally platonic way, of course.

Eric took her hand and led her to the center of the dance floor. Their dance was anything but seductive—it involved a lot of head banging, thrashing, and a bit of air guitar. Soon others began to join them until she was completely surrounded by family and friends and having the time of her life. Instead of playing their own songs, Exodus End took great liberties with the standard list of popular reception songs. This made it fun for everyone as they tried to figure out if the wailing guitar music, thudding drums, and hard core vocals was Eric Clapton's "Wonderful Tonight" or the Temptations' "My Girl." The band even did a metal version of "Ice Ice Baby," made awesome by Logan's skill on bass guitar. Jessica had never been to a more rockin' reception. She was drenched in sweat by the time Sed took her hand and led her off the dance floor.

"We need to leave!" he shouted over the metal version of "Twist and Shout."

She nodded. "Just let me get my bouquet."

She rushed back to the table and grabbed her pretty-much-demolished bouquet before heading to the stage with Sed on her heels. They waited for the current song to end and then climbed the stage to orchestrate their final tradition of the day.

"All the single ladies are needed in the mosh pit," Max said, winking at Jessica. "Time to toss the bouquet."

Jessica waited until everyone who wanted to participate was standing before the stage. She already knew who she was aiming for, so she took a mental snapshot of the crowd and turned to face the opposite direction. She tossed the bouquet over her shoulder and then spun around to see if she'd hit home. Aggie stood staring at the bouquet in her hands as if she didn't recognize what it was. Score! Jessica barely suppressed her victory dance. Aggie received numerous congratulatory pats, but she didn't seem to notice or remember how to blink. It was only when Jace approached her and gave her a playful shove that she awoke out of her stupor.

Jessica laughed when Jace interlaced his fingers and stretched his arms in front of him, limbering up to catch the garter. Jessica was directed into a chair on the stage, and Sed knelt on the floor between her feet.

The look he gave her could have melted the polar ice caps.

"All right," Max said in a farcical emcee voice, "it looks like the bachelors need to line up for the delivery of their life-without-parole sentencing."

Most of the younger men entered the dance floor only when shoved forcefully in that direction. Lawyers and rock stars alike fidgeted as they waited for the verdict.

"Jace," Jessica whispered to Sed, and he nodded.

He nibbled on his lower lip, as if hungry with anticipation while he waited for his cue. His cue was a chorus of "take it off, take it off" from the married gentlemen in the room. Sed delved beneath her skirt. Not just his hand but his entire upper body, including his head and both hands—which he immediately put to good use.

"What is he doing under there? Is he using his teeth?" Max asked.

"Yes!" Jessica squeaked. And that wasn't all he was using.

His mouth moved against her inner thigh, his tongue swirling against her skin between nibbles. The fingers of one hand tugged the garter slowly down her thigh; his other hand moved to the rapidly swelling flesh between her thighs. One finger found her cleft and slid its length, starting at her mound and working its way back until it slipped a scant inch inside her. Her jaw dropped in surprise as her body went from willing to eager in the span of a second. Her mouth opened wider as his mouth began to work its way up her thigh, closer and closer to the throbbing ache at her center. He wouldn't really put his mouth there in front of hundreds of guests, would he?

Oh fuck, he would. No one could see what he was actually doing under the wide skirt of her gown, but they had to be able to tell where his head was and where it was going. Dear lord, she should probably stop him before… His tongue flicked against her clit, and she nearly exploded out of the chair. Probably would have if he hadn't been gripping her thigh with one hand.

He suddenly withdrew, leaving her disoriented and needy for his body. The man was far more daring than most—she loved that about him—but one day he was going to go too far. At least he hadn't made her come in front of everyone.

Still kneeling at her feet but no longer beneath her skirt, he grinned up at her crookedly, clearly challenging her to admonish him for taking such liberties. She wiggled her eyebrows at him instead, and he laughed. He mouthed, *You rock, baby*, before climbing to his feet. He leaned in to kiss her before lifting the garter he'd received at Eric's wedding over his head in victory.

Everyone cheered until he turned to face the bachelors and took aim. Instead of shooting at Jace, he slipped his finger into the stretchy band and let it fly high. Being one of the more vertically challenged in the crowd, Jace was at a disadvantage. That didn't stop him from making a dive for it and landing hard on the wood floor with one hand extended, the garter gripped tightly in his fist. He climbed to his feet and stared directly at Aggie, pointing at his chest and then at her before making a twirling motion with his finger. She beamed a wide smile at him, a flush staining her porcelain-white cheeks, and nodded.

"Wanted to make him work for it," Sed said to Jessica as he helped her to her feet. "Is it time to get naked now?"

"Oh, it's past time for that," she said.

She snatched the microphone out of Max's hand.

"Thank you, everyone, for coming," she said. "Now it's my turn to do just that. Enjoy the rest of your evening. I'm sure I will."

The guys got her joke immediately, but she wasn't sure if many of the women had caught on to the double entendre. But she didn't have time to explain it. She needed her husband and she needed him immediately. She tossed the microphone to Max, who had definitely gotten her joke, if his appreciative grin was any judge, grabbed Sed by the jacket, and headed for the exit at a run.

While they waited for the limo outside, Jessica pulled Sed against her and kissed him deeply. One hand clung to the back of his head, the other began to work the buttons of his shirt. She wasn't going to wait until they got home to have him. If the limo didn't hurry the fuck up, she'd be having him right here on the sidewalk in front of the reception hall.

"Really, Jessica?" Her mother's voice was like a bucket of cold water over her head. "I have never been more mortified in my life."

Jessica kept right on kissing Sed, hoping her mother would take a hint and get lost.

No such luck.

"You have got to be the biggest slut to ever wear white on her wedding day."

More stunned than outraged, Jessica went still. Her mouth remained pressed against her husband's. Sed yanked her away from him and shoved her behind his body.

"I don't give a fuck who you are, lady. No one talks to my wife that way," he growled, cold venom dripping from every word. "You apologize to her and then get the fuck out of her life. She won't be tolerating your abuse anymore. I won't allow it."

Jessica stiffened as his words sank in. That was probably the most controlling thing she'd ever heard anyone say in her entire life. And it was such a huge and blessed relief that she began to shake uncontrollably.

"Apologize?" her mother screeched.

"Now!"

She narrowed her eyes at him before looking at Jessica. "I'm not sorry I called you a slut," her mother said, "but I am sorry you married an asshole."

Her mother stomped off, and Jessica stared after her, so astonished she could scarcely breathe.

"Are you going to let her talk to me like that?" Sed asked in a teasing tone.

Actually, no, she wasn't.

Jessica grabbed her skirt in one hand and raced up the stairs, catching her mother by the arm before she could reenter the building. She spun her around and could tell by the open-mouthed look of shock on her mother's face that she wasn't expecting Jessica to retaliate. Not when she'd so soundly put her in her place.

"I put up with a lot of bullshit from you because you gave birth to me," Jessica said, "but you've laced my life with poison for as long as I can remember, and I'm through with it. Understand? And maybe my husband brings out the slut in me, but unlike you, I don't choose a man to love based on how well he can financially support me. I am happiest when I'm with him and the most miserable when I'm anywhere near you." Jessica barely paused to suck in a breath. She had to get this out quickly because even though she argued with her mother, she had never made it personal. *This* was personal. And she was going to make it count.

"For the record, Sed is not an asshole. If you think he is, then you don't know him at all. He's caring and protective and challenging and a tad egotistical, but there isn't a vindictive bone in his body. So go fuck yourself, Mother. I'm sure it will be more pleasurable than screwing that perverted sleazeball you call a husband."

She didn't give her mother time to collect herself enough to fire back stinging words of retaliation. And maybe when Jessica's heart rate returned to normal and her thoughts cleared of rage, she'd feel bad for saying such horrible things to her mother, but at the moment, she felt light as air as she skipped down the steps and into the waiting limo.

Sed slipped into the car beside her just as a large crowd of guests swarmed out of the building to wave farewell. The driver shut the door, and Sed rolled down the window. She and Sed waved at their friends and family—and a few Hollywood actors neither of them knew—until the limo pulled away.

"Are you okay?" Sed asked, stroking her hair gently.

"Are you filing for an annulment after witnessing how poorly your wife treats her own mother?"

"Of course not. She had it coming."

"Then I'm more than okay. I'm perfect."

He pulled her onto his lap, and she wrapped her arms around his neck. They stared into each other's eyes, and she felt that something between them had changed for the better. Or maybe something had changed in her. Her mother's oppression had weighed her down for so long, she wasn't sure how to handle having it lifted so suddenly.

"Sed?" she whispered, searching his eyes for something deep and true. She found that and more in the man who stared back at her.

"Yeah, baby?"

"You really do bring out the slut in me," she said with a laugh and slid off his lap onto the floor of the car.

She gazed up at him as she unfastened his fly. She never took her eyes off his as she freed his rapidly hardening cock from his pants and licked its tantalizing head.

His belly tightened, his breath quickened, and he lifted a hand to toy with her hair as he watched her with a look of fascination on his handsome face.

"All this and brains too," he murmured.

Her cheeks tightened in a half smile as she descended on his cock, drawing it deep into the recesses of her mouth, determined to taste him before the limo reached their condo. She judged what excited him most by the hitch of his breathing. A combination of bumping his glans against her soft palate and applying hard suction as she backed off had him groaning in bliss. Usually Sed was a man with impressive stamina, so Jessica was shocked when he flooded her mouth with thick cum. She forced his fluids down her throat, not because she hadn't wanted to swallow, but because she had been completely unprepared to do so.

"Sorry," he gasped. "Something about you... Oh God!" His fingers tangled in her hair, pulling her onto him as he filled her throat with a second spurt. "About you..."

He shuddered violently and then went limp, his head dropping back against the seat and his fingers loosening their hold.

She released his spent cock with a loud slurp and then opened the minibar to grab a bottle of water. "Something about me what?" she asked as she opened the bottle and took a long drink.

"On your knees in that dress," he said with a laugh. "Hottest fucking thing I've ever seen in my life. I should have taken a picture."

"So it can end up as our next viral Internet sensation?" She closed one eye and shook her head at the disturbing thought. "No, thank you."

The limo pulled to a stop and Jessica rose from the floor to sit demurely on the seat and sip her water while Sed returned his cock to his pants and hurriedly fastened his fly.

"Sir"—the driver's voice came over an intercom—"it seems I need a code to get in the gate."

Sed hunted for a button and pressed it when he found one. "That's okay. We'll get out here."

"Very well, sir."

A moment later the door opened, and Sed climbed out of the car before taking Jessica's hand and assisting her to her feet. He gave the driver a huge tip—as was customary for Sed—and then led her to the pedestrian entrance to the side of the gated drive.

She gasped when he scooped her up in his arms and cradled her against his broad chest. Jessica had doubted the train of her gown could get any dirtier, but dragging it across a parking lot might do the trick.

"What are you doing?" she asked.

"Carrying you across the threshold," he said, nuzzling her neck and making her giggle.

"We aren't even close to our threshold," she pointed out. The building was across the parking lot, the entrance beyond a landscaped courtyard, and the condo was on the top floor. "Put me down."

"Nope. I want to make sure this threshold thing sticks."

"I'll stick you," she threatened with a grin, and then she wrapped her arms around his neck to lighten his load.

"I'll be doing all the sticking in this relationship."

"You'll hear no complaints from me about that," she said.

She rested a hand over his heart, its steady thud as comforting as his easy gait through the palms lining the walkway.

"We're going to have to start looking for a new house soon," he said. "My place is great for entertaining, but not so great for raising babies."

"We should be okay until the little one starts walking," she said. "Those open-backed marble stairs would give any mother of a toddler a heart attack."

"We created some great memories on those stairs," he said, devilishly lifting an eyebrow at her.

They'd created great memories on every available surface of the entire condo. And a few less available surfaces. She decided they'd better enjoy childless freedom while they had a chance. In a couple of years, fucking on the pool table in the middle of the afternoon might lead to awkward questions.

"Are you glad we decided to start having kids early?" she asked. "Our honeymoon will be cut decidedly short."

"We'll soundproof our bedroom walls," he said. "No worries."

"But we won't be able to make love on the kitchen counter or the sofa or on those hard marble stairs."

"We'll design a huge master suite in our new house. One big enough for a hot tub and a pool table and an entire kitchen if you want. But I've been thinking ahead. I already ordered your wedding gift. One that can bend you into a hundred different positions without taking up too much space. Unfortunately, it hasn't arrived yet."

"My wedding gift?" She smiled up at him. "Aren't *you* my wedding gift? I know you've bent me into at least a hundred different positions in the past few months. Though you do take up more than your fair share of space. You're a bed hog."

He chuckled. "I'm a required accessory for your gift. Ever heard of a tantric chair?"

Tantric? "Uh, no."

A doorman interrupted when he greeted them at the entrance with hearty congratulations. Sed nodded at him in thanks and then stepped onto the waiting elevator with Jessica still in his arms. The doorman helped Sed press the button to the top floor and offered them a knowing wink and a thumbs-up before the elevator doors slid shut. Normally Jessica wouldn't have let Sed carry her like this, but it seemed to make him content. And she loved that his dimples were showing, framing the perma-grin on his handsome face.

When the elevator doors closed, Jessica asked, "So what's a tantric chair?"

"A surprise."

"Is it what you've been teasing me about all day? You know I don't like surprises."

"You like surprises that make you come," he said, nuzzling her ear, his warm breath sending shivers of delight down her neck. "And both of these surprises should do the trick."

He wasn't wrong about her favorite kind of surprise. She was going to google tantric chair the first opportunity she got however.

The elevator opened on the top floor, and he carried her to one of two shiny red doors. There was a pair of sprawling two-story penthouses in the building and one of them belonged to Sed. The other was rarely used by its wealthy European owners, who only spent a couple months out of the year there. Good thing, because occasionally Sed and Jessica didn't quite make it all the way into their condo before succumbing to their insatiable lust for one another.

"Can you get the lock?" Sed asked, holding her next to the numbered keypad.

She punched in the code, and he balanced her precariously as he opened the door and carried her across the threshold. "Welcome home, Mrs. Lionheart," he said. Then he claimed her mouth in a deep kiss.

He kicked the door shut and set her on her feet, sending her spinning in a dizzying twirl so he could unzip her dress and let it drop to the floor.

"I still have sand everywhere," she said.

He made an unintelligible sound in the back of his throat. Apart from her partially loosened white corset and the kitten heels she'd rescued from the beach, she was naked. She glanced over her shoulder to find him staring at the lacings down her back and the cheeks of her ass, as if he was seeing her in a state of undress for the first time.

"Do you like?" she asked, doing the slow seductive stripper walk she'd perfected for the runway as she headed for the stairs and a much needed shower.

"Mercy, baby," he growled. "Show me the front."

She climbed the first step, pretending to ignore him as she threaded her fingers through her long tangled hair. She doubted she was doing a very good job of seducing him in her current state of disrepair.

"Jessica," he said, his voice harsh and raw.

She turned on the stairs to look down at him, her full breasts on display above the corset. Her nipples were as hard as diamonds. Surely he must be able to tell how turned on she was by his attention.

"Yes, Sed?" she asked, tilting her head coquettishly, knowing it made his motor run.

"I can't decide if you look better coming or going," he said.

"I assure you I look better coming," she said, grinning. "Wanna help me with that?"

She continued up the stairs slowly. Taking her time to tease. To lure. He stumbled up the stairs after her, catching her on the top landing with both hands on her chest and his cock planted firmly against her ass. God, how her breasts ached as he massaged her nipples. If sex was always this good while pregnant, she'd gladly carry all eight of the kids Sed claimed to want. She rubbed her ass against him, needing him hard, needing him to fill her.

"We'll have to multitask," he said, using her boobs like steering wheels and her ass like an accelerator to propel her toward the bathroom. "It's important that we aren't late for our evening rendezvous."

"Which would be…"

"A secret."

She sighed. "Of course."

In the bathroom, he turned on the shower and stepped away to look at her front in the mirror and her back right before his eyes. As she examined herself in the mirror—ignoring the rats nest she usually called hair—she had to admit that even though the corset wasn't cinched tightly, it did amazing things for her body.

"Is that thing waterproof?" he asked, tugging her toward the shower.

"I doubt it. And I wouldn't want to ruin it. I know how much work Aggie puts into these things. Unlace me, please."

He struggled with the lacings. Apparently her neat bow had become a not-so-neat knot at some point. By the time he freed her, he was really hurrying her along. "I don't think we have time to fool around," he said, shedding his clothes as quickly as he could and leaving them in a pile on the floor.

"There's always time to fool around, Mr. Lionheart. You just need to learn the place of a quickie."

"Quickie? What's that?"

"You owe me an orgasm for the one I gave you in the limo. Remember?"

"I would never forget that."

She stepped into the shower, and he followed. She turned to put her head under the stream of water and gasped in surprise when Sed sank to his knees, grasped her ass in both hands, and pulled her pussy to his face. His tongue darted in and out of her cleft, working her clit with thought-shattering speed and friction. She moaned in approval and clung to his head. She watched the water coursing down her breasts and belly and over the lips caressing her aching mound. She could get used to the look of him at her feet, wet and naked. Pleasing her. God, how he pleased her. Her breath hitched as his mouth pulled her higher, higher until she shattered with a loud cry of release. He licked her gently to bring her down slowly before patting her bare ass and climbing to his feet.

"Now we're even," he said and turned on the second shower head, so they didn't have to fight for water.

He jumped as water sprayed him in the chest. "Damn, that's cold, but I suppose a cold shower is in order."

She gazed at his rigid cock with appreciation. She knew that erection right there would probably get her through ten earth-shattering orgasms before he found release again, but apparently they were in a hurry. Tomorrow was another day. And she didn't really mind that *quickie* was not in the man's vocabulary.

They hurried through their showers, and he did allow her to blow dry her hair while he dressed, but claimed they didn't have time for her to apply any make-up other than lip gloss since they were already running late.

"You don't need any make-up," he assured her. "I'll be crushed if we miss our reservation time."

And she didn't want to crush him.

"Ah, so we're going to dinner," she said. Hopefully at a restaurant with very private booths so she could play with him beneath the table without prying eyes turned their way.

"Dinner will be included," he said.

She hurried into the walk-in closet—which was bigger than her bedroom had been in the apartment she'd shared with Beth in law school. She shimmied into her panties and bra.

When she turned, Sed lifted a hanger from the rack and held a sexy black dress out to her. "Wear this for me?"

She knew what it meant when he wanted her to wear a skirt in public. Her nipples grew hard in anticipation of what was to come, even if she wasn't exactly sure what was coming. Actually, she was sure what would be coming. *She'd* be coming. She just didn't know how or when or even where.

"Will you be wearing your leather trench coat?" she asked.

"It's in the car."

Chapter 7

JESSICA WATCHED THE COUNTRYSIDE speed by through the windshield of Sed's car.

"Where are we going?" she asked for the tenth time. Did restaurants even exist out here in the middle of nowhere?

"You'll see," Sed said, downshifting to ease the Mercedes around a hairpin turn. "We're almost there."

"I'm tired all of a sudden," she admitted, making a conscious effort not to yawn. "It's been a long day."

He reached across the car and fingered her hair. "So take a little nap. You'll want to be awake for my surprise."

She leaned back against the comfortable leather seat, blinking drowsily as they headed farther and farther out into the middle of nowhere. The next thing she knew, Sed was shaking her shoulder.

"We're here," he said.

She opened her eyes and sat bolt upright in her seat, her eyes wide with wonder. In a field, a colorful hot air balloon waited, tethered to the ground with ropes.

"Sed?" she said, for lack of anything more profound.

"We'll have dinner and bubbly floating high above the earth. And where it leads from there…" He shrugged.

"Can we do it in there?" she whispered, her heart thudding with anticipation.

He chuckled. "We can try. That was my plan."

She grabbed him around the neck and pulled him close so she could kiss him. "I love you," she said against his lips. "Did I ever tell you I've always wanted to make love in a hot air balloon on my wedding night?"

"Uh, no. I don't think so."

"That's probably because I didn't realize I wanted it until just now. Sometimes I think you know me better than I know myself."

He laughed and kissed her deeply. "You like to have sex in unusual places. It's not a mystery, only a challenge to figure out the best spots."

Antsy, she unfastened her seat belt and opened the car door.

"Hurry," she said. "I can't wait."

She fled the car, approaching the balloon in the valley using a half-run/half-skipping gait that made her feel utterly buoyant. Sed quickly caught up with her and took her hand in his.

"Good surprise, huh?" he asked, his voice deep and gruff.

"Great surprise!" she said. "It's so beautiful!"

The balloon was a bright blue with yellow stars and a curved quarter-moon decorating the fabric. The flame beneath the giant sphere glowed bright in the waning light as a man inside the basket pulled a cord and sent fire shooting up into the neck of the balloon.

"I was starting to think you weren't coming," he yelled in greeting.

"Sorry we're late," Sed called. "We had a hard time getting away from the reception."

"Congratulations on your marriage," the man said.

"Thanks. As far as wives go, I think I did all right," Sed said.

Jessica elbowed him in the ribs.

Standing beside the basket, Jessica stared up at the enormous balloon, her mouth agape with wonder. She'd seen hot air balloons in the sky before, but never up close. She couldn't believe how big it was. "Wow," she said.

"I'm Gary Bastion. I'll be flying our craft this evening."

"It's so big!" Jessica said.

"That's what she said," Sed quipped under his breath.

"First time?" Gary asked.

"Oh no, she hasn't been a virgin for a while," Sed said.

Jessica elbowed him in the ribs again. "It's my first time in an air balloon," she said.

"You're in for a treat," Gary said. "You're lucky the storm passed early."

"Lucky, he says," Sed murmured.

"We do have a few things to go over before we can lift off, but we need to hurry."

Jessica and Sed listened to his safety spiel. They even practiced the tuck and kneel position they were supposed to assume should they be in for a rare rough landing.

"Careful," Sed said as Jessica flattened herself face down on the ground. "You'll squash little Sed."

"Is she pregnant?" Gary asked.

"Yeah. We sort of started our family early," Sed said, giving Jess's belly an affectionate rub. "Couldn't wait for the honeymoon."

"How far along are you?"

Jessica looked up into Gary's concerned face.

"About ten weeks," she said. "Why?"

"We don't allow women in their third trimester to fly at all," he said. "There's always a slight danger of a rough landing, one that could trigger early labor."

"Should we cancel?" Sed asked, a mixture of concern and disappointment on his face.

"I'll leave that up to you. I've never had a rough landing— though there's a first time for everything—and she's not close to giving birth or anything. Have you had any complications with your pregnancy?"

"No," she said. "None."

Gary nodded, but his expression was serious. "The chances are slim that there will be any issues with the landing, but there's always a chance."

Sed looked to Jessica and squeezed her hand. She really wanted to ride in the balloon and she was far from her third trimester. How rough could a balloon landing possibly be? She couldn't imagine it being too extreme.

"I really want to go," Jessica said. "You went to all this trouble to arrange it and the danger is slight. It is slight, isn't it?" she asked Gary.

"Almost nonexistent."

She nodded at Sed. "Let's do it."

"If you're sure," Sed said. "I won't be upset if you're worried and want to cancel."

"I don't want to cancel. I'm not worried at all."

Sed smiled and nodded. "Everything will be fine."

"All right," Gary said. "Climb aboard."

Sed helped Jessica climb the ladder, and Gary gave her a hand over the edge of the basket and inside. Sed was soon standing beside her looking up at the balloon with as much wonder in his expression as she felt.

"Give me a minute to talk to Gary man-to-man," Sed whispered in her ear. She had a feeling he'd let his wallet do most of the talking, but she did want to make love to her husband floating high above the earth. She hoped Gary was accommodating. Sed and his wallet could be very persuasive.

Jessica leaned over the basket and noticed a woman sitting in the grass near one of the tethers. Jessica waved at her and got an enthusiastic wave in return. A cool wind rustled though Jessica's hair, and she rubbed her hands over her upper arms, wishing she'd thought to bring a sweater. But how was she supposed to have known that she'd need one when Sed refused to tell her his plans for that evening? A warm, hard body pressed against her side, and Sed wrapped an arm around her lower back.

"Cold?" he murmured into her ear.

"A little," she admitted, but that wasn't why she was shivering. It had been a very long day and she very much needed to get lost in her man's arms. "Well? What did Gary say?"

"He doesn't allow that sort of thing to go on in his balloon while he's watching."

"Oh," Jessica said, her voice flat with disappointment.

"But for a couple thousand dollars, he promised to look the other way."

With his sensual mouth, he caressed the skin just below her ear—nibbling, licking, suckling that delicious spot until her knees went weak and she groaned.

He stepped away. "Dinner first," he said. "Then dessert."

"I want dessert now, "Jessica said.

He captured her mouth in a heated kiss. Her entire body thrummed with pent-up sexual energy as she kissed him desperately.

He tugged away and leaned close to whisper in her ear, "I'm worth the wait."

She was well aware of that, but spanked his ass for being so full of himself.

He left her standing there and went to sit at a small rattan table next to one edge of the basket.

"Are you coming?" he asked, gesturing toward the seat across from him.

"Not yet, unfortunately," she grumbled under her breath.

But the table built for two was inviting—though not quite as alluring as its occupant—so she rubbed the chill out of her bare arms and took her seat. The table felt a bit awkward. The seats were higher than a normal chair—more like tall beanbags than anything—and when she was seated, the table was very close to the tops of her thighs. She wondered at the strange configuration until she peered out over the edge of the basket and realized she'd be able to see out while they dined. That would explain why the cushions were high, but why was the table so low in comparison?

Gary came to stand near the table. "My wife is an excellent

cook," he said proudly. "She's gone to retrieve your meals from the warmer in the SUV. Once the food is on board, we'll cast off, and she'll follow us in the chase car. You'll have to serve yourselves, I'm afraid. I'll be keeping the balloon on course. And we have to land before it gets dark."

"Why is the table so low?" Jessica asked.

"So your dinner doesn't fly overboard and spook the vineyard grapes," Gary said and then laughed.

"Oh," she said, smiling. "That makes sense."

"Is this your first dinner cruise?"

"Nope. My wife proposed to me on a dinner cruise," Sed said, nodding at Jessica. "But it was on a boat."

"*She* proposed to you?" Gary's eyebrows lifted comically.

"Yeah, she was a little desperate, I think." Sed grunted when she kicked him in the shin.

"You've got it all wrong. I proposed to Pes, remember?" Jessica said.

Sed laughed. "He's my evil twin."

"Is that why you put this together?" Jessica asked. "Trying to one-up my proposal dinner?"

"Of course not. I wanted to give you a wedding night you'll never forget."

She reached across the table and took his hand. "You know what it does to me when you're uncharacteristically sweet, don't you?"

He wiggled his eyebrows at her. "I am well aware of that, Mrs. Lionheart. I might have a few ulterior motives here."

"Boats are romantic," Gary admitted with a shrug, "but I think your husband might have you beat with the hot air balloon. Not that I'm partial or anything."

"We'll see," Jessica said. "If so, I'll have to come up with something even more splendid to reclaim my title as biggest romantic fool."

"Gary! A little help, please," a woman's voice said from the opposite side of the basket.

Gary went to help his wife load two lightweight Styrofoam coolers into the balloon.

Sed tilted his head at Jessica while they waited. "You look chilled."

"I have a feeling it's going to be even colder once we take off," she said.

"I'll be back."

"Where are you going?"

"Patience, love," he said with a grin.

Next thing she knew, Sed spoke a few words to Gary and was gone. She craned her neck to watch him jog across the field to the car. A moment later he was on his way back carrying his leather trench coat. Oh yeah, she knew what that meant. He only wore the trench coat when they were trying to keep their public liaisons as clandestine as possible.

Jessica looked up and smiled at Sed when he dropped the coat over her shoulders a few minutes later.

"Better?" he asked, placing a kiss on her temple.

She snuggled into the coat and inhaled the scent of leather and Sed—a heady combination. She felt instantly warmer, more than half of it due to anticipation, not the garment. "Yes, thank you. I'm glad you remembered it was in the car."

He took the seat across from her again, and Gary's wife approached the table. "You'll have to serve yourself," she said, "but everything that's warm is in the cooler with the red tape and everything cold is in the blue-taped one."

"What's on the menu?" Jessica asked, leaning over to lift the lid of the red cooler. The lid slammed shut before she could get a look at or a sniff of the contents. Sed's hand rested on the cooler, blocking her inspection.

"Patience, baby," he said.

"But I don't have any patience," Jessica said.

Gary's wife opened the blue cooler and placed a plastic bucket of ice in the center of the table. Jessica wondered if everything in the balloon was kept light or soft to prevent injury. Either that or Gary and his wife were cheap.

Gary's wife retrieved a bottle and forced it into the ice bucket, rattling and crunching ice as she pressed down.

"Utensils and glasses for your toast are in the basket there," she said, pointing behind Sed. "I think that should cover everything. Enjoy your evening. And congratulations on your marriage." She glanced specifically at Jessica when she asked her next question. "Was this really all your husband's idea?"

Jessica nodded. "It was a complete surprise."

"I think you have a keeper." She winked and turned to give Gary a kiss before climbing over the basket to leave.

"A keeper, huh?" Jessica said, grinning at Sed, who was looking very pleased with himself.

He cocked his head slightly, looking so sexy that Jessica had to cling to her squishy chair to keep from leaping across the table and tackling him.

"Was there ever any doubt?" he asked.

She chuckled. "Not in your mind."

Jessica felt increasingly light-headed and she realized that the balloon was free of its tethers and rising. She hadn't even felt it lift off. The burner roared as Gary pulled some rope that made the flames shoot high into the interior of the balloon.

"I'd think the thing would catch fire," Jessica said nervously.

"You're safe," Sed murmured.

He always made her feel safe. "I know."

She watched the earth slowly fall away as Sed rattled around in the basket and produced a pair of plates, utensils, and champagne flutes. She melted when she saw that their toasting glasses were engraved with a pair of wedding rings tied together with a ribbon, her and Sed's names, and the date. He'd thought of everything. He really was a keeper. Well, most days. Some days he was positively infuriating, but those days were becoming increasingly rare.

"I'm not sure how much I can eat after all that cake at the reception."

"I think you'll manage," he said.

He stood to get the food from the coolers. First he scooped tossed salad on her salad plate, then he opened the hot food containers. When she reached toward a spoon to help herself to some delicious-smelling herbed risotto, Sed snatched the spoon away from her.

"Allow me," he said.

"Sed, I can serve myself."

"I never doubted it," he said. "But just because you can doesn't mean you have to. Let me take care of you tonight. Without argument. It would really mean a lot to me."

She drew her eyebrows together. "Why?"

"Because I care about you."

"I care about you too, but I don't feel the need to serve you to demonstrate it."

"Well, tonight I do have that need. Can you handle it? Someone who loves you trying to take care of you?"

"I never said I couldn't handle it."

But as he filled her plate with food, she had to admit that it did bother her. She'd promised herself long ago that she'd never allow a man to rule her life and for some reason, this felt like a step in that direction.

"Can I serve you?" she asked, thinking that might make her feel a bit more comfortable about allowing him to choose how much and what kind of food she would receive.

"You can service me," he said, his voice gruff with desire.

Jessica pursed her lips. Was he trying to get a rise out of her? She knew her temper turned him on, but she really didn't want to argue tonight. Especially not here, where everything was so romantic due to his thoughtfulness.

"I think I'll let you service me," she retorted.

"I am willing, if not able," he said with a crooked grin. "The table is kind of low for me to get at you properly. Wasn't the shower enough?"

"You know I never get enough of you."

He grinned cockily and opened another container of food. The scents of basil and garlic, tomato and oregano stirred her appetite. She loved tortellini and couldn't wait to see what it was stuffed with.

When he had Jessica's plate full and arranged as he wanted it, Sed took his seat again. Everything looked and smelled delicious and the tortellini was stuffed with mushrooms and sausage—her favorite combination, which she was certain was not a coincidence. Still, she picked at her food, hardly sampling a bite.

"It really bothers you, doesn't it?" Sed said, having no qualms about devouring his own dinner.

"What bothers me?"

"The fact that I fixed your plate."

"What bothers me is that you decided what I wanted and how much and where on my plate it should go."

"I know you don't like me to make decisions for you, but don't you think you're over-reacting?"

"Probably," she admitted. "But I can't help it."

"Try," he challenged. "Learn to compromise."

"You don't compromise either," she said, spearing a bit of yellow squash and popping it into her mouth.

"I compromise with you more than I've ever had to compromise with anyone else," he said. "The problem is, we both like to be in charge."

She couldn't argue with that. It was blatantly obvious.

"So if you let me be in charge every once in a while, I'll let you be in charge occasionally, and we'll both have that need met. The rest of the time we can butt heads and argue if you like."

"I don't like to argue," she said.

"Right," he said, the word twisted with sarcasm. "And I'm sure that's why you became an attorney. Because you hate arguing so much you decided to do it for a living."

She flushed as she realized he was totally right. She loved to argue. In fact, no one argued with her the way Sed did. And few men would have been strong enough to give it to her as good as she gave it. Most men were afraid to cross her. Not because she was scary, but because they were attracted to her and thought by bending to her will, she'd be more likely to give them what they wanted. But not Sed. Sed pushed her relentlessly. It was one of the things she loved most about him. And the very thing about him that drove her crazy.

"So I like to argue," she said with a shrug. "I'm not the only one. You like to argue too."

Sed chuckled. "I only argue with you, babe. With everyone else, I boss and they obey."

"Just try to boss me and see if I obey," she said in a clipped tone.

"I know bossing doesn't work with you," he said. "I thought maybe taking you up in a hot air balloon and asking you nicely would do the trick."

"Do I not make you happy the way I am?"

"Of course you do. Never doubt that."

"Then where is this coming from?" she asked.

He stared out the basket at the passing treetops for a long moment. "It's hard for me sometimes. To step back. To let you do your own thing without interfering. It makes me feel less of a man."

She gaped at him. Had she really made him feel that way? "Sed, that doesn't make you less of a man."

"Yeah, well..." He shrugged. "I'm learning to compromise. But I do crave a bit more control. I can't lie about it. It's a struggle to keep that side of me under wraps. But you're worth the trouble."

He *was* getting better at compromising. They didn't fight nearly as often as they once had, but she hadn't realized it was because he was the one compromising the most, letting her get her way. She needed to meet him halfway. And if that entailed allowing him to choose what she had on her plate when he surprised her with a romantic dinner, she could handle that. Maybe with a little practice, she could let him have a bit more control of her life. But just a little. Their marriage would have to be a partnership. She would never tolerate living under a dictatorship. Of course, there was one place she never minded him being the boss.

"You know there are times when I like you to boss me around," she said.

He met her eyes and lifted a skeptical brow at her. "When?"

"In the bedroom," she said. "You know how hot that makes me, don't you?"

"I thought you obeyed in the bedroom because you know I never disappoint."

She laughed, choosing to take her husband's ego with a grain of salt. Besides, she couldn't argue with his boasting when it happened to be true.

"I guess that's part of it," she said. "But when you fuck me and make me say things—things I would never say anywhere else—it's exhilarating. Freeing."

"What kinds of things?" he asked.

"*This pussy is mine,*" she said gruffly. "*Say it. Say it, Jess.*"

He shifted in his seat. "Well, it *is* mine."

"Actually," she said, "it's mine."

He tilted his head slightly as he assessed her. "I never realized how much it must cost you to give me that much power over you."

"You know if I didn't like it, I wouldn't let you." She nibbled her lower lip as she put her thoughts to words. "So dominate me in the bedroom, but let me decide on my own dinner."

"Is that why you aren't eating?"

She nodded. "Ridiculous, isn't it?"

"I didn't mean to dominate your dinner, Jess. I just wanted to show you that I care about you."

"I know, baby. I'll try not to blow these things out of proportion."

"If you don't want to eat, you don't have to. I thought you liked tortellini."

He still wasn't quite understanding the reason it bothered her, but she needed him to get her. She knew how things got between them when they weren't perfectly clear. She reached across the table and plopped a spoonful of squash onto his plate. Sed didn't like squash. He'd ordered it because she liked it.

His brow crinkled. "What do you think you're doing?"

"Would you like another roll?" she asked.

"Um, I guess."

She placed another roll on his plate.

"So which method did you prefer? Me taking it upon myself to dump squash on your plate without consulting you or me asking if you'd like a roll before putting it on your plate?"

"Are you treating me like a kindergartner, Jess?" Sed chuckled and rubbed his forehead. "Okay, I get it. It isn't that you don't want me to show you that I care about you, you just want to be involved in the decision-making process."

"Yes!" she said, emphasizing the word with her hands. "That's exactly it."

"I'll work on that."

"And what should I work on to make you happy in this relationship? Because nothing is more important to me than making this work, Sed. I love you."

"I am happy in this relationship. You're perfect just the way you are," he said.

She rolled her eyes and shook her head. "Oh, please."

"You are. I don't want you to change—not a single thing about you. But I'll try to change if it will make you happy."

Oh no, she'd hurt his feelings again. She kept forgetting how sensitive he was about certain things because he was so good at hiding that sensitivity. She climbed from her cushion and squeezed in beside him on his.

"I don't want you to change, Sed. I just want you to be more careful about pushing my buttons."

"But I like pushing your buttons," he said close to her ear. "It makes your passion burn bright. But I wasn't trying to push your buttons tonight. I was trying to make the night special for you. A gift just from me and just for you on our wedding day."

And she'd made him feel like it wasn't special. Fuck. She was really screwing things up here. This was what she needed to work on, whether he realized it or would even admit to it. She had to be more careful with his feelings. Better at recognizing things that would hurt him *before* the fact rather than after, when the damage had already been done.

She touched his face, delighting in the slight roughness of a five o'clock shadow on his cheek. "Tonight is special," she whispered. "You made it special for me."

He smiled, his dimples cutting deep into his cheeks. "I did?"

"Mmm hmm." Her body recognized his close proximity and

instantly awakened, craving his touch. "Kiss me."

"Our dinner's getting cold," he murmured just before he claimed her mouth in a searing kiss.

The coat dropped from her shoulders as she wrapped her arms around his neck and got lost in him. His large, strong hands dug into her back, drawing her closer—closer—as if he wanted to meld their flesh. That wouldn't be happening while they were fully clothed, sitting mostly side by side, and with an audience.

Jessica tore her mouth from Sed's, breathing hard as she attempted to regain her wits. No good. Her brain was never fully functional in his presence, and it refused to start functioning again until her body found release. Sometimes several releases.

"God, I want you," she said with a groan.

"You'll have me after dinner."

A shiver of delight tingled at the nape of her neck. She wanted him behind her, his hands holding her breasts, teeth nibbling that spot under her hairline, cock buried deep.

"But I want you now," she insisted.

"But you have to wait," he said, his mocking grin making an appearance. "Are you cold, love?" he asked.

If she was, she hadn't noticed on account of the heat burning through her sex.

"Your nipples are hard." He cupped one breast and massaged the stiff point with his thumb.

"Not cold," she said, shuddering with delight. "Hot. For you."

She reached for his cock, but he caught her hand.

"After dinner," he said with an air of authority she couldn't argue against. Well, perhaps she could have argued, but she didn't want to. She wanted to be done with dinner.

She shifted, forcing her body from the place it most wanted to be—against her big, hunky husband—and moved to rise so she could return to her seat and finish the dinner that was getting in the way of more carnal delights. Sed's arm went around her back, and he grabbed her hip, tugging her securely against his side.

"You're not going anywhere, Mrs. Lionheart," he said. "I want you right here beside me."

Now that her body was burning for him, she didn't have the mental capacity to assert her independence. She snuggled into his side and sighed in contentment. He reached across the table and pulled her plate before her. There really wasn't enough room for two people to dine comfortably on one side of the small table, but comfort was far from her mind as she reached for her fork.

He took it from her. "I'll feed you."

The fire in her body died down as the fire in her heart flared back to life. "Oh you will, will you?" she asked, her tone hard with temper.

"What would you like first?" he asked reasonably.

She let a breath out slowly, reminding herself that he was just trying to be romantic and that if she got all defensive now, it would hurt his feelings. And then he'd pretend like he was angry instead of hurt and their whole evening would explode into another argument and then they'd fuck each other until they were raw and spent and too delirious with pleasure to be angry anymore. She was fine with that last part. It was the rest she wanted to avoid.

"Salad," she said.

He speared several leaves of romaine with her fork and carefully placed them in her open mouth. While she chewed and tried to conjure up romantic feelings about being fed, Sed took several bites of his tortellini.

"Would you like to try the tortellini? It's really good."

"Okay."

He fed her a bite of tortellini, and she murmured in bliss as the Italian spices, cheeses, and tomato sauce delighted her taste buds.

"That is good."

"Do you want some of this squash?" he asked, indicating the large mound on his plate. The mound she'd placed there to prove a point.

He fed her a lot more squash than she really wanted, but as the reminder of her lesson shrank in size, she relaxed more and more. She started to notice the scenery outside the balloon's basket as they sailed almost silently over vineyards and foothills. She also noticed how much care Sed put into feeding her—asking her what she'd like, selecting prime bites, gently placing them in her mouth, patiently waiting while she chewed. It made her feel cherished, not dominated. Weird.

When their plates were clean and their bellies full, Sed took her chin between his thumb and forefinger and kissed her gently.

Staring deeply into her eyes, he asked, "How was that?"

"Romantic," she said dreamily. She leaned toward him, a sappy grin on her face.

"You keep looking at me like that and romance will be the last thing on my mind."

This time when he kissed her, it was a bit raw. A bit rough. Jessica clung to his huge biceps as she opened her mouth to him and let him devour her.

He drew away, nipping her lip playfully before reaching for the bottle that was chilling in the blue plastic ice bucket. "Let's go watch the scenery," he said.

She opened her mouth to agree, and he said, "I mean, would you like to watch the scenery, Jessica?"

"I would," she said. "If you promise to keep me warm."

He slid his free hand down her back. "Will you settle for hot?"

"I suppose hot will do." Feeling positively giddy, she giggled.

She slid from the squishy seat and went to stand by the side of the basket, staring down at the lush green landscape below. Sed handed her the pair of engraved champagne flutes and gave the bottle a vigorous shake.

"Sed, don't shake it."

Too late. He lodged his thumbs firmly under the plastic cork, and it ejected from the end of the bottle with a loud *pop*. White froth exploded from the mouth of the bottle into the sky beyond the basket.

"Someone's cows might be a bit tipsy tonight," Jessica said, peering down at the miniature black and white spotted animals scattered across the expansive field below.

"Much more fun than regular cow tipping. But there's no alcohol in this since you're now drinking for two."

Sed took a champagne glass from her and filled it to the brim with sparkling grape juice before handing it back and filling the second glass.

"To us," he said, clinking his glass against hers and downing the entire glass in four long gulps.

"To us," she echoed, taking a tiny sip her own bubbly. It wasn't quite as delicious as real champagne, but she didn't get along with real champagne very well in the first place. The last time she'd gotten drunk on champagne, she'd been in Vegas and had said some pretty awful things to Sed. It was also when she realized why she'd hated him so much at the time. She'd hated him because no matter how much she fought it, she had never stopped loving him. And now she was glad she never would.

"Thanks," she said, covering her lower belly with one hand. "For thinking about the baby."

"I'm always thinking about the baby," he said.

She smiled in gratitude and took a long drink as he reached for the bottle and refilled his glass, tossing it back without pause. Neither of them would be getting drunk tonight, but Sed seemed to suddenly hope the bubbling grape juice had fermented since his first glass. And Jessica was wondering why.

Chapter 8

SED REFILLED HIS GLASS with more grape juice and swallowed a gulp. He wished it had alcohol in it; a little liquid courage never hurt. He wasn't sure why he was so nervous anyway. She'd already married him. And it wasn't as if he hadn't written songs about her before. Hell, he'd performed them in front of tens of thousands of fans, but this particular string of lyrics—the ones he wanted to sing in her ear—was too personal to share with the world. She'd be the only one to ever hear it. Well, except for Gary the pilot, if he was paying them any mind.

"It's so beautiful up here," Jessica said, leaning her forearms on the rim of the basket, her glass of bubbly held loosely between her elegant hands.

Sed moved to stand directly behind her. He shifted to lean against her back. Not too solidly—he didn't want to put too much pressure on the baby after the poor little tyke had been squashed into a corset earlier that day. Not that Jess hadn't looked fucking hot in that corset. She had. He'd just felt a bit sorry for Sed Junior. If his son was anything like him, he liked a bit of room to let it all hang out.

"I was going to do this at the ceremony," he said, "but things didn't go exactly as planned."

And maybe that unexpected deluge of rain had been a blessing.

"Do what?" she asked with a giggle. "Poke me in the ass with your junk?"

He rubbed his semi-hard cock against her ass. "My *junk*? Surely it deserves more respect than that."

"Very well. Poke me in the ass with your magnificent specimen of man-meat. Your love hammer. Your one-eyed anaconda."

He chuckled. "That's better." Maybe… "Our vows," he said, burying his face in her sweet-smelling hair. "We never said them. Not the real ones."

She stiffened and covered her mouth with her hand. "You're right. How could I have forgotten?"

She tried to turn to face him, but he held her front firmly against the basket. He cupped her breasts in his hands and nuzzled the back of her neck. His cock leapt with excitement, more than ready to be buried within her slick heat. Jessica instantly went limp in his arms.

He sang the words to her; somehow they meant more that way. He held her tightly in his arms, swaying back and forth to the cadence in his head.

"There are few things that steal my breath. They would be you, you, you. And few things that I'll love 'til death. Also you, you, you. From the moment that you caught my eye, and I knew I had to make you mine, I wondered if I should give my heart to you. I do, I do, I do."

"That's so sweet," she whispered.

He wasn't finished.

"Only one thing makes me more complete." He slid a hand low to cover her belly. Their child. "Part you, part me, inseparably. No way to ever untangle us two, when two become one and one becomes three."

"Or ten if you have your way," she said with a soft laugh.

"True. But that didn't rhyme," he said before continuing.

"There are few things that could steal my heart. Only you, you, you. And few things that could tear us apart." He spoke the next line. "Or nothing. You're stuck with me now, Jess. Like it or not."

"I like it," she insisted.

And then he finished the song in his baritone. "It's true, true, true. I love you, you, you. Say I do, do, do."

"I do!" She laughed. "I mean I did! But I still do. Did you write that?"

"Of course I wrote that. That's why it sucks so much. My lyrics come out better when I'm angry or pissed off. So forgive the lameness of my sap." He rested his chin on her shoulder and closed his eyes. His heart was still thudding like a spooked jackrabbit in his chest. Mushy love songs were so not his thing. He'd prefer to growl and scream about fire and brimstone any day.

"It doesn't suck, baby. It meant a lot to me and brought tears to my eyes."

"Oh yeah, sure," he said. "You and all the angels in heaven." He chuckled and rolled his eyes toward the weeping angels above them. They were probably weeping because it had been so ridiculous and stupid.

"My turn," she said and squirmed sideways. "But I want to look at you when I say mine."

He gave her just enough space to turn around before drawing

her against him again, belly to belly. He was surprised to see she really was teary eyed. So many females in his past had used tears to try to get him to respond or react in a certain way, so usually tears didn't affect him. But these tears—even though they hadn't left her jade-green eyes—had his heart clenching in his chest. Or maybe it was the look of utter adoration in her eyes. His Jess was really his now. He stole a kiss—unable to help himself—and then stared into her eyes as she spoke her heart to him.

"We will share many perfect and happy moments in our lives together, Sed. Unfortunately, we will also share heartaches and tragedies. For all the good times and the bad, as well as everything between, I promise to be by your side and ever in your corner—to support you and defend you. You are my greatest champion and my most difficult challenge, which is why, no matter what life throws at us, I know we'll make it through. Our love will be stronger for our efforts. It's a true and lasting love. One that cannot be denied or destroyed. It's forever, Sed."

She took his hand and rubbed the wedding band she'd already placed there, reminding him that these were her vows to him. "Today I take you as my partner in life and in love. I trust in you and in us. Separately, each of us is strong, but together, there is nothing we can't overcome. I promise to cherish each moment with you, my husband, and occasionally let you get your way."

She winked at him, and he laughed. He hugged her against his chest, his hand cupping the back of her head to hold her as close to his achingly full heart as possible.

"Well no angels are weeping over my spiel," she murmured, snuggling even closer.

He blinked the moisture from his eyes and kissed her hair. "No angels," he said in gruff voice, "but maybe one sinner."

"I'm not going to look," she said to his chest. "Or I'll be a blubbering mess."

He gazed out over the countryside as he held her close. The sun was beginning to set on the distant horizon, and as much as he loved embracing her, he couldn't rob her of such a beautiful sight.

"I think you should watch our first sunset as husband and wife," he whispered.

She lifted her face from his chest and turned her head. Brilliant pinks and streaks of orange decorated the few residual clouds in the sky.

"Breathtaking," she said, turning in his arms to face outward once again.

He stepped close behind her and cradled her lower belly in both hands. Resting his cheek against her hair, he closed his eyes and treasured the feel of her in his arms. He was definitely breathless. No sunset did that to him. But she did. "That's what he said," he murmured.

"I think you should grab your trench coat," she said. "Put it on now. You must be chilled."

Sed stiffened as he recognized what her suggestion meant; she wanted him to make love to her right here, right now. With nothing but a long leather duster to shield them from prying eyes. The pilot had assured him that he'd give them their privacy, but the basket was relatively small. There was little privacy to be had.

"You sure?" he asked, remembering a time when their lust for public displays of affection had nearly destroyed her happiness and her career.

"Yes," she said. "I'm sure."

He retrieved the trench coat from the floor of the basket and slipped his arms into the sleeves. It draped him all the way to the ground and was a few sizes too large on purpose. He wrapped his arms around her, completely enveloping her with his body and the cover of the heavy leather. She took the free edges of the coat in her hands so the sides would cover most of her and leave his hands free to do as he would. He'd touch her, he decided, and give her release, but he wouldn't risk penetrating her. Not here. He could wait.

He cupped her firm breast with one hand, massaging gently. She shuddered against him. Recently her breasts had become incredibly sensitive. He touched her far more carefully than he would have liked, but knew she couldn't handle rough treatment since he'd gotten her pregnant.

"Sed," she said breathlessly, "touch my bare skin."

He slipped the straps of her dress and bra down over one shoulder and lowered the fabric so that the top half of her breast was exposed. Arm crossing her body, his fingers delved beneath the cup of her bra to stroke her stiff nipple.

"Oh," she gasped.

While he had her distracted with pleasure, his other hand moved to her thigh and slowly slid the skirt of her dress upward. Her bare flank quivered beneath his feather-light touch. He glanced quickly over his shoulder to find Gary paying them absolutely no mind as he watched the scenery and controlled the balloon's flight.

Sed slid his fingers beneath the elastic at the leg of Jessica's panties, rubbing his fingertips against her skin from her hipbone to one soft, swollen lip. Her body jerked in response, thrusting her breast into his hand and pressing her ass against his burgeoning erection. Yeah, he could wait about five minutes before penetrating her, he decided. She did bring out the beast in him.

"Please, Sed," she whispered breathlessly. "Take them off."

"Take what off?" he growled low in her ear. He knew what that tone of voice did to her, and the trembling of her flesh proved she was as hot and eager for him as ever.

"My panties." She groaned as his fingers delved into the moisture pooling in her pussy.

He fisted the fabric in one hand and tugged. "These panties?"

"Yes, those. Unless you're wearing some. Then take yours off too."

He chuckled. "You know I always go commando, baby."

"Good. Because I want you inside me. Hurry."

He pinched her nipple, and she gasped.

"Maybe I don't want to hurry," he said. "Maybe I want to tease you a bit. Maybe I want you to beg for my cock."

The woman was all submissive and cooperative when she was aroused. So he wasn't really surprised when she said, "Please, Sed." She rubbed her ass over his throbbing erection. "Slide it inside me. I want it. I want it deep inside."

And the lady always got what she wanted. He inched her panties down her thighs, first one side, then the other, as he used one hand to remove them. His other hand was still very much occupied with her breast. Once her panties were down far enough to drop to her ankles on their own, Sed slid his hand between her legs and nibbled the back of her neck. He was rewarded with a flood of heat against his hand. He bent two fingers upward to tease her slick opening, but didn't slide them inside. Not even when she began to moan and rock against his hand.

"Shh," he whispered. "We're not alone, remember?"

"I'm sure he knows what we're doing," Jessica said.

"But we don't have to be obvious about it."

"Just slide it inside, Sed. You don't have to thrust if you're self-conscious about it."

Did she even realize what she was saying? He had her breast in one hand and her raw pussy in the other. There wasn't a self-conscious bone in his entire body. Hell, he didn't even need the trench coat. He'd have sex with her with Gary watching and taking close-up pictures on his camera phone to post on the Internet. He didn't give a fuck about propriety. But he *was* concerned for Jessica and knew how delirious she became when she was turned on. She didn't have a clue what she was asking him to do. He would be very upset if she got mad at him later because he did what she wanted.

She let go of one side of the duster and it immediately swung back. If Gary was looking their way, he would be in no doubt about what they were doing. He'd have a full view of Jessica's bare breast in one of Sed's hands and her slick pussy in the other. Jessica didn't seem to care that she was exposed. Her hand moved to his crotch and massaged his length through his pants.

"Please, Sed," she said breathlessly. "How many times do I have to beg before you take me?"

He released her breast to pull the coat around her again. "Hold the duster, and I'll give it to you. All of it." He bit her ear, and she shuddered.

She grabbed the leather and, as a man true to his word, he unfastened his fly and tugged his cock free. His mouth dropped open when his most sensitive skin brushed against the smooth warm flesh of her ass.

"Oh God," she said, inhaling the words in her excitement. "I want you so bad. Hurry."

His thoughts went thick with lust, and he became a creature of want and need. Nothing mattered but claiming her. Fucking her. She leaned forward, her hands on the sides of his coat tugging him down with her. He grabbed her hip with one hand and his throbbing dick with the other. Her pussy was sweet heaven as he dragged his cockhead through its warm moisture. She was fucking drenched. And he fucking loved that she liked having sex in unusual places as much as he did. He slipped inside her easily. And she tightened around him, her walls squeezing his tip, making his abs clench as pleasure consumed him and instinct claimed all rational thought. She relaxed around him, and he pushed deeper, pausing when she clenched again. She had the most sensational pussy on the planet. He knew that from experience.

"God, Jess," he groaned near her ear. "Let me in."

Instead of relaxing her amazingly strong internal muscles, she rotated her hips. His breath caught in his throat and his eyelids fluttered as sensations of pleasure rippled down his length, settling in his balls and pulsating deep inside him.

Cursing under his breath, he gripped both her hips and tugged her back, back, forcing himself deeper and deeper. Fuck, she was tight. So tight. She relaxed unexpectedly, and he claimed her last few inches, his balls bouncing delightfully against her.

"Deeper," she insisted breathlessly. "Oh please."

He couldn't take her deeper in this position, but he wanted deeper too. He had at least another inch to give her.

"Hold on," he instructed.

She reached for the edge of the balloon's rough basket, losing her grip on the duster. Gravity kept her covered this time as she leaned forward. Once she had both the basket and the flaps of the coat secured in both hands, he removed one arm from a sleeve and wrapped it around her waist inside the coat. He then carefully lifted her feet off the ground so that she was high enough for her pelvis to be above his. He stepped forward and tugged her down, groaning as she took all of him—every inch—deep inside her. He braced himself, feet apart for balance, and tightened his leather-covered arm around her lower belly for stability. His now free hand delved between her legs, fingers seeking her clit. When he found it, he rubbed fast and vigorously, sending her flying in seconds.

Her startled cry of release was quickly stifled. He kept working her clit as her body jerked and strained against him, and her pussy clutched him harder than ever. She went limp, leaning heavily against the edge of the basket—catching her breath, her bearings.

After a moment, she planted her feet firmly on the floor of the basket and began to rock ever so slightly to help him reach the bliss she'd already experienced. As much as he loved being buried balls deep inside her, the woman had a talent with the muscles just inside her entrance. He tugged back and took her with slow, shallow strokes while she squeezed and tugged him closer and closer to nirvana.

"Beautiful sunset," she murmured.

Sed forced his eyes open and tried to focus on the brilliant orange glow on the distant horizon, but he couldn't see a damned thing with his eyes rolled up in his head.

"Mmm," he said in agreement, his slow shallow strokes growing more rapid.

He sort of watched the sun sink beneath the horizon as he sought release and found only a slowly building pleasure that made his belly quiver and balls ache with lack of fulfillment.

"We'll be landing soon," a voice interrupted Sed's

concentration on his wife's glorious pussy.

He refused to finish their ride without finishing his ride. His thrusts strengthened, burying him deeper inside her again. She writhed her hips for him, in tune with his need to come. His breathing quickened and his muscles tautened as orgasm approached. She felt so good around him. So good. Oh God, Jess. He fought the urge to cry out when his fluids erupted from him at long last. He grabbed Jessica's breasts—one bare, one covered—and pulled her into him as he exploded inside her. Finally spent, he leaned heavily against her back, shuddering as aftershocks of pleasure rippled through him.

"God, I love you, woman," he said.

He gave her bare breast a gentle squeeze before tucking it back inside the cup of her disheveled bra.

"I wonder where my wife is," Gary said. "I don't see the chase car."

"One should never misplace one's wife," Sed whispered to Jessica, who giggled.

"I don't think you have to worry about that," she said. "You're stuck with me."

"More like stuck in you."

"For now. But eventually you'll have to pull out."

"Don't remind me." He growled in her ear and hugged her close.

"We're getting low on fuel," Gary said. His voice had an edge to it that hadn't been there before. "We need to land. You might want to uh... *separate*."

Sed tugged free of Jessica's body and made himself presentable again so he could find out if he should be worried.

"How can we be low on fuel?" Sed asked.

Gary refused to meet his eyes; a slight blush stained his cheeks.

"Uh, well. I flew a bit farther than usual. I didn't want to... *interrupt*. I didn't think you'd take so long." He glanced at Jessica, who was watching the scenery over the edge of the basket, as innocent as any regular passenger. "I wouldn't have lasted. She's a very beautiful woman," Gary said.

"That she is." Sed watched his wife, entranced by the copper glow of the sunset's final rays in her strawberry-blond hair.

"A handful?"

"More than one handful." Sed chuckled. "I wouldn't have her any other way."

"Are we going to hit that tree?" Jessica asked, pointing to a giant evergreen in their path. "We're drifting awfully low."

Gary pulled a cord to send a blast of fire shooting into the balloon. But only a small flame flickered in the fading light, before the fire sputtered out completely.

Chapter 9

JESSICA DUCKED LOW into the basket and covered her head with both arms as the balloon careened into the upper boughs of the tree. It just grazed the branches, but it was enough to rock the basket and make Jessica's stomach threaten an upheaval.

Sed was suddenly huddled over her protectively. "Are we going to crash?" he bellowed at Gary.

"We're in for a rough landing. Remember how we told you to handle a rough landing?"

Yeah, Jessica remembered. She also remembered being told that the chances of said rough landing were miniscule.

"You can't cover her like that," Gary shouted.

"I have to protect her!"

"Beside her, not above her. Remember? We practiced this."

Sed pulled away from Jessica's body and knelt beside her on the floor of the basket.

"It'll be okay," he said, the fear in his eyes so acute, she could almost reach out and grab it. "I will never allow you to be hurt, Jess. Understand?"

The reasonable person in Jessica knew there were some instances when Sed wouldn't be able to protect her, but the scared-shitless individual quaking uncontrollably on the floor of the basket clung to his words like they were a lifeline.

She'd be okay. The baby would be okay. The fates wouldn't dare defy Sed.

This wouldn't be like a plane crash, right? They weren't all that high and weren't moving at a high velocity. It was just a gentle hot air balloon. How bad could this be? Still… She covered her lower belly protectively and prayed for the safety of their child, remembering the warning they'd chosen to ignore prior to liftoff. If they got through this unscathed, she silently vowed not to do anything reckless for the rest of her pregnancy.

Sed's gaze was glued to her abdomen.

"I'm not in my third trimester," she reminded him. Reminded herself. A premature baby in the third trimester had a fighting chance, but if she went into labor now… She squeezed her eyes closed. She didn't want to consider that possibility. "The baby will be fine. The baby will be fine!"

Oh God, please let the baby be fine. She sucked her quivering lips between her teeth and braced for impact.

The basket hit the ground with a hard thud, bounced, hit the ground again with a teeth-jarring crash, and then tipped over on its side. Jessica clung to her belly, not caring if she face-planted into the rattan as long as she could cushion the baby's landing. Her face didn't land on rattan. Somehow Sed managed a tuck and roll maneuver that caught her on top of him as his body took the brunt of the impact.

"Everyone okay?" Gary shouted.

"Yeah," Jessica replied, struggling to crawl off Sed and out of the overturned basket. She didn't notice that Sed hadn't moved until she was standing beside the basket next to the deflated blue balloon with her knees shaking, but the rest of her surprisingly sound. "Sed?"

He answered with a groan of misery.

"Sed!" She dashed back to the basket and dropped to her knees beside him, running her hands over his body, looking for broken bones. She was pretty sure if she found one, she'd be sick all over him, but she had to find out if he was okay. "Where are you hurt?"

"I hope you want only one child," he said breathlessly and then curled into fetal position with a whine.

She slapped him on the shoulder. "Don't scare me like that! I thought you were hurt."

"You obviously don't have balls of your own," he said, rolling onto his hands and knees, crawling forward, and collapsing in the grass outside the basket.

Gravel crunched and sprayed as the chase car skidded to a halt on a nearby country road. A car door slammed, followed by the sound of running footsteps.

Gary's wife collided with her husband's body, then she kissed every inch of his face.

"I'm so sorry. I took a wrong turn and ended up on a dead-end gravel road and had to retrace my path. By the time I spotted you again, the balloon was already down. Is everyone okay?"

Jessica nodded. Sed staggered to his feet, still slightly hunched over as he tried to regain his bearings and protect his balls from additional threats.

"Our sex life is going to end up killing us," Sed murmured.

"I'd say it was worth it, but the baby…" She rubbed her belly, still not able to say what might have happened. It was hard enough just thinking about it. "We have to be more responsible. If something happened to our child, I—" Her voice cracked as the implications of what could have happened slammed down on her. Her knees buckled, and she grabbed Sed's arm to keep herself from crumpling to the ground.

"You're right," he said, looking more dejected than Jessica had ever seen him. "I put you and the baby at risk. I was thinking with my dick. As usual."

"You just wanted our wedding night to be memorable," Jessica said, patting his arm. "You can't take all the blame. I went against the advisement too."

She studied him and then slowly smiled with relief as the enormity of what *could* have happened was replaced with the realization that it hadn't. The baby was okay. She was okay. Sed was only slightly damaged below the belt.

"I was thinking with my pussy. As usual."

He chuckled and attempted to stand up straight, but winced and leaned forward again. "We'll just have to make love with our feet safely on the ground. And my balls safely away from your knee."

Jessica sighed. "I already had to give up hot-tub sex for this kid, now I have to give up ankles-behind-my-ears sex too? Just how much do I have to sacrifice to be a mother?" She was joking, of course. She'd willingly give up any of her own comforts and pleasures to protect her baby. But she needed the relief of a good laugh.

"We do have that new tantric chair arriving any day. Supposedly it makes all one hundred positions easier on the body."

"Are you sure there are only a hundred positions?" She gasped as if scandalized. "We'll be bored with it in a month, Sed."

"I could never get bored with you." He wrapped her in both arms and drew her against his warmth, surrounding her in a cocoon of leather-scented protectiveness. "You're my heart."

"And you're mine," she whispered.

They stood like that for a very long while, afraid to separate.

Having already packed the balloon on the trailer behind the SUV, Gary approached them. "Are you ready to head back to your car?" he asked. "I think we're all a bit rattled after that wild ride."

"I'm ready," Sed said. "Though I think our wild ride is just beginning."

Jessica hugged Sed tighter, needing his strength and stability now and for the long road ahead of them.

Sed tried to take a step, but Jessica held him fast.

"Jess? Don't you want to head for home?"

"Patience," she said. "I haven't quite found my strength yet. I need to borrow a bit more of yours." She never thought she'd willingly admit something like that, but it was true. Sometimes she would have to depend on him. And there was nothing wrong with that.

"Anytime, sweetheart," he whispered against her hair and drew her closer still. "Anything you need from me is yours."

"Right now I just need a strong pair of arms around me and a hard chest to lean against."

He chuckled. "Then I've got you covered, baby."

And she trusted he always would.

SINNERS ON TOUR ENCORE

November Rain

Epilogue to Hot Ticket

OLIVIA CUNNING

Chapter 1

JACE YAWNED as he inserted his key and unlocked the front door of his house. It was good to be home, no matter how temporarily. Sinners would only be off tour for two weeks as their stage equipment made its way by cargo ship across the Atlantic to Europe and Sed got married. And then he would be back on the road again for several months. At least Aggie would accompany him overseas. She'd become such an important part of his life, he couldn't imagine three months without his badass girlfriend by his side.

The instant he opened the door, he was yanked inside and smothered in the kisses of said badass girlfriend. She crushed him to the inner surface of the door, her hands sliding up his T-shirt to caress the bare skin of his belly. Her mouth sucked at his lips, and she straddled his thigh to move closer. Through the fabric of his jeans, he could feel the heat coming off her pussy. Jace groaned. The duffle bag in his hand dropped to the floor as his arms went around her to draw her closer. The woman always excited easily, but she'd obviously been worked up before he'd even entered the house. He wondered what she'd been up to. One of her hands slid down to rub his cock through his pants and as lust stole his more coherent thoughts, he decided whatever had gotten her all hot and bothered was a good thing.

"God, I missed you," she said between kisses.

It had been only five days since they'd last seen each other. While the band finished up several shows in New England, Aggie and the other Lady Sinners had gone home to take care of business before they all headed to Europe together. He and his four band members had flown home on a red-eye flight after last night's show in New York. Jace had slept a bit on the plane, but had been craving his mattress for some sleep. Now he was craving his mattress for a whole different reason.

"I missed you too," Jace said against Aggie's seeking lips.

One of his arms tightened around her as he pulled her closer and kissed her with the same enthusiasm she'd shown him. Cupping her full breast through her tight T-shirt, he found her nipple already hard and straining against his thumb for more vigorous stimulation.

"I could just fuck you right here," she said in that low, sexy growl of a voice his cock recognized as no-holds-barred sex coming its way.

"What's stopping you?" he murmured. "Are you working with a client in the dungeon? Is that why you're so turned on?"

When they'd spoken on the phone that morning, she hadn't mentioned doing any sessions as a professional dominatrix that day, but occasionally one of her clients talked her into an impromptu session. It wasn't a big deal. He just wondered what she'd been doing to the lucky son of a bitch that had her so on fire.

She chuckled. "No, no client today. There isn't a client on the planet who could make me want you this bad. But I do have a friend here."

A spike of jealousy speared Jace's heart. He knew Aggie would never fool around with a client, but she'd never gotten sexually excited just because a friend had visited. He couldn't help but wonder exactly what kind of fun she'd been having with her *friend*. And who the friend was. A past boyfriend maybe? She'd assured him none of the guys in her past had meant anything to her. So what had her attacking him at the door?

"Who?" he asked.

"Are you going to introduce us?" a soft feminine voice said from behind Aggie.

Jace stood away from the door so quickly that Aggie had to grab on to him to keep from tumbling to the floor. Behind Aggie stood one of the most stunning redheads Jace had ever laid eyes on. Tall and lithe, she exuded self-confidence and sexuality. Her brilliant red hair cascaded over her shoulders and had just enough waviness to make it full. The woman looked from Aggie to Jace and back to Aggie with grass-green eyes surrounded by thick lashes. The plunging neckline of her green silk dress drew his attention to a pair of large, round breasts. And he couldn't help but notice that she wasn't wearing a bra. Her huge tits seemed to defy gravity. Damn. If Jace had *friends* who looked like her, he might get sexually excited by their visits too.

"This is Jace," Aggie said, still breathless with arousal.

"I kind of figured that out, Ice," the woman said, a beguiling smile curving her soft pink lips. "What with you melting all over him and everything."

Ice?

"Jace, this is a friend of mine from Vegas," Aggie said. "We go way back. She's in town for the weekend, shooting a film."

So the redhead was an actress. Lots of actresses could be found in and around Hollywood, so that didn't surprise him. What surprised him was that she wasn't on the A-list and starring in lead roles that he'd recognize. He had no idea who she was. But she looked Aggie's age. For a budding actress, twenty-nine was fairly ancient.

"What kind of film?" he asked. He wasn't much of a conversationalist—especially not with people he just met—but he was genuinely interested. And not because she was hot. Because she was a friend of Aggie's.

"You weren't lying when you said you never told him about me," the woman said, crossing her arms and leveling Aggie with a harsh stare. "I thought we were friends."

"I wasn't trying to hide you from him or anything. You just never came up," Aggie said, releasing Jace and turning to stand beside him. She squeezed his hand.

"It's a pornographic film," Aggie's friend said to Jace, watching for his reaction. When he didn't gasp or give her a strange look, she added. "Typical gang-bang stuff—six guys, two at a time."

She definitely had the body for porn.

"This is Starr Lancaster," Aggie said. "Surely you've heard of her. She's one of the best-known porn actresses in the world."

Jace nodded slightly in Starr's direction. He had heard the name Starr Lancaster in certain circles—all-male circles. He was pretty sure half of the Sinners' porn collection featured her in the starring role, but he'd never been interested in watching porn, so even if it was on the big screen on the tour bus, he didn't really pay attention to the faces. Sometimes he took mental notes so he could employ new techniques, but it wasn't really his thing. Now that he knew who she was, however, his mind flipped through several mental images of her getting off. He remembered she was known for squirting when she came. He could feel the heat of embarrassment start to climb his cheeks.

"Did I actually make him blush?" Starr asked Aggie.

"It isn't hard to do," Aggie said, touching his cheek with her cool fingertips.

"My friend Eric would probably like your autograph," Jace said.

Starr laughed. "If he's as cute as you are, I'll sign his dick with my tongue."

Aggie winced. "God, Starr, do you have to be so crass?"

"Crass?" Starr lifted an eyebrow at Aggie. "When the fuck did you turn into Pollyanna, Ice?"

Ice? Why did she keep calling Aggie *Ice?*

"I didn't," Aggie said. "It's just Eric is married to a really sweet woman, and I know what a home wrecker you are."

"You can't wreck a home that isn't already wrecked," Starr said, lifting a hand and flicking her wrist. "So are we going to do this, or what?"

"Yeah, go get ready. I'll be right down."

"Be prepared to beg for mercy, babydoll," Starr said to Jace and turned on her heel to leave them alone in the foyer.

"What's she talking about?" Jace asked Aggie, trying not to stare at the green silk clinging to Starr's ass as she stalked away in her stilettoes.

"A little surprise for you. We used to work as a domme duo when we were first starting out and learning the trade. We were both trained under Mistress Z. When we worked a client together, Starr was called Fire and I was Ice."

"I wondered why she kept calling you that."

"We were highly sought after in Vegas back in the day, until…" Aggie's face took on a distant look before she shrugged and met his eyes. "It's been a while, but she stopped by out of the blue and got me talking about you and your… *tastes*. Then we started coming up with some ideas to get you worked up and—" She crushed him up against the door again, mashing her mouth against his and rubbing her mound against his cock.

So that's what had her so worked up—talking about him with another domme. He could live with that. He might be interested in playing their games, but there would have to be some boundaries defined and enforced. He didn't take orders from just anyone.

Jace pulled his mouth from Aggie and stared into her glassy eyes. She looked completely out of her head. "You haven't taken any ecstasy, have you?" he asked.

"You know I don't do drugs anymore."

"I've just never seen you like this, so I wanted to make sure you were thinking clearly."

She shook her head slightly. "I'm not thinking clearly at all, but it isn't drugs. It's you."

Jace grinned crookedly. "You know I'm happy to be involved

in your little experiments, but I have to set some boundaries with Starr."

"Of course."

"No sexual contact with her," he said. "At all."

Aggie nodded obediently. "She'll be my assistant," Aggie said. "Nothing more. I won't let her touch you in a sexual capacity. But I get to touch you in a sexual capacity, right?"

"If the mood strikes you," he teased.

"The mood already struck me," she said and laughed. "What are your other boundaries?"

"That's the only one."

Aggie shuddered with delight. "God, I fucking love you," she said. She grabbed him by the belt and tugged him toward the basement, where her private dungeon had been built. By the time they reached the door that led to the lower level, Jace's dick was rock hard with excitement and his thoughts cloudy with lust. He had no idea what kind of damage two sadists could do to him, but he was more than eager to find out.

"Happy birthday, baby," Aggie said at the bottom of the steps and kissed him gently. "I hope you enjoy your gift."

The dungeon was empty, but Aggie's dressing room door was open and he could hear Starr—or maybe he should think of her as Fire during this particular interaction—moving around inside.

"I'm sure I'll enjoy every moment of your thoughtful gift," Jace said. "But my birthday isn't for six weeks."

"Yeah, but we'll be in Europe then, and I won't have access to my dungeon to treat you properly." She grinned. "Or improperly, depending on your perspective."

"They do have dungeons in Europe," Jace said. "Real ones."

"We'll have to visit a few and see if they're up to snuff." She kissed his cheek. "I'm going to go dress as Ice for our session now. You go stand in the main dungeon and wait."

"Do you want me to undress?"

"Not until I can instruct you and watch you obey," she said.

His heart rate kicked up several notches. He had a feeling she was going to go all out because Fire would be observing her technique. Aggie went a bit easy on him now that they were together on a permanent basis; it had been a while since she'd driven him to his knees. Jace almost tripped over his feet in his rush to stand in the dungeon and wait for her—for them—to give him what Aggie promised with the heat of her gaze.

Half the excitement of a session with Aggie was anticipation. He could hear the two women talking and laughing in the room next door. He kept thinking the voices were approaching and that the women would arrive any moment, but apparently he was imagining things. When he could stand waiting no longer, he crept to the open door of the dressing room and peered inside.

Aggie was dressed in black patent leather from her thigh-high boots to her skintight corset. Fire's outfit was similar, but in shiny red instead of black. She was standing behind Aggie, braiding Aggie's long black hair. Jace preferred Aggie's hair down. The braid made her look too severe. Too cold.

"Did you tell your sub he could leave the dungeon?" Fire said without looking up from her task.

"He's not my sub," Aggie said and lifted her gaze to look at Jace standing in the doorway. "Not exactly. But, no, I didn't give him permission. He's just eager. Aren't you?" She winked at him.

"You've gone soft on me, Ice," Fire said. "Once upon a time, you were the brutal one and I showed them mercy."

"I am a touch soft with him," Aggie admitted. Her gaze gentled as she continued to stare at Jace. "I love him."

Jace smiled and hoped she could read the reciprocating emotions on his face, because there was no way he'd say them aloud in front of another domme.

"Well, I don't. He better get back into that dungeon before I'm done with this braid." Fire still hadn't looked at him. He knew it was part of the domme act, but he'd grown used to the way Aggie punished him and he much preferred it to the way past dommes had treated him. He had never liked the subservient part of the game. He just enjoyed the pain.

"I told you what he's like in the dungeon," Aggie said.

"And it made you cream your panties. Yeah, I recall. But I'm not you, am I? He'll listen to me or he'll suffer."

"I got tired of waiting," Jace said.

Fire lifted her gaze to his at last, and he was sure most men would have dropped to their knees to grovel at her feet. But he was not most men.

"He is a defiant one, isn't he?" Fire said.

Aggie chuckled. "You have no idea."

Fire tied a leather string around the bottom of Aggie's braid and then slid her hands over Aggie's shoulders as she stared Jace down. "I'm ready to make him beg, Ice. How about you?"

"We can try," Aggie said.

Knowing his wait was finally over, Jace retreated to the main dungeon. He wondered if they'd torture him as a unit or take turns. He also wondered if one of the women was more dominant than the other. He loved when Aggie dominated others—seeing the rush she got from her power was a total turn-on. He could scarcely imagine how hot she'd be dominating another dominant female. He wished he could sneak a moment alone with Aggie to bring it up, but she wouldn't want him to mention it in front of another domme. That would make her look submissive to him. And while she was open to suggestions from him when they were alone, the illusion of their power play would be shifted if he started making demands to her when she was already in her role as Mistress V or Ice. But maybe he could hint enough that she'd catch on and turn it into her idea. He was sure she'd be okay with that scenario.

The familiar click of Aggie's heels on the cement floor of the dungeon grabbed Jace by the balls. His body knew what was coming, and his dick was instantly hard with anticipation. The not so familiar cadence of a second set of heels made his belly quiver. He had no idea what to expect out of Fire. He'd had some vicious dommes in his past, dommes who'd had no problem taking his desire for pain much too far. But Aggie knew how to send him into his happy place quickly with minimal damage to his body. Still there was something exciting about not knowing what was to come.

He kept his eyes downcast as they approached, working hard to curtail his excitement. He shouldn't already be this turned on. They hadn't even touched him yet. Of course, he was used to twice-daily sex with Aggie, and he hadn't seen her for almost a week. He just didn't want to embarrass himself in front of Fire. A part of him wanted Aggie to be proud of how he handled himself with her friend. And watching him spontaneously come—spilling his seed all over the dungeon floor—while under the lash was probably not what she had in mind.

A pair of black patent leather boots came into his field of view, followed by a matching set in red patent leather. His cock pulsed in appreciation of footwear sexiness. He was already imagining what those pointed heels would feel like pressed into his chest. His back. His crotch. The women stood close together, so he couldn't help but lift his eyes to see more. Aggie had a flail in one hand and a riding crop in the other. Her expression was hard, cold. Jace's balls tightened. He knew that look well; he was in for a treat. He pulled his gaze from the familiar and perfect to Fire, who held a bullwhip in one hand and wore a look of mild amusement. Her arm was around Aggie's lower back, her hand resting with familiarity on Aggie's hip. The spike of jealousy that stabbed him in the throat caught him by surprise. What did he have to feel jealous about? They were just two friends barely touching. Yet he couldn't shake his concern over the possessiveness Fire showed toward his fiancée.

"Take your shirt off, babydoll," Fire said. "I want to see if the rest of your body is as cut as your biceps. I can tell you work out."

Was she fucking serious? He looked at Aggie for guidance.

"Is there something wrong with your hearing?" Aggie asked, her voice low. Cruel. Delicious.

"You know I don't take orders, Mistress," he said, which wasn't exactly true. He would eventually do what was asked of him, but he needed a bit of convincing first.

Fire's jaw dropped. Aggie just lifted an eyebrow at him.

"I think he doesn't want to take his shirt off because he's afraid to take your lashes against his bare back, Fire," Aggie said. "That's what I think."

Jace immediately tugged his shirt off over his head and tossed it to the side.

Fire chuckled. "You do know how to gain his cooperation, don't you, Ice?"

"Sometimes," Aggie said. "It took me a while to figure out what makes him tick."

Jace's jaw set in a harsh line. He didn't like to be talked about as if he wasn't there, and he had half a mind to collect his shirt and put it back on. The other half of his mind was already anticipating the zone, so he stayed where he was and didn't respond.

"What makes him tick?" Fire asked, snapping her arm out to the side unexpectedly and making the end of her whip crack.

At the sound, Jace's belly tightened and his nipples went hard. The small silver hoop in his piercing gave him a distracting jolt of pleasure in the tiny bit of erect flesh. Fuck. His nipples weren't the only things that were erect. He already ached for release.

"I'm not telling," Aggie said. "Figure it out for yourself."

"Afraid I'll take him from you?" Fire asked with a smirk.

"Not at all," Aggie said. "I want to see if you can handle someone like him without losing your head."

The way she had their very first session. She still apologized to Jace about it. Not that he needed or wanted her apology. He'd loved every minute of her harsh treatment. Sometimes he wished he was still capable of sending her into a rage. Sometimes he wanted her to beat the shit out of him. But most of the time, he liked how well she knew his body.

Aggie flicked his nipple ring with the end of her riding crop. "Maybe I should take the edge off before we get to work," she said. "You look like you're about to explode already. Do you need to come before we begin?"

She really was getting soft on him. Half of his torture today would be holding back his sexual release.

"No, Mistress," he said. "I can wait."

"He is filling out those jeans very nicely," Fire said, cracking her whip again.

Jace groaned in torment. He wished they'd quit talking and get down to business.

Aggie slid the tip of her riding crop down his belly in a Z-pattern, slowly bumping over each section of his six-pack, until the small square of leather rested against his low waistband just inside his hipbone. It was one of his most sensitive spots, and she damned well knew it.

"Unfasten your jeans," Aggie said.

Jace was more than ready to show her just how hard she made him, but two things made him hesitate. He wasn't sure he was delirious enough to allow Fire to see him in such an aroused state. And Aggie's retaliation was so much sweeter when he refused her demands.

"Unfasten them for me," he said, holding her gaze. "Mistress," he added as an afterthought.

She lashed her crop against his hip—once, twice—and then slid its tip down the solid bulge in his pants. He drank in the delicious sting in his flesh, craving more, *much* more.

"I'm going to whip him just for disobeying you," Fire said, and she lifted her arm to draw the length of her whip back.

Aggie caught her wrist. "No. You don't give him what he wants when he disobeys. You give it to him when he obeys."

Fire drew her eyebrows together. "And what does he want?"

"You can't tell by looking at him?" Aggie lashed his lower belly several times, and Jace's head tilted back as goose bumps rose to the surface of his awakening flesh.

Oh yeah, hurt me, Aggie. Please hurt me.

"You got yourself a pain pig here, Aggie," Fire said.

She wasn't the first domme to label him with that title, but it wasn't completely true. At least not since Aggie had discovered what really got him off.

"Do you want her to try out her whip on you, Jace?" Aggie asked.

"Yes."

He jerked when she brought the end of the riding crop down on his chest, next to his pierced nipple.

"Yesssss?" she prompted.

"Yes, Mistress," he said.

"Then unfasten your jeans. I want them at your ankles."

He struggled with the conflict between his desire for pain and his embarrassment at the thought of exposing himself to Fire. No woman but Aggie had seen his cock since he'd met her. He was surprised she was willing to allow another woman to look at it. Didn't she want it all to herself? Aggie waited patiently, and Fire tapped her toe on the cement while he contemplated his next move.

"I say we hit him until he does what you say," Fire said.

"Yes," Jace said immediately. "Do that."

Aggie chuckled. "Not a chance." To Fire she said, "That doesn't work on him. He'd let you hit him until your arm gave out or he was unconscious."

"Can't I at least hit him once? I obviously don't have your patience."

"You may hit him once," Aggie said.

"Goody."

He could just see her red patent leather boot in his peripheral vision as she drew the whip back and let it snap against his upper back. It stung, but was so far below his threshold that it would take him ten years to slip into his headspace if that was as hard as she could hit.

"Harder, Mistress Fire," he requested obediently. Because he could be obedient if it got him what he wanted. He knew this game well.

The whip scraped against the floor behind him as she drew it back and lifted her arm over her head. She didn't let it fly, though, because Aggie had raised her hand to halt Fire's action.

"She will not hit you harder until you unfasten your pants and drop them to your knees," she said.

"Are you sure you want her to see me naked?" he said.

"She didn't believe me when I was bragging about your size, so yeah, I want her to see it, and I want her to seethe with envy that it's mine and she can't have it."

Jace grinned. Well, when she put it that way, he kind of wanted to show off.

He jerked his fly open, watching Aggie's reaction as he pushed the fabric from his hips and let his jeans drop to his ankles.

"Jesus," Fire gasped.

Jace flushed with heat as both women drank in the sight of him.

"Now I see why you let him fuck you while you hit him, Ice. Just looking at him makes me wet. You could make some serious cash with a tool that big, babydoll," she said to Jace. "Let me know if you ever want to get in the business. You have a dick that belongs in porn."

"No," he said without hesitation.

"It's mine," Aggie said, running her riding crop down the length of him. "All mine."

The crack of the whip against Jace's back caught him by surprise. His belly tightened involuntarily, but he made no sound. He watched Aggie's face as Fire struck him several times in rapid succession. His eyelids fluttered as a particularly vicious lash struck his shoulder. It had been a while since he'd been under anyone's punishment but Aggie's, and all at once he realized how lucky he was to have someone who knew his body in command of the whip, because Fire's misplaced strike had fucking hurt. Sometimes Aggie let Jace serve as practice for women learning how to hit properly, but they always hesitated to unleash their full power. Fire wasn't so kind.

"Fire, that's enough," Aggie said, picking up on Jace's subtle cue of displeasure.

The end of Fire's whip scraped the floor behind him, and he released a breath he hadn't realized he'd been holding.

"How would you know?" Fire asked. "He doesn't make a sound."

Aggie ignored the question and touched her fingers to Jace's jaw. "Are you done?"

He shook his head. "Show her." Aggie would know what he meant—show her how to hit him properly. He didn't have to waste words on her. She knew him well enough to understand his wishes.

Aggie smiled. "She's not going to obey."

"Then punish her."

Aggie grinned. "So that's what you're after."

At times it was unnerving to be completely understood by this woman, at others it definitely played into his favor. The dungeon was no place to give his emotions free rein, but his heart swelled to unbearable proportions as Aggie strode across the room and tugged open the curtain that concealed the floor-to-ceiling mirror on the far wall. He couldn't deny he loved her and all her various personas for no matter what persona she played at, he could clearly see his Aggie at her core. Everything he could ever need or want was wrapped up in one beautiful package, and the other domme in the room faded into the background in comparison to his angel demon in black patent leather. He wished she'd let her hair down. He loved the way the waist-length black strands moved around her body as she walked and teased and finally worked him over.

"He likes to watch himself beg, does he?" Fire asked when Aggie moved to stand next to her.

Jace couldn't take his eyes off Aggie's reflection in the mirror.

"No, he likes to watch me work. On clients. On himself. He'll especially like watching me work on you."

"Me?" Fire gave Aggie an odd look. "Why would you work on me?"

"Because you aren't hitting him properly," Aggie said.

"So? Who's in charge here exactly?"

"Hmm," Aggie said, running the tip of her riding crop down Jace's spine.

He shuddered as anticipation and excitement followed in its course. She cracked the tip hard against his ass—once, twice. Perfection. She always made him hurt so good.

"Depends. Right now, it's me. But that could shift at any time."

"You two have a strange dynamic," Fire said.

"But it works," Aggie said. "Now hit him properly or suffer the consequences."

"What consequences?"

Aggie slapped Fire's bare ass cheek with her palm.

Fire jerked, but not half as hard as Jace's cock did.

"Hey! That stung," Fire protested.

"Do as you're told," Aggie said, her tone uncompromising and hot as fuck.

Fire took out her retaliation on Jace's back with a strike so brutal, his knees buckled. But he didn't crumple; he spread his feet to brace himself for the next blow. Two years ago he'd have begged for punishment this harsh, but he no longer needed pain to keep his emotions in check. Hell, to *survive*. But he still liked it—not because he thought he deserved it, as he had when he'd first met Aggie—but because it intensified the pleasure of his sexual experiences like nothing else could. Aggie had showed him that. Until that moment, he hadn't realized how completely his mindset had shifted since she'd come into his life. But something inside him wanted to watch Aggie take the brutal domme in red to her knees. His woman was queen of her domain, and he wasn't sure what he'd ever done to deserve her devotion, but all would bow before her while he stood proudly at her side. He wouldn't want it any other way.

Jace heard the crack of Aggie's riding crop against flesh, but didn't experience the welcome sting of her blows. She'd struck the inside of Fire's thigh.

"Mmm," Fire said, "you keep that up and I'm going to beat your boyfriend bloody. No one hits the way you do, Ice. You always did make my pussy hot."

Always? The thought was ripped from his mind as Fire's whip cracked against his lower back. He bit his lip so he didn't cry out. He wasn't sure when he'd become such a pussy; Aggie'd been taking it easy on him for too long. He could take Fire's brutality, he could. But he wasn't sure he wanted to.

Aggie's succession of lashes landed on Jace's ass, flanks, and thighs. Yes, like that. Just like that. He gasped brokenly with need as she took him to his next level, his balls heavy and aching for release.

"I thought you were going to hit me like that," Fire said with a pout.

"I will if you do your job properly."

Jace suppressed a grin of triumph as Fire's lashes against his back shifted from punishing to tantalizing. Aggie circled him slowly, her eyes locked with his. In time with Fire's lashes behind him, Aggie struck his hip with a flick of her crop. His lower belly. The inside of his thigh. She ducked her head slightly, still holding his gaze. The tap of her crop against the head of his cock made his entire body jerk. Pre-cum seeped from his tip, dripping on the floor. She'd have made any of her clients lick it up, but not him. Using a red-tipped finger, she collected a lingering drop from his glans and brought it to her tongue to taste him.

"You ready for some pleasure to go with that pain?" she asked.

He nodded, his throat too tight with desire to form words. Her crop struck the inside of his thigh, so close to his balls that his stomach tightened in knots.

"Spread," she demanded.

He spread his feet apart. She sank to her knees. He stared down at her, overwhelmed by pride and love and lust. She cradled his heavy nuts in one hand and stretched her mouth wide to take his thick cock into the warm recesses within.

"You're giving him head?" Fire said in disbelief.

Even though she was still working over the flesh of his back with practiced strikes, he'd forgotten the other woman was there until she'd spoken. He was far too lost in Aggie to care what Fire thought or did.

Aggie massaged his balls with just enough pressure to hint at pain. She completely distracted him with the power she held over him as she licked and suckled his cockhead with reverence. Pleasure and pain converged, sending him into a euphoric state, until a particularly hard slash across his shoulders brought him crashing back to Earth. He grunted in protest. Aggie paused, looking up at him in question. He shook his head slightly, trying to find his higher plane, but it had been snatched from his grasp.

Aggie placed a gentle kiss on the head of his cock before rising to her feet. Behind him, something clattered to the floor. Fire had dropped the whip. He didn't understand why until he saw the look of fury on Aggie's face.

"Assume the position, Fire."

As if controlled by puppet strings, Fire bent at the waist and grabbed her ankles, her long mass of red hair trailing on the ground at her feet. Aggie lifted a flail and brought the ends down, smacking Fire's ass and the swollen flesh between her legs. Fire was so obviously turned on, her swollen pussy was practically spilling from the fabric of her thong. Aggie moved to stand beside her.

"You brought him down on purpose, didn't you?" Aggie said.

The next strike hit Fire at a different angle, the lashes cracking over the backs of her thighs, her pussy, and asshole. Fire jerked and released a moan of deep pleasure before spreading her legs wider and tilting her pelvis to give Aggie open access to everything between her thighs.

"I might have," Fire said breathlessly. "I don't remember."

Aggie delivered three successive lashes to Fire's pussy that made Fire quiver with delight.

"Do you remember now?" Aggie asked, staying perfectly in her role of dominatrix as her friend tugged her thong aside and spread her wet and swollen lips with her fingers.

Jace's mouth went dry.

"No. I think I'll remember if you punish me," she said.

Aggie swung the ends of the flail so that they barely tapped Fire's opening and clit.

"Harder," Fire whimpered.

"Are you going to remember your place?"

Jace couldn't seem to stop his hand from circling his rigid cock. He'd never witnessed Aggie in such a position of power. If he didn't fuck her soon, he was sure he'd die on the spot, but he didn't want to interrupt.

"Yes, yes," Fire moaned. "I'll do anything you want. Send me flying."

Aggie's gentle lashes against Fire's center quickly had her sputtering with orgasm. Her knees buckled, and she sank to the ground, her body quaking and her breathing erratic. "Thank you, Mistress," she said and kissed Aggie's boot. "Thank you."

Jace was out of his mind with lust. He pulled Aggie against his chest and devoured her mouth. One hand gripped her soft ass while the other struggled to free her hair from its braid. He wanted the silky curtain of her hair around them as he fucked her. When her hair was loose, he clutched a handful and jerked her head back. "Panties off," he growled, too far gone to think about what he was doing. He just had to get inside her. Fill her. Surround himself with her. Lose himself in her. His Aggie.

She shimmied out of her panties and gasped when he pressed her against the nearest wall. She clung to his shoulders, and he used his hand on his cock to find her. He slipped into her hot, drenched pussy with a groan of bliss and used the wall for leverage as he thrust deep. He was vaguely aware of her legs around his hips, his hands on her ass, her breasts rubbing against his chest as he thrust into her. When lashes against his back added pain to his blend of pleasure and sensation, he called her name in tormented bliss. He couldn't separate the pleasure from the pain from the emotion. It was all Aggie. Aggie. His demon. His angel. His friend. His lover. His everything.

"Oh fuck," Jace cried as his body exceeded the pinnacle of rapture and his orgasm exploded, cum erupting deep inside her body. His fingers dug into her ass to hold her still as his final thrust buried his cock to the hilt and he filled her with vigorous pulses of his seed. The stinging lashes against his back intensified, sending him into a mindless state of euphoria far more intense than an ordinary orgasm. He wasn't sure when Fire stopped striking him or when Aggie shifted position so that her feet were on the floor and she was holding him in her arms, his chest pressed tightly to the soft mounds of her breasts. He'd been so caught up in whatever the hell that had been that he wasn't even sure if Aggie had come.

"Shit, Ice," Fire said somewhere behind him, drawing him partially out of the peace of his reverie. "No wonder you love the guy. He fucks like a maniac. Jesus, how many times did he make you come?"

Aggie's arms tightened around him, and she chuckled. "A few," she said.

Thank God. He'd hate to think that he'd been the only one to derive pleasure from that mind-blowing session.

"He is amazing in bed," Aggie continued dreamily, "but that's not why I love him. I love him because he feels emotions more deeply than any man I've ever known, and he accepts all that I am—good and bad—and doesn't want to change me or erase my past. I can be myself with him."

Who in their right mind would want to change a perfect woman or prevent her from being her wonderful self? He'd tell Aggie that later, when they were alone. Now that he wasn't delirious with lust, with pleasure, with pain, he was acutely aware of the strange woman standing behind him.

"You better marry the guy before someone comes along and steals him from you," Fire said.

"Is that a threat, Starr?" Aggie murmured.

"An observation."

Aggie leaned away slightly and cupped Jace's face between her hands. His entire body was aching, throbbing, stinging from the orchestrations of their punishments, but he was most conscious of the gentle press of her fingertips to his cheeks.

"Anyone who tries is going to have one hell of a fight on her hands. This man is mine."

Even though Starr was still observing them, he couldn't resist kissing Aggie deeply. Sometimes it was easier to show her how he felt rather than say it. He'd marry her tomorrow if she'd allow it. She kept telling him they'd know when the time was right—that a marriage license was just a piece of paper and it didn't mean anything—but being able to call her his wife meant the world to him. He just wasn't sure how to let her know that. He deepened the kiss and pulled her closer, needing her to experience the depth of his devotion. Her arms shifted so she could wrap them around his back, and she stroked the marked flesh with just enough pressure to bring back memories of the delicious blows he'd experienced only moments before. He sucked a breath through his teeth when the less pleasant sting of salt in an open wound interrupted his pleasure.

Aggie straightened abruptly and stared at her fingertips over his shoulder.

"Blood?" she growled, her gaze lifting to Starr. "You made him bleed?"

"Just a little," Starr said.

"I told you that was a hard boundary," Aggie said. "No blood."

"That's your hard boundary," Jace said. "Not mine."

In his past, he'd bled plenty of times after a session, but Aggie had only drawn blood on him once, and it had rattled her so completely that she'd dropped her guard and allowed him close enough to make love to her. He wondered if that was why she was so inconsolably pissed that Starr had made him bleed.

"I wasn't trying to make him bleed," Starr said. "I just got a little carried away when he was coming. I've never seen a guy come that hard and in my line of work, I've seen a fair share of male orgasms."

"Aggie, it's really okay," Jace said quietly.

"I disagree," she said, glaring at Starr over his shoulder. "But it's too late to prevent it now. Let's go clean you up so you don't get an infection."

Good idea. He hated hospitals, and trying to explain to a medical professional how his whip lashes had gotten infected might be a bit embarrassing.

Chapter 2

AGGIE WINCED as she eased Jace's hips back and his soft cock slipped from her body. She was going to be walking funny for days after being fucked so vigorously. It had been entirely worth it, and she knew how worked up he got when taking his pain with pleasure, but apparently watching her bring another domme to her knees with a whip-induced orgasm had taken him beyond even that. She grinned to herself and reached for a towel to catch the cum trickling down the inside of her thigh. Jace had released one hell of a load inside her, and she didn't want to get it all over her leather boots.

He flushed as he looked down and realized what she was doing. If they'd been alone, it wouldn't have bothered him, but they still had an audience, and she was sure that now that he'd regained his senses, he'd struggle with that.

"Put your pants on," Aggie demanded of him in her most authoritative Mistress V voice. "I don't want to have to look at your cock unless it's hard and ready to fuck me again."

She noted the look of relief on his handsome face as he obeyed her by doing exactly what he wanted to do. Starr seemed impressed by his sudden willingness to obey, but Aggie knew that he wouldn't have put his pants on unless he wanted to. The women ogled his perfect ass as he slipped into his jeans. They sighed in unison and then laughed when they realized what they were doing. Jace glanced at them over his shoulder as he fastened his fly. Aggie winked at him and approached to take a closer look at the crisscrossed welts on his back. Several of them were close to bleeding; she could see tiny beads of blood just under the skin. Only one lash had actually breached the surface. It was far less serious than when he'd made her lose her head during their first session. Starr'd had more restraint than she'd had. Of course Starr had had warning about the way he took his punishment and Aggie had gone in blind. That was still no excuse for drawing blood, Aggie chastised herself for the thousandth time. She'd promised him—and herself—that she'd never draw blood on him again.

"God, I'm still horny," Starr admitted as she followed them

out of the main dungeon and to the room where Aggie disinfected her implements and the occasional bleeding scratch. "Can you help me take the edge off, Ice?"

Aggie stiffened. Making Starr come to excite Jace was one thing; getting her off after a session, another thing entirely. Aggie had already told the woman that she didn't want Jace to know that she and Starr had once had a sexual relationship. It had been a long time ago, but it was the one relationship Aggie had never shared with Jace. Probably because no one had ever hurt her the way Starr had and because for almost a decade, Aggie had been trying to forget it ever happened.

"A spare vibrator I can ram up there. A fucking fist," Starr muttered. "Something."

Aggie's shoulders sagged with relief. That had been a close one. Starr had almost let Aggie's secret slip in front of Jace, and she didn't want to have to try to explain it to him. She was still a bit puzzled about it herself.

"You have ten perfectly functional fingers," Aggie reminded her.

"You're really going to make me do this the old-fashioned way?"

"Do you remember how?"

Aggie eased Jace down on a stool and went to rummage through her first aid kit for supplies.

Starr chuckled. "If I need help, Jace can remind me how to please a pussy. He seems to know what he's doing."

Aggie glanced at him so she could watch him blush and stare uncomfortably at his bare feet. She grinned to herself, loving that look. She had a difficult time making him blush these days, but others could still set him off without a problem.

Aggie turned back to her first aid kit and within a minute heard the unmistakable sound of a wet pussy getting worked over. Aggie closed her eyes and shook her head. Porn stars had no shame.

"Do you have to do that here?" Aggie asked casually and moved to stand behind Jace so she could tend to his back.

"Your man put me in this condition—I think he should have to watch me come out of it."

But Jace wasn't watching. He was staring intently at the floor. His face was so red, Aggie was surprised it didn't burst into flames.

Starr started making her obviously practiced porn sounds, moaning and groaning far more than the action of her fingers dictated. When she began to fuck herself with the handle of Aggie's whip, Jace turned on the stool so he was facing the opposite direction and crammed his fingers into both ears.

Starr's mantra of, "I'm coming, I'm coming, I'm coming, oh yeah, I'm coming," didn't faze Aggie in the least, but she found Jace's reaction of chanting "La la la la la, la la la la la," amusing.

She grinned to herself as she saturated his cut with antiseptic spray. Jace's spine straightened involuntarily, and his fingers slipped out of his ears just as Starr let out a final cry of release and then slowed her motions to bring herself down.

"Hope you like your new whip," Aggie remarked. Even if she could easily clean the remnants of Starr's orgasm from the handle, she'd never be able to hold it in her hand without thinking about where it had been.

"It's not as good as cock, but sometimes you have to improvise."

Jace snorted and then curled toward his knees as he was captured by an incontrollable case of the giggles. "Eric is never going to believe this," he said.

"What he's not going to believe is that you didn't watch her come, Tripod," Aggie teased, using Eric's nickname for Jace.

"He'll take away my man card if he ever finds out."

Aggie slipped her arms around his neck and kissed his ear, missing the closeness they usually shared after sex. "Love you," she whispered.

He glanced over his shoulder to observe Starr, who was still playing with herself, but a bit less enthusiastically than before. "Yeah," he murmured. "I'm just… tired."

She hadn't expected him to vocally return the sentiment—not with Starr as a witness—so she didn't press. Later, when they were alone, she'd make him say it a hundred times.

"Then you'd better head upstairs and take a nap," she said. "I'll need you well rested for what I have in mind for later tonight."

He reached up and clasped her wrist. "Just us," he said firmly.

She smiled and kissed his ear again. "Just us," she whispered.

His body relaxed before her. She hadn't realized he'd been so tense until his muscles went lax. While their experience with Starr had been incredibly intense and sexually satisfying, it had lacked the intimacy she and Jace usually shared. It warmed her heart to realize he craved those moments of connection—of tenderness and love— as much as she did.

Maybe she should marry the guy. He'd told her he was ready whenever she was, but something about being labeled as someone's *wife* didn't sit well with her. It seemed too ordinary for what they shared. Too conventional. Too... *subservient*.

Jace stood from the stool and stretched his arms over his head, ending with a wide yawn. "It was nice to meet you, Starr. Thanks for not taking it easy on me. I'm going to head upstairs for a nap."

"Nice to meet you as well, babydoll," Starr said and lifted her hand from her very exposed pussy to offer Jace a shake.

He took a step backward and nodded at her. "Yeah," he said to the floor, avoiding Starr's amused eyes. He opened the door to the small lobby where clients waited for their turn in the dungeon. Today it was empty except for a black and white cat who released a piteous *meow* the moment she laid eyes on her long absent human. Jace scooped Brownie off the floor and cradled her against his bare chest as he carried her to the stairs.

"Did you miss me?" he asked the cat.

"Brow rowww rown," the cat responded.

"No shit?" he said, as if he and the cat had a shared language only they understood. "No tuna at all? That sucks. I'll have words with her about that."

"Browww—" Brownie's unusual meow was cut off by her loud and persistent purr as she rubbed her face against Jace's jaw, one of her claws caught securely in his gold hoop earring so he couldn't escape her affection.

Through the dungeon doorway, Aggie watched them ascend the stairs until they were no longer visible. Starr's hand on her shoulder wiped the tender smile from Aggie's face.

"He's a cutie pie," Starr said, her breath hot against Aggie's shoulder. "No wonder you gave up your independence and career to serve his needs."

Aggie stiffened. She hadn't given up her independence or her career. Well, she didn't strip for a living anymore, but she didn't really have time for it when following Jace around the world as he toured. And maybe the number of clients she served in the dungeon had been reduced to a trickle, but any time she wanted to take on a dominatrix job, Jace didn't complain. The weird thing was, she no longer got the same joy out of being domme to those who'd pay her tribute. Not unless it was Jace under her lash. He gave her everything she needed to feel complete. Shit, maybe Starr was right. Maybe she *had* gone soft. Maybe she *had* given up her independence and career to serve Jace. And maybe it wasn't any of Starr's business, because for the first time in her life she was happy.

"Shut up," was the only retort Aggie could muster.

Starr's lips brushed her shoulder and her arm circled Aggie's waist so she could splay a hand over her lower belly. Aggie's brow furrowed with confusion. Why did this touch feel intimate and at the same time creepy?

"Of all the people who ever claimed to love me, you're the only one I regret hurting," Starr said quietly.

Aggie threw off Starr's hand and stalked across the room. "That's the biggest load of bullshit you ever shoveled at me," Aggie said, her heart twanging with pain. She'd gotten over Starr a long time ago, but the betrayal she'd suffered at Starr's hand still hurt when she was reminded of it.

Starr sighed. "Believe what you must; I'm just stating facts. But your friendship means a lot to me, so I won't ruin it again with sex. Even though all I could think about while you were whipping my cunt was your mouth on me."

"I'm not interested." As if Aggie would ever even consider hurting Jace by fooling around with someone like Starr. Or with anyone, for that matter.

"Are you going to tell him about us?" Starr asked.

"There's nothing to tell," Aggie said, striding purposely to the other room to retrieve the implements they'd used on Jace.

"Are you afraid of how he'll react, knowing you once loved a woman?"

"No," she said. *Maybe*, a little voice in her head countered. "I might tell him later." If she wanted to send him back to that closed-off place he used to frequent.

She didn't think he'd take her admission well. Mostly because she'd been hiding it from him for so long. He'd told her things about his past—about the deepest, darkest parts of himself—that no one else knew, and she couldn't even tell him that she'd once been in love with a woman. Why? Would she have had the same reservations if Starr had been a man who'd broken her heart? She honestly didn't know. A man had never broken Aggie's heart. She'd never given one enough power over her to do so. Before Jace, she'd never loved a man. Never even considered loving a man. But she loved *this* man, and she refused to jeopardize their relationship. He meant everything to her. And he did have the power to break her heart. To destroy her.

"You're afraid of losing him, aren't you?" Starr interrupted Aggie's turbulent thoughts.

She was surprised by the sudden tightness in her chest and the sting of tears in her eyes. "Terrified," she said breathlessly.

"Then you should probably marry him."

She was a touch terrified of that too. "Someday."

Chapter 3

AGGIE WRAPPED HER ARMS AROUND JACE and stole a kiss. Distracted, he kissed her back, but he didn't seem to mean it. She gave his ass an appreciative squeeze and drew away to stare into his dark brown eyes.

"What's wrong?" she asked.

"Just a bit…" His eyebrows drew together. "Cold."

While June in London wasn't as warm as June in southern California, it wasn't cold. Not even close.

"Cold?"

"I've been cold since we left the Tower of London yesterday." He pursed his lips and shook his head.

"Are you coming down with something?" She touched his forehead, then his cheeks. He didn't feel feverish. "Jet lag maybe?" He'd been a bit off all day. She hadn't even been able to convince him to join her in the shower that morning.

"Maybe," he said and wrapped his arms around his body to hold in a hard shudder.

Because she'd wanted to play tourist, she and Jace had rented a car to make their way from London to Donington Park for Sinners' stage performance at the Download Festival. The rest of the band had left on the tour bus the day before. Maybe Jace was just worried they wouldn't make it to the show in time. Their set didn't start until late that night and driving across England wasn't quite the same as driving across the United States.

"We'll make it. We just have one more castle I want to see, and it's only an hour and a half to the venue from there."

"Another castle?" He grinned crookedly. "I've seen a different side of you these past two days. I never knew you were such a history buff."

"History is so dark."

He chuckled. "Just the parts that interest you."

At her insistence, they'd spent the night in Mailmaison Oxford Castle—a creepy castle that had been used as a prison; their room had once been a cell. Jace had been a bit skittish the entire time, claiming some presence was lurking around him. She'd laughed his claims off, and he'd gone quiet on her, internalizing as he did when he didn't think anyone understood where he was coming from. She'd wanted to play tourist and had easily talked Jace into seeing some real dungeons, but while he'd started their adventure with enthusiasm yesterday morning, he'd been uneasy and listless the rest of the day. A restless night's sleep hadn't improved his disposition.

"Are you having any fun?" she asked.

"Do you really think I'd have fun touring the English countryside looking at old castles?"

"And dungeons," she reminded him.

His gaze lowered, and he smiled. "But not the good kind of dungeons."

"We don't have to leave home for the good kind. If you want to go directly to Donington and skip our last stop—"

He tipped his head to rest his forehead against hers and closed his eyes. They stayed like that a long moment while he mulled over his thoughts. They'd been together long enough that she knew he wasn't ignoring her when he was silent. He was merely thinking. At first, her natural instinct to demand a reaction had made it difficult for her to give him these quiet moments of contemplation, and they'd gotten into plenty of arguments over it, but she now understood if she gave him a moment to put his thoughts in order, he would share them with her. Eventually.

"I'm not having fun, not exactly," he said.

Her heart sank with disappointment.

"But I am enjoying my time alone with you away from the insanity of the tour. Even if I have to listen to history lessons all day, at least the British accents are entertaining."

Aggie chuckled. "What would you rather do?"

"Well, that would require one of those fun dungeons, but since I haven't seen one of those since we arrived, I'm content following your evil guidebook."

She pulled the dog-eared copy of *Tour the Scandals of England* from the back pocket of her jeans. "Not evil. Just a bit naughty."

They were working their way through the Tudor period, visiting sites where noteworthy members of society had done their dirty deeds or been punished for them.

"What's next?" he asked, his strong fingers sneaking under the hem of her T-shirt to stroke the bare skin of her back.

Pretending not to be affected by that simple touch, Aggie

flipped to the next stop on their self-directed tour. "Sudeley Castle, once home of Queen Katherine Parr. Only six months after the death of her husband, King Henry the Eighth, she married Thomas Seymour." She glanced up from her reading and met Jace's eyes. "Any relation?"

He shrugged. "Not that I know of. My father's family was originally from England, so maybe, but I really doubt it. Do I look like royalty to you?"

"You're king of my domain."

He chuckled. "That's more power than the King of England could ever claim."

She shifted on her feet. It was hard for her to admit that he held power over her. Not because he dominated her but because she loved him so much, she knew she'd do anything necessary to be with him. Not a comfortable position to find herself in, but Jace was worth the compromise. Unequivocally worth it.

"Let's go check out your ancestral home," she said and tapped his leather-encased arm with her book. "Maybe you're a baron or a duke and never even knew it."

He chuckled. "If I'm related to Thomas Seymour of Sudeley Castle, I'm sure my branch of the family tree was sawed off centuries ago."

"We can pretend; it'll be fun," she said and kissed him gently before opening the rental car's door and slipping inside. She inexplicably had a steering wheel in front of her. Crazy backwards cars. Grinning sheepishly, she slipped back out of the car and said, "I changed my mind. You should drive."

"You meant to do that, did you?" He winked at her knowingly.

"Of course," she said and hurried around to the other side of the car.

In her wrong-side-of-the-car passenger seat, she unfolded the large map of England and traced the road they'd be traveling to their next destination. "It's about a hundred kilometers from Oxford," she told him when he settled into the car beside her.

He scowled. "Which is how many miles?"

"Sixty or so."

"That's not far."

Once they were on the main road, they settled into a comfortable silence for several miles. It had been weeks since they'd been completely alone without interruptions. She enjoyed touring with his band all over Europe, but she was looking forward to getting back home in October. She missed her dungeon and her customers, but mostly she missed quiet evenings with Jace and his silly cat, Brownie. They'd had to leave the feline behind when the tour had brought them to Europe.

"I'm glad I decided to take a day off," she said, watching his face while he concentrated on driving on the wrong side of the road.

He glanced at her and smiled. "Me too. You've been working so hard on filling orders for corsets that I hardly see you without a needle in your hand."

Her business was definitely keeping her busy. Too busy. She'd collected so many orders while the band was touring the U.S. that she had enough to keep her fingers sore for months. She was horribly behind in her embroidery work, but everyone needed a day off every now and then, so she didn't feel too guilty.

"I've been thinking of working with some other fabrics. The silk corsets on display at that museum this morning were gorgeous."

"I like yours better," Jace said with a sheepish grin.

Hers were all made of leather, so of course he liked them better. He rarely went without his leather motorcycle jacket. And that was another thing she missed—riding behind him astride his rumbling Harley. But sitting on the wrong side of the car and taking in the sites was fun too. Smiling to herself as they passed through a quaint village, she caressed the platinum band of the solitaire engagement ring on her finger. Every moment with Jace brought her joy. She'd never thought she'd fall in love with a man. She definitely never thought one could hold her heart so completely and that she'd actually relish the feeling. She still pretended to be a badass dominatrix, but she'd come to terms with having an uncharacteristic soft spot for Sinners' silent bass player the day he'd crumpled at her feet and begged for mercy.

They arrived at their destination without mishap. Jace parked in a small lot. Through the trees, Aggie caught a glimpse of the enormous sandstone castle.

"I've seen this place before," Jace said.

"I thought you'd never been to England before."

He shook his head. "I haven't. I must have seen a picture of it or something. It looks familiar."

He opened his door and climbed out. He paused before the car's hood and stared up at the stone façade of the immense structure. Still inside the car, Aggie saw a shudder ripple through his entire body. He took a hesitant step in the direction of the castle. And then another.

He was halfway down the path to the gardens before Aggie opened the car door and climbed out. "Didn't you forget something?" she called after him.

He froze and turned to look at her. His breathing was uncharacteristically rapid and shallow. For a second he seemed not to recognize her. He lifted a hand to massage the golden hoop in one ear and tilted his head. "What did I forget?"

"Me!"

He held out a hand, and she trotted toward him to take it. As soon as his fingers wrapped around hers, he hurried down the walkway toward the entrance. After having to drag him through attractions for two days, his sudden change in enthusiasm baffled her.

"What's gotten into you?" she asked as he bounded the steps and swung the entrance door open.

"We're going to miss the last tour," he said, pointing at a sign.

This week only—Rare opportunity to tour the castle's private living quarters at 11 am, 1 pm and 3 pm. Tour space is limited.

So maybe he was having a better time than he'd let on. Or maybe there was something unique about this place. She wasn't sure why he was in such a hurry to catch another tour.

Luckily for them, there was space in the tour due to a last-minute cancellation. As they moved from room to room and the guide droned on about dates and lords and ladies, Aggie watched Jace with more curiosity than she held for any artifact or tidbit of historical information. Even though his eyes scanned every inch of every room, he didn't seem to be paying much attention to the tour. As they made their way through the luxurious castle, his stride became more and more stiff and his brow furrowed deeper and deeper with displeasure.

"Jace," she whispered as he glared at a set of drapes, "is something bothering you?"

"This is all wrong," he said. "She wouldn't approve of any of this."

"Who?"

"Katherine."

Aggie stiffened. "Who the fuck is Katherine?" While Aggie trusted him, she sure didn't like the name of another woman tumbling affectionately from his delectable lips.

Jace stared at her wordlessly for a long moment. If she hadn't known better, she'd have said he didn't know who she was.

"Jace?"

He closed his eyes, shook his head, and shuddered violently. The tour group had entered another room by the time he flipped his eyes open to look at her again. "Aggie?"

"You're acting weird," she said.

"I'm feeling weird. It's like I've been here before, but nothing is exactly how I remember it."

"Déjà vu?"

"I guess. I've never felt this way about a place before." He wrapped his arms around his torso and rubbed his upper arms. "It's chilly in here, isn't it?"

It wasn't. She touched her fingers to his forehead to check again for fever. She almost hoped he was coming down with the flu; at least his odd behavior would have an explanation. "You don't feel feverish, but I have to admit you're sort of freaking me out," she said.

He released a soft laugh. "You and me both, babe."

"Should we go? Maybe you should lie down for a while before you have to be onstage."

"No," he said hastily. "I like it here. I want to see every inch of the place, even though something feels a bit off and I don't know why that would be."

"Maybe you were here as a small child and that's why you remember it. And things look different to the adult you."

"Maybe," he said with a shrug.

She got the feeling he was only saying that to make her feel better about the bizarreness of what he was explaining, and she truly appreciated him for soothing her fears.

Based on appearances, the castle wasn't the least bit creepy. The décor was elegant and inviting, the ceilings high and the rooms filled with abundant natural light from the enormous windows. But she couldn't deny the shivers racing along her spine or the goose bumps on her arms. Maybe it *was* a little chilly in here.

At least she thought so until Jace leaned closer and captured her lips in a heated kiss. Nope. Not chilly in the castle at all. A bit too warm, if anything.

The chandelier overhead creaked. Aggie tugged her mouth from Jace's and glanced up at the enormous light fixture, her heart hammering.

"Are you sure you like it here?" she asked, taking his arm and moving him out from beneath the inexplicably swaying chandelier.

"Yeah," he said. "It's like I belong here or something."

She knew he didn't get that feeling often. Hell, he hadn't even felt like he belonged in his band, and it was obvious to everyone but him that he was tailor-made to fit their ranks. She patted his back and smiled, truly happy that he found a place that he connected to, no matter how many heebie jeebies were tickling her belly.

"Maybe you really are related to that Seymour guy. We should ask about him."

Expecting him to disagree, he surprised her by smiling brightly and nodding. "Yeah, I think I will."

They caught up with the tour group in the next room. Aggie stared at Jace in disbelief as he raised his hand and snapped his fingers to gain the tour guide's attention.

"Yes?" the woman asked, her head cocked slightly.

"Did someone named Thomas Seymour live here at one time?"

"Indeed," the guide said. "I usually talk about him in the chapel where his wife, Queen Katherine, is buried."

"His wife is buried there, but he isn't?" Jace asked.

"He was executed for treason less than a year after her death. Quite the scoundrel, that one. Well, depending on whom you ask." She giggled.

"Oh," Jace said flatly. His eyebrows scrunched together. "Would you mind telling me where he was executed?"

"In the Tower of London."

"Wasn't everyone?" an older man in the tour group asked, which elicited a round of laughter.

Jace didn't look amused. A bit nauseated maybe, but not amused.

"He was only lord of Sudeley Castle for two years," the guide continued. "He didn't have much claim to the place."

"I don't think *he'd* agree with that," Jace said under his breath.

The guide cocked a brow at him. "What do you mean?"

"Nothing. Please continue."

The guide gave him a long look and then took a deep breath to continue with her rehearsed spiel about a different lord of Sudeley Castle.

"Scoundrel, eh?" Jace said, and then he produced an unfamiliar soft laugh. "If only the truth were half as interesting as the lies."

"Have you completely lost it?" Aggie asked Jace.

He looped his arm through hers and trailed after the group, looking mildly amused for some inexplicable reason.

"It is a distinct possibility, my dear," he said in a perfect English accent.

She gaped at him, but allowed him to lead her into the next room. "You're full of surprises today."

"Am I?"

She nodded.

"Must be a side effect of basking in your splendid beauty, lovey," he said.

She stopped, drawing him to a halt beside her, and checked him for fever yet again. Jace didn't say things like that unless they were in bed and he was sure there was no one around to hear him. Or even see his lips move. She hadn't known he even knew the word *splendid*. And when the fuck had he started calling her *lovey*? "I think you need to see a doctor, baby."

"I think you need to kiss me." He drew her against him and brushed his lips against hers. A nearby door slammed. Jace pulled away and cupped her cheek. "She always was the jealous sort."

Aggie drew her eyebrows together and shook her head. "What are you talking about?"

"It's nothing. I'm just teasing."

She might have believed him if he were the type to tease. He wasn't. Jace turned and tucked her hand into the crook of his elbow again. He led her to a closed door, the one that had slammed for no apparent reason when Jace had kissed her. Even his gait was stiffer than usual as he opened the door and ushered her through it. He looked like Jace, but he didn't talk like Jace or act like Jace or even walk like Jace. If she believed in ghosts and the supernatural—and she didn't—she'd have insisted they turn back. Something was filling her with a dread she couldn't explain.

"Uh," Jace said, "I think we'll skip the next room."

"Why?"

"It's Mary's nursery. I don't want to go in there."

"How do you know that?"

"I… overheard the guide say as much." He nodded resolutely.

"Jace…" A chill raced down her spine as he took a step back from the room where the tour guide was speaking rather loudly about the child born to Queen Katherine and her fourth husband, Thomas Seymour.

"Very tragic," the guide said. "The baby was only days old when her mother died of puerperal fever."

"I don't think you should go in there either," he said.

Aggie straightened her spine, wondering when it had become a yellow wet noodle, and strode across the hall to the door with as much confidence as she could muster. "I'm going in."

When she was about to cross the threshold, the door slammed in her face. Aggie's breath caught in her throat.

She glanced at Jace, who was looking around as if completely lost.

"How did I get here?" he asked.

"You walked. I need to find a bathroom," Aggie said. "I suddenly need to go really bad." And she wanted to get away from that nursery as soon as possible. Part of her wanted to get away from *Jace* as soon as possible.

"We shouldn't leave the tour," Jace said.

"Do you want me to piss my pants?"

"Maybe." He grinned his usual adorable grin.

She hugged him against her tightly, relief settling over her. "You're you."

"Who else would I be?"

"Something weird is going on here."

"I'll say," he said. He squeezed her even harder than she was squeezing him and then took a deep breath before releasing his hold. "Let's find you a bathroom."

Aggie nodded gratefully. Ghosts didn't haunt toilets, did they? Hopefully they only did so in Harry Potter novels.

Chapter 4

JACE GAZED OUT A WINDOW while he waited for Aggie to come out of the bathroom. There was something about this place that soothed him. A strange connection. He almost felt like he'd been here before. At the same time he felt unsettled, as if he was supposed to be doing something, but couldn't remember what it was.

He caught a spot of color out of the corner of his eye and turned his head to see an elegant woman dressed in a green gown from the Tudor period. She stood directly beside Jace staring out the window next to his. Her face was flawless and a translucent white. He had the strangest feeling that even though she was standing right beside him, she wasn't actually there. The hairs on his arm stood on end.

"Hello?" he said.

She didn't acknowledge his presence. There were no sounds coming from her. Not the sound of breathing or the rustle of clothing. Dead silence. He took a step back, and she turned her head and smiled at him with recognition. *Thomas.* Her mouth didn't move, but he heard her voice in his head. *I've waited so long, my love. So long.*

"Jace, there you are," Aggie called to him.

Jace started and turned his head reflexively in Aggie's direction. By the time he turned back to the woman in green, she'd vanished.

"Where did she go?" Jace asked, peering down the hallway in both directions.

"Who?"

"The woman at the window."

Aggie craned her neck to look behind him and then met his eyes warily.

"There was no one here but you when I came out of the bathroom."

"But she was right there when you called my name," Jace said, indicating the empty space beside him with a wave.

"I didn't see her," Aggie said.

He closed his eyes. First he had blacked out for several minutes and now he was seeing and hearing things.

"Are you okay? You look a little pale."

He also had cold sweat trickling down his spine, but no explanation for who the woman was or where she'd gone or why he'd heard her voice in his head.

"I'm not sure. I should probably sit down for a second."

"Maybe we should just leave."

"No," he said hastily. He didn't want to leave. The very idea filled him with sorrow.

Aggie wrapped him in her arms. "I'm worried about you."

I'm worried about me too, he thought, but he didn't say it. He did welcome her embrace though, until the tour guide and a dozen or so people came out of a library.

"Civil ceremonies are sometimes performed in the library, but most weddings are performed in St. Mary's Chapel," the guide said. Her eyes landed on Jace. "There you are. We thought we'd lost you. Please keep up with the rest of the group; we're heading outdoors now. You missed much of the special tour."

Jace nodded slightly, thinking he'd had enough of the special tour, *thank you very much*, and loosened his grip on Aggie. He hadn't realized he'd been hugging her so tightly.

"We could skip out now," Aggie whispered in his ear. "I'll drive the rest of the way to the festival if you're not up to it." She leaned back and patted his chest. "Just be sure to wear your seat belt. No guarantees I'll get us there in one piece."

"I'm okay," he assured her. "I'd like to see the grounds before we go." It was as if something was tugging him to follow the group.

"You do look like you could use some fresh air."

"I'm fine," he said and pulled her questing hand from his forehead. Did he look like he was about to take his last breath or what?

They followed the group, keeping the others within sight, but didn't mingle with the crowd. The guide was giving details on hedges and other plants. Jace was content to look at them without knowing their names or what year they'd been planted. Hand in hand, he and Aggie rounded a corner, and Aggie stopped dead in her tracks.

Eyes wide, she covered her mouth with one hand, and her eyes filled with tears. "It's beautiful!" she squealed in the most girly display of excitement Jace had ever witnessed out of the woman.

He followed her gaze across the expanse of colorful gardens, symmetrical walkways, and perfectly shaped hedges to the notched roofline of a church.

"Jace!" she gasped, took his hand, and dragged him toward the building. "I want to get married here."

"Now?" he sputtered stupidly. Talk about spur of the moment.

She laughed and slowed her steps as they approached the open front doors of the church. "Not today," she said. "We'll have to make arrangements. But soon." She tore her awe-stricken stare from the romantic building to smile at him. "You're going to marry me here. Okay?"

He grinned, a bit overwhelmed by the sudden rush of emotion clogging his throat. He'd thought she'd never find *the* place, even though she'd insisted, "we'll know it when we see it," and she'd chosen here of all places.

"Okay," he said. "I'm ready when you are."

"Yeah?" she said, lighting up like a child on Christmas morning.

"Yeah."

She threw herself into his arms and kissed him excitedly. He was very much enjoying participating in her enthusiastic make-out session until someone cleared her throat. Jace pulled his reluctant lips from Aggie's and turned his head, expecting to see the tour guide. A woman he was sure he'd never seen before was standing at the top of the church steps, looking down at them with a knowing grin.

"Would you like to see inside?" she asked.

"Oh yes!" Aggie said, grabbing Jace by the sleeve of his leather jacket and yanking him up the steps before he could blink.

She entered the church a bit more respectfully and sucked in a deep breath while Jace tried to get his eyes to focus in the dim light.

"Oh, Jace, isn't it perfect?"

From what his spotted vision could see, yeah, it was nice.

The woman standing beside Aggie handed her something and she used it to dab at her eyes. Aggie didn't cry often. She'd cried when he'd been shot and they'd been reunited in the hospital. She'd cried when he'd told her of the most painful experiences of his past. She'd cried when he'd proposed to her. And she was crying now. Something monumental was happening for them. He was just going to go with it.

"It's even more romantic on the inside," she said and leaned her head against Jace's shoulder.

He took in the diamond-patterned floor, the rich mahogany of the pews, the intricately carved woodwork above the pulpit, and the spectacular stained-glass windows in arched frames along both side walls and behind the altar. It was the chapel most girls dreamed of getting married in. But Aggie wasn't most girls. Or maybe she was.

He kissed her temple and rubbed her lower back.

"When can we get married here?" Jace asked.

"That would depend on what kind of ceremony you have planned," the woman said, smiling kindly.

"What kind of ceremony do we have planned?" Jace asked Aggie.

She laughed and dabbed at her eyes. "We're open to suggestions."

The woman's smile broadened. "Would you like to go to my office and talk?" she said. "I'm Charity Watson—the event planner for the castle. I'd love to help you two make plans to tie the knot."

Jace nodded enthusiastically and with his hand on Aggie's lower back, directed his soon-to-be wife to follow Charity out of the chapel.

Aggie finally had agreed to marry him. He thought his chest might burst from the mix of love, excitement, and pride stirring within him.

Yeah, he was stoked that they were finally going to get married.

Even though the place she'd chosen was probably haunted.

Chapter 5

AGGIE WIPED HER INEXPLICABLY SWEATY PALMS on her jeans as she watched Charity circle her desk and sit across from her and Jace.

"We want to get married in that gorgeous little chapel as soon as possible," Aggie told her.

"Are you both American citizens?"

Aggie nodded. "Will that be a problem?"

"Potentially. You have to be in England for a minimum of fifteen days before the ceremony for it to be legally recognized."

"We could do a two-week honeymoon before the wedding," Jace suggested.

"Can we have a ceremony here and then have a legal get-hitched-quick courthouse wedding back in the States?" Aggie asked.

"I don't see why that would be an issue," Charity said.

"Would anyone be horribly offended if we got married in the chapel even though neither of us are members of the Church of England?"

The wedding coordinator smiled at them. "Who could be offended by two people so obviously in love as you two getting married in their church?"

Aggie glanced at Jace, who was very red in the face.

"So how soon can we do this?" Aggie asked. Now that she'd found *the place*, she wanted to get married as soon as possible.

"What's the rush all of a sudden?" Jace asked. "Afraid I'll get away?"

Aggie kicked him out of sight of the woman on the opposite side of the desk.

"If you want a spring or summer wedding, keep in mind that the castle is open to tourists," Charity told them. "It's not usually a huge concern, but if you wait until the castle closes for the winter, you'll have more privacy."

"I like privacy," Jace said.

Charity smiled. "I thought you might." She flipped through the day planner on her desk. "The first possible date in our off-season would be November first."

Jace breathed a sigh of obvious relief. Aggie scowled at him.

"That will give us enough time to plan something special," Jace explained. "We need a few months to organize. And you don't really want a bunch of strangers gawking at us while we get married, do you?"

Aggie patted his hand. He was right, she wouldn't. And she knew he would be very uncomfortable in that situation. Five and a half months wasn't all that long to wait.

"November first it is," Aggie said, a huge grin plastered to her face.

"Wonderful," Charity said. "Here's a brochure. We'll exchange contact information and make further arrangements."

"What happened to the rooms I had built for my lady?" Jace asked. "She cannot find comfort in these halls."

Aggie jerked her head to give him a strange look. "What?"

Jace blinked at her. "Why are you looking at me like that?"

"What did you just say? It didn't make any sense."

Jace shrugged and shook his head. "I didn't say anything."

"You did. I heard you." Aggie turned to Charity to back her up. "Didn't he just say something about building rooms for his lady and comfortable halls?"

The coordinator lifted a brow and shook her head slightly. "I didn't hear him say as much, but he is rather quiet for such an attractive man." Her cheeks went pink. She reached for an address book to record their personal information. "Names."

"Agatha Christine Martin," Aggie said. Soon to be Agatha Christine Seymour, which was an even worse name. She vowed that if they ever had children, she'd give them decent names to help counter the Seymour Butts jokes they were sure to endure.

"Jason Thomas Seymour," Jace said absently.

The woman stopped with her pen in midstroke. "Thomas Seymour?"

"Your middle name isn't Thomas, it's Michael," Aggie said.

Jace's dark eyebrows drew together. "You're right. I don't know why I said that. I'm kind of distracted."

This place seemed to bring that out in him.

"You're a Seymour?" Charity lifted a golden blond eyebrow at him.

Jace nodded.

"Thomas Seymour was the baron of this holding in the sixteenth century," she said. "Did you visit Queen Katherine's tomb in the church? He was married to her."

Jace shook his head, his face a shade paler than usual. "We didn't make it that far in the tour, but Aggie was reading about him in her guidebook and the tour guide mentioned him several times. That must be why I gave you the wrong name."

"I wonder if you're related," Charity said, sitting straighter in her chair. Head cocked to one side, her gray eyes assessed him with interest.

Jace laughed. "Not likely."

"Ah well, we can pretend," she said and winked at him. "I think you should go visit Queen Katherine before you leave today. Some claim to have seen her ghost. A tall, elegant woman in a green gown."

Aggie chuckled. Ghosts? Who in this day and age would believe in such nonsense? She rolled her eyes at Jace, but he did not look amused.

"We'll have to postpone that visit until we return in November," he said. "I have somewhere I need to be."

And by the way he was perched on the edge of his chair, Aggie assumed it was anywhere but here.

"You do want to get married here, don't you?" Aggie asked, grabbing him firmly by the elbow before he launched himself out of his seat.

"Can't wait," he said breathlessly.

But something about the way he held his body so stiffly made Aggie doubt his sincerity.

Chapter 6

Halloween

AGGIE DROPPED HER BAG wearily inside the bedroom door of the cottage she was sharing with her mother for the night. She felt that she got the short straw on that draw, but the other cottages just outside the Sudeley Castle grounds were occupied by couples, and since her new stepfather hadn't been able to attend the wedding ceremony, Aggie's mother had come to England without him. She'd been driving Aggie nuts since they boarded their flight in Los Angeles over eleven hours before. Sitting between her incredibly introverted fiancé and her obtrusively extroverted mother for that many hours had worn Aggie's nerves raw. This was supposed to be the happiest time of her life, and she just wanted to kick someone in the face.

"This is quaint," her mom said. "I expected accommodations at a castle to be a bit grander."

"The castle itself is breathtaking," Aggie assured her. "The guest cottages are newer. Besides, I like them."

"I saw the castle on the way in," her mom said. "It was beautiful. Very romantic. I always thought you'd get married someplace a bit gloomier."

"Why's that?"

Her mother chuckled, the sound low and throaty. "Well, you've always swayed toward the dark and macabre. And it is Halloween, after all."

"But I'm getting married tomorrow, not tonight."

"Close enough." Her mom grinned and began searching through her purse.

There was a knock at the door, and Aggie opened it at once. Jace smiled at her, but he looked almost as weary as she felt. She ushered him inside and closed the door to the chilly afternoon air.

"We need to meet with the event planner to make sure everything is ready for tomorrow," he said. "And apparently Eric has cooked up something special for everyone tonight, Halloween being his favorite holiday after April Fool's Day."

"I'm not sure I'm up for Eric's nonsense tonight," Aggie said with a tired sigh. "I have jet lag from hell."

He touched her cheek gently and stared into her eyes almost dreamily. "Maybe we'll have time for a nap before Eric's Halloween bash."

"Agatha! Come look at this view!" her mother called from somewhere in the cottage.

"In a minute, Ma!" she yelled. "Do you really think my mother is going to let me sleep?" Aggie asked Jace.

"*I* wasn't planning on letting you sleep," he said. "And I was inviting you to *my* cottage. The one without your mother."

"Aren't you rooming with Eric and Rebekah for tonight?"

"I'm sure they'll be busy with other things this afternoon." He leaned close and whispered, "Which leaves the cottage free for me to get busy with you."

She snorted at his use of "get busy." "You do know I'm in a really bad mood, right?"

He grinned and lowered his eyes. "Yep. I was kind of hoping you'd take your anger out on me."

She chuckled and kissed the tip of his nose. So he was after a little pain. Why hadn't he just said so to begin with? "I think I'll take you up on that nap."

"I thought you might."

He drew her into his arms and kissed her hungrily. Her cranky was rapidly being replaced by her horny. The man had that sort of effect on her.

"Save it for the honeymoon, lovebirds," her mom said from somewhere behind her.

Aggie stiffened and pulled away from Jace. He leaned close to her ear and whispered, "I love you."

Her heart warmed and even her annoying mother couldn't have put a damper on the joy brought from hearing those three words from him. "I love you too." Aggie turned toward her mother, who was grinning at the two of them. She looked almost happy for them.

"We're going to go talk to the event planner and make sure everything is all set for tomorrow," Aggie said, reaching around Jace to open the door. She prodded him toward the exit, trying to make her escape.

It had been a challenge planning and arranging everything by phone and email, but Charity was excellent at her job and had put Aggie's fears about the wedding to rest. Mostly.

"Just let me get a cigarette and retrieve my jacket," her mom said. "It's a bit chilly out."

Aggie winced, but didn't refuse to let her accompany them. Her mom was the only parent she and Jace had between them, and Aggie knew Mom wanted to participate in the wedding. She only had one daughter to marry off, and Aggie was only going to get married once, so this was her only chance to be mother of the bride. Aggie just hoped her mom would make her a believer of miracles by keeping her over-the-top personality reeled in a bit.

"We'll wait for you outside," Aggie said and stepped out onto the front step. Jace followed behind her and closed the door.

He took her hand, holding it gently in his warm grip, and they walked slowly toward the main castle so that her mother could catch up with them easily when she emerged from the cozy cabin.

"Do you think it's cold enough to snow?" Jace asked, glancing up at the overcast sky.

"Not quite," Aggie said. "But we might get some rain."

"I miss the snow," he said. "Let's go someplace cold for Christmas this year. It's just not the same when it's warm and sunny."

"As long as we stay huddled together in a cozy cabin. No driving."

His hand tightened on hers, and she knew they were both thinking about the last time they'd seen snow. It had been in Canada two years before, and they'd nearly lost their lives in a bus accident.

"Yeah," he said. "Some nice cabin in the mountains that allows pets."

Aggie smiled. "Christmas wouldn't be Christmas without Brownie," she said.

"She loves the decorations," he said with a gentle smile.

Jace's cat loved methodically stripping Christmas trees of all decorations, as if it were her mission in life. Aggie had been exasperated with the beast last Christmas until after the third time she'd decorated the tree and decided it was a losing battle. Besides, it made Jace laugh to watch his cat chase a wobbling Christmas bulb across the room, and anything that made him laugh was worthwhile to Aggie.

"Do you feel like we're already married?" Jace asked.

"We have been living together for over a year."

"Is this really the big deal everyone makes it out to be? I've felt like you are my wife for a long while now. Doesn't it seem like I'm already your husband?"

Until she stood before all their friends and spoke her vows to him, it didn't feel official to her. "No. I love you as if you're my husband, but I'm looking forward to marrying you tomorrow. Can't wait."

He squeezed her hand again, telegraphing all sorts of mushy feelings she knew he'd never voice, but she understood his affection.

"Me too," he said, grinning brightly. "Even if we won't be legally married until we return to California."

She stole a kiss, unable to resist his appeal when he unleashed that carefully concealed charm of his.

"I hope it doesn't rain on your wedding day," Aggie's mom said from several paces behind them. "Are you two at it again?" she asked.

Aggie drew away from Jace's delightful lips and tossed a look of annoyance in her mother's direction. "We're going to be at it for the next seventy or eighty years, so you'd better get used to it."

Her mom laughed. "You two are so cute together. Both hard on the outside and soft on the inside. You've cracked each other's shells and are all gooey and mixed up together now."

Aggie rolled her eyes. She had no idea where her mother had come up with such a silly idea. The idea that Aggie had a soft spot anywhere in her being was preposterous. Well, okay, so she did have *one* soft spot. But it was very small and well hidden. She only let Jace see it very occasionally. At least that's what she liked to make herself believe.

Mom took a drag off her cigarette and blew a long stream of smoke from between her lips. "That flight was the longest eleven hours of my life. I'm going to have chain-smoke for days to get caught up on my nicotine."

"You could have used the flight as an opportunity to quit," Aggie pointed out. She didn't like the smell of the smoke, or the nuisance of having a smoker in tow, but mostly she wanted her mother to quit because she worried about her health.

"And you could have used it as an opportunity to learn to speak Mandarin," Mom countered, taking another drag off her cigarette.

Jace chuckled, which earned him a squeeze around the shoulders from his soon-to-be mother-in-law.

"You are so cute when you laugh," she said, words that immediately wiped the smile off his face.

They crossed a wide field of grass, found a pathway around the immense castle—which was even more beautiful and romantic than Aggie remembered—and climbed the steps to the building's main entrance. Mom paused at the bottom of the steps to finish her cigarette near an ashtray. At least she wasn't crushing her butts into the landscaping. Aggie paused at the top of the stairs and turned to wait for her, but found her lighting up another cigarette as she scrunched out the cherry of the first. She hadn't been joking about her need to chain-smoke.

"I'll find you in a minute, don't worry about me," Mom said, waving them into the building.

Aggie shrugged and turned to Jace, who was gazing across the lawn toward a garden.

"Jace?"

He didn't so much as blink.

She waved a hand in front of his face.

"Earth to Jace."

He took a step toward the garden, and she jerked his arm. "Where are you going? We need to meet with the planner."

"But she's waiting…" he said, his voice distant.

"I'm sure she is. We're already late. Come on."

She pulled him toward the door. He sucked in a deep breath and rubbed his face.

"What's wrong with you?" she asked. "You're so out of it. Jet lag?"

He looked at her as if he hadn't realized she was standing beside him. "Nothing," he said and held open the door so she could enter the castle.

"You always act so strange when we're here," she said, glancing around the spectacular entry to get her bearings. Now, where was Charity's office again?

"I feel strange when we're here. Not bad strange, but strange."

She saw a familiar corridor and headed for the office. "What do you mean?" she asked, half her attention on him, half on finding their way.

"The way I feel when I get home after being on tour for a couple of months."

"Tired and horny. Gotcha," she said with a laugh. They tended to spend several days in bed when he returned from a tour. And usually they spent most of their mattress-time *not* sleeping.

"Settled," he murmured.

She was feeling particularly *un*settled, truth be told, but she was sure that feeling of nervousness in the pit of her stomach would vanish after the ceremony.

"Tripod!" Eric's voice echoed through the cavernous room.

If not for the crazy rock-star haircut, Aggie would have thought Eric had walked through a window in time. He was wearing a black coat with long tails over buff-colored trousers. He held a large top hat and cane in one hand, had some travesty of a floppy bow at his throat above a fitted cadet-blue vest, and wore brown calf-hugging boots on his feet. She really did do a double take of the lovely petite woman at his side. She wore a delicate pink gown with a ruffled bottom and ruffled sleeves all trimmed with ribbon and lace. Elbow-length opera gloves completed her look. Well, those and the splotches of crimson highlights in her blond hair.

"Rebekah?" Aggie said. "Where did you get that dress?"

"From our favorite costume shop," Rebekah said. "We had Malachi hunt down all sorts of costumes for the Halloween ball and ship them here from all over Europe and the United States, so everyone can find something grand to wear. Eric and I are vintage 1820s, but there are gowns dating back as far as fifteen hundred. We have nothing newer than the nineteen thirties and everything you can imagine in between. So it's not a period ball, exactly, but it'll be lots of fun."

"Did you know Rebekah doesn't have periods? It's awesome," Eric said, which earned him an elbow in the ribs from his wife.

"You decided to tell a period joke over a ball joke?" Jace said. "I'm stunned."

"I'm saving the ball jokes for later," Eric assured him.

"I thought you'd go for a Halloween theme for the party. Like monsters and zombies and stuff," Aggie said. When the couple had begged Jace to allow them to throw a Halloween party in lieu of the traditional rehearsal dinner, Aggie had expected it to be more, well... *Halloween*.

"Well, at first we thought you were getting married in a creepy old castle, but this place is grand," Rebekah said, twirling slightly as she gazed up at the ceiling high above. "It's so beautiful and romantic and fabulous. We decided a period ball would be more fun and far more fitting."

"At least she didn't decide on a tampon ball," Eric said, which earned him another elbow in the ribs.

Jace thought Eric's joke was funny. Either that or jet lag had him delirious. He laughed until he had to wrap his arms around his stomach to hold his merriment in.

"Are you done?" Rebekah asked her husband.

"Do you really need to ask me that?" he countered.

She lifted her eyebrows at him. "Enough with the period jokes already."

He grinned and nodded. "No problem, babe. I'll move on to the ball jokes then."

Rebekah rolled her eyes at him, but Aggie could see the mirth in her expression; she'd be howling along with Jace in no time. Aggie's sense of humor was a tad less fart-joke, but she loved to see her husband laugh so if he thought grand celebrations about periods and tampons were hilarious, good on him.

"Do you want to come see the decorations? They turned out really neat," Rebekah said. "Charity is a miracle worker."

"We need to meet with that miracle worker about the ceremony tomorrow," Aggie said, "but we'll stop by the hall on our way out."

"Awesome," Rebekah said. She hugged Aggie with excitement. "I'm so happy for you, hon. And you know I adore Jace almost as much as Eric does."

Aggie patted Rebekah's back a little. She wasn't much of a hugger. Though sometimes Aggie wanted to squeeze the stuffing out of Jace, she preferred to avoid personal contact with others as much as possible. And she'd been damned good at maintaining her distance from people until Jace Seymour entered her life.

"This place is so perfect for the exchange of your wedding vows," Rebekah said, forcing Jace to accept a hearty squeeze. He wasn't much of a hugger either and patted her back much the way Aggie had.

Eric gave Jace a bro tap with his knuckles and then swept his wife against his side and led her in the opposite direction, testing several ball jokes on her. At least that's what Aggie thought he was whispering that had her laughing so hard.

"I suppose we have to go to this Halloween party thing," Jace said. "Since they went to all that trouble."

"We should have a few hours between this meeting and when we have to attend the costume ball. I'm sure we can find time to take a little nap between now and then. Get you out of your jet-lag funk or whatever it is that has you so spacy since we arrived."

"A nap is exactly what I need," he said.

"Wow!" Aggie's mom hollered just inside the entrance. "These people must be fucking loaded!"

Aggie winced and pivoted toward her mother. Aggie waved her toward them so she could put a gag over her gigantic mouth if necessary. Mom hurried to catch up, and then linked one elbow through Aggie's arm and the other through Jace's.

"Exactly how much money do you rock stars make, Maynard? How can you afford to rent this place? You're just a bassist."

"Mother!"

"Did you add Agatha to your checking account?" she asked Jace.

"I—uh…"

Jace's face was the color of a tomato.

"I asked him not to, okay?" Aggie said. "Don't ask him questions like that."

"Why not? He's family."

"And he's probably wishing he wasn't."

"It's cool," he said. "I don't mind sharing. Uh, I make more than a paper boy and less than Bill Gates."

Aggie grinned, loving how he handled her mother. He was actually much better at it than she was.

"So closer to Bill Gates than a paper boy, am I right?" her mother said and laughed hysterically. Aggie was starting to wonder if she'd hit the wet bar while she'd been collecting her smokes from their rented cottage.

"Probably closer to the paper boy," Jace said.

"Huh…" Mom said, rubbing her nose on her shoulder. "Well, that's disappointing. Better luck next time, Ag."

"There isn't going to be a next time. Jace is mine for life." Aggie tilted her head to smile at him around her mother's slim form, but he was too busy blushing to back her claim.

"Well, I hope you don't have to go back to stripping to support his musician habit. I once dated a singer, you know," she told Jace. "Well, date is a strong word. Got knocked up by a singer. He was a total deadbeat. I heard being a deadbeat is common in your profession." She finger-quoted profession.

That's it. I'm going to kill her.

"Aggie's father?" Jace asked, not batting an eyelash at Mom's string of insults.

"That would be the deadbeat in question," she said and glanced around. "Where is this lady you're meeting? In *Africa*? I'm going to need to go out and have another cigarette soon."

"Well, don't let us stop you," Aggie said.

Their event planner, Charity, stepped out of a corridor to their left.

"There you are!" she said. "I was afraid you got turned around and ended up in the dungeon."

"Aggie would be right at home there," Mom said and guffawed at her own humor.

"Charity," Aggie said, "this is my mother, Tabitha."

"Nice to meet you," the sophisticated woman—who Aggie estimated to be around the same age as Mom—said. "Welcome to Sudeley Castle. Have you had a chance to explore the grounds and the building?"

"Not yet."

"You should have a look," Charity said. "Mr. and Mrs. Sticks went all out for the rehearsal dinner. Normally we don't do costume parties on Halloween, but your best man is very persuasive. Not to mention handsome." She giggled and touched her fingertips to her suddenly ruddy cheeks.

"Eric?" Aggie asked, wondering if Charity had somehow mixed up Jace's best man with any one of his groomsmen.

"Oh my, yes," Charity murmured. "Quite dreamy."

Aggie supposed Eric was an attractive man. His personality was so large it completely overshadowed his physical attributes, so she tended to forget how good looking he was. When he kept his mouth shut. Which was pretty much never.

"And he's so enthusiastic about everything," Charity gushed. "As is his wife. What a pair. They have brought such energy to the castle since they arrived yesterday."

Aggie was more likely to call said energy *obnoxious*, but she supposed Charity hadn't been living with them in close quarters for months. Their type of energy exhausted Aggie quickly, but she'd never meet a couple more suited for each other. Except perhaps herself and Jace.

"The chapel, with the exception of the flowers, is set up for the ceremony. Those will be brought in tomorrow so they're fresh," Charity said.

"What kind of flowers did you get?" Mom asked, sitting up straighter in her chair.

"Black and red roses," Aggie said.

Mom giggled like a schoolgirl. "Should have guessed."

"I believe both the bridal party and the groom's party have now arrived." Charity consulted a list and added checkmarks to the top two names—*Agatha Christine Martin* and *Jason Michael Seymour*. She ran a finger down the side of the list slowly, as if calling up the faces, or characteristics, of each person. "You have some, er, *interesting* friends."

Interesting? Aggie's bridesmaids included one notorious porn star and Jace's groomsmen were all rock stars. She supposed they would be interesting to some people. To Aggie and Jace, they were just friends.

"They'll be well-behaved," Jace said, looking uncertain.

Aggie rubbed his back. They would, but who cared if their entourage got a little rowdy? She liked them for who they were. And she knew none of them would go on a drug-induced rampage and destroy the castle or anything.

"I can't believe you asked Starr Lancaster to be in your wedding party," Mom said, craning her neck to read the list. "Isn't she that porn star you used to hang out with?"

"Well, yeah, when she's not stripping and not dominating her slaves," Aggie said. "She's a good friend of mine; I've known her for ages. Why wouldn't I ask her?"

"Uh, does Jace know about her?" Mom asked.

Aggie bit her lip. She still hadn't divulged how intimate her relationship with Starr had once been. Hadn't thought it important. Or maybe she was afraid of Jace's reaction.

Charity cleared her throat, the ruddiness in her cheeks increasing.

"Starr's a sweetheart," Jace said. "Not half as vicious as Aggie with a lash."

Now it was Jace's turn to go red in the face. "Uh, I mean…"

Aggie chuckled. She wondered if he'd feel awkward standing before everyone saying his vows with Starr in the wedding party. He hadn't questioned a single person she'd asked to stand up with her, but he was very good at hiding his true feelings—except embarrassment. Aggie would have been able to tell if Jace was embarrassed by Starr. When they were choosing their supposed-to-have-been *small* wedding party, he had mentioned in passing that Eric would be his best man, hinting that Aggie ask Rebekah to be her maid of honor. Even though she'd only known Rebekah for a year, she'd had no qualms about asking her to head her bridal party. To prevent hurt feelings, Jace had then asked the rest of his band to be his groomsmen, which made Aggie feel obligated to ask their significant others to be her attendants. They were left with Dave—Rebekah's brother and Sinners' lead soundboard operator—who was easy enough to pair off with Aggie's cousin Beth. Beth had been thrilled to walk with Dave as she hadn't shut up about the guy since she'd met him at Sed's wedding. Trey was walking with Aggie's mom because his significant others, Ethan and Reagan, had been unable to attend. And then there was Dare Mills—who Jace idolized second only to Eric. As Dare was rather tightlipped about his romantic prospects, Aggie had asked Starr to walk with him. Starr hadn't protested. More like swooned. And Starr really was her closest friend outside the Lady Sinners. She just hadn't told Jace how close. What happened in the dungeon, stayed in the dungeon. And her sexual relationship with Starr had never left the dungeon. Not once.

Aggie glanced up when she realized Charity was explaining how the rehearsal would go. She should probably pay attention, so she didn't make a fool of herself.

"So that about sums it up," Charity said. "Are you ready for your practice run?"

Aggie cringed. She'd missed more than she'd assumed while daydreaming. As in, she'd missed all of it.

"Could you repeat that one more time?" Aggie asked.

"It's easier to get instructions while you're all in your places," Charity said, standing and moving out from behind her desk. "Don't worry. You'll have it down by the time we're through."

The event planner followed Mom out of the office, saying how unusual it was for a mother to be a bridesmaid.

"Yeah, well, that's my Aggie," Mom said. "No one could ever accuse her of fitting a mold."

Was that a hint of pride in her tone? Aggie was sure she'd imagined it.

"Distracted?" Jace asked as he climbed to his feet and offered her a hand up.

"A little," she admitted.

"About?"

"Everything," she said vaguely. She couldn't very well say, *One of my few long-term romantic relationships was with a woman. And she's in our wedding party. And has seen you naked.* Maybe asking Starr to be one of her bridesmaids had been a mistake. Aggie didn't like to feel guilty, yet intentionally keeping secrets from Jace had that effect on her.

"Me too," he admitted.

He held her hand as they followed several paces behind chatting Charity and wide-eyed Mom. At least, he held her hand until the members of his band, along with Dare Mills and Dave Blake, came out of the ballroom. As soon as the rowdy bunch of men spotted Jace, he dropped Aggie's hand as if she'd suddenly contracted leprosy.

"You know," she said, "you're going to be saying some really mushy and embarrassing stuff to me in front of all these guys tomorrow. Are you sure you can handle it?"

Jace took her hand again and smiled crookedly. "Yep."

The guys were in various states of annoyance over Eric's rehearsal-dinner after-party.

"You don't really expect us to wear those clothes do you?" Sed said in his deep baritone.

"You better wear them," Eric said. "You were the most difficult person to fit. Do you know how rare it was for a human to reach your size centuries ago? You'd have been labeled a freak and had to join the circus as a giant."

"You're taller than I am," Sed pointed out.

"By an inch," Eric said. "It's those extra-wide shoulders of yours."

"That drive the ladies wild," Sed said with a wink.

"I'd say it's your ass that drives the ladies wild," Mom said. And she was not hiding the fact that she was checking it out. With excessive appreciation.

Sed wrapped an arm around her shoulders and drew her up beside him so she couldn't ogle what he had going on behind. "My wife gets very jealous when MILFs check out my ass," he said.

Aggie chuckled when her mom tripped over her feet as the definition of MILF sank in.

The guys followed them outside—ribbing each other as if they were brothers—and over to the church. Aggie's attendants were already congregated in the back of the building, surrounding the tomb of Queen Katherine.

"Did you know her third husband was Henry the Eighth and her fourth was Thomas Seymour?" Myrna asked anyone who would listen.

"So Aggie isn't the only woman willing to marry a guy with the last name of Seymour," Eric said.

"How did she die?" Rebekah asked and was immediately

engulfed in her husband's embrace.

"About a week after her and Thomas's daughter was born, Katherine died of childbed fever," Charity said.

"I bet Thomas was devastated," Rebekah said.

Charity lifted a scandalized eyebrow. "So devastated that he turned to the ladies of the court to ease his broken heart. He was courting a princess within months of Katherine's death."

"I can understand that," Sed said. "Nothing like copious sex with strangers to ease a broken heart." His words earned him an elbow in the stomach from his enormously pregnant wife.

"He was an ambitious man. Incredibly charming," Charity said. "And apparently attracted to powerful women."

All eyes turned to Jace and Aggie. Aggie grinned. She knew for a fact that her man was attracted to powerful women.

Trey whacked him on the back. "Maybe you *are* related to this dude," he said with a laugh.

Jace gnawed on his lip, but didn't respond.

"Did Seymour remarry?" Myrna asked.

"No." Charity shook her head. "He was beheaded for thirty counts of treason only six months later. He was accused of conspiring to kidnap his nephew King Edward—Jane Seymour's son."

"Nice relatives you have here, Tripod," Eric said.

"History has painted him in a rather villainous light," Charity said, "but I believe he loved Katherine. He loved her before she married into the royal family."

"I'm sure I'm not related to the guy," Jace said. "He didn't leave any sons to pass on the family name."

"But he and Katherine did have a daughter," Aggie pointed out. "What happened to her?"

"She was taken in by her mother's lady in waiting because her father wanted nothing to do with the child after Katherine's passing. There are no records of the girl beyond her early childhood. It's likely that she died."

"No records?" Aggie said. "Not even a death certificate?"

Charity shook her head.

"So maybe she is Jace's great-great-great-great-grandmother," Eric said.

"She would have passed her husband's name, not the Seymour name, to her children," Charity said.

Eric lifted a finger and pointed at an unseen idea. "*If* she married. Maybe she had a child out of wedlock."

Charity crossed her arms. "*Tut!* Pure speculation."

"Indeed," Eric said, "but it is possible that Jace is the descendant of a queen of England."

"Queen by marriage, not blood."

"He does sort of look like her," Brian said, tilting his head to contemplate the carved visage of Katherine lying in peaceful repose.

"He is quite lovely," Eric teased and poked Jace in the shoulder. "Definitely my favorite of all the princesses."

Jace started, released Aggie's hand, and turned toward the exit of the tomb. "Shouldn't we be rehearsing?" he asked. "I no longer wish to be in here."

Aggie stared after him, confused by the longing and remorse on his handsome face. Did he wish he'd found his roots here, or was something else bothering him?

Chapter 7

DURING REHEARSAL, JACE STOOD where he was told to stand and said what he was told to say and tried to listen to the battery of instructions that Charity relayed with utter professionalism and patience. It wasn't easy to get a twelve-member wedding party working as a cohesive unit. Especially when Eric was in such a good mood.

"Stand closer to her, Tripod," Eric said, shoving Jace in the back. "She doesn't have cooties."

Jace stepped closer to Aggie. She definitely did not have cooties and if she did, he was willing to be infected.

"Closer," Eric urged.

Jace and Aggie each took a step closer. Except where their hands were joined, they weren't touching, but her body heat warmed his chest and a familiar and welcome surge of longing throbbed in his groin. He had a powerful need to get lost in her so he could get over the unexplainable feeling of loss that had consumed him in Katherine's tomb earlier. He obviously hadn't known the woman, but as the others had discussed her, he'd felt as if he were yanked from his body, floating away to avoid the crushing reality of the death of someone he loved. He'd felt much the same when he'd learned of his mother's death and his first love's— *Kara's*—and even when he'd learned of his abusive father's passing. He was not a stranger to surviving unfathomable losses, but what was truly unfathomable in this case was that he'd never met the woman in question and she'd died almost five hundred years ago.

Standing back to examine the bride and groom, Eric stroked his jaw and chin with one hand, as if contemplating a work of art and finding something off. "Still too much daylight between you," he claimed.

Eager for distraction, Jace wrapped his arms around Aggie and tugged her against him—belly to belly, breasts to chest.

"Is this close enough?" Jace asked Eric.

"Not quite," Aggie whispered in Jace's ear. "I want your skin against mine. Your hard cock inside me. Filling my core. Making me whole."

Jace couldn't resist rubbing his overwarm face against hers as it was the only bare skin they currently had available. Her turtleneck sweater needed to go, even if it did hug her large breasts just right. His fingers tightened in the soft fabric at her hips as he fought the urge to make her naked so they could be closer.

"What do you think, Charity?" Eric asked. "Isn't that better?"

Charity pressed her fingers to her very red cheeks. "Yes, well, uh... I'm not sure... It's not quite... *proper*." The last word came out in a loud whisper.

"There is nothing proper about these two," Eric assured her.

Jace reached over and smacked him in the arm while the rest of the wedding party laughed at their expense.

"Indeed," Charity said.

Two practice runs later, everyone knew their parts and now seemed to think they were having their intelligence insulted. Charity proclaimed them ready and they filtered out of the church toward the ballroom where their rehearsal dinner/costume ball would take place as soon as everyone picked up the costumes Eric and Rebekah had selected for them based upon precise measurements collected weeks before. Jace didn't mind Eric and Rebekah throwing a party—he wouldn't have even known where to begin—but he did think they'd overreached their bounds by dictating what each person wore. Rebekah waved Aggie over to the rack of ball gowns in one corner of the room. Eric was arguing with Sed over a pair of velveteen knee britches on the opposite side of the room.

Aggie brushed a kiss against Jace's cheek. "Hurry back to the cottage. I need you buried balls deep inside me."

Jace flushed with heat. "One nap coming up," he said.

"Is that what you've decided to call it? Your nap?" Her hand brushed against the front of his pants. "I want to do wicked things to your nap, Jace. Don't let Eric distract you with nonsense."

Jace chuckled. Eric was an expert at nonsensical distractions. "I'll hurry," he promised. He strode over to Eric, who was now arguing with Trey and Brian over lace collars or some such nonsense.

"Why do I always end up wearing the most girly costume?" Brian complained. "Year before last, Trey and Myrna conspired to dress me as Prince Charming and now this? I'm not wearing a cape."

"It will look good on you," Trey said, flipping a cape around

Brian's shoulders and tying it under his chin. "See, you look—" He broke off with a snort before bending over to laugh himself breathless.

"Yeah," Brian said, yanking the bow at his throat to untie it. "That's what I thought."

"At least it's not blue velveteen," Sed grumbled, holding up his very poofy knee britches. "Who in their right mind would wear these on purpose?"

"It was the epitome of high fashion back in the day," Eric said, holding a surprisingly straight face. He glanced at Jace and winked before handing him a big white box with his name on it. No sense in standing there arguing, not when he'd soon be mixing nap and Aggie. Box in hand, he turned and stopped just in time to prevent himself from careening directly into Dare.

"This wasn't *your* idea, was it?" Dare asked, one dark eyebrow arching high over a piercing green eye.

"No, I voted for a pirate-themed rehearsal dinner," Jace joked.

"You know, if we didn't like you so much, we wouldn't put up with this bullshit."

Jace felt the familiar heat of embarrassment rise up his throat. He had no idea how to respond to declarations of affection from Dare Mills. "I—uh. Thanks. Eric convinced me that this would be fun."

Dare shook his head, smiling. "Yeah, well, his sense of fun is a little different."

"Everything about him is a little different," Dave Blake said. Jace hadn't noticed him standing, wheelchair-less, behind Dare. "I'm not sure why my sweet baby sister fell for the guy."

Jace didn't feel inclined to remind Dave that his sweet baby sister was a little different herself.

"So what's the story with you and the porn star?" Dave asked Dare.

Dare's dark brows drew together. "Porn star?"

"Yeah, that redhead you're walking with in the wedding. She's a porn star. A stripper. Prostitute?" He glanced at Jace for verification.

Jace shrugged and shook his head. He didn't know if Starr was a prostitute. She was a friend of Aggie's, so she was all right in his book.

"No story between us," Dare said. "Though I did notice she's a little hands-on."

"I'd think you'd be used to that," Sinners' soundboard operator said with a laugh.

"I think you're confusing me with my little brother."

The three of them glanced at Trey, who happened to be getting hands on with his best friend, Brian, at the moment. He had him in a headlock while Eric tried to force a white stocking on one bare foot.

"I figured he learned it from you," Dave said.

"Not me," Dare said. "I'm a paragon of self-control."

Jace busted out laughing. He'd spent four months on tour with the guitarist and his band, Exodus End, over the summer. Jace didn't think self-control was quite the right word for Dare's interactions with the female gender. Speaking of females... He could be enjoying his favorite female's company right now, rather than shooting the breeze with the guys.

He slapped Dare on the arm. "I'll catch up with you later."

"See ya. In the meantime, I'll try to retain my virtue from the porn star you set me up with."

"Don't struggle too hard," Jace said. "She's the kind of girl who likes a challenge." He winked at Dare and left him standing with Dave.

Jace hadn't gone five steps before being swept into the arms of the porn star in question.

"Hey, babydoll," Starr said in his ear. "Where did Aggie run off to? I haven't gotten the chance to talk to her at all since I got here."

"I think she's changing into her ball gown."

"If the two of you need assistance, let me know. She's the only woman who has ever topped me properly. Seems a crime that she'd marry a man."

Okay, that was a very odd thing for her to say. Aggie had mentioned that they'd trained together, but Starr made it sound as if there was something deeper between them.

Surely he was mistaken. Aggie would have told him something that important. Wouldn't she?

"Excuse me," he said. "Aggie's waiting for me."

"Let her know I'm available if she needs me."

Jace tilted his head, trying to make sense of the undercurrent he sensed in her words. She seemed to be hinting at something, but he wasn't sure what.

"Needs you for what?" he asked.

"Why taking care of you, of course," she said. "We all had a good time on your birthday. Remember?"

He remembered quite well. Remembered too the unfounded jealousy he'd felt whenever Starr had touched Aggie. Maybe that jealousy hadn't been so unfounded after all.

"I have to go," he said.

He scowled to himself as he stalked away. Aggie wouldn't fool around with someone, would she? She was always very clear about what she did with her submissive clients, and he trusted that she told him the truth. Trusted that she wasn't sexually attracted to any of them. Trusted that she wanted only him. *Loved* only him. But something about the way Starr acted had him wondering if Aggie had been playing him for a fool all along.

By the time he reached the cottage, he was seething. He slammed the door behind him and tossed the box containing his costume on the floor. He might have held on to his rage for a few more seconds if Aggie hadn't been leaning against the bedroom's doorframe wearing nothing but a pair of black satin panties and her red lipstick. He cursed the surge of lust that flooded his groin. Cursed her for looking so fucking hot and so uncommonly cold all at the same time. Cursed himself for being so goddamned weak to the woman.

Her come-hither smile faded as he remembered the reason for his anger and glared at her.

"What's wrong?" she asked.

"Why would anything be wrong?"

"You tell me. Last time I saw you, you were happy. And now, now you're obviously not."

"Have you been lying to me?" he asked.

Aggie's eyes shifted from his face to the space over his shoulder. "About?"

"Your clients. Your training. Fucking *everything*?"

"I thought we were past this," she said.

"Past what? Other men and women seeing your body, being privileged to your abuse, and you allowing them to worship you? What am I supposed to be past exactly, Aggie?"

"All of it. You said you were cool with me continuing to dominate clients. Remember?"

"Yeah, well maybe I'm not so cool with it." Not if she'd been hiding things from him. He could take it all if she shared that part of herself honestly with him, but if she hid it—*any* of it—he wouldn't be able to live with her not being his and his alone.

"It would be hard for me," she said, crossing the room to grip his chin and force him to meet her eyes, "but I'd give it all up for you, Jace."

She licked her lips and softened her hold, touching his cheek gently. He slapped her hand away. He didn't want her goddamned tenderness. He was too pissed.

Her fingertips pressed hard into his chest. "One of the things I love most about you is that you don't expect me to be someone I'm not. You allow me to be true to myself, but you're more a part of me than the thrill I get from serving clients, Jace. I could give them up. I will if I have to. But I can never give you up. Never. The choice is easy. It's you. It will always be you."

"I don't want you to have to *choose*, Aggie. I want—" What did he want? He wanted to be able to clearly express his feelings to her, to say what was in his heart, but as usual, words failed him, so he turned to face the wall, fighting the urge to punch it.

"What do you want?" Aggie said.

He was so acutely aware of her, the hand she laid on his back seemed to burn through his leather jacket.

And he knew she would push. She always pushed. It drove him fucking insane, but God he loved her for forcing him to face his deepest fears. For knowing that she wouldn't walk out on him no matter what kind of weird shit he struggled through.

"Tell me about, Starr," he said. "Don't leave anything out."

The hand resting on his back fell away.

"Starr?" she whispered. "How did you find out about Starr?"

Jace felt like the floorboards beneath his feet had vanished. His stomach and heart sank as if he were rapidly descending straight into the yawning chasm of Hell beneath his boots. He let Aggie have her way most of the time because he wanted her to be happy. But not this time. He should have realized that if he allowed her to continue working as a dominatrix that eventually she'd get personal with one of her subs. Have sex with one of them. Fall in love with one of them. Finding out about it the night before they were to get married wasn't ideal, but he should have seen it coming.

"Jace," Aggie said, "how did you find out? Did she say something to you? That stupid bitch. I told her I didn't want you to know."

Jace spun and grabbed her by both arms. He gave her a shake. "I'm sending her home. And you aren't going to see her again."

Aggie stiffened, and her eyes narrowed. "If you think you can dictate my life—"

"I gave you free rein and you abused it, Aggie. I allowed you to keep your slaves, allowed them into my fucking house. But not this. I won't let you cheat on me."

"You think I'm cheating on you?"

Did she think he was a complete idiot?

"You just said you didn't want me to know about your relationship with Starr, Aggie."

"My *past* relationship with Starr. *Past!* It's been over between us for years. How could you think... Why would I ever..." Her brilliant blue eyes turned glassy with tears. "Jace Seymour!" She stomped on his foot. *Hard.*

"Ow!" Startled by her unexpected retaliation, he released his hold on her arms, and she spun on her heel—black hair flying out behind her—and stormed off into the bedroom.

He stared after her, trying to process what she'd said. *Past* relationship with Starr. Okay, he could live with that. He'd misunderstood. But why was Aggie angry and why had she been hiding a past relationship? That made no sense. They were completely open and accepting of everything about each other. At least he'd thought they were on even ground. Perhaps he'd been fooling himself into believing she was as open with him as he was with her. He puzzled over this revelation for a long moment before striding into the bedroom. He wanted the truth out of her, no matter how much it frightened him.

As soon as he passed through the bedroom door, Aggie tossed her thigh-high boots at him. He caught them against his chest and gaped at her.

"You will dress me before I punish you," she snarled at him.

Yes, please. But not if her lashes were motivated by anger. She was the one who'd taught him the difference, after all. He craved her punishment, but wouldn't tolerate abuse.

"Why are you pissed?" he asked, dropping her boots on the floor and moving toward her.

She yanked a cat o' nine tails from his open suitcase and lifted her arm over her head.

"Do not hit me out of anger," he said calmly.

Her grip went slack, and the whip clattered to the floor behind her. She slapped her hand over her mouth, her breathing erratic, eyes swimming with tears. That's when he realized she wasn't angry, she was hurt. Shouldn't he be the one hurt? She'd been hiding things from him. It didn't matter who should be hurting the most. Not when she looked so upset. No stranger to pain—emotional or physical—Jace was willing to endure any agony, but he couldn't stand seeing it in her.

"Aggie, just tell me. Do you still have feelings for her?"

"No," she said, her hasty reply muffled by her hand. She dropped it and took him by the arm, giving him a hard shake. "Of course not. I have feelings only for you."

"Then why have you been hiding this relationship with Starr from me?"

"Because I wanted to forget about it. It should have never happened."

She sat on the edge of the bed, rested her heels on the bedrail, and curled her body toward her knees, her hands pressed into her eyes. He could see the tremble of her body even at a distance.

Aggie didn't tremble.

Aggie never faltered.

Aggie was strong.

Aggie was...

Aggie was human.

Her hints of weakness always caught him by surprise. And made him love her even more.

"A lot of things should never happen," he said. He approached the bed cautiously, not sure if she wanted him to touch her, but the need to do so overwhelmed him. He stroked a long strand of silky black hair from her bare shoulder.

She slid her arms around his waist and rested her forehead against his chest. She talked to the floor, but at least she talked.

"We met when we were both in training under the same domme—Mistress Z."

He already knew that. Aggie had told him about Mistress Z when he'd asked her how she'd gotten her own domme moniker—Mistress V. When she'd reached the end of her training, Mistress Z had given Aggie that name and she'd given her other pupil, Starr, the name Mistress X—apparently because Mistress Y and Mistress W weren't threatening enough. Aggie had laughed herself silly when Jace had admitted he'd thought *V* was short for vagina or something.

"Starr and I trained together and if a client had enough money, we worked together. We became highly sought after in the BDSM scene in Vegas. As you know, they called us Fire and Ice. Starr was

Fire for her red hair. I was Ice because, well, I've always been cold."

"You're not cold to me," he whispered, stroking her hair.

She glanced up at him and offered a wavering smile. "Only because you melt me, Jace Seymour."

He resisted the urge to kiss her, knowing that if he did, they'd ignite in passion and lose track of their conversation. He wanted to hear this. Needed to hear it.

"So is that when you two became lovers?" The last word squeaked out of him as if he was going through puberty again. He didn't want to be the jealous sort, but the thought of Aggie loving someone else made his throat tighten and his chest ache.

She nodded. "Not right away," she said, "but as you know, dominating puts me in the mood. And part of Fire's act was to touch me. It made the clients hemorrhage cash to watch two dommes in training touch, so Mistress Z encouraged it. At first I tolerated the touches, but then I began to crave them. Crave her. And the friendship between us began to change." She paused and her eyes focused on Jace's. "Do you want all these details?"

He wasn't sure he *wanted* details, but they both needed them out in the open. "Continue," he said quietly.

"It took me months to get up the courage to tell her how I felt about her. I wasn't sure if Starr really wanted me or if it was all an act for the clients. But when I finally confessed, she said she felt the same way about me, and we uh, had sex." A blush stained her cheeks. "A lot of sex. I'd never had sex with someone I cared about before. I couldn't get enough. Like with you."

A hard, cold lump settled in Jace's stomach. So he didn't want the details after all. It must have showed in his expression, because she captured his face between her hands.

"Not like with you," she amended. "She never got to see my soul laid bare the way you do. I never trusted her to love me enough to see all of me."

"Aggie…" Saying her named threatened to pull his heart out of his chest.

"It's okay, baby. This story doesn't have a happy ending."

He saw the hurt shadowing her eyes and knew that Starr had broken her heart.

"Once we became intimate, Starr began to get bolder in the way she touched me in front of our clients. Kissing. Putting her fingers… places." She gave him a hard look, as if trying to telegraph her thoughts to him. "It made me feel violated. Like our sexual relationship wasn't really about our love for each other, but only another way to make cash."

"Maybe she just liked you so much she couldn't keep her hands off you." He knew what that was like.

Aggie shook her head. "I wish that had been the case. One night after a session, we were both really turned on. She'd seen the client out and we were alone in the dungeon—at least I thought we were alone—and she drags me to the floor and goes down. So I'm lying there and her mouth is on me and her fingers are inside me and somehow over the sounds of my own moans, I hear this other sound. I open my eyes and I see the client—who was supposed to be gone—peeking out from behind a velvet drape and he's got his dick in his hand and he's jerking it while he watches us."

Can't blame him, Jace thought, but he sure as hell wasn't going to say that.

"I go after him—so mad I can't see straight—and he says, *I paid her to watch.*" She quivered, but didn't look away from Jace. "He was talking about Starr," Aggie clarified, her voice hard with anger and betrayal. "He paid Starr to watch us have sex and not only did she take his money, she didn't tell me."

Jace tried to find something to say, but he came up lacking.

"I'll never forget what she said to me in defense. *What do you expect from a whore? Stop pretending you're better than me, Ice. You're just as much of a whore as I am.*"

"But you're not a whore," Jace said.

Aggie released a derisive huff of air. "But if she hadn't said that to me, I probably would have become one. So even though she broke my heart, she saved me. Even though she hurt me, I can't hate her. She's always had my back, and I've had hers. Is it strange that our friendship survived a romance gone sour?"

"I don't think so. You've been through a lot together."

Aggie nodded and lowered her gaze. "Yeah, we have. It's hard to find people who don't judge you when you lead the kind of life I've led. Someone like me has to hold on to those who care that they still breathe."

"Then hold on to me," he whispered and pulled her against his chest. "Hold on and never let go."

Chapter 8

Aggie tried to slip into her dominatrix frame of mind, but she was just too damned emotional to pull off anything but a smile as Jace knelt at her feet and slipped her foot into one of her boots. She should've told him about Starr ages ago. It was as if the final demon that haunted her had been sent back to Hell and she was truly free to love this man with all her heart. She'd been certain that he wouldn't understand her strange relationship with Starr, but as usual, Jace surprised her with his empathy, his compassion, his acceptance. And the man was hers.

Jace tugged the supple leather up her leg and then tightened the lacings of the boot, starting at the back of her ankle and working his way up. She'd always loved having a man at her feet, but she never would have guessed how much she enjoyed Jace helping her dress in her corset and boots. There was something intimate about him assisting with her transformation from Aggie to Mistress V. With her slaves, she'd never let one see her with her guard down like this, but Jace had never been her slave. At times he was submissive, at other times he was completely in charge. He could make love to her with absolute tenderness or fuck her until she begged for mercy. They were constantly exploring the dynamic between them. She never knew what to expect from him, and it rocked her to her core that neither of them adhered to a specific role.

But roles were for games, and this wasn't a game to her. It was her heart. Her soul. Her life. Her love.

He tied the lacings of her boot at the back of her thigh and grinned up at her. "Does this please you, Mistress?" he asked, looking about as submissive as a caged tiger when his gaze met hers in challenge.

"Yes," she whispered. Everything he did for her pleased her.

He buried his face in her crotch, caught her black satin panties in his teeth, and gave them a tug. When she didn't demand that he stop—because frankly she didn't want him to—his teeth nipped at the flesh beneath the fabric, sending sparks of pleasure and pain along her nerve endings. Heat flooded the emptiness between her thighs, making her swell and throb with anticipation.

He grabbed the top band of her panties, tugged them down in front, and slid the tip of his tongue into her cleft. He teased her clit just enough to make it tingle and tilted his head back to look up at her. She saw the defiance in his eyes. Knew exactly what he was after.

"Did I say you had permission to lick me there?" she asked.

"It's mine," he said, lifting both hands to grab her ass. "I can lick it if I want."

"I think someone needs to be punished," she said, forcing herself not to hold the back of his head and encourage him to lick her more rigorously.

"Is it you?" he asked.

He nibbled her mound and then sank his teeth into her throbbing flesh. Her knees buckled.

"It's definitely you," she said breathlessly, trying to find the hardness in her demeanor, but only finding her soft spot for the man at her feet. "Put my other boot on." The demand sounded too much like a request, so she half expected him to refuse. He did enjoy his punishments for not obeying, but he reached for her boot and carefully lifted her foot to slip inside it. She rested her hands on the top of his head for balance and tried to control the quivering in her thighs and belly as he slid the boot up her leg and tightened the laces up the back. The little licks and kisses he bestowed on her flesh as he nuzzled her crotch were driving her mad with need, but she tried not to show her eagerness for his attention. He was doing as she'd instructed—dressing her in her boot—so he obviously wanted this dynamic to continue a while longer.

He tied the lacings at the back of her thigh and lifted her panties to cover her aching pussy.

God, she wanted him. Would that lessen with time? Not if her body had a say in the matter.

"I was rather enjoying that," she said.

He grinned up at her and then rose to his feet. He cupped her bare breasts in his palms and massaged them gently.

"Do you need your corset?" he asked. "I like to watch your tits bounce when you hit me."

"Did I ask you what you like?" she asked. This time her voice managed the hard edge of Mistress V, and Jace shuddered.

She stepped around him, tossing her long hair back over her shoulders as she strode to the open suitcase on the dresser. Her Mistress V persona took another sentimentality hit as something in her suitcase caught her eye. Among her instruments of torture rested a familiar, lacy white and blue garter, the one she would wear on her thigh the next day when she made Jace her husband. She smiled at it and touched it gently with her fingertips. It was a bit out of place in her mix of leather and nylon, but she had to wear it— *wanted* to wear it. She knew how much it meant to Jace to be part of Sinners, so of course she'd wear the girly thing with pride to carry on the lady Sinners tradition. Every member of Sinners had peeled that same piece of lace and ribbon down his new wife's thigh, and she knew Jace would want to be a part of that bond. She moved the garter aside, because it had no business being witness to what she was about to do to her man. She could feel his interested gaze on her as she selected a long wooden paddle and a flail with three lashes.

"Take off your shirt," she demanded quietly. She didn't bother to look at him and hid a smile when she heard the rustle of his clothes as he obeyed. He always wanted to obey and sometimes he did so without argument, but boy did he struggle with it at times. She loved the challenge he presented. She doubted she would have ever fallen in love with him if he were truly submissive. She set the paddle aside on the dresser and turned to approach him, slapping her flail against the leather of her boot. Each time it cracked, he released a little gasp of excitement.

She stopped to stand before him and trailed the dangling ends of the flail over his flat belly.

"So you think my pussy is yours, do you?" she asked.

"Oh yeah."

"Since it's between my legs, don't you think I should decide who it belongs to?"

"I already know," he said. "It's mine."

She snapped her wrist, and the flail slapped his chest. He bit his bottom lip, but didn't jerk or make a sound. He just stared at her with those dreamy chocolate-brown eyes of his.

"You may touch it only when I allow it," she said.

"Which is whenever I want," he said, lifting a brow at her in challenge.

Completely true, but only because she always wanted him. Always. Two years in his arms, his bed, and she still always wanted him.

"And what would you do if I said no?" she asked, cracking the flail against his belly. "Take what you wanted anyway?"

"No, I'd pleasure you until you thought it was your idea, until you submitted to me."

Submit? She hit his chest twice with her flail for his audacity.

"I never submit," she said, knowing it was a lie. "Not to you. Not to anyone."

He chuckled. "Maybe you can claim you've never submitted to anyone *before* me, just as I never submitted to anyone before you, but we both know I let you dominate when it suits me."

"You're trying to get a rise out of me, Mr. Seymour," she said.

He chuckled again. "Only because you're not hitting me hard enough yet."

So she remedied that situation until his entire chest and belly were crisscrossed with red lash marks and his fly was about to burst under the strain of his erection. When she took a step back to catch her breath and allow him to experience the sting in his flesh, he moaned in torment. Not because he wanted her to stop, but because she was only giving him half of what he really wanted. He preferred his pain served with a contrasting dose of pleasure.

"Please, Mistress," he whispered and rubbed a hand over his crotch. His abs clenched in excitement, and his eyelashes fluttered as he got his first taste of pleasure.

She lashed at the back of his wrist in warning. "Don't touch it until I give you permission."

When he unfastened his fly and the thick, hard length of his cock sprang free of his jeans, Aggie's pussy clenched, and her pelvis jerked involuntarily in his direction, which threw her shoulders back to lift her breasts high. Yes, she wanted him, but for fuck's sake, she couldn't let him know that yet. He bit his lower lip and stared into her eyes as he gently wrapped a hand around his cock and skimmed his palm down its length. The look of rapture that came over his gorgeous face almost made Aggie regret that she'd have to punish him for disobeying. Almost.

She turned her back on him—because watching that man pleasure himself always made her weak and horny—and went back to her suitcase for more supplies. He obviously needed to be restrained and then tortured with pleasure, but not in the way he expected.

He didn't resist when she fastened the leather cuffs around his wrists, or when she used long straps to secure his right cuff to one post at the head of the four-poster bed and his other arm to the post at the opposite end. His cock stood rigid just above the mattress, and his bare back was exposed for her to work her magic.

"Did you ask my permission to touch yourself?" she asked near his ear, the tips of her breasts just grazing the skin of his back. She fought the urge to grind her body against his, because then he'd know how much she wanted him already, and they were still playing games.

"What are you going to do about it?" he asked, his tone full of challenge. The man knew how to get her worked up and exactly how to top her from the bottom. But she had a surprise in store for him.

She slid down his back, rubbing her nipples against his skin as she squatted. She jerked his jeans down to his knees to expose his ass. Her breath caught as its perfection came into view. She massaged his firm cheeks for the sheer pleasure of it. God, she loved this man's ass. She almost hated to cause it pain. Almost.

He tensed when the first blow of the paddle landed on his cheek. She purposely struck him way below his tolerance for pain. In fact, for someone who got off on pain as much as Jace did, her blows were probably more annoying than stimulating.

"Harder," he pleaded.

"You'd like that, wouldn't you?"

"Yeah."

She grinned, feeling a bit evil for tormenting him. Much more evil than she ever felt when she was delivering the pain he craved. "You're being punished, so no, I won't hit you harder."

"Please."

"You know I love it when you beg, baby," she said. And she was certain he'd be doing a lot of begging by the time she was finished with him. She paused to squirt lube on her fingers and rubbed them over his ass, making him nice and slippery. He went completely still.

"Aggie, what are you doing?"

"Whatever the fuck I want to do," she said.

"Don't you dare put anything in my ass," he said, fighting his restraints now.

The bed shook and creaked as he yanked on the straps, but they held.

"Oh, I dare, baby. You should know better than to challenge me."

She inserted her index finger into the ring at the base of a curved rubber tool. It was only a few inches long and very slender.

She doubted he'd be able to feel it except where she wanted him to feel it.

"Aggie!" he said as she slipped the prostate stimulator inside him.

Apparently he'd been expecting her to ram a ten-inch phallus up there, because his body went limp with relief. He remained relaxed until she began to move the tool inside him, and then he began to twitch.

"Oh," he gasped. "What are you... Mmm."

She continued to stimulate him internally while she used her free hand to smack his bare ass. Her palm tingled each time it connected with his flesh. When he began to rock his hips involuntarily, she moved up close against his back and peered over his shoulder to check his level of excitement. His cock was as hard as granite, flushed darker than the rest of his skin. Tortuous veins coursed along the entire shaft, and the tip glistened with moisture. He was seeping so much pre-cum that it was dripping. She'd never wanted to drive his cock into the achiness between her legs so badly before in her life. But she was in control here. She wouldn't shatter that illusion just yet.

"If I let your arms loose right now, would you touch yourself?" she asked.

"God, yes," he groaned.

"Then you haven't learned your lesson yet."

She rubbed his lower belly, delighting in how his cock jerked each time she came within inches of touching it.

"I wonder if I can make you come without touching your cock at all," she said, increasing the speed at which she moved the stimulator inside him.

He cried out, and she craned her neck to find his eyes squeezed tightly shut. She grinned deviously and then smacked his ass. His body tensed, and he whimpered.

"I've learned my lesson," he said. "Oh God. Please don't make me come this way. I won't touch it. I don't even want to touch it."

"Liar."

"I want you to touch it," he said with a groan.

She could have released his restraints then, but she knew if she did, he'd be fucking her the instant he was free and the power would tip in his direction. She wasn't quite ready to give up her power to him just yet.

She pulled the stimulator free of his body and tossed it into the garbage. She took a moment to clean his ass, knowing how distracted he'd be by the wetness; she wanted his concentration on her.

Jace glanced over his shoulder. "What are you doing?"

She shrugged, slipped her panties off, and wearing her thigh-high boots but nothing else, climbed onto the bed in front of him. "We came here to nap, right?"

She curled up on the mattress, snuggled into a pillow, and closed her eyes.

"You cannot leave me like this, Aggie," Jace said.

She opened her eyes and stared at his enormous cock.

"I do want you inside me," she said. "Jace."

"Yes."

"But I don't want you to fuck me right now."

"Huh?"

"I'm still craving control."

"So take it," he said between clenched teeth. "Do with it what you will, but for fuck's sake, Aggie, don't leave me like this."

Aggie shifted onto her back and opened her legs, scooting on the mattress until her legs were dangling off the edge of the bed and Jace's slim hips were between her thighs. She reached for his cock and the instant she touched him, he sucked a tortured breath between clenched teeth. She rubbed his head against her clit, sighing in bliss.

He backed away from her slightly, and she scooted even closer toward the edge of the bed.

"I want inside you so bad right now," he said, moving his hips to try to direct his cock into her body.

She slipped his head down into her opening, and he stepped forward, sliding deeper.

"Wait," she said.

She sat up on the edge of the bed, the only contact between them her hand on his shaft and his cockhead buried just inside.

"Allow me," she said.

"*To?*"

"Control."

She released his solid length and gripped his hips, directing him closer. Deeper. His breath came out in a hot huff against her hair. Hands on his hips, she guided him out and then in again, deeper this time. Deeper. She encouraged him to rotate his hips, then draw out again, and press in, deeper still. Under the instructive touch of her hand, he made love to her slow and deep—exactly how she wanted him to take her. Exactly.

She rested her head against his shoulder and closed her eyes so she could concentrate on the feel of him inside her. Thick and hard. Filling her. Stretching her. Rubbing her oh so right.

"You don't have to restrain me to have this kind of control," he whispered.

She didn't want to discuss or debate, she just wanted to feel. She slid one hand to rest on the upper curve of his tight little ass and pressed down to encourage him to tilt his hips, take her at a different angle. Drive deeper and rub within her there, *right there. Oh yes, Jace. There.* Moaning with pleasure, she rubbed her face over his bare chest. Higher. Higher he pulled her toward bliss.

"Aggie?"

Her back arched as she found her peak, waves of rapture clenching deep within her. She pushed him into her—balls deep—and rocked with him, intensifying her orgasm until her entire body was quaking with release. Spent, she collapsed back on the bed, trembling with aftershocks of pleasure.

"Have I been doing it wrong all this time?" Jace asked.

Her eyes flew open, and she lifted her head to look at him standing between her legs—still buried inside her. Still restrained. "Of course not!" she said. "Why would you even think that?"

He shrugged and averted his gaze. It was never her intention to hurt him on the inside, no matter how much pain she inflicted on his flesh. She forced her weary body to sit up and wrapped her arms around him. She thought carefully about the words she wanted to say, because she'd made him vulnerable. She knew from past experience how hard it was for him to allow her to see that vulnerability.

"I shouldn't have used you like that," she said. "I'm sorry."

He relaxed into her. His still-rigid cock slid deeper. "Don't be sorry. I just... when you get me all worked up like that, I always want to fuck your brains out until I explode. I never even considered that what you needed was something entirely different."

"I like it when you fuck my brains out," she assured him. "I just..." She wasn't sure how to explain it to him without making herself vulnerable. Because even though she trusted him enough to allow him to see that vulnerability in her, she sure as hell didn't like to feel that way. "Being your wife," she said. "Certain expectations." Hell, she was really blundering this. How could she explain without hurting him?

"You don't want to be my wife?"

She smacked his ass none-too-playfully. "Never think that again, much less say it."

"I don't understand what you're trying to tell me."

She laughed, the movement allowing her to feel exactly how deep her lover was buried within her.

"I know it's stupid, but to me, the word *wife* just rubs me the wrong way. Like in the traditional ceremony when the vows are sealed with man and wife. Why not husband and woman?"

"This day and age, they do say husband and wife," he said.

"Yeah, but why not wife and husband? Wife always comes second."

"Aggie, I think you're overreacting. Nothing is meant by it."

"So why is the woman expected to take the man's name? Why didn't you offer to take my last name?"

"I thought you wanted to hyphenate your name."

"I do," she said. "But you didn't hyphenate yours."

"So you associate the word *wife* with a submissive role."

She shook her head. "I don't know."

"You realize that's a strange thing to think when you have your soon-to-be husband tied to the bedposts, don't you?"

She chuckled. "I know you understand our dynamic, but others? Others expect me to fall into a certain role as your wife."

He snorted. "Since when do you give a fuck about doing what others expect of you?"

"Since never."

"So where is this coming from?"

"I don't know. I promised myself that I'd never get married. Never give myself to a man."

"So you think you'll regret marrying me?"

"No. No, Jace! I won't regret it. I just want to feel like I'm still in control of my life."

"You know I won't stand in your way. I'll support you no matter what. You *know* that."

She snuggled against him. "I *know.* It's me who's struggling with this. You're perfect."

He chuckled against her hair. "Hardly."

"You are," she whispered. "I love you so much, I don't know what I'd do if I lost you."

And maybe that was what was really bothering her. They were

so meshed at this point in their relationship that she wasn't solely her own person anymore. Part of her identity would always be known as Jace's woman. His *wife*. Ugh, that word.

"Release me, Aggie," he said. "I want to show you something."

"What is it?"

"I could tell you, but you know I'm not good with words. Let me show you."

Curious about what he could possibly want to show her—and more than a little excited about the prospect—she reached for the cuff on his left wrist. She couldn't quite reach it and keep him buried inside her, so she scooted back, surprised by how rock hard he still was as his cock popped free of her body.

He closed his eyes and groaned. "It will be a true test of my restraint not to fuck you hard and fast as soon as I'm free."

She grinned, thinking she wouldn't mind it so much, but she didn't let him know that. She liked it when he struggled for control. They both had a certain obsession with being in control at all times—self-control and, in her case, control of others. It was why their relationship was always challenging and exciting. The kind of relationship they both needed to be satisfied.

The buckle on his cuff came free and he rotated his shoulder to get full mobility in his arm as she worked on unfastening his other cuff. Once both of his arms were free, she looked at him in anticipation. He didn't jump her bones as she'd expected, he simply stared at her as he stretched his arms over his head, drawing her attention to his well-muscled chest, cut abs, and that huge fucking cock of his. She was more than ready for him to pound her with it.

"Come here, wife," he said, still standing alongside the bed. He opened his arms wide and beckoned her closer with flicks of his wrists.

She didn't move, just lifted an eyebrow at him. "Perhaps I wasn't clear when I said I don't *like* that word."

"Only because you associate the word with the wrong thing. With subservience," he said. "Allow me to show you what the word wife means to me. Maybe it will change how you feel about it."

"Doubtful," she said and flipped her long hair behind her before moving against him.

"Wife," he whispered, holding her securely to his chest. "The only one I hold in my arms."

His heart was thudding so hard, she could feel it against her chest.

"Wife, the only one who holds my body, who holds my heart."

Aggie sucked her lips into her mouth to stop their trembling. He spoke his feelings so seldom that when he did, she could scarcely handle the enormity of his sentiments.

"Wife," he said and stroked her hair. "She has the only hair I want to caress, the only eyes I want to get lost in, the only lips I want to kiss."

Aggie lifted her face to look at him, and he smiled softly. He cupped her face in one hand and traced her trembling lips with his thumb. "Wife, whose face is the first I want to see each morning and the last I want to see before I close my eyes at night, so I can meet her in my dreams."

"Jace," she whispered, her eyes swimming with tears. He never opened up like this.

"Wife," he said, taking her hands in his and drawing her knuckles to his lips. "Who possesses the hands that give my body everything it craves. The pain. The pleasure."

He pressed her down on the bed and leaned over her, trailing kisses along collarbones, her breasts, and her belly. "Wife, owner of the only body I desire."

He continued down her body and opened her legs gently. "Wife, who conceals a wondrous place between her thighs. The only pussy I'll ever taste."

His lips moved against her, rough beard stubble rubbing sensitive skin, soft tongue collecting her cream. She quickly lost herself to the pleasure. "Jace," she called to him as her desire bloomed.

"Wife," he said, "the only voice I want to hear call my name in ecstasy."

He rose above her and used his hand to guide his thick length into her.

"Wife, who accepts me into her body, holds me within, blinds me with pleasure."

She reached up to pull him into her arms. He joined her on the bed, careful to stay buried within her as he found a comfortable position above her.

He rocked slowly, staring into her eyes as he possessed her most intimately.

"Wife, who I love above all things and will cherish until the day I die. My wife. My one. My *only* love. My Aggie. My *wife*."

She was really loving the word *wife* at the moment, she couldn't deny it. As long as she was *his* wife—his and no other's—she'd bear the title proudly and with love in her heart.

"That's what wife means to me, Aggie. So when I call you my wife, know that it isn't a word that means subservient to me. It's a word that encompasses every wonderful thing you are to me. Do you understand now?"

She nodded mutely, her throat much too tight to form words. She drew him against her, and he nuzzled her neck as his hips began to move more vigorously to drive himself deep inside her. She knew how long it took him to find release when he was being tender, but she was totally fine with him making love to her slow and gently for as long as he needed to get off. It wasn't exactly a negative quality of his, though he'd eventually get frustrated as orgasm eluded him.

"Thank you for loving me," she whispered, one hand clinging to his firm ass that tensed and relaxed with each penetrating thrust. Her other hand touched the soft hair on the back of his head, and she rubbed her cheek against the roughness of his beard stubble, delighting in all the various textures of his body. "Nobody has ever made me feel the way you do, Jace. Tomorrow I will be proud to call you my husband, proud to be your wife."

He lifted his head and stared down into her eyes. Apparently he was all out of words, but she could see his feelings for her in his brown eyes.

His entire body was drenched in sweat by the time he finally lost himself inside her. He clung to her shoulders, forehead pressed to her collarbone, excited bursts of breath warming the sweat-slick valley between her breasts. She met him, her belly slapping against his as her back arched in bliss and her pussy gripped him tightly in earth-shattering waves of orgasm.

Arms trembling, he collapsed on top of her and gathered her close while he caught his breath.

"Wife," she heard him whisper between gasps of breath.

She smiled and hugged him tightly, remembering all he said that word encompassed. "Husband," she answered, her word meaning just as much.

And tomorrow they'd be recognized as wife and husband by the others who were important to them. Would their friends and family be able to tell how much their union meant to him? To her? Somehow, she thought they might.

Chapter 9

JACE'S HEART THUDDED at the sight of his wife as she sat at a vanity arranging her long black hair into an elegant twist. They hadn't said their I-dos yet, but in his heart, Aggie was already his wife and everything that sentiment meant to him.

He'd always loved the way she looked in thigh-high boots and leather corsets, but there was something about her being dressed in a luxurious sixteenth-century gown that totally did it for him. Perhaps it was because she was naturally well-endowed on top and her breasts were fighting for room in her tight bodice, settling as beguiling cleavage above the neckline of her forest-green dress. It made him want to bury his face—and his cock—in the sweet crevice between the soft mounds of flesh. He was used to her cinching her waist tight in corsets, but the wide skirt of the gown made her waist look impossibly tiny and her hips even fuller than her luscious tits. He hoped she'd gotten her fill of slow and gentle sex that afternoon, because there was no way he'd be able to restrain himself after having the tantalizing swell of her breasts in sight all evening.

Jace wasn't quite as keen on his own attire. The fitted forest-green jacket wasn't so bad, but the knee breeches and buckled shoes were asking far too much of him. He didn't care how many eyelashes Aggie batted at him or how many threats she muttered, he wasn't wearing either of them. So yeah, he was wearing a formal sixteenth-century jacket with his worn blue jeans and his biker boots, and if anyone had a problem with it, he'd call it a night and leave early. He didn't particularly want to go to this party, but he knew how upset Eric would be if he bailed, so he'd show up. No promises that he'd stay, however.

"You're going to be the only one dressed like that," Aggie said, grinning at him in the mirror and shaking her head at his mismatched style. Mismatched *style*? Hell, his millennia were mismatched. He knew Eric and Rebekah liked to play make-believe, but he preferred to keep his head firmly planted in reality. And right now his reality was how stunning his wife looked in that fucking dress. He didn't care if he made a complete ass of himself by showing up half baron/half biker. No one would be looking at him anyway. Not with that stunning woman on his arm.

Thomas, a voice whispered through his head.

Jace started.

The bedroom door slammed.

Aggie paused with her lipstick halfway too her mouth. "A draft?" she asked.

"Must have been," Jace said. "Did you hear someone say the name Thomas just now?"

Aggie's eyes darted to one side. "No," she said, drawing out the word. Her eyes darted in the opposite direction and she bit her lip.

She actually looked unsettled. Jace had never seen Aggie anything but badass and confident. He'd seen her attack an armed mugger once. In the end, Jace had been shot twice, and she hadn't had a scratch on her. The woman didn't do frightened. It was as if she didn't possess a fear response. At least that's what he'd always assumed. He didn't like the trembling of her lips as she smeared them with a soft pink lipstick, a shade he hadn't known she'd owned.

"Me neither," he said with a chuckle he hoped didn't sound false. "Just messing with you. You aren't *scared* are you?" He hoped a challenge would remedy her of any lingering anxiety.

"Well, it *is* Halloween," she said.

The bedroom door creaked open again. Jace turned to stare at the empty doorway, his heart thudding high in his chest. He didn't see anyone. But he felt someone there. Watching them.

Something cool brushed his cheek.

A chill slid down his spine.

"Wow, that's some draft," Aggie said, rubbing her hands over her arms. "I think we'd better get going."

She rose from the dressing table and for a split second, Jace caught the reflection of a light-haired woman in the mirror. She was wearing the same green gown that Aggie had donned, but the resemblance stopped there. He blinked and stared hard into the mirror. It was just Aggie now. Apparently he'd been seeing things.

As well as hearing things.

And *feeling* things.

He grabbed Aggie's hand and tugged her toward the front door.

"Yeah, we'd better hurry," he said. "I'm sure we're late."

Lights glittered in lanterns posted along the otherwise dark pathway that led from the cottages toward the field that separated the quaint set of cottages from the main castle. Jace's breath plumed before him in the chill of the night.

"It's cold out here," Aggie said. "Let me go grab my wrap. You pulled me out of there so quickly, I left it on the bed."

"I'll get it," Jace volunteered, though he honestly did not want to go back into the cottage. He suddenly had a bad feeling about the place. And as little as he wanted to go in there, he wanted Aggie to brave it alone even less.

"Don't be silly. Just wait for me," she said and went back inside.

The expansive field between their accommodations and the castle was dark. Fog slowly rose from the ground in twisted wisps. Jace looked up at the castle in the distance. The windows glowed with inviting warmth. Every nerve ending in Jace's body was on high alert. He wanted to be inside the castle, surrounded by others, not out here alone in the dark. Normally he preferred to be alone or in an intimate group of those he loved, but he was craving a big anonymous crowd to get lost in at the moment.

Jace caught movement out of the corner of his eye. A pale mist moved through the field of grass beyond the cottage lane. It was human-like in shape and moving toward the castle. A trick of the light reflecting off the fog, he told himself.

Thomas, who is she? A voice whispered behind him.

He spun around. Aside from the pale stone of the nearest building, there was nothing there.

Thomas?

"Okay, who the fuck is in here?" Aggie yelled inside the cottage. "This isn't funny, Eric. Where are you? Hiding under the bed?"

Suddenly the cottage seemed like a very nice place to be. Jace dashed inside and found Aggie yanking the closet open and pushing through the clothes hanging there.

"What are you doing?" Jace asked.

"Some jerk is trying to scare me," she said and pointed at the mirror.

He is mine was written on the glass in pink lipstick.

"Uh, yeah," Jace said, grabbing Aggie by the arm and pulling her out of the closet. "Let's go now. Right now."

Aggie grabbed her wrap off the bed and allowed him to haul her out the front door again. He shut it before taking her hand and dashing toward the castle as if the ground was caving in behind them and they were trying to escape falling into the depths of Hell.

"What's gotten into you?" she asked.

"That message on the mirror didn't freak you out?"

"It's just someone's idea of a prank," Aggie said.

"There was no one in that cottage but you."

"Just because we didn't see anyone doesn't mean no one was there."

Right. But someone—some*thing*—was in there. Jace had seen her. Heard her. He was pretty sure that *he* was the "he is mine" mentioned in the mirror message. But if Aggie wasn't afraid, then neither was he. Nope. Not him. Not scared at all.

She grinned at him crookedly. "You look a bit freaked out," she teased.

A *bit*? "Whatever. Let's just get this party over with."

"And then we can go back to the cottage and fool around under the covers."

Oh second thought, partying until dawn sounded fantastic. While time spent with Aggie under the covers was always phenomenal, he preferred to be anywhere on Earth other than that cottage.

They entered the castle and followed the loud music and voices to the ballroom. An attendant took Aggie's wrap and opened a set of double doors that was actually muffling the sound far more than Jace had realized. The hall had been set up with a long buffet table along one side. Round dining tables, each seating six, were arranged on a plush patterned carpet to designate the dining area. The rest of the room had wooden floors and a DJ who was currently playing the worst club music Jace had ever heard. But people—members of the wedding party and guests who had arrived early enough to attend—were dancing. And looking a bit odd in their ball gowns and suits as they bumped and grinded and bounced and swayed to the rapid tempo of the pop song. Perhaps the haunted cottage wasn't so bad after all, Jace decided.

"There you are," Eric said. "Thought you might have been eaten by zombies or something." He did his best impression of an evil laugh, which grated on Jace's already raw nerves.

"That dress looks so great on you." Rebekah squealed at Aggie. "I knew it would be perfect for you when I saw it." She took Aggie by both hands and made her sway side to side to set the skirt swinging.

Aggie's mom, Tabitha, came over to give her daughter a hug. "I'd never be able to pull off that dress, baby girl. You've always had the most beautiful skin."

Every inch of her was beautiful. And his. He couldn't seem to help but stand a bit taller when she was on his arm.

"I stay out of the sun," Aggie said.

"Because you're a vampire?" Eric asked.

Aggie's white teeth flashed as she smiled. "You guessed it, Sticks. I'm queen of the dead."

"That would explain her cruelty," Eric said, jabbing Jace in the ribs with a sharp elbow.

But Jace knew a different Aggie. A loving Aggie. Maybe he was the only one who recognized the gentleness and vulnerability inside her because she didn't allow anyone but him to see it. Jace squeezed her hand and even though she was chattering with the women and apparently paying him no mind, she squeezed back.

Aggie and Rebekah complimented Tabitha on her flapper dress—whatever that was. It was covered with long shiny strings that reminded Jace of spaghetti. Which sounded delicious. His stomach rumbled in agreement.

"What's for eats?" Jace asked Eric, releasing Aggie's hand and slapping Eric on the back to get him to head toward the buffet table.

"Rebekah thought we should eat British foods popular in various time periods." He glanced at his wife to see if she was paying attention—she was still fawning over dresses—and then he crinkled his nose in disgust.

"Oh," Jace said.

Out of the corner of his mouth, Eric whispered, "And they ate some really weird shit back in the day. Kidney pie? Did they not realize that kidneys are where piss is made? Blood pudding?" Eric gagged.

"Uh, I think people still eat those things in this country," Jace said.

The corners of Eric's mouth turned down. "You're kidding?"

Jace shook his head.

"I think it's time the fine people of Great Britain were introduced to hot dogs and scrambled eggs. Separately and together."

It was Jace's turn to gag. "You do realize what hot dogs are made of, don't you?"

"Sunshine and happiness," Eric said.

They met Sed picking through the buffet selections and filling a large plate. Apparently he'd decided to try one or three of everything.

"You hungry?" Jace asked.

"Mmm, yeah, but this is for Jessica," Sed said, glancing at his wife at a nearby table.

Jessica was hugely pregnant and nibbling on the after-dinner mints set in a little bowl in the center of the table. Jace decided the woman was even more beautiful when she was expecting. She appeared radiantly happy. Alive. And he admittedly liked a woman with a little meat on her bones. He fleetingly wondered what Aggie would look like with a baby growing inside her—*his* baby—but immediately quashed the idea as soon as it occurred to him. He had no business being a father, didn't exactly have a good example to go by. He sure didn't want to fuck up some kid's psyche as much as his own father had fucked up his.

"So how many little Lionhearts are you going for, Daddy-O?" Eric asked.

"As many as she'll agree to," Sed said and sported a cocky grin. "I owe our species the perpetuation of my superior genes."

Eric snorted and then turned to Jace. "Speaking of jeans. Where are your pants, Jace? Didn't they fit? I made sure they were extra short, which was far easier than finding historic garb in size tall. You'd have blended in well two hundred years ago, little man."

Jace was too used to short jokes to rise to his bait any more. "I don't know if they fit; I didn't bother trying them on. I'm not wearing them."

"That was an option?" Sed growled, glaring down at his own knee-length trousers with disdain.

"Is this where the real party's at?" Trey asked, joining their little Sinners huddle. "I'm about to jab sharp objects through my eardrums. What is that fucking music they're playing?"

"That's music?" Sed asked, glancing toward the flashing DJ booth suspiciously. "Could have fooled me. Sounds like shit."

"This *shit* is far more popular than our music," Eric said. He reached around Sed for a plate but was blocked by the shift of Sed's body, as if they were playing one-on-one basketball instead of raiding a buffet.

"Put me out of my misery." Trey grabbed a butter knife, gritted his teeth, and aimed the knife at his ear canal.

"I wouldn't do that if I were you," Eric said, "Small as it is, your brain is rattling around in there somewhere." He grabbed Trey's wrist and they made a big theatrical scene of fighting over embedding the butter knife in Trey's ear.

"I'll do it," Trey said, cringing as the knife slipped and scrapped against one of the piercings in his ear. "I'll end it all. Make the noise stop."

"Get the knife, Jace," Eric said, "before Mills bleeds all over the blood pudding."

Jace squeezed Trey's wrist and took the butter knife out of his loosened grip. He dropped the dull blade on the table. "Maybe you should talk to the DJ," Jace suggested. "Ask him to play something more to your liking."

"But that would be the sensible thing to do," Eric said.

"And the DJ happens to be a *her*," Sed remarked, adding several crumpets to Jessica's already overflowing plate.

"Oh really," Trey said, his body going erect with interest.

"Does Reagan know you still flirt with every woman who will hold still long enough for you to harass her?" Eric asked.

"Of course she knows. She isn't stupid or blind," Trey said. "She also knows a little harmless flirting leads to nothing."

"Except anything you want," Jace said with a grin.

Eric released Trey, who tugged on his form-fitting burgundy brocade vest and straightened a very large lacy cuff. Did men actually *wear* this stuff back in the day? How did the human species not go extinct? Dressing like a chick couldn't have done much for their ancestors' testosterone secretion. Trey smoothed an eyebrow with one spit-wet fingertip and headed toward the *umph umph umph* blaring from giant speakers across the room.

"I don't know why Reagan puts up with him," Eric said, crossing his arms over his chest. "If I acted like that with other women, Rebekah would put me on pussy restriction for a month."

Jace laughed. "Does Rebekah have trust issues?"

"I don't think so," Eric said. "She's just very territorial."

"Aggie is as well," Jace admitted. But like Reagan, he understood that his mate could be trusted to enjoy others without breaking their emotional bond or cheating.

"Jess is also territorial," Sed added, resting the full plate on his forearm and grabbing a second plate to add a selection of desserts.

"Territorial? If you keep feeding her like that, she's going to end up as her own sovereign territory," Eric said.

"No worries, she shares." Sed grinned. "And she's been so horny lately, I can scarcely keep her satisfied."

"Maybe you should hire some assistance," Eric joked.

Sed hit him in the forehead with a crumpet.

An unexpected silence filled the room. Jace had been tuning out the music in the background, but its sudden absence was very noticeable.

Trey's voice came over the speakers. "I hope you all can dance to Exodus End," he said. "I can't stand the club music for another moment."

Everyone on the dance floor gawked at him as the familiar intro of "Bite" filled the large room. Apparently no one knew how to dance to Exodus End, so Trey entered the dance floor to show them.

A hand pressed against Jace's lower back.

"Is anything on the buffet edible?" Aggie asked.

He glanced at her and smiled. "I wouldn't know. Sed is holding up the line."

"I'm almost finished." Sed added another slice of cake to his second plate.

"Yeah," Eric said, "but there won't be anything left for the rest of us."

"I'd hit you, but I don't have a free hand."

"I'd be willing to take on the task," Aggie said. "For a price. I don't work for free."

"Does she still charge you, Jace?" Eric quipped.

"Not after tomorrow," he said. "Marrying her makes good financial sense."

"Bassists do make a little more than paper boys," Aggie said.

"But not by much," he said.

Eric lifted an eyebrow at him. "Didn't your contract give you an even cut of Sinners' profits?"

"Yeah." Jace shrugged. He really didn't care about the money. It was nice to make a living off what he loved, but he could do without. It wasn't as if he'd never been destitute. He didn't particularly want to go back to wondering where his next meal would come from, but he'd survived it once and could survive it again.

"Inside joke," Aggie said. "My mother was trying to get him to tell her how much he makes."

Sed snorted. "Sounds like my mother-in-law."

"I thought you and Jess cut all ties with her after the way she acted at your wedding," Eric said.

"Yeah, well, she decided she could control herself if she was allowed to see her grandchild. She's been marginally successful at not pissing off Jessica so she doesn't get disinvited from the delivery room."

"Jessica looks pretty hungry if you ask me," Aggie said. "If anyone is pissing her off, it's you."

And Sed finally left the buffet to allow the growing line a chance to score some food.

"You're brilliant," Jace told Aggie.

"Eh, Sed thinks like a typical guy. He's easy to manipulate." She kissed the corner of Jace's mouth. "I'm still trying to figure out how to get you to do what I want you to do when I want you to do it. You're still a bit of an enigma to me."

"Tripod is not complicated," Eric said. "Just bring out the short jokes. They get him all flustered, and he forgets he's brooding and that he lacks a sense of humor."

"He's not short, he's perfect," Aggie said. "Maybe you're just freakishly tall."

Jace lifted his eyebrows, the corner of his mouth twisting in a smirk. "Eric's just jealous because my dick is bigger than his."

Eric stared at him with his mouth hanging open, apparently without a proper comeback.

"Yeah, well," Eric said finally. "My dick's not small. It's perfect. Maybe yours is just freakishly large."

Aggie and Jace laughed.

"And I like it that way," Aggie said, giving Jace a courteous slap on the ass.

Eric grabbed two plates and, as if on cue, Rebekah sidled up to him, bypassing the entire line.

"Hey," Aggie chided. "We were here first."

"Eric was holding my place," Rebekah said, the red streaks in her blond hair matching her ball gown perfectly.

"I was?" Eric said, his lips twitching with amusement.

"Yes."

"And where have you been, Miss Reb?" Aggie asked. "Setting up more pranks to scare the piss out of me and Jace?"

If the looks of confusion on Eric and Rebekah's faces were fabricated, they should have gone into theater instead of music.

"What are you talking about?" Eric asked.

"The message you wrote in lipstick on the mirror," Aggie said. "Very mature, Eric." She crossed her arms over her large breasts and scowled at him.

Jace had almost forgotten about the creepiness they'd experienced before they'd entered the castle. He shuddered as the feelings of unease settled upon him once more.

"What did it say?" Eric said with a snigger as he filled his plate with food. "Get out! Get out of Aggie's pussy, Jace. You're late for your own rehearsal dinner?"

"You know damned well what it said, jackass," Aggie grumbled.

"*He is mine*," Jace told them. He lifted a heavy white china plate from the end of the buffet as Eric followed after his wife down the spread of food.

Eric's head swung in Jace's direction, and his eyebrows shot up toward his bizarre hairline. "Do you have something in the closet you'd like to share, little man?"

"No." He prodded Eric in the ribs with his elbow. "That's what the message said."

"I'd love to take credit for rattling the unrattleable—"

"Is that even a word?" Rebekah interrupted her husband.

"If not, it should be," he said.

"It wasn't you?" Aggie asked, leaning around Jace to look at Eric. Her ice-blue eyes were pleading with him to admit he was lying.

"Nope. We've been here waiting for you to arrive," Eric said. "Maybe Jace's fangirl—he only has one that I know of—has come to sabotage the wedding."

"Or maybe the place really is haunted," Jace spoke his thoughts aloud.

"Did you see a ghost?" Rebekah said excitedly. "I heard the queen's ghost haunts the grounds. I've been hoping to catch sight of her all evening."

"I saw..." Jace crumpled his forehead as he tried to make sense of what he'd seen out in the field. "Something."

"You did?" Aggie squeaked.

"It was just some reflection of light on the fog." Jace shrugged, trying to convince himself—more so than his captive audience—that what he'd seen hadn't been a ghost. He didn't believe in such things, did he?

"*Rawr!*" Eric growled and bumped into Jace, trying—and

failing—to startle him. Eric earned a stomped-on foot for his efforts.

"You're sure you didn't write the message on the mirror?" Aggie asked.

Eric shook his head. "Maybe you're seeing things."

"I saw it too," Jace said.

"So you're having sympathy hallucinations," Eric said with a shrug.

"This is cool!" Rebekah said. "I want to see it. Did you wipe it off?"

Aggie shook her head. "We'll show you later."

Much later, Jace thought. Maybe after the sun rose and Halloween was over. Rehearsal dinners usually continued until dawn, didn't they? He hoped so. Jace bit his lip and continued to fill his plate, not paying much attention to what he was going to have to eat once he sat down.

The four of them joined Brian and Myrna at a nearby table. The couple had already finished eating, but they were still trying to convince their stubborn son to ingest unfamiliar foods in a place that had far more interesting things to watch than the spoon making daddy-derived airplane noises at him. It seemed Mal wasn't a fan of British fare, if one was to judge by the state of his father's food-splattered shirtfront.

"He doesn't like that," Myrna said.

"He doesn't like anything," Brian said, closing his eyes as Mal blew out a spoonful of red mash. Beets? Brian reached blindly for a napkin and wiped the bright red muck from his face. "Are you going to eat anything, Mal?"

"No!" Malcolm said.

"If you eat your dinner you can have cake." Brian tried bribery.

"No!"

"Are you tired?" Myrna asked.

"No!"

"What do you want?"

"Down!" Malcolm tried to snake his way down out of his high chair, but a strap between his pudgy legs thwarted his escape.

Brian tugged the baby back up into his seat and tightened the tray to keep the squirmy child in place.

"Down pwease, daddy," Malcolm said, his most heart-melting expression plastered to his face as he lifted his chubby arms and opened and closed his hands repeatedly.

Brian was made of stronger stuff than Jace was. Jace knew without a doubt that he'd have succumbed to the child's wishes immediately.

"Maybe he just needs to crawl off some energy," Myrna suggested.

The youngster must have been sucking energy out of his parents while they slept and stockpiling it for his own use; the two of them exchanged weary smiles.

Yeah, Jace decided. Parenting was not something he'd be any good at. He needed his sleep, if nothing else. Sleeping until noon wasn't something he'd be able to enjoy with a baby in the picture.

"You're not getting down until you eat your supper," Brian said to his pouting little one.

"Twey!" Malcolm screamed at the top of his lungs. "Twey!"

The godfather in question appeared at the table a moment later. "What are you doing to my favorite buddy?" Trey swept a hand over Malcolm's fluffy black hair.

"Making him eat," Brian said.

"Who wants to eat when you can party?" He bestowed an ornery grin upon his godson. One that was immediately mirrored by the child. "Do you want to party, Mal?"

"Twey!" Malcolm said, reaching for the dangling cuff of Trey's shirt and giving it a tug. "Pwease."

Brian rubbed his forehead and shook his head. "I give up."

Trey rescued his godson from the high chair. Free of his prison, Malcolm immediately spotted his favorite object to yank—Eric's hair—and leaned over to wrap his fist in a long red strand resting temptingly on Eric's shoulder. Eric rose to his feet to prevent being scalped and trailed after Trey and Malcolm, now making for the dance floor, until he was able to extricate his hair from Malcolm's grip.

"I do believe your friends are a bad influence on our child," Myrna said to Brian. "Especially that *Twey* character." Her crooked grin indicated she was teasing, but Brian rested his head on the table and rubbed his face over the table cloth.

"We're doomed," he murmured. "Doomed!"

"He talks so well already," Aggie commented. "Do they usually talk that much at nine months?"

Myrna beamed. "Not usually. His pediatrician says he's never met a more gifted child."

"Doomed!" Brian repeated.

Jace laughed and sampled what he believed was kidney pie. The dish was a bit salty, but not as disgusting as he'd feared.

"He's so goddamned cute, it should be a crime," Aggie said, watching the baby giggle and squeal in Trey's arms as the pair energetically took up a mix of disco and swing dancing to the Metallica song blaring from the speakers.

Eric returned to the table, rubbing his scalp, which was likely down a few hairs at Malcolm's insistence. "Your kid hates me."

Myrna shook her head. "He adores you, Eric. He just knows Trey is his little bitch, so he gravitates toward him."

Brian lifted his head. He rested his elbow on the table and his chin on his knuckles. "Hear anything from the adoption agency?" he asked Eric.

"We're still on the waiting list for a baby," Rebekah said, "but when we get back we're going to check into fostering some older kids."

"Kid*s*?" Brian said, enunciating the *S*.

"We figured we'd start with two or three," Eric said, picking over his food. "They have a hard time placing siblings in the same home. But we're very open to that."

"You sure you want to start that big?" Myrna asked. "This child-rearing stuff is exhausting."

"We're sure," Rebekah and Eric said in unison.

Jace glanced at Aggie, who was scowling at her plate. He decided it wasn't because she was trying to figure out what to try next. He took her hand under the table and whispered, "What's wrong?"

"Just wondering if you've changed your mind about having kids," she said.

The table fell silent as four sets of eyes were suddenly staring directly into their business.

"Uh," Jace said. "I'm not good with kids."

"It's different when they're your own," Brian said.

"Or adopted as your own," Eric said hurriedly. He placed a protective hand on his wife's back.

Yeah, then he'd be entirely responsible for screwing them up.

"Do you want kids?" Jace asked Aggie under his breath. He squirmed in his seat, not sure he wanted the answer.

"Only if they're yours," she said.

"Aw," Eric said and reached over to pinch Jace's cheek. "I think she likes you, Tripod."

Jace felt the heat rise up his face to greet Eric's fingertips. He'd been trying for years to control his blushing, but it was no use. "I should hope so," he said. "She's marrying me tomorrow."

When they finished their meal, Eric rose to his feet and clanged on his glass with a spoon. The thundering music died, and everyone turned to look at him.

"A toast!" Eric called and those on the dance floor returned to their tables to find their glasses.

Aggie took Jace's hand under the table—probably for moral support. There was no telling what was about to spew from Eric's lips.

Jace offered her an encouraging smile and lost his breath as a face not belonging to Aggie smiled back at him. A face he recognized as the likeness of the long-dead Queen Katherine Parr. Heart thundering in his chest, he squeezed his eyes shut and opened them again, releasing a sigh to be staring into the bright blue eyes of his fiancée. Perhaps he should lay off the booze tonight. Not that he'd had any yet.

"Thanks for taking time out of your jet lag to join us this evening," Eric called out to the crowd. "I know it's not customary to throw a Halloween ball in place of the rehearsal dinner or to invite more than the wedding party to the event, but I have a feeling that the happy couple will cut the reception short tomorrow afternoon before I'm drunk enough to spout sentimental drivel in front of all our friends and family. Lucky for you all, I'm on my fourth whiskey sour." He downed his drink in several gulps and clunked the empty glass on the table. "Make that my *fifth* whiskey sour." Laughter chased the downing of his whiskey.

"Even though these two are doing things out of order..." He lifted an eyebrow at them. "You're supposed to consummate the marriage *after* the wedding, you know."

The jibe was greeted with shouts of approval, catcalls, and whistles.

"You can talk," Jace mumbled.

"...they're finally going to make it legal. *When* they return to the States and get their actual marriage license. Do you have to say your vows again?"

Aggie nodded.

"Twice the opportunity to get it wrong."

"Or right," Aggie countered.

Eric winked at her and then turned his attention back to the crowd. "We all know that even though that piece of paper entitles her to half his shit, what's important is that we all get to see the groom turn the color of cranberries as he tells this wonderful woman that he'll never be worthy of her in front of God and everyone."

Jace was turning the color of cranberries now.

"He's worthy," Aggie said. She squeezed Jace's hand beneath the table.

"Raise your glasses in toast."

Glasses were lifted.

"To the happy couple—Katherine and Thomas. May your love transcend time."

Jace froze. Was he hearing things?

Rebekah slapped her husband's thigh. "That's not funny, Eric."

"What's not funny?"

"Saying their names wrong," she whispered loudly through clenched teeth.

"I did?" Eric scrubbed at his mouth with his fingertips. "Maybe I should have stopped at four adult beverages. I meant to say: To Jace and Aggie. May it never come to her taking half his shit."

Many of the onlookers laughed, but Jace didn't and neither did Aggie. Saying their names wrong in jest wouldn't have been a big deal, but why those particular names? Had Eric done it on purpose knowing how it would affect Jace after all the weird tricks his mind kept playing on him? What other explanation was there?

Jace downed his glass of champagne with everyone else, but inside he was rattled.

"Eric's the one playing tricks on us," Aggie said in his ear. "I'd bet my dungeon on it."

It did seem like something he'd do, but the pieces didn't quite fit.

Trey's voice came over the sound system. "I think it's time for the soon-to-be-Seymours to take a turn on the dance floor. What do you all think?"

Enthusiastic applause drew Jace to his feet. He hated dancing, but he loved being in Aggie's arms, and this would fulfill his need to be close to her. Maybe he'd stop shaking with her to hold on to. He offered a hand to Aggie, but didn't look her in the face. Part of him was afraid he'd see another woman in her place. He wasn't sure if he'd be able to handle it a third time. He felt like a complete coward—a feeling that did not sit well with him—but he had no experience with the weird and the creepy. He hadn't figured out how to steel his emotions against all the strange things he experienced in and around this castle. But Aggie always gave him strength. He hoped she could lend him a little now.

Aggie took his hand and followed him onto the dance floor amid more applause.

"I dedicate this song to you two," Trey said. "And my dog, Sparky. May he rest in peace."

Sinners' most famous ballad, "Goodbye Is Not Forever," began to play. Jace drew Aggie into his arms and so he wouldn't be reminded that everyone was watching them, he focused on the feel of her body against his. His hand rested against her lower back, and her breasts brushed his chest, but her skirt was too wide to allow him to hold her as close as he'd like.

As they swayed to the music, a different song began to play in his head, competing for his attention. A song he was pretty sure he'd never heard. A waltz played on the strings of a talented quartet.

I waited, a voice whispered to him.

"What?" Jace whispered aloud, his body suddenly cold. He shuddered, but kept his eyes closed. He knew he was hearing things. If Aggie found out he'd lost his mind, would she leave him? He tugged her closer.

"*What* what?" Aggie asked.

"Nothing," he said, burying his face in her neck and inhaling her scent. It was familiar and calming.

I waited and waited and you never came, the voice said. *Were your words a lie, Thomas? Did you never love me? Why did you reject our daughter? Why did you break your promises?*

Jace answered her aloud, but wasn't sure where the words were coming from.

"My world ended the day you died, Katherine. I could not bear to love anyone again. Not even our daughter."

Aggie stopped suddenly. "Who is Katherine?" she asked, her voice hard and cold. "And *what* daughter? What the fuck are you talking about, Jace?"

"Actually, I didn't say that," he admitted. He almost wished he *had* said it. It would have been less weird than having to tell her that he was being haunted.

"You did say it," she said. "Explain to me what exactly is going on with you."

He pulled her against him, hoping that somehow her proximity would put an end to the strangeness surrounding him. At least the only music he heard now was the aching melody of "Goodbye Is Not Forever." Maybe it was just the stress of the wedding making him certifiably crazy. And when it was over, he'd stop hearing voices and seeing the ghost of Katherine Parr.

"Just dance with me," he pleaded. "Just dance."

Her arms tightened around him as she swayed with him.

"Jace, I know something strange is happening to you," she whispered in his ear. "Whatever it is, you can tell me. You can trust me."

He did trust her, but he wasn't going to tell her. What could he say? *Hey, baby, I've completely lost my mind. I hope you don't mind participating in conjugal visits in a padded cell.*

"Jace? Please don't shut me out again."

He couldn't bring himself to put her fears to rest with words, so he kissed her, hoping that the press of his lips to hers would soothe her. A chill raced up his spine, and the chandelier overhead rattled. Jace deepened his kiss, hoping it would center his attention on Aggie enough so he could ignore the weird things going on around him. When he'd been fixated on her in the cottage earlier, he hadn't heard a single voice, felt any cold chills, or witnessed any object move on its own accord. Aggie had chased away the figurative ghosts of his past, so a few literal ghosts shouldn't be a problem for her.

Apparently Aggie wasn't too keen on his methods of avoidance. She pulled her lips from his and caught his face between her palms.

"We don't do this anymore, remember?" she said.

"What?" he said gruffly. "Kiss?"

"No, we will do that plenty," she said with a smile. "But we don't hide things from each other."

"You hid Starr from me," he reminded her.

She ducked her head and stared at his chest. "That was a mistake," she said. "I hope you won't make the same one I did. Whoever this Katherine is, you should tell me about her."

Uh, no. He should not. Not entirely. But he didn't want to worry Aggie, so he settled for half-truths.

"This isn't what you think it is. I don't love Katherine, Aggie. I never did."

There was a loud creak overhead. Jace caught the downward movement of the chandelier in his peripheral vision. He shoved Aggie as hard as he could, and she stumbled backward, falling unceremoniously on her ass as the chandelier smashed to the floor between them.

Aggie stared at him in wide-eyed shock for a heartbeat and then scrambled to her feet before dashing from the room among the startled gasps and whispers of the guests who'd witnessed the near accident.

Jace raced after her, his heart thudding in his chest.

"Is she okay?" he heard Eric call after him, but Jace didn't stop long enough to answer.

I can't lose her. Not again. I've been searching so long, unable to find my way back to her.

Jace stopped in the long corridor, looking in either direction for a sign of his lady, and spotted the hem of an elegant green ball gown disappear around a corner down the hall.

A cool breeze blew over the back of Jace's neck, propelling him forward.

I have to explain. Have to see her again, have to hold her. I've been wandering alone for far too long. I need her in death even more than I needed her in life. Don't let her get away.

Jace drew to a sudden halt. Where were those thoughts coming from? He pressed his hands to his skull and tried to force them out.

"Shut up," he growled.

Thomas! The name echoed through his mind.

His legs started to move again, carrying him down the passageway he'd seen her take, out a side door, into a garden. Flurries of snowflakes fell from the dark sky, melting as soon as they landed. His breath billowed like a cloud before him as he panted to catch his breath.

"Katherine?" he called.

Stay away! He heard her wrath within himself. Felt it even.

He caught a motion up ahead and his heart stuttered. Aggie stood in the garden with both arms wrapped around her body as she tried to hold in wracking sobs.

"Aggie?" He stepped closer. "You okay?"

She shook her head and headed farther into the garden. Running from him. Aggie was never supposed to run from him.

"Aggie, don't run. I need..." He swallowed and started after her. "I need to tell you something." He gained on her rapidly, chasing her through the garden and toward the chapel. Toward the tomb of Katherine Parr. He wasn't sure why she was headed in that direction, but he had to stop her before she reached the building. After her near miss with the chandelier, he was starting to believe that ghosts could harm a person. And he could not let that happen.

When she was finally within reach, he grabbed her from behind and encircled her body, wrapping his arms around her waist, pressing her back securely to his chest. He tried to inhale her, pull her inside him where she'd be safe. Protected. Warm.

She didn't struggle, just sagged against him.

"Why did you run from me?" he asked.

"I wasn't running from you," she said. "After the chandelier fell, I saw someone—someone who wasn't you—standing there looking at me."

"Thomas," Jace guessed.

"You don't sound surprised," she said. "Why don't you sound surprised?"

"I don't think it's Thomas you need to worry about." He was pretty sure it was Katherine slamming doors and ripping light fixtures from ceilings.

"He scared the shit out of me. Do you know what's going on? Am I losing my mind?"

"If you are, we both are," he said, pressing his forehead to her shoulder. "Aggie, I think I'm being haunted."

"Well, that makes two of us," Aggie said. "Any idea what we should do about it?"

"Not a clue."

Chapter 10

AGGIE RUBBED THE STIFFNESS from her icy fingertips. She'd almost shit a brick when she'd seen some stranger standing in Jace's place on the dance floor. Almost being beaned on the head with a chandelier had been nothing compared to that.

"Do you think we should leave?" she asked. She hated to cancel their wedding, but this was some freaky shit they were dealing with, and she was not keen on being the mark of some crazy, dead Queen of England.

Jace sighed and his arms tightened around her. He felt so good behind her. So solid and real and... and un-ghost-like. She shuddered at the thought of what she'd seen back in the castle.

"Maybe we need to help them reconcile. That should make them leave us alone. I think I'm the one who brought Thomas here from the Tower of London, and she's been here waiting for him all this time."

Aggie shook her head, glad her senses were returning. She'd completely freaked out in the ballroom, but now she was half-convinced that she hadn't actually seen Thomas Seymour's likeness. It made a heck of a lot more sense to think she'd just imagined it.

But Jace was talking about both of them—*two* ghosts—as if they were real.

"Okay, this is just too bizarre," she said. "I don't believe in this kind of thing at all."

"Me neither, but it's kind of hard to deny it's happening when you're living it."

She begged to differ. "I am perfectly capable of remaining in denial, thank you very much."

"Have you heard the voices too?" He squeezed her as if trying to force agreement from her lips.

"No, I just *see* things. You can hear them?"

"Unfortunately. I hear him a lot. I even hear her. And I see her sometimes. In you. I thought I was losing my mind."

Aggie shuddered. "Maybe you are."

"Maybe."

"Then I am too." Aggie turned in Jace's arms and clung to him. "I don't have much experience with this kind of thing."

He snorted through a small laugh and nuzzled her neck. "Does anyone?"

"Maybe the guy from *Crossing Over.*"

"I always thought that was fake."

"Me too."

"I don't think these two intend any harm," he said, pulling her tighter. "Or I didn't until that chandelier came crashing down. It could have killed you."

"I'm okay," she assured him. "Not something I'd like to repeat, however. Maybe we *should* let them talk this out."

"And how do we do that?"

She shrugged. "No idea. Like I said, I don't have much experience with this kind of thing."

"Where's a good ghost whisperer when you need one? Or maybe an exorcist is better qualified for the job."

She chuckled and pulled away so she could turn to stare into his eyes in the dim light of the lanterns that lit the garden. The snow had changed over to a dreary drizzle, and she began to feel the cold seeping into her skin. Before, she'd been too freaked out and juiced up on adrenaline to notice the temperature. She snuggled close to Jace again, telling herself she just wanted to be next to him for warmth, not because she was afraid of things she didn't believe existed and because Jace made her feel safe.

He seemed to be more sensitive to this bizarreness than she was, so she asked, "When did you first hear the voices?"

It was infinitely easier to talk about it if it was *his* problem, not hers.

"When we stepped out of the car five months ago."

She stiffened. "You heard them the first time we visited? Is that why you were acting so strange that day?"

"Yeah."

"And you agreed to come back to this place? I'd have run for the hills."

"I felt drawn to this place. I still do."

"So have you been possessed by the spirit of Thomas Seymour your entire life?"

Aggie felt the lift of Jace's shoulders as he shrugged. "Never met him before that last visit. I think he's using me as some sort of guide. He can't find this place unless I'm here."

"But why you?"

"Hell if I know. It isn't as if he tells me his plans or how these things work."

"And you see her too?"

"Sometimes," he said, "when I look at you. And I'll be honest, it freaks me the fuck out."

"I still think maybe we should just leave. It isn't as if Thomas bothers you when we aren't here, and our chandeliers at home are brand new."

"You don't think we should try to help them? They want to be together, but they suck at communication."

Aggie laughed and gave Jace a squeeze. "We used to struggle with that."

"Are you guys out here?" Eric yelled from the steps of a side entrance.

"Yeah," Jace called.

"Is she still breathing? We banished the evil chandelier from the dance floor. You can come back now."

"We're sort of busy at that moment," Jace returned.

"Are you two having sex out there?" he asked. "Can I watch? It's been a while since I've watched anyone but myself and Reb."

"No and no," Aggie yelled.

"Dammit," he muttered before turning away. "You should come back inside soon. It's cold."

Aggie covered Jace's chilled ears with her hands. "I hardly noticed," she whispered. "I'm kind of afraid to go back to the ball. People must think I'm crazy for running out like that."

"I'm sure they just think you were rattled from a chandelier attempting to kill you."

"Well, I guess that's better than what *really* has me rattled," she said.

"Let's walk the gardens for a bit. I'm not ready to face the crowd or the questions."

He was staring at her with a rare intensity. If she wasn't mistaken, his eyes were misty.

"What's wrong, baby?" she asked.

"When that chandelier came crashing down, I thought…" He swallowed. "I thought I might lose you."

"The night before our wedding?" Aggie said. "You should be so lucky."

Aggie moved away from Jace and took his hand. She could

definitely feel the cold now that he wasn't pressed firmly against her. She couldn't believe he'd been suffering with this in silence. Actually, she could believe it. And she suddenly felt like a complete jerk for intentionally messing with him earlier.

"Jace, I have a confession. And an apology." She squeezed his fingers. "I'm sorry I tried to scare you. If I'd known that you really were hearing things and seeing ghosts, I wouldn't have done it."

"Scare me? When did you scare me?" he asked.

"*I* wrote that message on the mirror. A kind of Halloween practical joke. I figured we'd get a good laugh out of it tomorrow, but I don't think it's funny anymore."

Jace kissed her soundly on the lips. "Thank God it was you. I was starting to think these ghosts could do real damage. Maybe that chandelier falling right after I said I didn't love Katherine was just a coincidence."

"Maybe," she said, but she kind of doubted it.

"But we need to make sure," he said, drawing her to a halt at the steps of the chapel.

"Why are we here?"

"We're going inside. To visit Katherine's tomb."

Aggie stopped in midstride. "Oh no, we're not," she said, shaking her head vehemently. "I'm not going in there on Halloween night."

"Why not? You don't believe there are really ghosts in there, do you?"

"Maybe. I'd love to say we could explain all this away, but if they're talking to you and you're seeing things…" She patted his shoulder. "Let me put it this way, I'd rather believe in ghosts than believe you're crazy."

"Good. Because I need to deal with this, this *haunting* or whatever it is," he said. "Now that you know what's been happening to me and you haven't called the loony wagon yet, I feel like I can face the problem head on. I want to face it. With you. Does that make sense?"

She squeezed his chilled fingers and smiled. "Yeah and it makes me happy that you feel that way."

Well, happy in a *I don't really want to do this but can't refuse the man anything because he asks so little* kind of way. Jace was the type who didn't put his whole heart into many things—with the exception of his band and their music, his woman, his cat, and apparently the troubled romance of a couple who'd been dead for nearly five hundred years—so Aggie supposed she had no choice but to follow him to Queen Katherine's tomb. On Halloween night. When the woman's jealous spirit was pissed as hell at her.

Chapter 11

JACE ENTERED THE DIMLY LIT TOMB ALONE. Aggie hung back in the corridor, peering around with wide eyes. Now that Jace had come to terms with what was going on, he and Aggie had shifted roles. It was common for that to happen in their relationship, so he didn't waste time pondering why Aggie was afraid of things that probably couldn't hurt her and he was paralyzed by the things that could. The sight of that chandelier on the floor where Aggie had been standing split seconds before—and the very *thought* of losing her—had immediately put everything into perspective for him. Jace refused to let a pair of wayward souls endanger his woman or encroach upon what would be the happiest day of his life, so he was going to put an end to this nonsense right now. At least that's what he told himself until a breeze swept into the room, causing the few lit candles around the perimeter of the tomb to sputter. He wondered if they burned candles in the tomb every night or if Halloween was a special occasion.

"Jace!" Aggie whispered loudly. "Let's go back to the ball. People are probably worried about us."

"Not until these two agree to leave us alone."

"They can't follow us back to L.A., can they?"

"It wasn't likely," he said, smirking at his shoes, "until you just told them where to find us."

"I refuse to be haunted the rest of my life," Aggie said. She darted into the tomb and grabbed Jace's hand, squeezing it hard enough for the pain to rob him of his breath.

"Katherine, I know you're in here. Come out and talk to us."

I won't talk to her. Your whore. *Did you wait until my body was cold before you took her to your bed, Thomas?*

Aggie glanced around curiously, her full lower lip trapped between her teeth, but didn't seem upset. She obviously hadn't heard Katherine's insult; Aggie didn't take shit from anyone. Not even queens or ghosts of queens.

"You have me confused with someone else," Jace said. "I'm not Thomas."

"Are you talking to her right now?" Aggie whispered.

Jace nodded.

"I can't hear her."

"She said she doesn't want to talk to you. She thinks you're the one Thomas slept with after she died."

I know you slept with her. I saw you together in the cottage.

Okay, a ghost watching them have sex was even weirder than when his cat decided to play captivated audience.

"What did she say?" Aggie asked.

"Uh… She… well…" His cheeks burned with the heat of embarrassment. It quickly spread to both ears. "…saw us together."

Aggie lifted an eyebrow at him. "Saw us together? When?"

His cheeks flamed hotter.

"In the cottage this afternoon?"

He is mine! Katherine's voice roared through Jace's head.

Aggie stiffened. "Okay, I heard that."

"She thinks I'm Thomas."

"Probably because he's latched on to you for some reason," Aggie said. "Is he with you now?"

Jace went still and listened, hoping for the first time to hear those weird voices in his head. Jace's shrink would have a field day with the entire experience. If he ever told him about it. He hadn't been to therapy in ages, no longer felt a need for it. Strange that he'd consider it now.

"I think he's gone. I haven't sensed his presence since we were in the garden. It seems he's more afraid of facing Katherine than we are."

"I'm not afraid of her." Aggie grabbed Jace by the lapels of his jacket and pulled him close so she could take his mouth in a deep, passionate kiss. At first he was too stunned to push her away and then, as the heat between them escalated, he didn't want to. His arms circled her back and drew her closer as his lips and tongue met hers.

The sounds of sobs echoed through Jace's head, growing fainter until he could no longer hear them.

"You two seriously aren't going to do it in a tomb, are you?" a soft voice said behind them. "I have a taste for the macabre myself, but that's pretty hardcore, even for you, Ice."

Jace stiffened. He'd purposely been avoiding Starr—*Fire*—since Aggie had told him they'd once been lovers, but there was no way out of the tomb except the way they'd entered, and Starr happened to be standing in the doorway.

Aggie tugged her mouth from Jace's. "I hadn't planned to take it that far," she said to Starr, and then lowered her voice to a whisper, "but if we're trying to upset a jealous ghost, I think that would do it."

"I don't want to upset her any more than we already have," Jace said quietly, hoping Starr wouldn't overhear. Aggie knowing that he was being haunted was one thing. Starr knowing it was entirely different. "I want her to find peace, even if it's with a philandering traitor who abandoned his own child and put his ambitions before his family."

What would you have me do? Thomas's voice echoed through Jace's head. *I would have gladly laid down in the grave beside her and died to spare myself the last miserable months of my existence.*

"He's back," Jace whispered. "I can hear him again."

Aggie released Jace and turned to Starr. "Were you looking for me or did you just happen upon me making out with my fiancé in a tomb by accident?"

Starr grinned. "Perhaps I shouldn't have interrupted. Looked as if it were about to get interesting."

"You have no idea," Aggie muttered.

"I wasn't looking for you—just trying to avoid that tall whack-job who keeps asking me to autograph things—but I'm glad I found you. I don't have anyone to talk to but you."

Jace snorted. Eric was a whack-job, but he couldn't believe Eric would actually hound Starr for autographs. On second thought, he could totally believe it.

"I thought you had a thing for Dare Mills," Aggie said.

"Oh, I do. Unfortunately he doesn't have a thing for me." Starr scratched her ear and met Jace's eyes before swinging her gaze back to Aggie. "Can we talk?" This time she gave Jace a pointed look. "*Alone?*"

"Anything you need to say to me, you can say in front of Jace," Aggie said.

Starr shook her head. "You don't want him to hear this. This is about that *thing* you're trying to pretend didn't happen."

"Do you mean our past sexual relationship?" Aggie asked bluntly.

Starr's eyebrows shot toward her hairline. "Uh, I thought you didn't want him to know." She nodded toward Jace.

"I told him. Because *someone* gave enough hints to make him question my relationship with you. And *someone* is giving enough hints now that if the first round hadn't tipped him off, this encounter certainly would. Why are you doing this, Starr?"

"You're okay with marrying a lesbian?" Starr directed the question at Jace.

"I'm not marrying a label. I'm marrying Aggie and everything that comes with her—past, present, and future."

Starr shook her head and rolled her eyes. "Now isn't that touching?"

"Don't make me regret asking you to be here for me," Aggie said. "I've been trying to hold on to pieces of my old life so I never forget where I came from, but maybe it's time to let all that go."

Jace stared at Aggie in disbelief. She wasn't serious was she? Her past had made her the woman she was—the woman he loved. Would she change into something unrecognizable if she let it go?

Aggie chuckled. "Of course that would mean admitting my mother was right and that ain't never gonna happen. So why are you really here, Starr?"

"I just came to check on you. If you need to talk to someone about the way he treats you, I'm all ears."

"The way he treats me?" Aggie swiveled her head in Starr's direction. "What's that supposed to mean?"

"I just know how guys treat women like us. We are alike—you and I—and men see us a certain way. They treat us a certain way. Don't pretend you don't know what I'm talking about, Aggie."

Jace saw very few similarities between Aggie and Starr, so he wasn't sure why Starr insisted they were lumped in the same category.

"Oh my God, Starr," Aggie bellowed. "Are you fucking kidding me? You know he doesn't treat me like his slut. I'd never put up with that bull. Now stop being a jealous bitch and pull your shit together."

Starr's jaw dropped, and for a moment Jace thought he was going to have to break up a cat fight, but then Starr laughed.

"You're right," she said and shook her head, sending her dangling earrings swaying. "You are right. I'm jealous. I am. I admit it. And I'm not jealous of Jace for winning you. I could have had you if I'd wanted you. I'm jealous of *you* for finding someone to accept you the way he does. *Christ*, he saved your life tonight, Aggie. Did you even thank him?"

Aggie glanced at Jace, who suddenly wished he was invisible. He didn't need her thanks. He was just glad she hadn't been hurt.

"Thanks, baby," Aggie said and placed a rather platonic kiss on his cheek.

"It was nothing."

"It wasn't nothing," Starr said. "I don't have *anyone* who would stick their neck out for me like that."

Jace tilted his head to the side. "I would." He'd have shoved a perfect stranger out of harm's way. It wasn't a big deal.

"You would?" Starr squeaked.

"Of course he would," Aggie said. "I'm not sure what you're so worked up about."

"Do you know how fucking rare it is to find a man like him, Ice?"

Aggie nodded and turned her head to look at Jace. "Yeah, I do. And that's why I'll never let anything come between us. Not you or anyone else; living or dead."

The redhead is exceptionally attractive, Thomas's voice sounded through Jace's head unexpectedly. *Do you think I could have a go at her?*

"Where do you find a guy like him?" Starr asked. "You wouldn't happen to have a brother, would you, Jace?"

Jace shook his head, answering Thomas and Starr simultaneously. But he did have an annoying ghost Starr was welcome to have.

"Let's go back to the party," Aggie said. "People probably think we're fighting."

"Most of them know better," Jace said.

Aggie laughed. "Yeah, most of them probably think we bailed early so we could spend time dancing between the sheets rather than on the dance floor. No telling what Eric told them we were up since he was the one who checked on us."

He'd love to be alone with Aggie dancing between the sheets. Unfortunately, they weren't alone no matter where they went while at the castle. And Jace sure didn't want Thomas and Katherine yelling in his head when he was pouring his heart out to Aggie the next day. The ghosts had to go and he had to be the one to make them leave.

"You two head on back," he said. "I'll be there in a minute."

Aggie's eyebrows drew together. "What's going on?"

Jace chuckled. "Voices in my head."

Starr gave him an odd look, but Aggie nodded before kissing him gently. "Don't keep me waiting too long. I don't want anyone thinking I murdered you and buried you in the garden."

He grinned. "I won't."

He watched her walk away with Starr, and then he sat on the ledge of Queen Katherine's tomb.

"You still there, Thomas?" He spoke to the stone floor.

I am.

"Go after her. Go after Katherine. Don't hesitate. Go now."

She doesn't want me.

"She waited for you for five hundred years. She wants you. She loves you. But you hurt her, so you have to fix it. You don't want to spend eternity alone, do you?"

A deep sorrow settled in Jace's heart. He didn't know if it was his sadness or Thomas's. An eternity alone? And he'd once thought a life lived alone was unbearable. He couldn't imagine spending all eternity alone.

If I'd known I'd see her again, I wouldn't have tried to forget her in the arms of other women. Kat was different. Kat saw me, the man beneath the scoundrel. She knew what I was and loved me anyway.

"I have a woman like that," Jace said.

Treat her well.

Jace nodded. "I'll do my best."

He sat quietly for a moment, wondering if his best was really good enough for Aggie. Even with a lifetime of loving stretching before them, he wasn't sure if that was enough time to give her all that she deserved. But if they could be together forever—beyond death—then maybe... Maybe she could come to realize the depth of his devotion.

He couldn't imagine the devastation that Thomas must have endured when Katherine died; first watching his child grow within her, seeing her hold that child, love that child, then watching her die days later, leaving them to carry on without her. Jace didn't know that he'd have made the same decisions Thomas made—being unable to love the child they'd created—or if he'd have clung to and cherish the little piece of her left on Earth, but he knew that if he ever lost Aggie, his heart might as well stop beating.

"You still there, Thomas?" Jace said.

Yes.

"Go tell Katherine what's in your heart, man. Just tell her."

And if she doesn't forgive me?

"At least you tried."

Will you tell your lady what's in your heart as well?

"Tomorrow," Jace promised. "When I marry her." He would lay his heart at her feet and pray she didn't stomp on it.

Chapter 12

JACE STIRRED. The sound of rain lashing against the windows was a muted lullaby that made finding consciousness a challenge. He slowly opened his eyes to be confronted by a direct blue-eyed stare. He flinched, releasing a gasp of surprise.

"I'm not that scary in the morning, am I?" Eric asked with a wry grin.

"Why are you staring at me like that?"

"Trying to wake you with the power of my mind. Did it work?"

Jace smacked him in the face with a pillow. "You are so fucking weird, Sticks."

"That's a given." He gripped the pillow between both hands, stood up straight so he was no longer leaning over the bed staring in Jace's face, and shrugged. "Did you sleep well?"

Jace stretched lethargically and grinned with contentment.

"Good," Eric said. "I thought you might like to know that your wedding starts in twenty minutes, he-who-sleeps-like-the-dead."

"What!"

Jace kicked the tangle of covers aside and leapt from the bed, searching the cottage in a mixture of disorientation and panic. Eric was already dressed in his tux, and the clock on the fireplace mantel made it clear that Eric had not been joking about the time. It was a quarter till one in the afternoon. "Where's Aggie?"

"Somewhere getting ready with Rebekah and the rest of the women. They wouldn't let me watch them dress. Can you believe it?"

Jace dashed to the closet and pulled out the garment bag that held his tuxedo. He tossed it on the bed and yanked the zipper open. "Yeah, you perv. Most women think that's creepy."

"They just don't know what I'm missing." He wet a finger and smoothed one eyebrow with it.

Jace shook his head and laughed. "Once a perv, always a perv."

His highly polished black shoes tumbled out of the bottom of the bag, and he reached for his slacks. He decided he didn't have time for a shower. Good thing he'd taken one last night before he'd climbed into bed alone. No Aggie, but also no ghosts, thank God.

"Takes one to know one. Rebekah made me feel better by promising that I could watch her undress later."

"Good thing you met that woman."

"And I say the same of you and Aggie. I guess there really is someone out there for everyone."

Jace hurried through dressing, one eye on the clock. "Why didn't you wake me when you left this morning?"

"I did. Several times. You said you were up. Aggie sent me to check on you since you hadn't shown up yet. Good thing she did. Only you would sleep through your own wedding."

Jace didn't remember Eric waking him at all. He had gotten to bed rather late. Once he'd made his way back to the ball—without Thomas infiltrating his thoughts—everyone had given him a hard time about trying to kill Aggie with a chandelier but chickening out at the last moment. His friends had strange senses of humor.

"I suppose I don't have time for caffeine." Jace slipped the tuxedo jacket on and then sat on the edge of the bed to put on his socks.

"No, but do take the time to brush your teeth. You don't want to melt Aggie's face off with your dragon breath."

Jace slipped on his shoes and darted toward the bathroom. Managing not to piss on his shoes while multitasking brushing his teeth and relieving his bladder, he went over his vows in his head. Forgetting what to say was not an option. Almost every person he knew would be there, but he figured he could get through it if he just kept his eyes on Aggie the entire time. Still, his stomach began to do its best impersonation of a roller coaster.

"You can do this," he said to his reflection as he dabbed some gel at the ends of his bleached-blond tips to spike them haphazardly.

He gargled a bit of mouthwash and washed his hands. He ran a hand over his jaw and winced. His beard stubble was a little longer than he normally kept it, but he didn't have time to trim it. Damn it, why hadn't he woken sooner? Aggie would be furious with him if he was late. And as much as he'd enjoy her punishing him, he did not want to disappoint her.

Deciding he didn't look half bad for ten minutes of prep work, he hurried toward the sitting room at the front of the cottage. Eric was waiting for him with a large umbrella in his hand. He seemed to be tempting fate as he opened and closed the contraption indoors.

He glanced up when he noticed Jace had joined him. Eric twisted pursed lips to one side as he assessed Jace's attire. "So you'll wear a penguin suit for your wedding, but refuse to wear knickerbockers to your rehearsal dinner."

"Is that what those ugly fucking pants are called? *Knickerbockers*? For real?" Jace chuckled and then burst out laughing, glad for something to release his tension. Eric was usually good at turning Jace's naturally dark mood lighter. He wasn't sure what he'd do with himself if he didn't have the obnoxious goofball in his life.

"Those pants are not funny," Eric bellowed indignantly. "They are historically accurate." Eric tried to keep a straight face, but was soon busting a gut along with Jace.

After a moment, Eric wrapped an arm around Jace's back and whacked him on the shoulder. "Better?" he asked.

"Uh huh," Jace said, wiping tears from his eyes.

"Ready to get married?"

"Yep."

Eric opened the umbrella, and Jace opened the front door. It was pouring.

"Sucks that it's raining," Jace grumbled.

"Rain on your wedding day is good luck," Eric said. He tried shoving the large open umbrella through the door, but it was much wider than the wooden frame.

"This is a bit too much good luck for my tastes." Jace scowled up at the dark clouds overhead. At least he wasn't getting married outdoors. He remembered the disaster Sed and Jessica's beach wedding had been due to rain. Funny how the happy couple hadn't been upset about it in the least. Had he been in their position, he'd have been pissed.

Grunting with feigned exertion, Eric attempted to get the black umbrella out of the house sideways.

"It's not going to fit no matter how much you want it to," Jace said.

"That's what she said," Eric said automatically. "Maybe this is why you aren't supposed to open umbrellas indoors. Has nothing to do with luck and everything to do with geometry." He tried sending it out handle first to no avail.

"Dude, I'm going to be late if you don't stop fucking around."

"She'll wait," Eric assured him, but he folded the umbrella slightly so it would fit through the door.

Jace was scarcely aware of his surroundings as they hurried

toward the beautiful chapel where he would say his vows. What were his vows again? He wrung his hands together, trying to remember the words he'd agonized over for so long. The words that expressed exactly what Aggie meant to him. He couldn't remember a damned one.

"Nervous?" Eric asked, giving Jace's arm a much needed squeeze.

"I can't remember," he said dully.

"You can't remember if you're nervous?"

"I can't remember what I wanted to say."

"No one pays attention to that part anyway," Eric said.

Eric's assurance made Jace feel marginally better, even though he knew Eric was lying. Maybe the guys in the crowd would be thinking about the football season or which bridesmaid was the most doable, but the women—and one woman in particular—would be hanging on his every word, and he damned well knew it.

"Did you write them down?" Eric asked, looking at him as if he'd just checked into intensive care with no hope of recovery.

"About a thousand times," Jace said.

"So just read them to her. She knows you get stupid in front of crowds and even more stupid when faced with topics of a romantic nature. She won't care if you just read them to her. She'll understand."

Jace rubbed a hand over the scruff on his jaw. "I shredded all the papers. I didn't want her to find them."

Eric snorted at him. "Real smart, dude."

"You're not helping, *best* man."

"Was I supposed to be helping? I thought I was just supposed to stand behind you at the altar and catch you if you faint."

Jace slugged him in the arm and when Eric jerked to the side to avoid a second blow, Jace got a face full of ice cold rain water from the edge of the dripping umbrella. Rivulets dripped down the back of his neck beneath his collar. He shuddered from the chill and sidled in next to a wary-looking Eric once more. Jace might have been a bit damp now, but at least he felt slightly more alert. He was surprised by how alert Eric was. The guy had drunk so much the night before that he and Rebekah had to practically carry him to bed.

"How are you not hung-over this morning?" Jace asked.

"Myrna," Eric said.

Jace lifted a brow at him. What did Brian's wife have to do

with anything? "Myrna?"

"Yeah. She made me consume her banana and drink all her fluids."

Baffled, Jace gaped at him. "What?"

"I always knew that chick had a thing for me." Eric winked at him.

Jace chuckled. "Don't they all?" He then muttered under his breath, "In your imagination."

"Keep talking like that and I won't catch you when you faint."

A few people were standing outside the chapel under umbrellas. Aggie's mother happened to be one of them. As usual, she had a lit cigarette in one hand, but she looked quite elegant in her black bridesmaid gown.

"Wasn't sure if you were going to show up, Maynard," she said, taking a puff off her cigarette and releasing smoke in a drawn-out cloud as she looked him over.

He was used to her trying to sum him up, and he knew it was because she was overprotective of her daughter—the woman just had a weird way of showing it.

"You knew I'd be here," he said.

She tossed her cigarette into a puddle and nodded, avoiding his eyes. He extended a hand in her direction and touched her chilly bare arm. She glanced up and blinked back tears.

"You make her happy," she said, her voice quivering slightly. "Don't ever stop making her happy."

"I promise."

Before he could dodge her, she was hugging him. Jace normally didn't do hugs, but he made an exception in this case. He surrounded Tabitha's slight frame with both arms and embraced her. Gently at first, but then more securely so she'd know that he meant it. Her entire body was trembling, at least partially from the cold.

"Don't make me cry, damn you," she said, and then she tugged away to slap him on the chest. "I'm not the emotional type."

She looked up at him—eyes so similar in shade to Aggie's that it was a bit disturbing—and then pinched his cheek *hard* before trotting into the open door of the chapel with her umbrella still in hand.

Had he just had a moment with Aggie's mother? Maybe she'd stop calling him Maynard now.

Heads turned as he walked up the aisle. He knew he should

greet the people in attendance and thank them for flying thousands of miles to witness his wedding, but he was afraid that if he focused on anything but the pulpit at the end of the aisle, he'd either come down with a case of the dry heaves or Eric would get to tease him for the rest of his life for actually fainting at his own wedding. Why couldn't he be infallibly confident like the other guys of Sinners? None of them had been this nervous on their wedding days. Or if they had, they'd hidden it well.

"You were supposed to come in the back," someone at his elbow said.

"I was?" He was so light-headed he wasn't even sure who was talking to him or what the woman meant by "come in the back." Sounded kind of kinky.

"Are you feeling unwell, Mr. Seymour? You look a bit pale."

He glanced at the woman and recognized the wedding planner, Charity.

She smiled kindly and took his hand, which he recognized was like ice only when she patted his frigid fingers between her warm palms.

"A tad nervous?" she asked.

He swallowed and nodded.

"You perform music in front of thousands of fans, don't you?"

He nodded again, and stared at her cream-colored lapel. There was a small ruby flower pinned there, and it gave him something to concentrate on other than the backflips his stomach insisted upon doing.

"How do you deal with that?"

"I hide," he said, and his mouth twitched in an attempted smile.

"But those are strangers. These are your friends. Would you be nervous in front of them at a gathering?"

"Probably not," he admitted.

"And that's what this is, Jace. It's just a gathering of your friends. It's just a bit more formal than most gatherings." She leaned close and whispered, "Some say imagining them all in their underwear helps."

"I'd rather just not look at them."

"Whatever gets you through this," she said agreeably. "But when that wedding march begins, you *will* look at your bride. Promise me that."

At the mention of his bride, Jace's vision tunneled.

"Jace?"

He gave himself a hard mental shake. "I promise," he said quietly.

"Don't forget."

He nodded mutely. He didn't have long to stand in front of the crowd and perspire. Within minutes, a harp began to play. His head jerked up, and his gaze fixed on the head of the aisle, but he was disappointed to find it wasn't Aggie standing there. Dare Mills was headed in his direction with Starr on his arm. Jace took a deep breath and watched the pair approach, hoping Dare couldn't tell that he was freaking out. He craved the man's respect and owed him a world of gratitude. Perhaps that was why it startled him so completely when Dare slapped him hard in the shoulder.

"Buck up, bro," he said with a devilish grin. "This isn't your execution."

Starr laughed, and Dare shook off her clinging hold so they could separate and go to opposite sides of the pulpit. The rest of the bridal party entered two at a time. Each member of his groom's party whopped him a good one as they passed. Brian punched him in the gut. Sed slapped him on the back of the head. Trey, with tears-streaming-Tabitha on his arm, gave Jace's nose a hard yank. Jace was a bit confused by their physical retaliation until the final pair approached. Eric didn't stop at a slap in the arm or a jab in the ribs; he released his wife's hand so he could put Jace in a headlock and rub his bony knuckles over Jace's scalp.

"Feeling better?" Eric asked when he released him.

"Huh?"

"You looked like you were about to pass out there for a minute."

And he'd been effectively distracted by the mild physical pain they'd each delivered. It had kept him on his feet. So Eric had instructed the guys to knock him around? It had worked. Jace no longer felt like he was going to faint. He'd have to remember to thank Eric later with an equal number of physical blows.

The first chords of the bridal march began and everyone stood to have a look at the bride. With his heart thudding like a jackhammer against his ribs and his knees a bit on the wobbly side, Jace forgot to breathe. Then Aggie stepped into view, and breath didn't seem to matter anyway.

Everything around him faded into the background as she took a step closer and then another. With each step, his heart swelled larger and larger until he feared he'd suffocate. He'd never seen anything so beautiful in his life. Her long black hair had been artfully arranged around a small sparkling tiara. Curled tendrils framed her face. Her beautiful, smiling face. Oh, Aggie. His Aggie.

There was so much love in her expression that he felt it tugging at his chest until he couldn't resist its pull and his feet started carrying him toward her. There were a few delighted chuckles from the spectators, so somewhere in his addled thoughts he knew he was doing something out of place, but it felt right to meet her in the middle. It felt right to touch her cheek when she was standing before him. Felt right to get lost in her brilliant blue eyes. Felt right to finally suck a decent breath into his lungs before leaning toward her and kissing her soft lips.

"Tripod," he heard Eric call from the front of the church. "You're doing it wrong."

Maybe. But it felt right. *She* felt right. From the moment he'd seen her dancing at Paradise Found in Vegas, the woman had felt right—as if she'd been designed exclusively for him. And he knew he'd never feel right again if he ever lost her.

Their lips lingered, parting slowly as he drew away and opened his eyes. She smiled and touched his cheek.

"Did you lose yourself there for a moment?" she asked.

"Found myself," he said, his voice thick with emotion.

She tilted her head slightly, her smile brightening. "Do you want to marry me now?"

He nodded eagerly, his cheeks aching from the smile that couldn't possibly reflect the immense joy trying to burst from him. He took her hand and placed it in the crook of his elbow as they walked the rest of the aisle together. He was glad she was paying attention to where they were going, because he couldn't take his eyes off her.

She halted unexpectedly and tugged at his elbow to get him to stand beside her.

Someone cleared his throat loudly, and Jace dragged his gaze from Aggie's face to the priest who was staring at him with one eyebrow raised. Jace licked his lips and tried to swallow, but his mouth had suddenly gone dry.

"She looks beautiful, doesn't she?" the priest asked.

"Yes," Jace said, unable to stop himself from stealing another glance at her. Wow. Even the gaudy gold-foiled plastic heart dangling from her necklace looked perfect. He knew it was the only token she had of her father's and was glad she'd thought to wear it today no matter how much it contrasted with the rich fabric of her white gown.

"Do you think you can keep your wits about you long enough to marry her?"

"God, I hope so," he said, still staring at his bride.

Aggie released a soft laugh, and a blush tinged her cheeks pink as she stared down at the bouquet of black roses she held at waist level.

Jace no longer felt nervous. Or self-conscious. He felt proud. Confident. As if he could tackle even the most daunting task—including speaking about mushy feelings in front of his peers—as long as Aggie was beside him.

"Take each other's hands and turn to face one another," the priest instructed.

Aggie handed off her bouquet to Rebekah, who arranged the long train of Aggie's gown for her, and then she offered her hands to Jace. He took them in his, noting that they were trembling slightly. He lifted her hands to his lips and kissed her knuckles reverently before dropping his head forward to press the backs of her hands to his forehead. He loved this woman—*worshipped* her—and he really didn't care who knew. In fact, he wanted them all to witness his devotion and recognize it for what it was.

The priest cleared his throat again and Jace reluctantly straightened. The tears swimming in Aggie's eyes as she offered him a tremulous smile squeezed at parts of his soul he'd thought he'd surrendered to pain long ago.

"You've made me whole again," he said.

A single tear coursed down her cheek. She bit her lip, her thumbs stroking his fingers, sending sparks of pleasure and awareness between them. Incapable of maintaining any distance between them with her looking so shaken and vulnerable, Jace released his loose hold on her hands and pulled her into his arms. Much better, he thought as she melted against him. His fingers found a crisscrossing ribbon down the length of her back. It reminded him of the lacings of one of her corsets, only more delicate. Later he was definitely going to have to take a moment to admire her wedding gown before he stripped it off her.

"You're not good at taking orders, are you, Mr. Seymour?" the priest said.

Jace wasn't the least bit sorry for not following protocol, so he didn't bother to apologize.

"You have no idea how right you are," Starr Lancaster said from the end of Aggie's line of bridesmaids.

"One of his best qualities," Aggie murmured and dropped a kiss on the sensitive pulse point in his throat.

He reluctantly loosened his hold so he could stare into his bride's eyes and prevent himself from getting overly aroused in front of God and everyone.

"Can I proceed with the ceremony, or shall I wait until you've fondled her a little more?"

He's just jealous, Jace thought, grinning deviously at Aggie.

"You shouldn't have given him options, Father," Eric said. "Any man in his place would choose fondling without ceremony."

"Eric!" Rebekah hissed a warning and glared at him over Aggie's shoulder.

"Just stating a fact," Eric said.

Jace chuckled along with his wedding guests, but he turned to look at the priest. "Proceed. I'll save most of my fondling for later."

When the priest turned back to his Bible to continue, Jace lowered his hands and gave Aggie's ass a firm squeeze. She squeaked in surprise.

"I said *most*," he whispered.

"Do you know what I do to naughty boys?" Aggie whispered in his ear. She wasn't paying the slightest bit of attention to the formality of the priest's speech either.

"Mmm hmm," he murmured, doing his damnedest to listen to the priest's inspired words and not let his mind wander to all sinful things he knew Aggie did to naughty boys.

Jace was lost in a haze of possibility when the priest said, "Do you have any words you'd like to share with each other?"

Jace froze, his heart rate doubling in an instant. Aggie looked at him expectantly, and he couldn't remember the words he'd wanted to say to her. Not a one. Luckily, she knew him well. While the priest rubbed the edges of his Bible impatiently and the crowd shifted in their seats and the wedding party drummed their fingers and twiddled their thumbs, Aggie patiently waited for him to find his voice.

The priest cleared his throat. "I could—"

"Shh," Aggie interrupted the priest's attempt to move the ceremony forward. "Wait."

Jace concentrated on her face, allowing everything but her to fade into the background. It wasn't difficult; she was more radiant than the sun. All things paled in comparison. As he stared at her, his pulse slowed, his thoughts focused, and he found himself in that perfect headspace that at one time he'd only been able to find after he'd suffered enough physical pain to blot out the emotional agony he didn't think he'd ever escape. But he had escaped it. And he had to tell her how much that meant to him—how much *she* meant to him. He took a deep breath and forced the words from that wounded place inside him that he'd never revealed to anyone but her.

Chapter 13

AGGIE COULD SEE THAT JACE WAS STRUGGLING to find his voice. And she was struggling with a powerful protective instinct—the one that no one brought out in her more than Jace did. Part of her wanted to let him off the hook and not make him say whatever he'd thought it was she should hear from him on their wedding day. But the wiser part of her knew he needed to do this for himself more than for her.

She couldn't stop thinking about how he'd met her halfway down the aisle. She wasn't even sure if those dozen steps in her direction held the same significance to him that they did to her. They were partners. Lovers. Friends. They always met in the middle. That's why when he'd looked at her, kissed her, and touched her in the middle of the aisle with absolute reverence, she'd fallen to emotional pieces. As a dominatrix, she was used to men worshipping her, but in her head and her heart, Jace had always been her equal. So when he showed utter adoration in front of a hundred witnesses, the gesture meant something. Hell, it meant everything. She still had a fucking knot in her throat.

"I've been trying to find the right thing to say to you for months," he said at last. "I never did find perfect words, but I ran out of time to come up with something better, so you'll have to forgive me if I botch this."

She wanted to tell him she knew whatever he said would be perfect to her, but was afraid if she interrupted, he'd stop talking.

"My entire life people have only see pieces of me," he said, his voice strong and unwavering. "Some see what they want to see. My mother only saw the parts of me that stood in the way of her dreams. My father looked at me and saw nothing but loss and pain and rebellion. My first love, Kara…" He swallowed. "Kara saw adventure and recklessness, the bad boy in me."

These were all people Jace had lost before he'd become a man, but Aggie knew how much they'd shaped him. Correction: had shaped *pieces* of him. But not the whole of him. The whole of him was amazingly resilient and talented and compassionate and loving. And hers.

Jace pushed on. "Some see what I let them see. My boxing

coaches see the violence that needs an outlet. Past dommes saw the perversion that twists my perceptions of pain and of pleasure. Fans, they see the music that burns within. To my band, I'm still the new guy who just wants to be accepted as one of them and can't help but worship them to this day. To my cat, I'm a provider and a somewhat entertaining plaything. But *you*, Aggie, you're different. You see *all* of me. The best pieces and the worst. Everything in between. You worked so hard to get all my pieces to fit together like the world's most frustrating puzzle."

She smiled. That was exactly what he'd been like at the beginning, and his insight amazed her.

"I didn't think I was worth the trouble. I was so damaged. So *broken*. And I didn't even realize it."

She shook her head and squeezed his hands. She'd never seen him that way. Lost. Confused. Hurt. But not broken.

"Despite my best defenses, you persisted relentlessly to make me whole. And you could. You could. Do you know why?"

Not trusting her voice, she shook her head.

"Because you saw all the pieces. Even the pieces I didn't want you to see. You saw them all and accepted them. You put me back together one piece at a time until I realized there was only one piece missing. The piece that holds all the rest together."

She stared at him wide-eyed as she steeled herself for whatever bombshell he was about to drop on her. Something he'd managed to hide from her all this time. She was sure whatever it was, she could handle it. She just wished he'd picked a better place to tell her about that one missing piece.

He smiled gently and squeezed her hands.

"You, Aggie. You're the piece that holds me together. The missing piece that made me whole. You, Aggie."

She sucked her trembling lips between her teeth.

"I'll probably never understand what you saw in me. What kept you from giving up when I fought so hard to push you away."

"I love you," she whispered.

"Thank you for being so strong and stubborn. So harsh and tender. Thank you for being *you*. For never giving up on me."

Never, she mouthed.

"I only make one promise to you today, wife," he said.

When he called her *wife*, she felt the power behind the word because he'd so clearly showed her what it meant to him just the day before. "I promise to love you with *all* of my pieces forever. I just don't know how to love you any less." He lifted her hands to his mouth and kissed her knuckles, staring deeply into her eyes with that look of reverence on his face again. She could definitely get used to seeing it.

Someone in the pews began to clap. The enthusiasm for Jace's words spread through the entire room until everyone was cheering. Jace turned his head slowly, as if surprised they weren't alone. And maybe that was how he'd opened up to her the way he had. By pretending they weren't surrounded by a hundred riveted spectators. He blushed and lowered her hands, peeking up at her sheepishly.

"That was beautiful," she said. "Perfect."

The priest raised a hand and eventually their guests quieted.

"Not sure how I'm supposed to follow that," Aggie said. "I knew I should have gone first."

Jace bit his lip, his eyes trained on her cleavage. She tucked a finger under his chin and forced his gaze up. She could only imagine how hard it had been for him to pour his heart out to her like that, but he was going to have to fight off his inherent shyness for a few more minutes, because she had things to say that he needed to hear.

"We make an interesting pair," she said. "A cold-hearted bitch and a selfless, misunderstood man."

Jace opened his mouth to protest, but she covered his lips with her finger.

"My turn to talk."

He inclined his head ever so slightly in agreement.

"I eat men like you for breakfast and pick my teeth with their bones," Aggie said.

A few people chuckled.

"At least, I did. Until I discovered who you really are. You weren't what I expected. You brought out something in me I thought I'd lost." She closed a fist over her chest and pressed it against her breastbone, crushing her father's heart-shaped pendant into her skin. "My heart. I didn't think I needed it. It only ever caused me pain. Got in the way of my ambitions. I did a really good job of pretending it didn't exist anymore. That I didn't need a heart. Or love. And then you happened. I still don't know how you managed to not only remind me how to love, but how to need love. To want it. How to need you and want you. I should be pissed off that you took my life by storm and made yourself the center of my universe. I had plans, aspirations, goals, and none of them involved a man."

"I'm sorry," he said, and then he grinned. "Actually, I'm not."

"You shouldn't be sorry," she said, her voice softening. "I've never been happier to have been so wrong about what is most important to me. It's you and the love we share. It can get me through anything." She stroked the stubble on his jaw, delighting in its rough texture against her fingertips. "You only made one vow to me today, but I have dozens to make to you."

His eyebrows drew together.

"I promise never to make you buy me tampons."

He laughed.

"I promise I will not choke you in your sleep for leaving the toilet seat up. I promise to hug you hard when you need it and even harder when you think you don't. I promise to tell you exactly what's on my mind and wait patiently for you to tell me what's exactly on yours. I promise to support you in your career and allow you to support me in mine. I will be your partner and your wife for the rest of my life, but I promise to love you forever."

She glanced at the priest expectantly. He twitched, as if she'd cracked her whip at him, and then he cleared his throat.

"Do you Jason Michael Seymour take this woman to be your lawfully wedded wife, with God as your witness?"

"I do," he said without hesitation.

"Do you Agatha Christine Martin take this man to be your lawfully wedded husband, with God as your witness?"

"Hell yeah, I do," she said, wanting to make Jace smile. It worked.

The priest again cleared his throat. "The rings."

Eric produced the rings from inside his pocket and handed them to the priest. He said some words that Aggie didn't pay much attention to. She was too lost in Jace's brown eyes to be fully cognizant of anything but him.

Jace took the smaller of the gold wedding bands and slipped it onto Aggie's left ring finger. "With this ring I thee wed," he said.

Aggie reached for Jace's ring with trembling fingers and slipped it over the knuckle on his left ring finger. She stroked the band, rubbing it into his flesh to solidify the physical evidence of their lifelong bond. She was surprised by how emotional the simple gesture of putting a ring on his finger made her.

"With this ring I know Jace Seymour belongs to me, and I thee wed."

Jace's grin of happiness made Aggie's heart soar.

"By the power vested in me," the priest said. "I now pronounce you husband and wife."

Eyes a bit watery with tears, Jace drew her against him and kissed her as if he never planned to stop. Passion and emotion warred within Aggie until her senses were so overwhelmed by Jace—her *husband*—she could do nothing but cling to him and let him have his way.

"You may kiss your bride," the priest said unnecessarily and slammed his Bible shut.

The guests and bridal party clapped and cheered as the kiss deepened and their passion intensified. Tears of happiness leaked from beneath Aggie's eyelids, and she didn't bother trying to stem their flow. She and Jace were now one. In her heart, they'd always been one, but now she understood the importance of weddings. It allowed a couple and those they cared about to celebrate the rare and wondrous love that two people found in each other. What could possibly be more glorious than that?

A brilliant glow lit Aggie's face from the enormous stained-glass window behind the altar. The sun had found a break in the clouds.

The cheers and applause died at once, replaced with gasps of astonishment and whispers. Aggie tugged her lips from Jace's and turned her face toward the window. A pair of human-shaped, misty apparitions embraced before the glass. Aggie smiled. Thomas and Katherine had found their way back to each other. It was about damned time.

"I think they're kissing," she said to Jace.

"I guess they finally sorted things out."

"Thanks for coming to our wedding," Aggie called to Katherine and Thomas.

The fading figure of Thomas lifted a hand in farewell, wrapped an arm around his wife, and then they vanished together.

"Maybe love really is forever," Aggie said, turning back to Jace, "and we really can spend eternity together."

"I hope so, baby," he said, squeezing her hand and staring deeply into her eyes. "But we've still got a lot of living to do first."

"And loving," she said, crushing his handsome face between her palms and grinning until she was sure her cheeks would explode. "That's the best part."

Special Sneak Peek of

SINNERS ON TOUR

in Paradise

A Sinners Encores Anthology

OLIVIA
CUNNING

Coming Soon!

Need even more Sinners? The weddings are over, but the honeymoons are just beginning...

from *Take Me to Paradise*

Chapter 1

FOR BRIAN, THERE WAS ONLY ONE THING in the world more wonderful than waking up with his cock in the mouth of a skilled lover and that was knowing this *amazing* morning wakeup-call was being delivered by his spectacular wife, Myrna.

"Well good morning to you too," he said, lifting his head from the pillow to watch her work her magic.

Since her mouth was otherwise occupied, she smiled a greeting with her pretty hazel eyes. She took him deep into the back of her throat and increased her suction as she pulled back.

His belly tightened in an involuntary spasm of delight and he dropped his head back on the pillow wondering what he'd done to deserve this fantastic alarm clock.

Myrna bobbed her head until he was so hard he could have used his dick as jack-hammer and then she pulled back until his cock popped out of her mouth. He watched her in silent awe as she crawled up his body to straddle his hips.

"I just took my temperature. It's optimal," she explained and reached between her legs to press his cockhead into her slick opening. His flesh rippled with pleasure as her tight pussy swallowed him inch by glorious inch.

Myrna wanted a baby almost as much as he did, and though they'd been trying for months, so far they hadn't found success. She had recently resorted to taking her temperature near the middle of her cycle hoping to find her fertile time. She'd switched from a romantic approach to a more scientific one when fucking like rabbits anytime they were in the same room together hadn't produced the desired results.

"I should be on top," he said, "so gravity isn't working against us."

She pursed her lips together and nodded, blinking against the sudden flood of tears in her eyes. He understood her upset. It did seem like more than gravity was working against them.

Brian sat up and wrapped both arms around her. "Don't cry, baby. It will happen."

"How can it happen when you're always on the road?" she said and snuggled her face into his neck.

She clung to him as if afraid he was about to desert her. Again. He knew most of their problem was that the current tour with his band kept them apart so frequently.

"I'm not on the road now," he said.

"Only because the tour bus was ripped in half."

"Maybe your ovaries planned it that way," he said and rolled her onto her back. He was hoping to bring a smile to her face, but she just scowled at him.

"Don't joke about the crash. I thought we were all going to die."

He kissed her deeply and began to rock his hips, willing memories of that horrible experience to leave her mind and his. When she relaxed beneath him and began to explore his back with gentle fingertips, he churned his hips to give her more pleasure. He knew he could give her pleasure. He just wasn't sure if he'd ever give her the baby she wanted so badly.

Myrna moaned softly, grinding against him as her pleasure built. He lifted onto his elbows, so he could watch her as he plunged into her, receded, plunged into her again. He would never tire of looking at her face or its countless expressions—her joy, her anxiety, her passion, her fear, her sorrow, her anger and tenderness and wonder and love. He cherished every nuance of her beautiful face and doubted he'd ever grow tired of watching her—not even when they were both old and wrinkled like a couple of enamored raisins.

"I love you," he whispered when the emotion became too raw to hold inside any longer.

She smiled up at him and lifted a hand to touch his beard-stubbled jaw. "I love you too, Brian."

They deserved to have the ultimate expression of their love. They deserved to have a baby. So why was making one so fucking difficult for them?

He made love to her slowly, filling her deeply, waiting for her to find her peak. He followed her in orgasm, making sure he was planted firmly against the entrance of her womb as he found release inside her. He withdrew slowly, trying not to disrupt what he'd left behind and then rested his head on her chest as he slowly regained his breath. She ran her fingers through his hair while he prayed that they'd made it happen this time. Please God, let her be happy. Let her have a baby. My baby. Please.

"Let's go away somewhere," she said after a moment. "Just the two of us. We never got to have a real honeymoon after our wedding and Jerry said it will be weeks before you're able to get back on tour."

That sounded like a great idea to him. "Where would you like to go?"

"I'll go anywhere as long as I'm with you," she said. "Except Canada. Canada doesn't seem to like me much."

The bus accident had occurred in Canada, and they both knew it had nothing to do with a place *liking* anyone, but he understood her hesitation in wanting to return there so soon after tragedy had struck the family of their little metal band.

"I'll call a travel agent," he said. "Are you hungry?" He bent his head and kissed her flat belly. He wondered what she'd look like with his baby growing inside her.

"A little. Are you?"

"Starving," he said.

"I'll get up and make you breakfast."

He pressed her firmly into the mattress. "You stay here and incubate," he said. "I'll bring you something."

"I appreciate that," she said, her eyes growing moist again. Damn she was emotional while trying. He couldn't even imagine how emotional she'd be once she actually got pregnant. He wouldn't mind being there for her though. He was more than happy to make midnight runs for pickles and ice cream to keep a smile on her face.

"No problem," he said and kissed her pouty pink lips. "It's the least I can do after that wonderful wake-up you gifted me with this morning."

"When my ovaries say it's time, it's fucking time," she said with a laugh.

"We have at least twelve more hours to take advantage of their cooperation," he said.

"Better make that breakfast a large one," she said and patted his ass. "I think we're going to need our stamina."

Acknowledgements

Special thanks to my beta readers Cyndi McGowen, Wendy Christy and Jill Anderson for helping me make this the best book possible. And to my patient and talented editor, Beth Hill. One day I will learn how to use a comma properly. Or should that be: One day, I will learn how to use a comma properly. Consider my punctuation weaknesses, your job security.

Much love to my fans and readers, who bring a smile to my face every day with their love and enthusiasm for a fake rock band. If Sinners were real, I believe they'd need more condoms and tighter security.

And extra thanks to my family and friends, because they're the ones who have to listen to me bitch when the muse isn't cooperating or when I'm on my fifth edit and I'm convinced that every word I've ever written sucks. I appreciate you all.

About the Author

Combining her love for romantic fiction and rock 'n roll, Olivia Cunning writes erotic romance centered around rock musicians. Raised on hard rock music from the cradle, she attended her first Styx concert at age six and fell instantly in love with live music. She's been known to travel over a thousand miles just to see a favorite band in concert. As a teen, she discovered her second love, romantic fiction—first, voraciously reading steamy romance novels and then penning her own. She's going to have to buy a new snow shovel because soon she's moving from the warm beaches of Galveston, Texas to her hometown in western Illinois. Sometimes family trumps geography. But no matter where her itchy feet take her, she'll continue to write about the rock stars that exist in her head. And her heart.

Made in the USA
Lexington, KY
11 March 2014